The Covenant has been kept. The blood of the priest has bought my freedom—his pain has absolved my sin. And I have come here tonight to claim my liberation. . . .

Suddenly I feel Judas enter the hidden room. He has come as silently as a shadow, with no more substance than a dream, yet so terribly real.

Look at me.

His command invades my mind like rolling thunder. "I have done your bidding. The priest is dead. The Covenant is complete," I say.

I know.

"How?"

I am always with you. You cannot escape me any more than you can deny me.

"Release me."

No. The Covenant is not complete. There will be others. Many others.

When he is through with me, I hear the slap of his sandals on the dirt floor—his retreating footsteps. My muscles begin to relax and I take a deep breath.

What he has asked . . . told me to do is so monstrous I can hardly comprehend it. I came here tonight to free myself of this force, but I am bound to it more than ever. There is no escape.

The Covenant must be kept. . . .

THE JUDAS VOICE

ANTHONY JOHN

J

JOVE BOOKS, NEW YORK

THE JUDAS VOICE

A Jove Book/published by arrangement with the author

PRINTING HISTORY
Jove edition/April 1989

ISBN: 0-515-09989-9

Jove Books are published by The Berkley Publishing Group,
200 Madison Avenue, New York, New York 10016.
The name ''JOVE'' and the ''J'' logo
are trademarks belonging to Jove Publications, Inc.

PRINTED IN THE UNITED STATES OF AMERICA

10 9 8 7 6 5 4 3 2 1

Prologue

The house, decayed and weather-beaten, stands derelict at the end of the long gravel road. It is camouflaged by overgrown trees, bromegrass, and brindle shrubbery. It has become a part of its background and almost invisible, even from the road. Its isolation is a reflection of my own lonely life.

I have always hated this house. The unspeakable things done to me here still make me shudder with revulsion. Yet the house draws me back. For it was here that the Covenant was made, the pact bound in blood. And it is here that he waits for me.

Crossing the threshold, I feel I've stepped into my past. The interior of the house has been vandalized by time and neglect. It is musty, damp, and smells of animal droppings. I set straight an overturned chair and I wait.

It comes gradually, almost silently, like the faint, insinuating step of a rodent. A spasm convulses my rigid body, as I strain to focus my entire consciousness on the sound.

It is terrifyingly familiar—the soft slap of sandals on the creaky basement stairs, the whisper of his voluminous robes.

I want to turn and face him, but I cannot. I remember my vision of his eyes, burning with hellish intensity. Haunted and condemned. The eyes of Judas Iscariot.

The distant pealing of church bells breaks the spell. I count each ring. When they stop I sense him withdrawing, and I am able to move again. But I understand the meaning of the bells. They are a death knell.

I am home. . . . It is time.

The Covenant must be kept.

PART I
The Covenant

*"We have made a covenant with death,
and with Hell are we at agreement."*

—Isaiah 28:15

Chapter One

On the roof of an abandoned tenement in the South Bronx, the transvestite clutched a screaming baby to his foam-rubber breasts.

He pressed the polished edge of a straight razor into the pink folds of the baby's neck, drawing tiny drops of blood that rolled down the blade and onto his hand. Periodically, he licked his fingers and smacked his thick, painted lips. The taste of blood and lipstick aroused his confused sexual desires; he felt himself grow hard under the red silk dress he was wearing. It was wonderful, he thought, to be in drag, high, and fucking-up gringo cops.

He did a little dance of pure joy and sang out in a screeching tremolo, *"Mamē mí chocho . . . cho cho cho!"*

"What's he saying?" the tall man with the field glasses asked.

Smiling slightly, Detective Lieutenant Vincent Ciano answered, "He wants you go eat his pussy, Captain."

Captain Andrew Talbot never took his eyes off the transvestite, nor did his expression change. "It's his most lucid request yet," he said, annoyed with Ciano.

Ciano frowned. They had been on the rooftop for two hours in the sweltering July heat listening to the transvestite's insane threats and bizarre demands. If it were my decision to make, Ciano thought, I would stop jerking around and blow the bastard away.

But it wasn't his decision. Vince Ciano was a street cop. His regular assignment was working undercover with the Midtown-South Anticrime Unit. He hated the Bronx, but then again, he wasn't in love with Manhattan, either. He was on the roof at Captain Talbot's request because he knew the transvestite from a previous investigation. He had no authority to do anything.

Six months before, Ciano had raided a drug factory in the Times Square porn district and had found the same transvestite beating and sodomizing a six-year-old boy. Enraged and sick-

5

ened, Ciano had taken great satisfaction in knocking the man's poorly capped teeth down his throat. But because of his gratuitous action, the case had been thrown out of court. The pervert was back on the streets long before Ciano's reprimand was out of the typewriter.

Ciano's reputation as a cop was marred by his tendency to react violently to violent crime. He had a string of commendations for bravery to his credit, but an equally long list of reprimands for dangerous heroics and a marked insensitivity to the rights of murderers, rapists, and child abusers. This made him an outcast with the brass downtown. They considered him a dinosaur, a relic of another age, who had very little to do with their world of financial planning, computerized statistics, and community relations luncheons. Ciano would never make captain and he didn't give a damn.

All he wanted was a chance to bring a little street justice to the scumbags who deserved it. There was a rumor that he had indirectly iced two rapists who had brutally assaulted a nun. The two men, charged with more than fifty assaults in three years, were turned loose by a judge who didn't like the D.A.'s method of gathering evidence. Laughing and joking, the rapists had walked out of the courtroom taunting Ciano and even throwing the finger at the sympathetic judge who believed that two rapists were worth more than one violated nun.

Ciano didn't see it that way, and took a leave of absence to follow the two men, making sure they knew they were being watched. In a panic, the rapists found an ACLU lawyer who hauled Ciano into court for harassment. But the charges didn't stick and Ciano kept up his private vendetta. Finally, the two men decided to leave town, figuring a few months in sunny Florida might be just what they needed.

That's when Ciano was supposed to have dropped the dime, that is, called a certain party he knew in an organized crime family in Brooklyn. Three months later, the bodies of the two rapists turned up in a South Miami wrecking yard. Someone had used a chain saw to make sure all their body parts fit neatly in a fifty-five-gallon oil drum. A mob hit, the cops said. No charges were ever brought, nothing was ever proven, but the rumors persisted.

Ciano and Talbot were crouched in the cupola that led to the H-shaped rooftop. The transvestite was in the middle of the "H", pacing back and forth, shouting, screaming, holding the baby close to him. His real name was Juan Batista, but when he

6

was strung out on angel dust he liked to call himself Eva. Eva Prime. His twenty-six-year-old court-appointed psychologist reported that the name he had chosen was significant because it was an approximation of "Eva Prima," or the first Eve, an obvious allusion to the Garden of Eden. Ciano thought both the psychologist and the transvestite should be locked up. Together.

A strand of limp red hair from his cheap wig fell across Eva's forehead, giving his overly made-up eyes a feminine appearance. But a two-day growth of beard betrayed his sex. It itched in the fierce heat and reminded him he couldn't afford costly facial electrolysis; shaving was a daily indignity to his female alter ego.

The infant squawled, piteously uncomfortable, hungry, and wet, unaware of the thin thread of sanity upon which her life depended.

"You'd better move now or you kill the kid," Ciano said, peering over Talbot's shoulder, from the shadows of the cupola.

Talbot put down the field glasses and wiped the sweat from his eyes. The knife-sharp creases in his uniform shirt were beginning to wilt in the oppressive heat.

"What do you want me to do, Ciano?" Talbot asked, exasperated. "Start blasting away?"

"You've got marksmen stashed all over the area, Captain. Use them," Ciano answered.

"Sure," Talbot said. "And blow both of them away. They're standing too close to the edge of the roof. One errant shot . . ."

The baby's screams grew even more tortured. They ripped through Ciano's gut. Both men turned back to the rooftop.

Eva Prime held the screaming baby by one tiny foot and began swinging her slowly in front of him, working up a 180-degree arc. In his other hand he held the razor; his eyes were wide and glassy, and with each pendulum-like swing, the baby was brought closer and closer to the glinting razor. Eva very much wanted to kill the baby, but he wanted other things, too.

"Money!" Eva screeched in a rough falsetto. "Get my ducats, man, or I cut her. And no chump change, *maricon*! You get me two million in small bills, man, like on T.V. You hear me, motherfucker?" He used the razor to make a small cut in the baby's foot. "You hear me?" he shouted again, forgetting the falsetto and licking the blood from the baby's foot. It smeared his lipstick, making him look like a demented clown.

"We hear you, Juan. Just calm down and relax. Everything's

7

being arranged," Talbot lied smoothly. "It takes time to gather that much money. Just be . . ."

"Stop calling me Juan, *coño*!" Prime shouted. "My name is *Eva*, motherfucker!" With that, he grabbed the baby by both its chubby arms, held her in front of him and began to gyrate his hips, simulating intercourse. Ciano could see Prime's erection poking through the red silk dress.

Talbot's right hand went toward his cap. It was an innocuous movement, but it was a signal. Once his cap came off, Emergency Service marksmen would open fire. Ciano tensed for the kill, but almost as if he sensed that his life was in danger, Prime pulled the baby back up to his chest, looking around wildly, and the opportunity was lost.

Ciano was overcome by a confusing mixture of emotions. He could feel something snap inside his head; the headache that had dogged him all day flaired with a white-hot intensity.

"Let me take him out," Ciano urged Talbot. "Let me take him out or he'll kill that baby."

Talbot continued to stare through his binoculars.

"Be quiet or be gone," Talbot said.

"You're making a mistake, Captain. That scumbag gets off on violence. It's like sex to him. His outrageous demands are just foreplay, a little fooling around before the big bang. He'd have killed that little boy in Times Square if I hadn't stopped him."

"If you'd done your job, Ciano, we wouldn't be here now," Talbot hissed. "Now get off this roof and report back to your commander. I've had enough of you."

Ciano could feel his vision blur and hear a roaring in his ears. He was close to exploding, but he clenched his fists until the knuckles shone white. Then he backed down the narrow stairs to the landing below. It smelled like boiling urine.

Still grappling with his pent-up emotions, Ciano nodded to two patrolmen lounging on the dark, airless landing. With them was a small Hispanic man dressed in a bright lemon-colored leisure suit, white shoes, and a panama hat. Ciano had been told this was the transvestite's "husband," Antonio Maldonado. The swarthy little man stroked his pencil-thin mustache. Ciano had an idea.

"I'm Vince Ciano," he said pleasantly, holding out his hand.

Maldonado stared angrily. He hated cops and he wasn't afraid of them. He spat on the floor.

"You have a name, don't you?" Ciano said, his hand waiting for Maldonado's.

8

"Sure, pig. I gotta name. Chu got a mother?"

Ciano smiled. It wasn't a pleasant smile, more like the grin of a predator.

His hand still outstretched, he reached up and slapped Maldonado across the face. Hard.

"I asked you your name," Ciano said, unruffled.

Maldonado backed away from Ciano; the two uniformed cops began studying the ceiling with exaggerated care, ignoring the scene.

Maldonado was confused and scared. He had pushed and abused cops before and they had all taken it—taken his shit with calm faces and polite smiles. They had to these days. If a cop struck back he could lose his job. But this one didn't seem to care.

Ciano slapped him again. "I can keep this up all day, asshole."

"Antonio . . . Antonio Maldonado."

"That's better," Ciano said, extending his hand again.

Maldonado took it tentatively; Ciano clamped his hand down on Maldonado's and pulled the man toward him.

"Can you talk to that other asshole on the roof?" he growled directly in Maldonado's face. "Can you get him to give up the baby?"

Maldonado tried to draw back, but Ciano's grip held him impaled like a butterfly. He didn't know how to answer. If he told the truth—that Juan was so strung-out on PCP anything could happen—the cop might beat the shit out of him. Lying seemed safer.

"Sure, man, sure. Just don't hurt Juanito. I love him, man. You promise you won't hurt him?"

Ciano released the man, pushing him toward the wall. "He gives me the baby unharmed and I'll drive him to the hospital myself. He needs a doctor, right? Not cops."

"*Sí, sí.*"

"You got my word, Antonio," Ciano said, smiling strangely. "But hear me, good. You pull any tricks up there, or if your 'Juanito' hurts that baby, both of you fall off the roof with nothing but your well-worn asses to break the fall."

Maldonado nodded. Beads of perspiration rolled down his forehead; his face was the sickly color of his yellow leisure suit. For the first time in his life he wished he were going to jail. Anywhere, but out on that roof.

• • •

9

Talbot was hunkered down in the cupola, talking to Prime. Standing on the stairs behind him, Ciano could see that the captain's uniform was now limp and soggy. He thought he could smell Talbot's fear and indecision. But that didn't matter anymore. Ciano had decided to act. It was as if he were moving on an involuntary course, sliding on a greased track.

Eva Prime was agitated. He wasn't receiving enough attention. He thought the roof would be crowded with photographers, reporters, and television news cameras. He decided it was time to do something about it. Before the horrified eyes of Ciano, Talbot, and four ESU marksmen watching through sniper scopes, Prime swung the baby by one leg out past the roof's edge and back.

Ciano felt as if he had been hit in the stomach; he could hear his breath whistling through his teeth. Maldonado closed his eyes tight, as the snipers slid the safeties off their rifles at Talbot's signal.

Prime was laughing hysterically. *That* had gotten their attention.

"Get me Geraldo Rivera," he demanded. "I want to tell him my life. I want to tell him my troubles. I want to suck his cock and I want . . ." He pursed his blood-smeared lips and blew a kiss to Talbot, then began to stroke the razor against the baby's stomach.

That did it for Ciano. He shoved Talbot aside and pushed Maldonado out onto the roof. Before the surprised Talbot could react, they were out of his reach.

"What the hell are you doing?" Talbot shouted, a blue vein in his neck pulsing wildly, his face crimson. But it was too late. Ciano was in action.

Prime had to shade his eyes in the glaring sun to see who was coming toward him. It couldn't be cops, he thought wildly. They wouldn't dare. But it was too soon for Geraldo Rivera.

Pressing the baby to his chest like a flak vest, Eva Prime hopped about nervously. He was coming down from his high fast; he felt spiders crawling up his legs and his skin seemed loose and sagging, like it was slipping off his bones. Prime's eyes darted about wildly; he was finding it difficult to focus. He tried to brush the phantom spiders away, but his reactions were slow; his head hurt.

Holding Maldonado firmly by the arm, Ciano pushed him closer to Prime. He had no real plan except to get into a position to fire. He felt as if something outside him were driving him on,

10

demanding that he save the child. He trusted his experience and instinct to save the situation.

The instant Eva Prime recognized Ciano he threw back his head and began howling like a dog. Ciano used this time to edge closer, dragging a reluctant and fearful Maldonado.

Prime flashed the razor, ready to slash the baby's throat, but when he saw Maldonado, his arm froze in mid-swing. He couldn't trust his senses. *Was it really Tonio or was it a trick?*

"*Tu? Estas bienes, Popi?*" he asked in a quavering voice.

Maldonado gave a frightened nod.

Ciano released Maldonado's arm and grabbed the man's greased-down hair. Maldonado's instinct was to resist—he didn't like anyone touching his pomaded hairdo—but Ciano had drawn his gun.

"Let's make a deal, Juan," Ciano said, yanking Maldonado's head back and jamming the barrel of his .38 into the surprised man's open mouth. "You give me the baby and I won't blow your boyfriend's molars all over the South Bronx. *¿Tu sabes, coño?*"

Maldonado made gagging sounds; his prominent Adam's apple bobbed up and down.

Eva Prime, his attention riveted on Ciano's gun, began to shake and cry. In his mind he saw Ciano's gun violating his friend's soft warm mouth. The baby slid from his arms and fell to the roof; the hot tar made her cry even harder.

Ciano sighed with relief as he removed the gun from Maldonado's mouth. Releasing his grip on the man's hair, he prodded Maldonado toward Prime, hoping to keep the transvestite busy until he reached the baby.

As Ciano bent to pick up the baby, Maldonado turned abruptly, cursing him in Spanish and English, and lashed out with a kick, knocking Ciano on his ass.

Seeing this, Prime screamed insanely and raised the razor high. He was laughing to himself, sure that the cop was going to die.

Ciano, seeing the blade arcing toward him, knew he'd never be able to fire in time. Instead, he kicked backward, hitting Maldonado in the knees, sending him into the direct line of the razor. Maldonado screamed as Prime's razor halved his right eye. He kept on screaming, the bright blood spraying all over his yellow suit, as he staggered about the roof blindly.

"Shoot, damn it, shoot!" Ciano yelled, rolling over into firing position. *Where the hell were the snipers?*

11

Ciano dodged just as Prime's blade reached out for him again. The knife slashed his shirt, and he could feel it rip like a burning brand through the skin and muscle of his right arm. His hand hung limp and useless.

Quickly, he switched the gun into his left hand and squeezed the trigger.

A jet of flame roared out of Ciano's .38; the bullet slammed into Prime's forehead, pulping it and smashing into the soft gray matter behind it.

Prime's head jerked back. Then a curious thing happened. He began to dance, like a dying puppet, as the snipers' bullets hit his back and mushroomed into dark stains as they exited from his chest.

It was several seconds before Prime crumpled to the roof, but he had been dead since Ciano's bullet had destroyed his brain.

Drained and shaking, Ciano rolled over and grabbed the screaming baby. He sat there on the roof wiping Prime's blood off her with a curiously maternal gesture. His mind was in neutral; he didn't notice anything until the fiery sun was suddenly blocked by Talbot's tall figure.

"You stupid son of a bitch!" Talbot was raging, when Ciano finally heard him. "What the hell do you think you're doing pulling a stunt like that?"

Ciano tuned him out, getting stiffly to his feet.

"I'm talking to you, Lieutenant!" Talbot screamed, purple veins in his neck corded and throbbing. "You dumbass. . . ."

Ciano handed the baby to an ESU cop. Then he turned to face Talbot.

"Stand at attention, Lieutenant!" Talbot yelled, poking a finger into Ciano's chest.

The roof was filled with cops now and Ciano, pushing Talbot's hand away, turned his back on the captain.

"You're finished, Ciano," Talbot swore. "I'll have your badge for this!"

Ciano walked away, mumbling.

Talbot stopped his tirade and demanded to know what Ciano had said.

"I don't know what you're so pissed about, Captain," Ciano said loud enough for all to hear. "You can have the collar, if you want."

A wave of muffled laughter rose from the cops on the roof.

Chapter
Two

Monday, November 1

Vince Ciano fought a fierce southerly crosswind as he drove the battered station wagon across the Verrazano-Narrows Bridge toward Staten Island. The sun was just beginning to come up, but his thoughts remained dark and confused. He had been driving around aimlessly all night, too tense to sleep, too nervous to light anywhere.

He slammed his fist down on the steering wheel in frustration. The gray plastic wheel creaked. Unexpectedly, the radio crackled to life. "Fucking car," Ciano said aloud. Fucking trial, he said to himself.

The departmental hearing had been mercifully short, if not particularly merciful. Ciano had been suspended for three months and transferred to a country-club precinct. That was bad, but it could have been worse. Much worse.

At first, he was sure he would lose his badge. Then two things happened. The first was that he had some powerful supporters in the upper echelons of the department, cops who admired his guts and determination. Unknown to Ciano, they began an unofficial lobby to persuade the board to keep him. The second was the blistering commentary by New York *Post* columnist Freddy Jermezian, who headlined one story: TALBOT GETS CREDIT, CIANO GETS SHAFT.

Annoyed at the untoward publicity and the surprising pressure from within the department, the police bureaucracy, in the words of Assistant Chief Charles Ahearn, decided to "slap Ciano's wrist before placing him gingerly out of harm's way."

Out of harm's way was defined as the 122nd in central Staten Island, the precinct that had consistently posted the lowest crime statistics in the five boroughs, a place other cops talked about with a mixture of awe and scorn.

"It's so quiet out there," Ahearn told the Chief of Detectives. "Ciano will probably quit within a year. Or die of boredom.

That will get Jermezian off our backs and keep Talbot from having a stroke.''

So the compromise was reached, the sentence passed, and almost everyone involved was unhappy about it. Captain Talbot, outraged and humiliated, wanted Ciano fired and was shocked that his personal ''rabbi'' in the department, Deputy Chief Sal DeFeo, would allow himself to be manipulated so easily. Ciano, on the other hand, was equally furious. He had saved the child, and to him any other action was justified. The rest was just politics. He felt defeated, misunderstood, and betrayed by the department to which he had devoted fifteen years of his life, the department that was now sending him to the boonies to write traffic tickets. What hurt most, he thought, was not being able to function as a real cop anymore. The street, the action—that was what Ciano craved. When he wasn't working, he felt flat . . . dead inside.

As he thought about it, Ciano decided that the only person who was going to make out in this mess was Antonio Maldonado, the late Eva Prime's lover, now a one-eyed flake with a whopping fifty-million-dollar lawsuit against the police department and Ciano personally. Being sued by that scumbag Maldonado had irked him at first, but Ciano's lawyer had assured him the case would drag on for years and probably be settled out of court by various insurance companies. But it didn't matter to Ciano. He didn't have much money anyway. All he owned fit neatly into the two cardboard boxes in the back of his station wagon. Not much to show for a man nearing forty, but at least he had a salary, even though most of it went to his ex-wife and six-year-old son.

The wind hammered the station wagon, threatening to lift it over the guardrail and drop it into the choppy water below. As he neared the center of the bridge, Ciano could just make out the neat rows of clapboard houses, punctuated by church steeples poking out of the foliage like white skeletal fingers.

It looked forbidding to Ciano. Forbidding and familiar, for he had been born on Staten Island and had lived there until his divorce. His childhood, once pushed deeply into his subconscious, now seemed a whirling montage of pain and disappointment. Just looking at the dark landscape seemed to dredge up uninvited memories. His marriage, once the happiest part of his life, had later caused him almost unbearable pain, so he had escaped.

Now he was coming home. Disgraced. What is there about

14

this place that keeps trying to destroy me? he wondered. He knew that to other people, Staten Island represented security, safety, a sheltered middle-class oasis far from dangerous urban streets. Yet, except for the first years of his marriage, Ciano had hated every minute he had spent there.

He hunched his shoulders, as if physically warding off thoughts of despair, determined to fight the rising tide of hopelessness. He wondered, not for the first time, if he could get back with his ex-wife. They had been happy once, perhaps they could be again. Maybe it wasn't too late. Maybe he could change. Of course he could change! She used to say that he was more wedded to the department than to her. Well, that certainly wasn't true anymore. His career was down the toilet and there would be plenty of off-time in a suburban precinct. It had only been three years since he'd left, perhaps she still loved him. Yes. That was a good thought. If she didn't still love him, she would have married somebody else by now. And his son would have a new father.

The boy, Ciano sighed. He'd try to spend more time with his son, even if it killed them both. He didn't want his child to be shackled with the memories he had of his own parents. It could work, he thought. It *would* work.

With this burst of irrational confidence, Ciano gunned the engine hard, expecting a surge of power. Instead, the engine bucked, backfired and almost stalled. A cloud of smoke belched from the rusted exhaust. Ciano fought to slow the 1975 Hornet down, but like him it was well past its prime, falling apart and hard to control.

Coming off the bridge, he steered into a toll lane, leaving behind clouds of noxious fumes every time he accelerated. The toll attendant took his bills, handed back change and a receipt, and warned him about the illegal exhaust. Ciano smiled, rolled the receipt into a little ball and flicked it out the window. Then he peeled out, leaving the toll-taker choking in a cloud of black, oily smoke.

Merging with the westbound traffic, Ciano looked into his rearview mirror and laughed for the first time since July.

He had things to do.

Six miles from the Verrazano Bridge, Jeanette Kidder Eddins took a deep breath and waited. No pain. That was a good sign, she thought, rinsing out a gold-and-white Limoges tea cup. She

15

decided to give special thanks to Saint Jude, the patron saint of lost causes, for yet another pain-free day.

"Lost cause," she muttered to herself, thinking about what the doctors had told her: The next heart attack would be fatal. But with the inherent pragmatism of her seventeenth-century Dutch ancestors and the zealous conviction of a Catholic convert, she accepted her plight and regarded each day as a precious gift from God. She saw no reason to allow a flock of young doctors to operate on her, especially since the only thing they could guarantee was their outrageous bills. No, she put her trust in God, which was a lot cheaper and a lot surer.

She left the kitchen, walking gracefully for a woman only two months away from her eighty-second birthday, and into the study where she had erected an altar forty-five years earlier. Kneeling, she recited her morning prayers, remembering the special thanks to Saint Jude. When she had finished, she blessed herself with holy water from a small porcelain bowl and rose gingerly to her feet. Wonder of wonders, she thought, her ankles weren't swollen badly this morning. It *was* going to be a good day.

Leaning forward, she cupped each of the altar's four votive candles, carefully blowing them out, not wanting to spray the statue of the Lord with hot wax, then took another deep breath to assure herself she was still feeling well.

She glanced at the tiny gold watch pinned to the bosom of her simple navy-blue dress and decided it was time to leave for Mass. In the spacious foyer of the old Dutch mansion, she pulled aside the starched, embroidered curtains to check on the weather. The sun was just beginning to come up; it would be clear and cold, she decided. She preferred early Mass because there was less chance of meeting foreigners, who were notorious slug-a-beds, and because old Monsignor Bryan always officiated, rather than that young twit Father Layhe.

Her sweater, coat, and purse hung neatly from a walnut coat-rack near the front door. She dressed quickly, pulling a black kerchief over her head and knotting it firmly under her chin. Because she didn't believe in canes, crutches, walkers, or eye-glasses—all signs of weaknesses—she plucked the umbrella from the rack and used it to lean on. I'd rather have them think me eccentric than feeble, she said to herself, pulling open the massive oak door.

Closing the door behind her, but not bothering to lock it as was her custom, Miss Eddins stepped off the porch ready to face the world. Or at least the part of the world she would encounter on the half-mile trip to Holy Cross Church.

She walked with brisk efficiency, head down, umbrella clicking on the cement sidewalk, thinking that the sidewalk had once been a dirt path. She had ridden her horse on this very spot as a child. So many changes, she muttered to herself, thinking about the endless rows of identical matchbox houses that had replaced the commodious homes of her father's friends; the ceaseless traffic that had erased the quiet lanes and dense woods of her youth. It was the fault of the foreigners, she thought, those people who began arriving after the Second World War and who had virtually inundated the pastoral island by the time the Verrazano-Narrows Bridge was completed. Foreigners. People from the city. Italians. Colored. Who knew what else? Foreigners, she thought contemptuously, conveniently forgetting the fortune she had amassed selling off her land to "foreign" real-estate developers.

But there was one spot left on Staten Island which met with her approval: Richmondtown Village. As chairwoman of the Historical Society, Jeanette Kidder Eddins had been a driving force behind the restored village. She felt that it was geographically, culturally, and spiritually the center of the island. She had raised funds, contributed money and land and had interviewed hundreds of so-called experts (mostly foreigners), about creating an exciting, historically accurate village, much like Williamsburg, though on a smaller scale. The houses and places of business, such as the blacksmith's shop and the apothecary, were from the seventeenth to the early nineteenth centuries, allowing visitors to view the changing patterns of life on Staten Island. Miss Eddins felt that because her home had been invaded, the conquerors should be forced to see what they had destroyed, and be overcome by guilt.

At this time of the morning, Richmondtown Village had a serene, haunting quality that appealed to Miss Eddins. She could almost see ghostly inhabitants of the past going about their morning chores and imagined herself joining them, becoming a part of their quietly fulfilling lives. She slowed her pace and, leaning on the umbrella, stood there absorbing the village's beauty and tranquility, drinking in the damp, earthy smells.

She walked on, looking for signs of progress. But the reconstruction was going slowly—scaffolding, construction equipment, and tarps littered much of the ground. That's the price you have to pay, she thought, when you want something done

17

right. For she had insisted on employing only historically correct methods of rebuilding the village. She had fought, bribed, and browbeat the committee into transferring whole buildings from other parts of the island; screamed at them when they wanted to erect prefabricated facsimiles, and clutched her heart in dismay when they thought of using nail guns and glue when old-fashioned methods were the best. It had been a struggle, but in the end she had won. Unfortunately, she was now paying the price for winning in the one commodity she could ill-afford: time. She wondered if she'd live long enough to see it through.

Miss Eddins paused outside Stephens General Store, a graceful seventeenth-century building next door to the Courthouse. The Courthouse was built in the early 1700s as a symbol of British rule and prestige, and currently served as a visitor's information center. She was thinking that it might have been better if the British still reigned, when she heard a strange creaking noise that intruded on her reverie. She turned around slowly, trying to locate the source of the sound, but everything seemed to be in order. In front of the courthouse, the empty wooden stocks, that had once held malefactors, stood in mute testimony to today's penchant for mollycoddling criminals. Like the stocks, the scaffold was grossly underused these days, she thought. That's when she noticed that someone had strung up a noose on the scaffold. It was creaking in the stiff wind. Vandals, she thought, vandals and foreigners. But secretly, she decided that the noose added a nice touch of realism to the restoration. She vowed to persuade the committee to let it stay. Musing about the noose, she hurried on.

When Holy Cross Church came into sight, just behind the courthouse, Miss Eddins paused to inspect it critically. The two-story fieldstone structure was a bit of a fraud, she thought, having been built in her father's time and technically beyond the boundaries of Richmondtown. But Miss Eddins loved it, as she loved her own house and the restoration, the trinity of her earthly passions.

She gazed at its cheerful stained-glass windows and arched double doors that had, to her consternation, been painted bright red. There was a man in a blue flannel shirt standing—most unseemingly, thought Miss Eddins—with arms akimbo by the front steps. As she moved toward the man she determined to find out what he was doing there. In the dawn light, the man remained motionless, and just as she was about to address him, she glanced up at his face.

18

Miss Eddins gasped, feeling a twinge of pain in her heart.

She backed away slowly, her mind flipping through a catalogue of possible horrors. But there was only one explanation. The grinning orange face must belong to the angel of death. She was sure her time was over and that this creature had come to carry her off. But not without a fight, she decided, using her umbrella as a sword. With surprising strength she poked at the apparition, but it just stood there, transfixed.

Ha, thought Miss Eddins, the blood roaring in her ears, the Devil's sent a poor substitute. She poked at him again, even harder this time, and to her amazement its head landed at her feet with a soft, juicy plop.

Curiosity overcoming her fear, she moved closer to the creature. Its badly damaged head lay broken on the pavement. It looked familiar; she touched it gingerly with the umbrella. A pumpkin, of all things, she thought, perplexed. Then it dawned on her that she had been battling a scarecrow. What in the name of God was a scarecrow doing in front of the church? It was enough to frighten an old lady to death, she thought, wishing she had worn her glasses this morning. No doubt it was young Father Layhe's doing, some kind of practical joke, she thought, unaware that the scarecrow with its pumpkin head had been used as decoration at the Halloween party on Saturday.

Father Layhe will certainly get a piece of my mind, Miss Eddins thought, catching her breath and beginning to climb the seven steps to the church. Breathing easier now, and somewhat ashamed of herself for acting like a foolish old woman, Miss Eddins finally arrived at the top of the stairs and stood resolutely on the flagstone landing.

She tried the door on the left. It was locked. She bounced the tip of her black umbrella on the flagstone in frustration, remembering the time Monsignor Bryan had been ill and young Layhe had opened the church fifteen minutes late. He's probably done it again, she thought savagely, reaching for the door on the right, fully expecting it to be locked.

But before she could grasp the brass fixture, the red door was flung open from the inside and a hunched-over figure rushed past her, almost knocking her down. Foreigners, she thought, startled, but she was relieved that at least the door was open. "Foreigners," she said aloud. "Even in God's house."

The inside of the church was cold. The lights hadn't been turned on, but Miss Eddins was thrilled to see the early morning sunlight streaming through the rosette window high above the

19

main altar. It cast a rosy glow on the dark walnut pews and over the jumbled collection of workmen's scaffolds and equipment, for like Richmondtown, Holy Cross Church was being refurbished, another project dear to Miss Eddins' heart.

Peering intently toward the altar, Miss Eddins could see that the huge cross that was once suspended above it was lying negligently near the rail. Preposterous, she thought, then stopped in mid-stride. There was something else that caught her attention, something on the cross. A man. Upside down. But surely, I'm imagining it, she thought, like I imagined that scarecrow to be a man. With her umbrella clicking hollowly on the marble floor, Miss Eddins moved closer to get a better look.

When she was five feet away, she chided herself for being so silly, for the figure on the cross was too crumpled and bent to be human. He didn't seem to have a head. Another scarecrow, she thought, vowing to speak to Monsignor Bryan about his young assistant's dubious sense of propriety.

She poked at the figure with her umbrella.

It was real.

She couldn't believe it. Her senses told her that the stringy strips of meat could never have lived. Then she recognized the crucifix lying in a pool of blood.

Miss Eddins moaned. She felt dizzy and weak. Her vision blurred, her legs turned to rubber. She began vomiting before she hit the floor.

She tried not to think about the horror that had once been Monsignor Byran, her friend and confessor. It made her heart hammer and jump; she felt as if she were on fire.

Suddenly the burning sensation in her chest turned into a searing pain that swept down her left arm. Then the pain quickly became an explosion and Miss Eddins shook spasmodically for several seconds before she died on the new marble floor she had so joyously chosen.

Chapter
Three

It was almost 8 a.m. when Ciano pulled into the parking lot behind the 122nd Precinct. He shut off the engine and sat staring at the manicured lawns and flower beds, now bare, that lined the back entrance to the station house. It was quite a change from the urban tenements he had worked in before. Flowers, he sneered, wondering if the cops here had tea and crumpets for lunch.

Keep thinking of this as an opportunity, he told himself, an opportunity to build a whole new life. But the extravagant optimism of dawn had given way to the harsh reality of morning.

Entering the precinct through a door marked POLICE PERSONNEL ONLY, Ciano found himself in the locker room. It was lined with standard gray metal lockers and smelled of dirty clothes, stale sweat, and disinfectant.

A few men were lounging around talking, smoking, and playing cards. They didn't notice him, or if they did, they paid no attention. In a high-crime precinct, a guard would have pounced on him the moment he entered. Here no one seemed to care.

To his left was the now-familiar plywood wall separating the changing room for policewomen. Carved into the makeshift wall were several peepholes with huge letters marked "Peephole" and "Hole Peek—5 Cents." Nickel pussy, Ciano thought, everything's cheaper in the suburbs.

"Hey, chief," he said to an almost naked fat man reading the racing form. "Which way to the desk?"

Without looking up, the fat man pointed a chewed cigar butt toward a green door to Ciano's right.

"Thanks," he said, and pushed his way through to the precinct's main room. He told the desk sergeant who he was, then waited for someone to show him where to go.

A man about his own age or a little younger introduced himself as Detective Sergeant Joseph Dugan. He had sandy hair that was turning to gray and a boyish Irish face with an upturned nose. He looked pleased to see Ciano, pleased to be a cop, and pleased to be alive.

"It's a pleasure to meet you," Dugan said. "Nice to have somebody around who knows what he's doing."

"Who do I have to see?" Ciano asked, embarrassed at Dugan's reception.

"Captain Smith's the precinct commander," Dugan said. "And you have a special visitor from downtown."

"Who?"

"That famous sleuth, Deputy Chief of Detectives Salvatore DeFeo."

Shit, Ciano thought, Sally the Shit, Talbot's friend and a slimeball deluxe. The man would stroke your dick while he stabbed you in the back, a bastard whose career had been built on the bodies of the poor assholes he had screwed.

"Wonderful," Ciano said. "Lead the way."

"Captain Smith will be delighted to make your acquaintance," Dugan said, walking up the long flight of steps to the second floor. "A fine man and a credit to his race." There was a slight brogue in Dugan's speech, Ciano noticed.

"A credit to his race?" Ciano asked, outside the captain's door.

"Absolutely," Dugan said. "The last of the family men." He knocked and pushed the door open.

"Lieutenant Ciano?" Frank Smith asked. He pronounced it *Sigh-ano*.

"Ciano. *See-ano*."

"Mmm," Captain Smith muttered, as he fiddled with a handsomely carved pipe.

Ciano took a seat and lit up a cigarette, watching his new commander. The captain was short and broad-shouldered with a thatch of wavy red hair. His face was jowly, shot through with freckles, but the total effect was almost cherubic.

Ciano smoked and looked around the office as Smith tangled with a bent pipe cleaner. Dugan had it right, the captain was a family man. One wall of his office was a showcase of family photographs. Some were old snapshots of Smith as a rookie, some of his wife and two small daughters. By looking around the room, Ciano could follow the chronology of Smith's life and career. As he moved steadily up the ranks, Smith and his wife got smaller and older; the daughters grew and blossomed into womanhood. The most recent photographs showed Smith as a doting grandfather.

The pictures made Ciano feel guilty. He couldn't remember the last time he had had his picture taken with his son. At least three years, he sighed, but he noted with perverse satisfaction that the captain's wall of family pictures was almost full. He'd be retired or dead before he could start on a new side of the office.

"You have a family don't you, Lieutenant?" Smith asked, his sharp blue eyes focusing for the first time on Ciano.

Ciano nodded, not wanting to get into the truth.

"Fine, fine," Smith said. "It's important for a policeman to have a family to provide a safety valve. A family man is more likely to be a safe man, Lieutenant, a man who puts caution above reckless bravery, a man who thinks rather than reacts, a man who follows orders rather than forgets them," Smith paused. "That's the kind of man I want in my precinct."

Ciano shrugged. What could he say? It didn't matter what the hell Smith thought of him. The captain was in charge of the uniformed officers and the maintenance of the plant, the station house. Ciano reported to Borough Detectives, and although Smith outranked him, he couldn't say jackshit about Ciano's command.

Smith frowned, then stood up from behind his desk and moved around front to face Ciano.

"But failing that, Lieutenant, let me say that I'm glad you're here with us, anyway. We could use a man of your experience," Smith said, smiling. He extended his hand. It too was covered with red hair and freckles.

Surprised, Ciano shook Smith's hand, saying, "Thanks, Captain. It's nice to hear something positive for a change."

Smith planted himself on the edge of the desk. "I figured I could dispense with my usual welcoming speech, Ciano," he said. "You have one hell of a record, both good and bad. I followed your departmental trial through sources of my own and I want to tell you that you came within an ace of being a crossing guard in Elephant's Breath, Montana. But you've got some friends, believe it or not, and they went to bat for you."

"I didn't ask them to," Ciano said, feeling bitter again.

"So? Who cares? They saved your ass and you should be grateful," Smith said. "Even if you have to sit out here and rot."

"I still get paid," Ciano said. "That's all that counts, anyway."

"Bullshit!" Smith roared. "You'd trade a year's vacation and your left nut for an 'A' precinct assignment. We both know nothing happens on Staten Island.''

"It can't," Ciano said. "It belongs to the Mafia."

Smith laughed. "You're right about that. They took the two best locations, Todt Hill and Grimes, to build their villas and nothing keeps crime out of a neighborhood like *la familia*. If we could only get them to direct traffic, we could all pack up and go on vacation.''

Ciano was silent, wondering what would come next.

"DeFeo's here," Smith said.

"So I hear. Come to ream me out before I get started?" Ciano asked.

"Probably," Smith shrugged. "You want to see him alone or would you rather have, uh . . .''

"A witness? Yeah, a witness is what I'd like," Ciano said. "Where is he?''

"Cooling his heels in your new office," Smith said. "That's why I had Dugan waylay you.''

Apparently everyone had heard about Sally-boy.

"Give him a holler," Ciano said. "Might as well get it over with.''

Smith spoke briefly on the phone, then relaxed and played with his pipe again.

Sal DeFeo came bursting through the door, a grin on his flat, dark face.

"Vinnie, Vinnie, glad to see ya," he said, holding out his arms.

The son of a bitch is going to kiss me, Ciano thought for a second, but all he got was a bear hug from the Deputy Chief.

"Goombah," DeFeo said. "We're really gonna shake the leaves out here in the sticks.''

Ciano's smile was a sneer.

"Vinnie, my boy," DeFeo said with his most sincere voice. "We're not only gonna have the best precinct in the city, we're gonna have *fun*. I can't tell you how glad I am to have you on my team.''

So you can shaft me, Ciano thought, so your buddy Talbot can piss on my grave.

"Chief," Ciano nodded. DeFeo was no more than five-feet-six, but his shoulders were much wider than the rest of his body. He looked about forty-five, but Ciano knew he must be close to sixty. The chief's hair was black, probably dyed, his skin dark and oily like his personality. His nose was bumpy and crooked, again like his personality, Ciano thought.

"Fun?" Ciano said.

"Right, Vinnie. Us greaseballs gotta stick together. Right, Captain?" he winked at Smith, who smiled wanly.

"So if the good precinct commander doesn't mind, we'll mosey over to the other room for a chat about how we're gonna run this show," DeFeo continued smoothly. "Then we'll all have lunch."

"That'll be fun," Ciano said, instantly wishing he had kept his mouth shut. The man is out to get you, he thought, don't even *look* disrespectful.

"Great," DeFeo said, pretending not to have noticed Ciano's tone. "Shall we . . ."

He didn't get a chance to finish because Joe Dugan came bursting into the room.

"We just got a 911," he said. "A bad one. Two people murdered at Holy Cross Church."

"My God," Smith whispered. "That's the first murder we've had here in eighteen months and it's a double homicide!"

"I thought you said nothing ever happens here in Staten Island," Ciano said, grinding out his cigarette.

"It didn't," Smith said. "Until you arrived."

At Holy Cross Church a crime scene had been established. Blue N.Y.P.D. barriers cordoned off the area around the church and official vehicles were parked at odd angles near the scene. The flashing lights from police cars overlapped each other in sharp points of yellow, red, and white light.

Ciano and Joe Dugan walked toward the church while DeFeo was being briefed by the first cop on the scene. The day was bright and crisp, reminding Ciano of a trip to the country, not a murder investigation. He stopped in front of the church, and eyeing the headless scarecrow, thought the scene looked too bucolic, too clean, to be the site of a gruesome crime. Murder seemed much more acceptable to him amid the burnt-out tenements and garbage-strewn streets of Manhattan. Staten Island was an unlikely place to be murdered, Ciano thought, feeling the violation that had taken place around him.

Except for a few parishioners and neighborhood housewives who stood well back from the barricades, there wasn't much activity. The hordes of urban vultures weren't there laughing, joking, and sometimes screaming. It was too quiet.

25

As he and Dugan went through the red church doors, Ciano noticed another difference from the normal crime scene. Ashen-faced young policemen, hatless and with open collars, milled about, shaken. There were none of the usual wisecracks; the smell of vomit was strong. These guys, Ciano thought, have never been in the trenches.

They signed the Crime Scene Log and were issued disposable plastic gloves so they wouldn't inadvertently add to the evidence.

Ciano went first, retracing the steps of Jeanette Kidder Eddins. Near the altar, he looked down at the old woman's crumpled body. Her face was frozen in a snarl of pain and terror. Her false teeth had slipped, and shocking pink gums protruded from her curled lips, making her look like some kind of fierce animal; the smell of feces and vomit was penetrating. But what he saw on the altar was brutal enough to shake even Ciano. Silently he apologized to the weak-stomached young cops; it was all he could do to keep from throwing up himself.

"Oh, my God," Dugan gasped behind him, and quickly closed his eyes, shutting out the sight of death. But the smell was everywhere. He spun on his heels and marched out of the church.

Monsignor Bryan had been crucified upside down on the huge mahogany cross that had been taken down from its place over the altar for renovation. The old priest's left arm was tied to the cross, but three large nails had been driven through his right hand and into the wood. The priest's feet were bloody and mangled, the result of several unsuccessful attempts to hammer more of the long nails through his insteps. His feet, or what was left of them, were tied with nylon clothesline. Ciano recognized a half-hitch knot from his Navy days.

The priest's almost naked body had been torn apart, his vestments reduced to bloody strings of cloth. From his ankles to his neck, thin fragments of black cloth and bloody white skin intermingled like streamers hanging from the sickeningly white bone underneath. His genitals had been pounded into an unrecognizable clot of blood, skin, and hair.

Ciano squatted down in the coagulating pool of blood beneath the priest's head. He noted the ivory crucifix, coated with blood. Then he looked into a pair of empty eye sockets.

He stood up quickly and lit a cigarette. There was virtually no skin left on the priest's face. Ciano had been staring at a white and red, slimy skull. All the features that make up a human face had been erased; the eye sockets were empty and staring. Ciano thought he saw something where the left eye should have been, but he wasn't sure. He stared at the stained-glass window behind the altar watching the play of colors. He dragged deeply on the cigarette, disgusted by the incredible savagery of the attack.

His thoughts were broken by an Oriental man who said he was Dr. Young, the Assistant Medical Examiner.

"You in charge here?" he asked Ciano.

"Nope."

"Then do you mind getting out of the way? And put out that cigarette," the Assistant M.E. said.

Ciano stood aside while the Assistant M.E. dragged his black leather medical kit over to the altar. The inside of the case was covered in red felt, each instrument rested in its own niche. He was working fast now, concentrating totally, ignoring Ciano.

"I can't quite figure out the wounds," Young said to no one in particular. He used a scalpel to probe the shredded flesh. "The intensity of the wounds varies significantly from minor contusions to deep punctures and they appear in patterned groups of threes and fours."

He poked at the priest's Roman collar, lying near the body. It was smeared with blood, twisted and bent, indicating the frenzy with which it had been ripped from Monsignor Bryan's throat.

Young forced himself back to his work. "The shape of the individual wounds," he said in a studied monotone, as if recording an autopsy, "is consistently wedge-shaped, approximately six-by-two centimeters. There seems to be no discernible residue within the wounds and no compelling pattern to them."

"What's that mean?" Ciano asked, still staring at the stained-glass window and away from the corpse.

"It looks like he's been hit with a shotgun spray of some kind, though probably not from a gun. He's been whipped. Flayed alive," Young said as if he were discussing the weather.

"Jesus," Ciano said, forcing himself to look again at the battered remains of Monsignor Bryan. It was eerie, he thought, that although the body was severely damaged, the skin from the face was almost entirely gone. He was looking at a skull with an almost human body attached. A Halloween nightmare.

"Did you take a close look into his eye sockets?" Ciano asked, feeling like puking.

"Yeah. There's something in there, but it ain't eyes. It's metal," Young said. "I'll check it out back at the shop."

The shop, thought Ciano, a strange way to refer to the Medical Examiner's building.

"You want to guess at a time of death?" Ciano asked, lighting another cigarette, field-stripping the spent one and putting the butt in his pocket.

"Hard to tell, but I'd say he's been dead for only a couple of hours. Maybe less. We'll have to see when rigor sets in."

Young stood up and gathered his equipment. "But I'll tell you one thing, whoever worked him over did a thorough job. Took a long, long time to kill him. Some of these wounds are obviously hours older than others. The brutality, the . . . look, I've had enough. Let's go outside," Young said. Ciano was glad to follow.

The sparkling autumn morning did little to lessen the horror inside the church. Young had already given Miss Eddins' body a cursory inspection and had gone to make his preliminary report. Ciano sat on the rail of the landing, smoking a cigarette, biting his thumbnail and feeling ignored. He tried to think about what kind of person would flay a priest to death, what kind of maniac would spend hours torturing a man, then—

His thoughts were interrupted by Sal DeFeo.

"Ciano, over here," he beckoned. "This is your case now. You're supposed to be a detective."

Ciano pushed himself off the rail and walked slowly over to the little knot of men conferring in front of the church's red doors.

"Now, look," DeFeo said. "What with the reorganization of the detective division—for the tenth time in as many years it seems—the 122nd is responsible for the primary investigation of all homicides within its boundaries. I was just in communication with Chief Purcell," he said, referring to the Chief of Detectives, "and he's going to throw it at you. You can get help from downtown if you need it, but I told them you were perfectly capable of doing it on your own."

Setting me up for a fall, you bastard, Ciano thought.

"I want you to do this one quick, Ciano, and I want this killer ASPCA. Understand?" DeFeo continued, meaning ASAP.

"Right, Chief, ASPCA," Ciano grimaced. He didn't want this case. He didn't want to have anything to do with it. All he could see was unending work tracking down a psycho who probably had no record and who would strike again and again before it all ended. Ciano could envision the hundreds, perhaps thousands, of man-hours, devoted to a fruitless search. The promises he had made to himself—was it only this morning?—about making a new life, about spending more time away from the job, had just evaporated. If he took this case, he'd be consumed by it for months, years. Or more likely, fired from the case after a few frustrating weeks.

"Wouldn't you rather have them handle this downtown?" Ciano said, hoping he didn't sound like he was whining. "Set up a task force?"

"Let me spell it out for you, Ciano. First, it's out of my hands. The party line these days is 'decentralization.' Here on the local precinct level you are supposed to be able to solve crimes better than the old centralized detective division," DeFeo said.

Ciano was about to say something when DeFeo waved his arm, continuing, "Who knows if it's true? The new Police Commissioner says it's true, so we think it's true. Whatever. Second, you're in charge of this case, whether you like it or not. It's a murder, maybe two, but it's only murder. Priest or not, it's nothing that hasn't happened before and downtown isn't interested."

DeFeo paused. "Where was I? Oh, yeah. Third," he held up three fat fingers. "This is your chance to get it back on with the brass. You pull the solution to this case out of your ass and you're a hero."

"And fourth," Ciano said, holding up four fingers, mimicking DeFeo, "if I do fuck it up, which I probably will, because you know as well as I do that this kind of psycho is never really caught by standard police procedures, what then? We'll get him if he *decides* to get caught—some guilt complex or something—or he'll just disappear some day after slaughtering twenty-nine people. It stinks, Chief, it really stinks."

"Fifth," DeFeo said. "Do it or I'll put you on a scooter and make you a meter maid."

"Sixth," said Ciano, holding up five fingers of his left hand and the middle finger of his right, "what choice do I have?" He lowered his left hand. "You've got yourself a fucking whipping boy."

DeFeo smiled. "Correct. It's your ass on the line, so watch it."

"Sure," Ciano said, moving away. That's when Captain Smith grabbed him by the arm. Ciano shrugged him off.

"Easy, Ciano," Smith said. "I'm going to give you a bit of information I got from my sources. There's talk downtown about a certain group of cops, led by your old friend Captain Talbot,

29

who are out to get you. This is a made-to-order situation for them and they'll be watching you like a dick eyeing a virgin.

"Also, you've got to submit an Unusual," Smith continued, referring to an Unusual Occurrence Report, which would go right down to the Thirteenth and Fourteenth floors of One Police Plaza, home of the brass. "So everybody'll be watching."

"Wonderful," Ciano said, pushing his way past the captain. He had no choice—they had him by the short hairs. He walked over to the Assistant M.E.

Attendants came out of the church with Jeanette Kidder Eddins in a black body bag strapped to a gurney.

"What about the old woman?" Ciano asked Young. "Anything yet?"

"Probably died of a heart attack. There are no marks on her. She might have stumbled onto the murderer or onto the body and it killed her. Did you notice the strong smell of feces about her?" Young said.

"Yeah."

"I'd say she literally had the shit scared out of her."

Ciano frowned, then looked up to see Joe Dugan striding toward him.

"What'll we do next, boss?" Dugan asked. "Go downtown and steal some man power?"

"We're going to stay as far away from HQ as we can," Ciano said. "Those bastards want to tack me up on my own personal cross and they'll probably do it."

"Yeah, but think of the view," Dugan smiled.

"Ain't funny, Dugan. When they nail my ass you're an accessory."

"So? What are they going to do?" Dugan said. "Transfer me to Staten Island?"

"That's a point," Ciano laughed. "Come on, let's go play detective and find out who discovered the body . . . bodies."

"It was the other priest, one Thomas Layhe. He's waiting for us in the rectory now," Dugan said, adding, "I'm very efficient."

"You're also nuts, but come on," Ciano said, suddenly wishing he had slept a few hours the night before.

Chapter
Four

Inside the rectory, Father Thomas Layhe was thinking about the phone calls he had just made. It had been to the Cardinal's secretary requesting permission to excavate a crypt beneath the marble floor of the church, just behind the altar, to receive Monsignor Bryan's earthly remains. It was done as much to honor the dead priest as to appease his own guilt.

The thought of his predecessor's body entombed less than thirty feet away from the pulpit where he preached made Layhe uneasy. His whole adult life he had dreamed of running his own parish and now he'd feel Bryan's presence every time he entered the church.

The two priests had been at odds since Layhe had first arrived. Monsignor Bryan knew he was being replaced by Layhe, but he held on tenaciously, using all his power and authority to block any moves Layhe made. Their disagreements over the future of the parish had degenerated into heated arguments which invariably ended in one of Monsignor Bryan's contrived coughing spells. After the first time, this ploy hadn't worked again with Layhe, but in the aftermath of the horror, Layhe felt guilty.

Holy Cross had been Bryan's first love, he thought. The man had taken a sleepy country church and had turned it into a thriving parish. Then, old age, inertia, and changing times had caught up with the priest. Old parishioners died and had not been replaced, while youngsters laughed openly at the church and refused to attend. Then came Vatican II, the English Mass and innovations Monsignor Bryan had trouble accepting. It was as if the church were becoming Protestant, a thought so totally alien to the old priest as to be incomprehensible.

Monsignor Bryan continued to celebrate Mass in Latin and for his disobedience the Archdiocese had retired him, sending Layhe to replace him. In retrospect, however, Layhe saw that he might have been more sympathetic to Bryan's feelings. A new broom, he thought, should sweep clean, but not raise so much dust.

The constant friction between the two priests became a topic of gossip in the parish, each man having his own supporters and detractors. Now he supposed he'd have to officiate at the old man's funeral. It seemed hypocritical to Layhe for him to address the congregation while reading a cliché-ladened homily dedicated to a man he disliked. He could see a church full of Bryan's friends frowning knowingly as he lauded the old man. It was a distasteful prospect. That was why he was waiting for another priest, Father David Graff, perhaps Bryan's only friend. He told Graff on the phone about Bryan's murder and Graff had said he'd come right over.

Graff was as opinionated and stubborn as Bryan, but the two old priests had known and liked each other for years. He would be the perfect choice to deliver the eulogy, Layhe thought.

Layhe was on the phone with a local funeral parlor when Father David Graff knocked loudly on the oak door of the office.

Layhe, the phone wedged between shoulder and chin, motioned to the older priest to come in. Father Graff was drunk; his eyes were red and swollen. Layhe wondered if it was from crying or drinking. He motioned for the priest to sit down.

"Thank you very much, Mr. McCarthy," Layhe said into the phone. "I know you were a good friend of the monsignor's and we appreciate your help in this matter." Amen, Layhe thought, hanging up the phone. The funeral parlor was taken care of, at least.

"Thank you for coming, Father," Layhe said, looking distastefully at the older priest's rumpled clothes. Graff was not a big man, but he seemed bloated, as if a lifetime of drinking had finally caught up with him. Graff's nose was large and covered with broken veins, as were his puffy cheeks. His large hands drooped between his legs; he looked ready to pass out.

"Can I get you something?" Layhe asked, knowing he'd refuse the man another drink, but Graff shook his head. He started to say something, but his voice cracked with emotion and he fell silent.

How eloquent, Layhe thought, the perfect choice to deliver the eulogy. He looked at Graff's ruined face and thought idly that this priest must be the last man in New York to still wear a crewcut. He probably wears a hair shirt under his cassock, Layhe mused, waiting for the decrepit priest to speak.

But before Graff could say a word, Ciano and Dugan barged into the office.

"Father Layhe?" Ciano asked.

32

"Come in," Layhe said, standing up behind his desk. "I'm Father Layhe."

Ciano introduced himself and Dugan, and discovered that the rummy in the priest's suit was David Graff. The room smelled like a distillery.

Ciano dismissed Graff from his thoughts and concentrated on Layhe. His first impression was . . . brown. The priest, a solidly built man in his early thirties, was wearing dun-colored cords and an orange-and-brown Norwegian sweater knitted with prancing reindeer and swirling snowflakes. His running shoes were brown as were his eyes and hair. But the man himself wasn't brown and nondescript: he moved and spoke with energy and purpose, his handshake was firm, his voice was cultivated and low.

The study was richly paneled in oak and was lined from floor to ceiling with books. Ciano wasn't surprised to find that the thick carpeting and good leather chairs were also brown. Layhe seemed to disappear like a chameleon into his brown habitat. Ciano wondered why the priest was camouflaging himself. Only the man's voice penetrated the dark atmosphere.

"Would you gentlemen like coffee?" Layhe asked.

"Lovely," Dugan said.

"No thanks," Ciano said. "We'd like to hear about you finding the bodies."

Layhe shrugged and began his story while Ciano took meaningless notes. He was more interested in how the priest told his story than in what he actually said. Making the witness repeat his story over and over would bring out any inconsistencies.

Ciano was also absorbing the atmosphere of the room. Except for the nodding wino it made him feel as if he were in an exclusive men's club, and perhaps he was. Ciano remembered the secretive ways of the Jesuits who had taught him in school—remembered the beatings and the arrogant air of self-satisfaction those priests wore around themselves like their vestments. He sensed some of that superior attitude in Layhe, but the priest seemed intent on projecting a "just one of the guys" image. That annoyed Ciano more than smug sanctimony.

He led the priest through the usual questions. Had he heard or seen anything unusual? What time had he found the body? Had he touched anything? Layhe answered each question precisely, but with a hint of playfulness, as if he were trying to curry favor with the detectives. Unfortunately, he added nothing new to the investigation.

After a few moments of awkward silence, Ciano asked, "Did the monsignor have any enemies?"

"No," Layhe said casually. "Not even a disgruntled altar boy, or God forbid, an amorous nun." He laughed, but Ciano pursed his lips.

"What was your relationship with him?" Ciano asked.

"He was a monumental pain in the ass," Layhe said. "He was crochety, abrupt, rude, and difficult to deal with. I was his replacement and he resented it. Resented getting old, I suppose. No, he was not a candidate for canonization, but he didn't have any enemies either."

"You didn't answer my question," Ciano pressed.

"That's because it's a stupid question. I didn't have anything against him," Layhe said, losing his forced charm for the first time.

"Sometimes dumb questions lead to smart answers," Ciano said smoothly, but he let the matter drop. With skill and ease, Ciano began sorting through the pieces to this puzzle. He heard all he wanted to hear about the deceased, his relationship with Miss Eddins, and about Layhe's strained relationship with them both. He got the feeling that the young priest was secretly relieved to be rid of his two antagonists. But murder? Ciano found it difficult to believe. However, he had been fooled before.

"How about threats to you or the church? Hate mail, vandalism, that sort of thing?" Ciano asked.

Layhe stared at his hands for a moment. "Not really. We're pretty middle class out here. I mean, somebody spray-painted, 'Father Layhe Sucks' on the parking lot pavement once, but that's about it."

"Anything unusual happen recently?" Ciano asked, getting ready to terminate the interview.

"Like what?" Layhe asked. Ciano thought the priest was becoming wary again.

"Oh, I don't know. Anything out of the ordinary," Ciano said, watching the priest's eyes. If he were lying, the eyes would give him away.

"Well, on Saturday we had a party, a Halloween party for the kids. We had a good turnout, but there was some trouble."

"What kind of trouble?"

"One of the girls, Kathy Santini, was all upset because she saw someone looking in at her when she was in the girls' room," Layhe said. "But you know kids, probably just some of the boys horsing around. You know."

34

"Sure. But what else?" Ciano said, noticing that the priest's eyes had flickered slightly.

"Well, it sounds crazy, but Kathy said it was a, uh, troll looking at her."

"A troll?"

"Sure," Dugan said, speaking for the first time. "One of the little people. They live in caves and under bridges."

Ciano never took his eyes off Layhe. The priest shrugged and said, "That's what she said, Lieutenant. I tried to tell her that it was one of the boys with a mask, but she stuck to her story."

"Have you got her address?" Ciano asked. "Maybe we'll talk to her."

Layhe opened a folder on the leather-topped desk and read out an address in Todt Hill. Ciano made a note. He also made a note of Layhe's number. Then he turned to Graff, who was half-dozing in the chair next to his.

"How long did you know the monsignor?" Ciano asked. The old priest shook himself out of his stupor.

"Long time," Graff mumbled. "Long, long time."

Ciano noticed for the first time that the priest seemed not so much drunk as in shock and decided to let him off easy.

"We'll be in touch, Father," he said, as they left. "And we'll talk to your housekeeper as soon as she's pulled herself together."

"What do you think?" Ciano asked Dugan when they were outside in the sunshine walking toward the car.

"About what?"

"About the whole package," Ciano said. He lit a cigarette and dragged the smoke into his lungs. Funny, he thought, he hadn't lit a cigarette in the priest's study.

"Well," Dugan said. "I think we got problems. What was the motive? What could the monsignor have done to deserve to die like that? No, it's my feeling it was a ritual murder of some sort. The victim could have been any priest in any parish. We should look for some kind of off-the-wall cult."

"How about the troll business?" Ciano asked.

Dugan shrugged. "Reliable witnesses have seen weirder things."

"And the priest, Layhe?" Ciano asked.

"Ah, the good father. A man destined for big things, I fear. A man who would climb the ladder of success wearing track

35

shoes. Never mind that he planted the spikes into the bodies of his friends," Dugan said.

"You suspect him?"

"No, I don't think so. Murder would be bad for his corporate image."

"How 'bout the rumpot?"

"Now, there's a man who's had a hard life, a stinking life, that has tested his vows and ruined his taste buds."

"Taste buds?"

"Each of the little darlin's has been annihilated. Couldn't you smell it? Bar scotch, boss. The bottom of the barrel, as it were— the kind of whiskey most bartenders use to polish up the shine on the mahogany and to remove the road tar from their wheels."

"I take it that's expert testimony?" Ciano asked.

"It is," Dugan said. "And here's a bit more advice from the same source. You can expect this killer to strike again. Soon. And I just hope we can stop him."

"How we going to do that?" Ciano said. "If he wants to kill again, he will." They got into Ciano's station wagon and drove out of the parking lot.

"Then maybe the priests can stop him," Dugan said.

"The priests?"

"Sure. Let me tell you a story that my Uncle Sean swears is true." He spoke as Ciano drove. "It happened in a remote part of Galway many years ago. It seems that one day both the parish priest and the local doctor were called to the sick bed of my Great-Aunt Mary. Ninety she was, if she was a day. But she had a vision that told her she was about to take her last breath, so she sent for the priest and the doctor, one to help her into the next world, the other to stop her from going if he could.

"Both men came in a shiny black car in the midst of a terrible rainstorm. They both practiced their specialties for a time, and Great-Aunt Mary took a sudden turn for the better. Lived more than ten years longer, she did.

"Anyway, the priest and the doctor finished up their business and dashed out to the car. Well, they got to the car, escorted by my Uncle Michael, as was the custom of the day, when the doctor suddenly remembered his umbrella, open and drying in the hall.

" 'Michael, my boy,' the old doctor said to my uncle, 'run back to the house and fetch my umbrella.' So Uncle Michael ran through the rain, grabbed the umbrella, then stopped dead. He could see right off that the big old umbrella would never fit

36

through the door. So he called Great-Uncle Brian, who was known for his phenomenal abilities to solve any sort of problem. 'I'll take the frame off the door,' said the inventive Brian, and in ten minutes the frame was lying in the rain.

"But alas, the umbrella was still too wide to fit through the door. 'I believe if we take out the stones from around the door, it will work,' said Brian, relishing his task and delighted to have a monopoly on the brains in the family.

"But while he was hammering away at the stones, the priest got tired of waiting, so he dashed into the house, grabbed the umbrella, unfurled it and ran back out to the car, giving Michael and Brian a strange look.

"The two men stood there in the rain looking at the priest. 'Well, what do you think about that?' Uncle Michael said, with great wonder. 'Say what you want about priests,' old Brian says. 'But it's good to know that they've still got the power.'"

Ciano snorted.

"I hope the priests still have the power," Dugan said, looking infinitely pleased with himself. "They'll need it."

His hands covered with blood, his mind rolling with images of death, Joseph Steppe crawled deeper into his hiding place high above Richmondtown Village. From his vantage point beneath the porch of the abandoned Victorian house, he could see the lights of the police cars strobing in the distance. It was hypnotic; he wondered if he'd ever be able to look away.

He lay on his stomach for several minutes, dazzled by the lights, reliving the scene in the church. He shivered uncontrollably, picturing the priest's ruined face and the blood. All that blood! His hands had been covered with it. Even now he could see the rusty remnants of it lodged in dark crescents under his fingernails.

Without taking his eyes from the lights, Steppe reached into the pocket of his green work pants and brought out a lumpy, stained Kleenex. It was warm, soft and strangely comforting. He put it to his nose and inhaled, trying to remember every detail of the slaughter.

It came back to him in a rush: the tattered flesh, the blood seeping over the marble floor, pooling, coagulating, collecting in little rivers, following the grout canals. . . .

He stuck out his tongue to taste the soiled tissue and reveled in its coppery tang. It was almost electric. He wanted to open the little package, but he didn't dare because the lights in the distance were still flashing, signaling something to him. If he could only read the code, he might have the answer to a question that evaded him, haunted him since childhood.

What he never could understand was why God gave him polio. His had been one of the twenty-eight cases reported nationwide that year. The chances of catching that rare disease were infinitesimal, convincing Joseph Steppe that he had been singled out by Divine Providence for special punishment.

He fondled the Kleenex, at last looking away from the flashing lights. The thought of what was in the tissue was making him excited, as excited as he got when he gave into his *other* compulsion—showing himself to little girls.

Joseph Steppe weighed the soggy tissue in his hand, enjoying the heft of the object wrapped within. Holding it close to his face so he could see it well, he slowly unwrapped the tissue. He smiled and bounced the object in his palm, then popped it into his mouth. He savored its salty taste as he had savored his latest victory. It made him excited again, especially when he thought about the girl at the church party last Saturday. He could still hear her screams echoing in his head. It was one of the many victories he had won, always over young girls. He didn't like women to see him, they would laugh. But girls, little girls, always screamed, giving him a strange excitement, allowing the power to flow into his penis, making it large and hard, not small and weak. For except for showing himself to little girls, his life had been sadly lacking in power. He controlled no one, everyone controlled him. He had taken a job at the Richmondtown restoration, but he was only a handyman. They ordered him around, treating him as though he were stupid. They told him to do this and do that, as if he couldn't see what had to be done. He hated them all, especially his boss, Abigail West.

He chewed lightly on the object in his mouth, then spat it out in his hand.

"Look at me! Look at me!" he said.

It looked back at him with an approving stare.

"I see you," he giggled, rewrapping Monsignor Bryan's eyeball in the wet, dirty tissue.

Chapter
Five

Ciano eyed the ceiling of his new office with contempt. There were more than a dozen pencils stuck into the acoustical tile above his head, a forest of yellow stalactites poised ominously, ready to fall on him. He had played that game before—flipping sharpened pencils into the tile—but it irritated him now, reminding him he had a whole new crew to control, all unknown quantities.

He looked at his watch. Mickey's big hand was on the four, his little hand on the twelve. That meant it was probably noon or a little later. Mickey was always a bit vague about the precise time, but Ciano had kept the watch because his wife had given it to him—what?—six years before. He had found it sifting through the clutter of his old apartment, and although he knew it was some kind of slam about his job, somehow it seemed important to wear it.

The phone at his elbow rang. He picked it up. It stuck to his hand.

"Lieutenant Ciano?"

"Yeah?"

"Dugan. You want me?"

"Yeah. And bring some towels from the men's room. This place's a shithouse."

He leaned back in his chair, hoping it wouldn't tip over, and put his feet up on the gray metal desk. The top of the desk was a riot of coffee rings and unidentified stains. Ciano didn't want to touch it. The floor, gray linoleum tile, had been freshly waxed, but whoever had done it hadn't bothered to sweep first. It was disgusting, but it was typical.

"The luxury suite," Dugan said, standing in the doorway of the cubicle. A six-foot-high green plastic wall separated Ciano from the open expanse of gray linoleum. An island of shit in a sea of shit, Ciano thought, nodding to Dugan and telling him to sit in one of the gray plastic chairs in front of his desk.

"The guys aren't going to like it," Dugan said, slumping down.

"Like what?"

"You taking over their card room, cum lunch room, cum private telephone booth," Dugan said, tossing a stack of rough, brown paper towels on Ciano's desk. "It's been a while since we've had a boss around here."

Ciano looked at him, and without losing eye contact, spit on a paper towel. Rubbing at the coffee stains, he asked Dugan to fill him in on the personnel.

"Well," said Dugan. "You got six detectives, three third-class, three second-class. None are first class in any sense of the word. You got two spades, two micks, a Guinea and a Marty Abel, who says he isn't Jewish."

"Is he?" Ciano asked, spitting again to moisten the towels.

Dugan smiled. "Who knows? He's certainly not able."

"Well, round them up and send them in. Might as well meet them."

"It's almost time for lunch," Dugan said.

"Fuck lunch. Get those guys in here," Ciano said, leaning over his desk to get at a multiple coffee-ring combination that looked like the symbol for the Cerebral Palsy Olympics. "Tell them to get here ASAP. No, make that ASPCA."

When Dugan had gone, Ciano stood gingerly on his chair and snatched a pencil from the acoustical tile. Then he began doodling on a clean paper towel, trying to clear his mind. He wrote down $M = PF^2$ in bold capital letters. It was a formula he had learned long ago from an old frog-faced line cop who had burped it up between bites of an onion-smothered meat burger. The advice and the smell of onions were inexorably entwined in his memory. $M = PF^2$. It simply meant that murderers were caught with hundreds of phone calls and an enormous amount of footwork. The more men you had on the job, the easier it was. Except, of course, with a psycho. Then it really didn't matter at all. He crumpled the towel and threw it at the wastebasket in the corner of the office. He missed. The wadded-up paper towel joined the others lying near the empty trash container.

With the last towel, he picked up the gummy phone and dialed the M.E.'s office. He got Dr. Young on the third ring.

"Give me a break, Ciano," Young complained. "The bodies are still warm."

"How about the thing in the priest's eye socket? What was it?" Ciano asked. He could imagine Young sitting amid beakers,

40

flasks, bubbling distillers, and jars filled with floating body parts. It made him feel better about his own grunge-encrusted office.

"Well, you're not going to believe me, but somebody shoved a coin up the guy's eye socket," Young said.

"What kind of coin?"

"Old coin. Antique. Greek or Roman or something. Shoved the sucker right up there."

"You're having it analyzed?"

"No, I'm going to use it to tip the pizza man," Young said.

"Good."

"Oh, and one more thing. Whoever inserted the coin, removed the eye. Can't find it anywhere. One's all mashed up, but looks complete. Other one's gone," Young said. "Vanished."

"You probably left it under a pew. I'll send a man back to the church. I don't want some old lady complaining there's somebody looking up her skirt on Sunday." He paused. "Keep on it, huh?"

"Give me a little time," Young said.

"That's what you've got," Ciano said. "Little time."

Dugan showed up with four of the six detectives. They stood around uncomfortably, looking at Ciano as if he were a leper.

"You probably know my name," Ciano said, not asking anyone to sit; there weren't enough chairs anyway. "I'll get to know yours. Right now we got work to do."

"Who's missing?" he asked Dugan.

"Abel and Mancuso. They're at the church talking to the priest's housekeeper and keeping an eye on things."

Ciano laughed. "Appropriate," he said. "Tell them to be on the lookout for an eyeball."

"Left or right?" Dugan asked, but the four detectives stared at him impassively, as if they expected this kind of crazy talk from him.

"No shit," Ciano said. "Assistant M.E. says the priest lost an eyeball. I want those two guys to scour the church for it. If they don't find it, and I don't think they will, we can figure our man took a souvenir of his late-night consultation with the priest."

Then he began to hand out the assignments, telling the four detectives that this case took priority over everything else they were working on. He had already pried eight uniforms out of Captain Smith and had them doing a house-to-house canvass of the neighborhood surrounding the church. They were looking for early-morning dog walkers and joggers, as well as insomniac busybodies who monitored the nocturnal doings of their neighbors.

He assigned the two black cops, Darren Henderson and Calvin Richards, to cover the sanitation department. They were to interview the street sweepers and garbage men who worked the area. He also told them to check on any delivery services—bread, milk, and mail—that might have been on the scene. Then he told Bobby O'Reilly and Sam McClurg to pull all the psycho files.

"After that," Ciano said, "get out in the field and help the uniforms. I'm particularly interested in retracing the old lady's steps this morning."

He stopped. "And tell those other two guys about the eyeball." They stared at him with insolence.

"Well, get to it," he said.

As they filed out of his office, he heard one black detective say to the other. "Sure, *we* get the fucking garbage detail."

Ciano sighed. Was there ever anything new?

After telling Dugan to call the radio stations that did live traffic reports, in case any of the helicopter pilots had seen anything unusual, Ciano spent an unproductive half hour making notes.

Not knowing what else to do, Ciano called his ex-wife. He let it ring ten times before hanging up the sticky phone. Then he grabbed his jacket and left the office. He knew from experience that it would be several hours before the reports started coming in. That would give him plenty of time to see his new apartment, the one he had sublet sight unseen from a real estate agent on Victory Boulevard. It would take pitifully few minutes to unpack his two cardboard boxes, then be back at work.

Outside, in the precinct parking lot, he found Joe Dugan lying on the hood of his battered station wagon. His eyes were closed.

Ciano slammed his palm down next to Dugan's ear; the sergeant opened his eyes slowly.

"Didn't I tell you to get to work?" Ciano asked, more amazed than angry.

"All done," Dugan said. "Like any good executive, I delegated the responsibility to certain uniform-types who know which side their bread is buttered on. And speaking of bread and butter, let's go to Hanratty's for a bite."

Ciano ignored him and opened the door on the driver's side.

While he was hunting for his keys, Dugan jumped to the ground and said, "Come on, you've got to meet Hanratty."

"Why?" Ciano asked.

"Because he's Hanratty, that's why. Come on, see for yourself."

Ciano slammed the door and shrugged. "I could use some coffee." His apartment could wait.

Hanratty's Place looked like somebody's house. It occupied the bottom floor of a two-family, wood-shingled building across the street from the precinct. Except for a half-dead neon sign flickering out the dubious message RATTY'S, Ciano would have walked right by it.

Dugan pushed his way past a white front door decorated with Indian corn and went down the three steps into the restaurant.

There were about twenty tables, each set with mismatched silverware, a white citronella candle, and a Perrier bottle filled with dried flowers.

Some of the tables had bright red-and-white checkered tablecloths, others sported blue place mats, but all were crowded with cops noisily having lunch.

"Trés chic," Dugan said. "In a tacky sort of way."

Ciano followed him to a corner table, where Dugan began undressing. He took off his coat, hat, and gunbelt and piled them neatly in an empty chair. Then he kicked off his shoes and toed them carefully under the table.

"You moving in?" Ciano asked, sitting down.

"Nope," Dugan said, scratching himself under the armpit. "Just getting comfortable."

Ciano frowned, but before he could say anything a gaunt man of about sixty came over to the table and sat down. He was wearing baggy, pleated pants with the waistband turned over to keep them up, a blue nylon shirt, and a droopy black cardigan sweater. He had closely cropped white hair and a small, white mustache. His round wire-rimmed glasses magnified his watery blue eyes.

"I got a reservation," Dugan said, slouching in his chair.

"Just making sure my customers are happy," the white-haired man said.

Ciano stared at them. They were playing some sort of game.

"Bring Joe his Coke," the man said to a passing waitress. "Can I get you boys something to eat?"

43

Dugan ordered three fried eggs, french fries, toast, and a side order of pancakes.

Ciano thought about his heart and ordered black coffee.

"Ed," Dugan said. "I want you to meet Lieutenant Vince Ciano, our new whip."

"Ed Hanratty," the white-haired man said in a mild voice, but Ciano could sense authority behind the neutral pose. Definitely some kind of game, he thought.

The waitress returned with Dugan's Coke, which was really a beer in a soda can. Ciano could smell it.

Dugan drained half the can, then reached into his back pocket and produced a silver flask.

"Blood medicine," he said, pouring a healthy slug of Jack Daniels into the beer and swirling the mixture around.

Here's part of the game, Ciano thought. See how far you can push your new commander. As an expert at that particular ploy, he wasn't about to play.

"Ed's an ex-cop," Dugan said. "Former captain and now proprietor of this juice bar. You should get to know him."

Part two of the game, Ciano thought, but he still wasn't playing. He'd let Ed Hanratty, retired Captain, N.Y.P.D., make the first move.

Hanratty began by playing, "Who do you know?" and quickly moved on to "Where have you worked?"

Ciano was irritated. He didn't like to be grilled. His answers were curt.

"So you put in time on the Great White Way?" Hanratty said. "I spent time there myself in the late '50s. Of course, then it was still great and white."

Ciano nodded. "I don't understand why it's a tourist attraction anymore."

"Maybe it's the smell of urine," Dugan volunteered, realizing at once he had made a mistake.

"I'll get your orders," Hanratty said quickly, standing up and heading for the kitchen.

After Hanratty had disappeared behind the swinging door to the kitchen, Dugan continued in a somewhat subdued tone, "Ed's a good guy. But he's kind of, uh, precise, I guess you might say. Prissy's too strong a word. He's probably real upset over that Monsignor Bryan's death. They were good friends, you know. Went way back together, I hear. So if he quizzes you on the case, play it cool, huh?"

Ciano nodded, shaking out a cigarette from a fresh pack of

Camels. Here was the game plan. "I gather you told him the bad news earlier," Ciano said. "Over a few Cokes."

Dugan smiled. "Well now, aren't you the detective, Mr. Ciano?"

"Shove it."

"Okay, you nailed me, chief. I figured I needed a back bracer after this morning's visit to the Twilight Zone, so I told him. Never saw him show so much emotion before. But this one went through him like shit going through a goose. Thought he'd keel right over on the floor."

Ciano grunted and took the opportunity to look around. The restaurant was warm and home-like because it was a home, not because some fancy designer had filled it with old tables. It seemed to Ciano that running a greasy spoon was quite a comedown for a retired captain. The old guy should be grilling his body in the Florida sun, not grilling hamburgers over a hot stove, but maybe he was broke. Business, however, looked good. The tables were full of cops laughing, shouting, and chewing with their mouths open. Civilians were always leery about places like this and stayed away in droves. The patrons were too raw and raucous, too crazy for normal people to handle. Fortunately for the public, cops usually hung out together—not because they enjoyed each other's company particularly, but because they couldn't stand anyone else either.

A few minutes later, Hanratty returned with their orders. Ciano sipped his coffee, wishing he had ordered bacon and eggs.

Hanratty sat down again and Ciano winced. Here it comes, he thought, the old war horse is going to tell me how to do my job and about how cops aren't real cops these days.

"I don't know if Dugan told you, but Francis Bryan was a good friend of mine," Hanratty began. "I'd like to be of some help on the case. Get a little involved, if you will."

"What if I won't?" Ciano said, feeling cornered and angry. He didn't like being set up by Dugan and used by this old cop. He looked at Dugan, who looked away.

"I don't want to interfere with your case, Lieutenant," Hanratty said. "Or tell you how to run your investigation. All I'm offering you is my forty-plus years of experience to help catch a friend's murderer. That's all I'm doing."

"Well, do it somewhere else," Ciano muttered, sipping his coffee.

Hanratty smiled and shrugged before excusing himself and disappearing back into the kitchen.

"That wasn't too swift," Dugan said. "I thought you were going to be cool."

"You didn't tell me he wanted to run my case," Ciano shot back. "And what the hell business is it of yours?"

"Come on, all you had to do was jerk him off a little. He's good people, why the wise guy routine?"

"I have a thing about bosses," Ciano said, thinking about Captain Talbot.

"He's retired, for chrissake. But he still has a lot of friends downtown," Dugan said, runny fried eggs dripping off his fork.

"You know something, Dugan? Both him, his friends, and you can go fuck yourselves." Ciano stood up and threw a dollar bill on the table.

"Aw, sit down, Lew," Dugan said, using the slang for lieutenant. "Relax."

Ciano was about to go when he felt someone behind him. He shuddered involuntarily and spun around, tensed to fight. But what he saw made him tense for another reason.

She was tall, almost as tall as Ciano, with long thick auburn hair that cascaded over her shoulders. Her eyes were deep emerald, laughing at him. She was wearing a white wool dress that clung to her like a second skin, revealing a lush figure that made Ciano's balls tingle.

She smiled, emphasizing her high cheekbones and giving her flashing green eyes an upward, almost Oriental, slant. It was an intriguing smile, a mysterious smile, one that Ciano realized could easily become a sneer. Unfortunately, the smile wasn't for him.

"Hello, Sergeant Dugan," she said. Her voice was pleasantly husky. Refined.

"Darlin'," Dugan grinned. "A breath of springtime in the autumn of my sad life."

She smiled again. "How's the biggest Irish bullshitter this side of County Cork?"

"When he comes in, I'll ask him," Dugan said. "But I'd like you to meet Vince Ciano here. He's angry looking, but basically okay. This is Erica Hanratty."

"James," she corrected.

"James Hanratty?" Ciano said, trying desperately to be witty.

"Hardly," she said. There was an air of superiority about her that was not a sham. She *was* superior and she knew it. Ciano wondered how she would look spread-eagled on a bed, her na-

46

ked body writing with pleasure. He fought to clear his head of this image, but damn it, she even smelled good.

Ciano couldn't think of anything smart to say, so he said nothing, hoping she would think he was deep. It didn't seem to work.

"May I sit down?" she asked, sitting down. Ciano was still standing, trying to decide what to do next. He caught a flash of her thigh and he sunk slowly into his chair.

"You're Ed Hanratty's daughter," he said, as if he were making a profound statement. Erica looked at him oddly.

"That's what I like about your friend, Joe. He's so bright. Must be a detective."

Dugan, who hadn't stopped grinning the entire time, launched off on a monologue about the vagaries of a police career, all the while thinking that this woman didn't have the slightest interest in him. He had noticed, however, that there was something happening between Erica and Ciano; he couldn't believe it.

Every cop in the precinct had tried to get close to Hanratty's daughter during the two months she had been visiting her father. But no one, not even Dugan, with his con man's spiel, had ever managed to get her to sit down at a table. Now she was sitting, but it was Ciano who had attracted her. Amazing. Ciano sure didn't look like much to Dugan. Maybe ten years ago, but not now. His dark, craggy face was puffy and wrinkled with worry. He couldn't even carry on a conversation with her, yet she was sitting, Dugan thought, and if you can get them sitting, the next step's to get them lying down. Amazing.

Erica asked Dugan for a cigarette and while he fumbled for one in his jacket, Ciano pushed the pack of Camels in her direction.

"Thanks," she said, tapping the cigarette on the table. Ciano lit it for her and noticed she cupped his hand while he held the match. A good sign, he and his buddies had always said when they were kids. Means the girl likes you. He also liked the way she had taken the unfiltered cigarette without hesitation. No protests about how strong they were. This was a woman who was in control.

Dugan scraped his chair over the linoleum floor, hoping the sound would interrupt the handholding. "Your father's taking his loss pretty hard," he said.

"What loss?"

"Why the monsignor, of course," Dugan said, arching an eyebrow.

"Oh, yes," Erica said. "I suppose they were great friends."

47

"Friends? They were almost like brothers to hear him tell it," Dugan said. "Did you know the monsignor?"

"Yes, but I hadn't seen him for years," Erica said, looking back at Ciano.

She didn't seem at all interested in the priest's death, which surprised Dugan.

"I've never seen Ed so upset," Dugan said, trying again.

"That's because you've never lived with him," Erica said, laughing. Ciano joined in halfheartedly; Dugan was silent.

"Oh, come on Sergeant Dugan," Erica said. "Lighten up a bit. After all, he was an old, old man. It's tragic, of course, but then life's tragic, isn't it? Why should his death be any worse?"

"But he was *murdered*," Dugan said.

"Murdered, hit by a bus, cancer," Erica said, blowing a cloud of blue smoke at him. "None of it's pleasant. Ed will get over it."

"Perhaps," Dugan said doubtfully.

"Do I shock you?" Erica asked Ciano.

"Who me?" Ciano said, tearing his eyes off her. He hadn't been listening.

"Yes, you," Erica said. "Well, I have to run. It's been a pleasure."

The noise level in the restaurant fell off abruptly as every man in the room watched her glide across the floor.

"Jesus," Ciano breathed. "That's some woman. She makes me feel like a fourteen-year-old with a hard-on and no place to stick it."

"I told you you'd like Hanratty's," Dugan said, stirring the remains of his eggs without much interest. He took another slug of his boilermaker.

"What's her story?" Ciano asked, signaling the waitress for more coffee.

"Mrs. Erica Hanratty James," Dugan began, as if he were reading a police report, "white, female, about thirty, married to some guy with a ton of cash. She's been here a couple of months, her first visit to dear old dad in a long, long time, I gather. She's been all over the world with her husband, but he's supposedly away alone now. To me, that means they're having problems and she's here with poppa to teach him a lesson.

"But I'll tell you one thing, if that lady were mine, I'd be damned if I'd go farther than the men's room without her. Might even take her in with me, to help me shake it off."

48

Ciano said nothing.

"Smart broad, too," Dugan continued. "Like her father. He sent her to all kinds of fancy schools in Europe. She's got almost too much for one woman, if you ask me. But I'd give up half my pension to find out if she's really . . ."

"A redhead," Ciano finished absently. He was staring at her swaying ass. "You know, Dugan, I think this case may be more difficult than I thought," Ciano said.

"You might like some help from a certain retired police captain, would you?"

"I just might. See if you can set it up."

Ciano felt like a fool. This morning he had been full of optimism about getting it on with his ex-wife and living as a normal human being again. A few hours later, he had been saddled with a case that would probably destroy what was left of his career, and had met the most beautiful woman he had ever seen. Worse, he had acted like a clumsy schoolboy in front of her. "You're Hanratty's daughter?" Jesus. What a jerk, he thought.

He drove slowly down Victory Boulevard, past the real-estate office that had subleased him the apartment. This area of Staten Island was all built up now, but Ciano remembered it from his youth as small town, rural. He turned off Jewett Avenue onto Fiske Road and headed toward the place he would hang his hat for a year, with an option to renew. He hoped he wouldn't be there that long. He wanted desperately to get back to an "A" precinct.

His new apartment was located in a sixteen-building complex called Stonehenge. Stupid name, Ciano thought, wondering if they hired druids as janitors. Living in someone else's apartment made him feel like he wasn't good enough to have his own home.

Maybe in his old age, the loner is getting lonely, he thought, entering the development.

The apartment buildings were even uglier and more depressing than he had imagined. Each unit was square, five-story brick and dingy. Row after row of these squat, identical buildings looked like a military compound or an institution.

He drove through the maze of roads connecting the buildings until he found the correct address, then parked the car where it said NO PARKING. Hefting one of his two cardboard boxes on his shoulder, he followed the narrow cement path that divided two sections of brown lawn to the entrance of the building. An old

49

woman in a black dress and black kerchief eyed him suspiciously and refused to let him in the door until he produced the keys the real-estate office had sent him. There were three keys and naturally the last one he tried fit the glass front door. The old woman shrank from him, expecting to be robbed or raped or murdered. Ciano growled at her and she fled to the safety of her ground-floor apartment. Ciano knew buildings like this. They were the last refuge of the elderly, before death or the nursing home got them; they were filled with young couples just starting out and short on cash; they were also full of middle-class minorities who thought they had it made in the white world.

Ciano looked around. The lobby was L-shaped, painted a dark, oppressive green and empty of furniture. He walked up two steps to the mailboxes. He read the names. Lots of Italians. Good, he thought. I probably won't be shot to death in the hall unless I do something radically wrong. He looked for apartment 1-A. G. Stabille. Poor old Mrs. Stabille. He had frightened the old woman and that would keep the rest of the tenants off his back. She was obviously the concierge, the gatekeeper, the granny patrol, for this building. Nothing would escape her attention. By the time she got through gossiping about him, he'd be a homicidal maniac, and perhaps even a man possessed of an evil eye. Friendly place, the suburbs, he thought. But at least the building didn't smell like piss.

He took the coffin-sized elevator to the third floor. The hall was covered in puke-green industrial carpet that made astroturf look like the White House lawn. Putting the box down in front of the blue-green metal door, he fumbled with the keys until he got both locks open.

The nameplate on the door said CHRIS & DAN FREEBURG, the couple who had sublet the apartment. As Ciano made a note to have it changed, he noticed the center of the blue door had been cleaned with a caustic detergent that had bleached the paint. Using the box to hold the door open, he switched on the hall light and examined the faded area, trying to read what had been wiped out. It was a single word beginning with a capital "F," but it was too long for the ubiquitous "fuck." He kicked the door inside, letting the door slam behind him.

It was cold and dark inside the apartment. On his left was the kitchen, which looked like a normal kitchen. Straight ahead was the living room. He searched for the light and snapped it on. He was sorry he had.

My God, he thought, it looks like a French whorehouse. The curtains were dark burgundy with gold trim; they clashed with the wine-colored velour sectional couch that dominated the room. Two overstuffed gold chairs flanked the couch; a brass-and-glass coffee table completed the room. There were plants everywhere, hanging from the ceiling, growing out of huge wooden tubs on the floor, perched precariously on tiny tables strewn around at random. The deep-pile carpeting was black.

Frowning, he shut the light off again. If the living room was done in porno-movie modern, he could imagine what the bedroom was like.

When he turned on the bedroom light, he realized he didn't have the imagination to imagine what it was like.

It actually made him dizzy. Hundreds of do-it-yourself mirror tiles had been installed from floor to ceiling, creating a fun-house effect that was truly staggering. Thousands of Cianos stared back at him in open-mouthed amazement; the seams between the mirrors distorted and blurred his image, fragmenting him in a thousand pieces. Here and there, foot-square mirrors were missing, leaving black holes in the gleaming background, reminding him of an evil, gap-toothed grin.

The major piece of furniture in the room was a huge round bed perched on a two-foot-high platform. It was covered with a peach-colored comforter and heart-shaped red pillows were lined up neatly against a red, heart-shaped velour headboard. Ciano didn't know whether to laugh or get angry. A stereo-TV unit was suspended above the bed. Ciano liked that, he could watch the Jets without getting up—but could he really sleep in a round bed? With mirrors?

He walked around the room in wonder, all the myriad Cianos following him, and he began to laugh. What the hell else did you expect, asshole, when you rent an apartment without seeing it first? he thought.

On the bed was a TV remote control unit. Taped to it was a piece of pink paper. It read:

Welcome to our home . . . sorry we couldn't meet, but maybe when we return. . . . I've cleaned out my closet for your use (it's the one with the big "C" on the door) and the hall closet's practically empty. If you need more room, just push our things aside. The fridge is full of yummy leftovers, so help yourself! And please, please take care of my darling plants. They're like my children (ha, ha!). Hope you enjoy this place as much as Danny and I do—tho Europe will be heavenly!

Love,
Chris

Ciano opened the closet with the ornate "C" on the door. It was empty, but it reeked of cheap perfume. Chris with the C should change her scent, Ciano thought, deciding not to hang his clothes in there. He went to the closet marked D, for Dan he supposed, wondering why a married couple couldn't remember whose closets were whose.

Inside of Dan's closet was a full-length black-and-white poster tacked on the door. On it was written, "Dan and Chris. Married July 26th. Live happily ever after!" It showed a bride and groom, surrounded by their friends, smiling ecstatically. The groom was wearing a top hat, shoes, and spats; the bride was wearing a veil and carrying a bouquet of flowers. And that was all they wore. They were nude. They were also men. Both of them.

Ciano kicked the door shut and walked to the kitchen, trying to remember where he had put the rental agent's card. Holy Christ, what a place! When old Mrs. Stabille found out where he was living. . . .

Using the wall phone in the kitchen he dialed information, but the operator, who barely spoke English, couldn't help him. Frustrated, he slammed his hand down on the counter by the sink. A cockroach scurried out of the drain, looked at Ciano, then plunged back toward safety. Ciano turned on the hot water, hoping to boil it, but knowing it was useless.

What a fucking day, he thought. I need someone to share this happy experience with. And he knew just the person.

He dialed his ex-wife. On the third ring she answered.

"Diane? It's Vince," he said, then waited for her reply; when none came, he continued.

"Is Vincent home?" he asked, feeling his stomach knot. "Diane," Ciano repeated, putting an edge to his voice. "I didn't call to fight, I just want to talk to my son."

His ex-wife answered in her ice-queen voice, "Nobody is fighting, Vince. Your son has been waiting to talk to you for the last four months. You haven't called since the end of June and you've been too busy to return his calls. So excuse me if your sudden interest in our son doesn't overwhelm me."

"I know that. I'm sorry. I've had some problems."

"I know all about your problems. I read the papers. But you

still should have called. There is no excuse for what you put that child through."

This was not going as he had planned. He knew he was using his son to get to her. And so did she. It made him feel even more guilty than before. One of the reasons he had stopped calling in the first place was that he hated to be reminded of how lousy a father he was. He already knew.

"Look, Diane, I've been transferred out here to Staten Island and I'd like to try to straighten things out with you and Vincent. Maybe I can come over and we can have dinner or something? You should see the place I've rented, it's . . ."

"That would be nice, Vince," Diane said, her voice less harsh. "Vincent's at school, but you can call back tonight."

"No phone," he lied. "I'll call you tomorrow at seven p.m."

"That'll be fine," Diane said, then hesitated before adding, "Vince, I'm glad you'll be close by now and that you want to see Vincent. But if you start with the same old nonsense, I warn you, I won't allow it. Vincent is beginning to accept living without you and I won't let you start playing with his emotions."

"Look, Diane, I'm trying to set things straight. Just give me a break and don't bust my balls. Instead of calling, I'll come over and see you both. Maybe I can explain things, so that you and Vincent will understand some of the shit I've been up against." He hoped he didn't sound like he was whining.

"Not tomorrow," she said.

"Why not?"

"Because you can't, that's why."

Ciano's stomach tightened. That meant there was someone else. He wondered if he should question her. But he really didn't want to know.

"I understand," he said and hung up. Staring at the yellow phone, he lit a Camel and tried to calm down. He shouldn't have called when he was upset. All he wanted was a little sympathy, not the Third World War.

That was the thing about Diane, she had a way of opening old wounds and making him angry. She couldn't help it, he thought, she just had the knack for pissing him off. The trouble was, most of the time she was right and that always made him madder. He had always thought that she could take care of herself during their violent arguments, but she took them more seriously than he ever did. Ciano would be livid one minute, horny the next. But Diane held everything inside. He remembered she had once said she was like the Hapsburgs: She forgot nothing, forgave nothing. Whatever that meant.

She had loved him once, he knew, even though he had screwed it up royally by being more of a cop than a husband. He always thought she could take it, but one day she gave up on him and that was it. He didn't realize how much he missed her until she was gone, he didn't realize how much she irritated him until he talked to her. The police shrink, to whom he had been forced to go before his trial, had told him he loved her in the abstract, not in reality. Maybe that made sense, he thought, but maybe all shrinks were nuttier than their patients. It was a mystery to him, a mystery he couldn't solve.

He looked at his watch. Mickey's hands were frozen at 12:20. He shook his wrist violently and Mickey's big hand dropped limply to the six. So much for good intentions, he thought, my own personal Disney World is already running behind schedule.

He opened the refrigerator, hoping Chris and Dan had left some beer among the "yummy leftovers," but standing on the top shelf was a foot-high, white plastic statue. It looked like Michelangelo's David, except that this one had an erect penis. Attached to the penis was a slip of Chris' pink notepaper. It read: "Eat me! (Ha, ha!)"

So much for leftovers, Ciano thought, wild to get away from the apartment.

He checked the dim hall to see if Mrs. Stabille was waiting for him, then slammed the front door. The phantom graffiti on the door suddenly became clear—*Faggots*.

Chapter Six

The Covenant has been kept. The blood of the priest has bought my freedom—his pain has absolved my sin. And I have come here tonight to claim my liberation.

I am outside the old house. In the moonlight it looks weary, ready to collapse in upon itself. I pray it does, for it is an evil place with a cold, cankered heart.

I push past the elaborately carved front door and close it softly behind me. Inside, the darkness is strangely mottled, leprous. Deep wells of blackness erupt, pustule-like, in the gray velvet gloom. Small things scurry away at my approach.

The darkest and most forbidding spot is on my left, the hall leading to the basement door. That is where he lives. . . .

Normally, I would be paralyzed with fear, but tonight is different, tonight I will be free. I must go to him before he comes to me.

As silently as I can, I open the door to the basement. I close my eyes, for there is no light and no need for it. I have been down these stairs a thousand, ten thousand times. I can see everything in my mind—my eyes are not necessary here, only my senses. Judas draws me to him like the insistent pull of the tide.

I walk down the creaking stairs, carefully until thirteen are behind me, then I reach out to use the rough, clammy wall as a guide. I count thirteen more steps and I know I am facing the furnace, the source of my terrifying childhood nightmares. I feel its massive bulk blocking my way. To reassure myself, I touch its cold, sloping shoulders and its yawning doors—doors I once believed were the very gates of Hell. But the flames are gone forever, as is my mother, who took sadistic delight in corrupting my soul with such lies. Only the truth . . . and Judas . . . remain.

I make my way across the airless basement to a shelf built into the back wall. Near the floor, I find and light a kerosene lamp, then I grip the left corner of the shelf and pull. It opens easily, a hidden door to a hidden room.

The dark and dampness are familiar. I can see my breath in the flickering lamplight; under my feet, I can feel the softness of the slugs as they are crushed beneath my shoes. There are more lamps hanging on the stone wall. I light one and watch the shadows dance and flutter like the spirits of the dead.

The room—my room—was a godsend, a refuge I discovered by accident the summer I was eight. It had once been used by colonial settlers to hide from Indians and pirates. But that didn't matter to me then—it saved my life. I needed—still need—a dark place to crawl to, for I am a creature of darkness and seek safety from unwanted thoughts and hallucinations. This was the one place where my mother couldn't find me, the one secret I kept for my own.

The room is a square, ten feet on each side and perhaps ten-feet tall. There is no furniture. I have to sit on the dirt floor. I feel the cold through my clothes but ignore it.

I sit cross-legged, close my eyes, regulate my breathing and will him to come to me. But there is no answer. Intruding on my thoughts are the tortured screams of the priest. His shrieking howls echo endlessly in my mind, causing my heart to pound irregularly, keeping Judas away.

I gasp for air, thinking it cannot be guilt that makes me feel this way, for the martyrdom of the priest was ordained. I was simply the divine instrument of his death. I took great care, planned everything, rehearsed. . . .

The church doors were open. The old priest, who wore a white alb and embroidered stole, sat praying in the confessional, the door open, waiting for me. I had told him I wanted to make a general confession to him. Alone. The hour was strange, but he was strangely willing.

When I approached, he smiled a welcome. Or did he recognize death coming toward him and exalt in its imminence? He closed the door and I pushed open the right side curtain, carrying my black canvas bag.

"Bless me, Father, for I have sinned. It has been five years since my last confession," I began the traditional preamble, not really understanding the irony of my words. Then, like Saul on the road to Damascus, I was blinded by the enormity of my task, immobilized by the forces at work on my mind.

"I . . . I . . . I . . ." It sounded like a chant, for I was unable to think what to do next. *"I . . . cannot,"* I said in a whisper.

"Try, my child," he said, his high, clear voice full of authority.

The dull throbbing pain in my head exploded into a searing, white-hot torment. The light seemed to change color, from a misty gray to a cold blue, then to a deep sea-green. *"Try, my child,"* the priest had said, and I knew then that he was ready to die. He was the patient martyr awaiting his death, the lamb ready for the slaughter. *"Try, my child."*

I staggered from the confessional and ripped open the center door.

He looked startled, his eyes wide with fear and confusion.

I seized the apostle by the throat and pulled him upright. He was small and weak, unprotesting.

I brought the mallet down on his thin, white-fringed skull. It sunk in with a ripe sound that repulsed me. I saw the whole scene in slow motion, saw his head and features balloon into impossible sizes. Fearing his head would burst, I flung him to the cold marble floor, searching for the black canvas bag that contained the tools of his martyrdom.

I dragged his limp body over to the enormous cross resting on its side behind the altar. I touched it and felt its power course through my body, confirming the rightness of my act. Like Iscariot, I knew I was being used by and for a higher purpose, for without death there is no resurrection.

With all my strength, I tilted the cross into an upside down position. Then arranging the body I took the iron spikes, cold and unyielding, and began pounding them into his palms. The blood spurted and the pain must have roused him, for he began a high-pitched keening that nearly drove me from the church.

I used the mallet on him again and he subsided, but he had ripped the nails from his hands. I tried again, but it was useless. I had to tie his arms to the cross, a compromise made in the name of necessity, in the name of Judas.

I removed his shoes and socks, positioned his feet together as I have seen thousands of times on countless crucifixes, and began to pound in the long spikes.

It was a difficult task because the bones did not break neatly, but cracked in successive snaps like small bursts of gunfire. It is difficult to believe how loudly human flesh cries out when it is torn and punctured.

He moaned again, fighting for consciousness. The blood from

the wounds on his head began trickling down to his partially opened lips . . . he was drinking his own blood in silent mockery of his beloved sacrament.

For some time I had been seeing everything bathed in a deep emerald glow, but when I reached for the scourge, suddenly the church was enveloped in a numinous aura of blue-white light that changed quickly to bloodred as I swung the steel-tipped whip—again and again.

I lost track of what happened next. I remember he opened his eyes once and smiled at me, absolving me. Or perhaps it wasn't a smile, only his teeth protruding from his ruined lips.

But all that is over. Forever. And I am prepared to believe he reveled in his martyrdom. . . .

Suddenly, I feel Judas enter the hidden room. He has come as silently as a shadow, with no more substance than a dream, yet so terribly real.

He stands behind me. Waiting. I realize now I never should have come here. He is too . . . powerful. Yet I have no choice.

The air has become colder and my breath hisses in small bursts of vapor.

Look at me.

His command invades my mind like rolling thunder. I open my eyes, but all I can see is the hazy golden light of his terrible epiphany. It hurts my eyes.

"I have done your bidding. The priest is dead. The Covenant is complete," I say.

I know.

"How?"

I am always with you. You cannot escape me any more than you can deny me.

"Release me."

No. The Covenant is not complete.

"Release me!"

My scream is loud, but Iscariot will not hear. He has no conscience or compassion, only a burning vengeance as intense as the fires of Hell. His manipulation of me is total. I tremble in his presence. I am blind before his glory.

"I am too weak," I say.

Do you forget? I helped you accomplish your childish plans. The Covenant was signed in blood.

"But I have paid my debt," I insist.

No. There will be others. Many others.

• • •

When he is through with me, I hear the slap of his sandals on the dirt floor—his retreating footsteps. My muscles begin to relax and I take a deep breath. It seems like the first one in hours.

What he has asked . . . told me to do is so monstrous I can hardly comprehend it. There are no subtleties with Iscariot. He is crude, forcible, and demanding; his pound of flesh is not metaphorical. My mind reels. . . .

I came here tonight to free myself of this force, but I am more bound to it than ever. There is no escape.

The Covenant must be kept.

Chapter
Seven

Tuesday, November 2

"Elevenses?"

Ciano looked up from the pile of pale blue Supplementary Complaint Reports, the Form 5s.

"What?"

"Elevenses," Dugan said, holding out a blue-and-white paper cup with a picture of the Parthenon on it. "Coffee break."

Ciano took a sip. "That's the worst fucking coffee I ever tasted," he said, spitting the cloudy liquid back into the cup.

"That's because it's tea," Dugan said. "More than two cups of coffee a day will kill you. Tea nourishes the spirit."

"You're full of shit," Ciano said, drinking the tea anyway. At least it was hot. Ciano was not. He had been at his desk since seven a.m., the victim of an overactive imagination. All night he had kept thinking about the grotesque body of the priest, and the even more grotesque antics Chris and Dan had probably engaged in on the round bed. Finally, he had abandoned the mirrored bedroom for the plant-choked living room, hoping to avoid whatever lurked between the satin sheets. Even the new precinct felt more like home than the apartment.

"Dugan," he said, fishing around in his pocket for the real-estate agent's card. "Call these people and tell them I'll bust them all if they don't let me out of the lease."

"What's wrong with your apartment?" Dugan asked.

"It sucks. And so do the people I rented it from," Ciano said, looking back at the 5s. The six detectives assigned to the case had generated a mountain of paperwork and a molehill of information. Shopkeepers, homeowners, dog walkers, bus drivers, truck drivers, and joggers had been interviewed, but no one had seen a damned thing. Every license plate within a ten-block area had been noted and was being processed by the National Crime Information Center. That might yield something, but Ciano doubted it.

Ciano took out the original crime scene report from the center drawer of his desk and read it for the third time. It contained the cold facts: time and place, name and number, body, but no soul. The overnight crime report—the 60 sheet—listed the usual fistfights, broken windows, and stolen cars. Nothing interesting.

He flipped to Detective Abel's report. No eyeball had been found at the church. That meant the killer had taken a trophy or that Abel was a shit detective. Or somebody else glommed it as a giggle. Cops did strange things. So did civilians.

He skimmed the 5s again, catching the key words and phrases with unerring accuracy. The police jargon and semiliterate style had long ceased to irritate him, but by 11:30 he felt the immensity of the brick wall in front of him.

"Hey, Dugan," he called from his office. "Any word on the apartment?"

Dugan shook his head sadly, making a thumbs-down sign.

"Shit," Ciano said, as the telephone rang.

"Ciano? It's James Young, M.E.'s office."

"It's about time," Ciano said, opening his second pack of Camels that morning.

"I've got a few things for you," Young said.

"Shoot."

"Well, first off the official cause of death is internal hemorrhaging. The victim was repeatedly beaten by a whip or whip-like instrument. The priest's lungs were filled with blood—he literally drowned in it."

"Wonderful."

"Second, as I said, the weapon was a multi-thronged whip. The marks on the body were wedge-shaped punctures. They appear like on a cat-o'-nine tails, but this cat had only three. The tips must have been weighted to produce those marks.

"Microscopic examination of the wounds shows animal bone fragments, which might indicate that the business end of the whip was made of bone. The pattern of the blows would indicate that the perp was right-handed and stood above the victim.

"There are almost two hundred wounds on the body, not counting the incredibly savage blows which ripped the skin from the skull," Young said.

"You ever see any weapon like it?" Ciano asked.

"Never."

"Go on."

"The victim was alive and kicking—kicking hard—when he died, but somehow someone managed to affix him to that cross before whipping him to death."

"How about the missing eyeball? You find it anywhere?" Ciano asked.

"Nope. If you don't have it. . . ." He didn't have to finish.

"You send that coin in his eye socket over to the lab?" Ciano asked.

"They picked it up."

"I'll go get it," Ciano said. "Can you give me an approximate time of death?"

"Between two and six a.m. Probably on the later end of that scale. It took a long time to kill him, a long time for him to die," Young said, trying not to remember the blood.

"The victim also had nail holes in his hands and feet," Young continued, consulting his notes. "Spike holes, actually."

"Like Christ?" Ciano asked.

"Well, sort of. The spikes were pounded into the victim's palms, and naturally they ripped out. To crucify someone, you've got to nail them through the wrists. There were also puncture wounds on the feet, but as you saw, the psycho gave up and tied the old guy to the cross with rope.

"The spikes, by the way, look handmade. They're square and about ten-inches long. I sent them over to Forensic with the coin," Young said.

Ciano dragged deep on his cigarette. "What do you make of all this?" he asked.

"Well," said Young. "It was a carefully planned production. Crucifixions need forethought, you don't just buy the tools at K-Mart.

"But the perp fucked up. He couldn't nail the hands and feet of the victim to the cross. He had no medical knowledge or he'd have known that the soft tissues of the palm wouldn't support a man on a cross. Despite the crucifixes you see in churches, it's anatomically impossible.

"Also, I think you have to have a platform for the feet, but then, this guy was upside down," Young said. "Like what's his name?"

"Saint Peter," Ciano replied automatically.

"Yeah, well, I prefer a good, old-fashioned shooting any day. It's much neater," Young said, his voice trying for levity he didn't feel.

"Anything else you can tell me?" Ciano asked.

"Not at the moment. You'll have the complete autopsy report tomorrow sometime. Maybe. If that asshole assistant of mine finished the blood work this morning.

"Oh, and by the way, I had a buddy of yours here bright and early. A reporter named Jermezian. Looking for a headline," Young said.

"You give it to him?"

"Not me. The Medical Examiner would have my ass," Young said, thinking of the directive from Sidney Glossman, the Chief Medical Examiner: Anyone caught talking to the press without his authorization would be cut into little pieces and fed to the Hudson River striped bass. And everybody knew striped bass were tough mothers. So was the M.E.

Ciano made Young repeat what he had said to make sure he had gotten everything. It felt good to have a few solid facts, no matter how bizarre. If he could trace the coin or the nails, he'd be close to his man. Maybe he'd get lucky. It had to happen sometime.

"Do me a favor," Ciano said, scanning his notes. "Leave Jermezian to me."

"You got him," said the Assistant M.E. and hung up.

Ciano dialed the Forensic Unit and spoke to Sergeant Larry Kooperstein.

"Koop, it's Vince Ciano. What have you got on an antique coin and some nails the M.E.'s office sent over?" he asked.

"I got nothin'. Ain't even had time to sort through half this shit," Kooperstein said. He and Ciano had worked together for years. Kooperstein, a Phi Beta Kappa from NYU, affected a street cop's language. Ciano was a street cop who tried his best not to act like it—most of the time.

"Well, dust them off," Ciano said, referring to the fingerprints, "and I'll come down and pick them. It's my only lead and I'll do the investigation personally."

"Gimme an hour, for chrissakes," Kooperstein said. "You know how many prints ya find in a fuckin' church?"

"Do the coin and the nails first. Please, Koop, it's important," Ciano said.

"It's all important," Kooperstein said.

Ciano put on his brown leather jacket and wandered out into the squad room. He tapped Dugan on the shoulder and told him to grab his hat. They were going to Manhattan.

Hidden in the dense autumn woods, Joseph Steppe felt safe. In his arms he held a black-and-white kitten named Duke, the much-loved mascot of the Richmondtown complex below. Steppe made soothing, cooing sounds as he limped painfully through

63

the undergrowth. In his pocket was a razor-sharp, four-inch knife, a pair of twelve-inch pinking shears, a fist-sized rock carved with odd symbols, and Monsignor Bryan's eye, wadded in tissue.

It was going to be a good day, he thought.

Dugan drove. Ciano chain-smoked.

"I fixed it up," Dugan said, as they crossed the Verrazano Bridge.

"What?"

"The meet with Captain Hanratty."

"Oh, yeah." Ciano had forgotten about the retired cop, but he had remembered the daughter, Erica. He had thought about her during his long vigil last night.

"Tonight at around seven. They live above the restaurant," Dugan said, as they rolled toward New York and the Forensic Lab. "With your permission, I'll give him copies of the 5s and some of the pictures of the crime scene when we get back."

"Mmm," Ciano said, not wanting to talk about it.

"You're really fucked, aren't you?" Dugan said, ignoring the silence.

Ciano looked around sharply.

"I mean, you signed that contract for the apartment without reading it. Right?" Dugan said.

Ciano nodded, thinking that he was fucked in more ways than one. This case he had caught would cut him off at the knees. He knew it. Dugan knew it. The whole fucking world knew it. Nobody wanted to say anything about it.

"They said they'd try to find another tenant," Dugan said. "But until then . . ."

I'm responsible, Ciano thought. And until they find someone else, I'm in charge of this damn case.

"Just what's so bad about the place?" Dugan asked, intent on starting a conversation.

"You wouldn't believe it if I told you," Ciano said, trying to end all discussion.

But Dugan wouldn't be silenced. "Freddy Jermezian called before we left," Dugan said. "I told him you were out."

"I am." But he owed the reporter for standing by him in print. He wondered how he could pay the debt and still maintain his independence of action.

He glanced at Dugan.

"Are you going to bother me all the way into town?" Ciano said, finally.

"Yep."

"Well, let's talk about the case, then," Ciano said, discussing what he had learned from the Assistant M.E.

When he was through, Dugan whistled respectfully. "A first-class, A-number-one nut job," he said. "And right up Ed Hanratty's alley."

Ciano resented Dugan's reverent tone, but he had to admit he needed help on this one—unless the coin lead worked out.

When they pulled up in front of the police academy, which housed the lab, Ciano sent Dugan to get the coin and nails from Sergeant Kooperstein while he waited.

When Dugan returned, they drove uptown toward the 72nd Street shop of Arthur M. Howell Associates. While they fought the traffic, Ciano examined the coin. It was cold, powdery, and slimy. There had been no prints.

"I'd say it was a Turko-Russian ghazooky from the ninth century," Dugan said, glancing over at Ciano.

"Yeah?"

"But then again I don't know my ass from my elbow about coins," Dugan laughed.

"Asshole," Ciano muttered, turning the coin between thumb and forefinger. It seemed heavy for such a small coin.

Dugan parked the car in a tow-away zone and got out while Ciano slipped the coin back into the plastic evidence bag.

They walked up the steps to the brownstone and Dugan rang the bell. Through the intercom they identified themselves while a camera slowly panned back and forth. Finally, the electronic buzzer released the door.

They were greeted by a frail old man in a gray herringbone suit. He was bent over with arthritis and was slightly hunchbacked. His pale features were obscured by huge round black-rimmed glasses which made his brown eyes look absurdly large and inquisitive. Almost owl-like. Sticking to the top of his head like the stump of an antler was a loupe—a jeweler's glass he used to examine coins.

"I'm Arthur Howell," he said, bowing from the waist. He rubbed his hands in anticipation. Ciano recognized the type immediately. Arthur Howell was a cop groupie—a civilian who wanted desperately to be of assistance to the police. They all wanted love, acceptance, and respect. They came in both sexes, all sizes and ages. Mostly they were a pain in the ass, but sometimes groupies like Howell proved to be invaluable by providing free, expert analysis on obscure subjects—like coins.

Howell led them past the stairway, down a dark, narrow hall and pushed open a green metal door.

"My study," he said, standing aside and allowing Ciano and Dugan to enter his private world.

The room was at least twenty-feet wide by thirty-feet long and two stories tall. Floor-to-ceiling bookshelves ringed the space and the oak floors were covered with thick Oriental rugs in hues of red, blue, green, gold, and purple. There was a fireplace and an ancient carved desk. The desk, chairs, and a couch were all covered in leather. The room smelled musty, but it smelled like money. A lot of money.

"Sit down, gentlemen," Howell said in a squeaky, high-pitched voice. "How may I serve you?"

You could serve us a drink, Ciano thought, but handed him the plastic evidence bag.

Howell, humming with excitement, opened the bag, brought out the coin and slid the loupe down over his round glasses. He peered, mumbled, squinted, and said, "Ah," several times. Finally, he pushed the loupe away and tossed the coin on the desk.

"Just as I suspected," he said. "A reproduction."

"A reproduction of *what*, Mr. Howell?" Ciano asked.

"Why, a lepton, of course," Howell said, as if Ciano should have known. "This is a reproduction of a coin minted by Pontius Pilate in Jerusalem between about A.D. 15 and A.D. 40. This particular coin was probably minted between A.D. 30 and A.D. 40, or rather it would have been if it had been real."

"How do you know this, uh, lepton is a phony?" Ciano asked.

"You can see on the sides here that the coin is composed of a metal alloy," Howell said. "Leptons were pure silver."

"Why would somebody go to all this trouble of counterfeiting a coin like this?" Dugan asked. "Are they worth a lot?"

"Oh, several hundred dollars, I suppose," Howell said. It was obvious that he didn't think the coin was particularly valuable. "Depending on its condition. But this reproduction wouldn't fool even the most amateur numismatist."

"Numis— coin collectors are pretty sharp then?" Ciano asked.

"Exactly. I would suggest that this coin was made as a theatrical prop or by one of those private mints which sell reproductions by mail," Howell said.

"A coin-of-the-month club?" Dugan asked.

"Exactly."

"We'll check it out," Ciano said, rising and slipping the coin into his pocket.

"Oh, don't go yet," Howell pleaded. "Please tell me what case you're working on. I find police work so fascinating."

"Sorry," Ciano said. "Right now it's classified. But thanks for your help. We'll let you know how it turns out."

He walked quickly to the door. He didn't want to go back over the crucifixion—and Pontius Pilate, for chrissakes.

"Please, please," Howell called after him. The suspense was excruciating. He lived for the brief moments when he became a part of the police department—one of the officers, somebody's buddy. But Ciano was already out of the door. Dugan lingered a minute, feeling sorry for the old man.

"I'll give you a complete rundown by phone," Dugan said, winking conspiratorially. "But don't breathe a word to anyone. Death cult. Devil worshippers. Black Mass. Very hush-hush. The mayor may be involved."

Howell, his eyes gleaming behind the thick glasses, sank into his chair, almost breathless.

"Devil worsh—"

"*Shhh*. Not a word," Dugan said, looking around with paranoid intensity.

Involuntarily, Howell brought an index finger to his lips, sealing their bargain. Then he reached down and solemnly handed Dugan the plastic evidence bag Ciano had forgotten.

"Thank you, Mr. Howell," Dugan said. "We wouldn't want to leave without what you might call our 'lepton tea bag'."

The long, flat rock was Joseph Steppe's special place. If he stood on the rock he could see Richmondtown below him, and watch the people walking around totally oblivious to his presence. In back of him was the old Victorian house with its dark secrets and air of crumbling gentility, but he felt like being in the open today, not hidden away in the dank interior.

Gripping the black-and-white kitten in his left hand, he opened his coat. The sun felt warm and good shining down on him. It was a sign.

Slowly, as if he were doing a striptease, Joseph Steppe began to remove his clothes. First, his knit hat, which he twirled on his finger for a moment, before flipping it to the ground, then his patched and worn Army field jacket. He placed that on the ground reverently, for it represented one of his highest aspirations: to join the military service. If they had only given him a gun, he thought, he would have shown everyone what he could do. But his withered leg and curved spine barred him from the world of men and weapons, of heroics and bravery. He knew he could be a fine soldier—if only they would have given him a chance.

One button at a time, he undid his plaid wool shirt, feeling the cool breeze instantly erect his nipples. He ran a hand over his smooth sunken chest, wishing as always he had grown hair there. Then, using two fingers, he slowly undid his belt, pulling it tight, then releasing it, inch by inch. He could feel his heavy, green work pants begin to slide down his hips.

Suddenly, he let go and was naked in the sun, his penis already expanding with the pleasure of it.

He grasped the kitten in both hands, bringing it in contact with his hard penis. The feeling was electric. The cat's soft fur felt just like a woman, he thought, knowing that was a lie. Joseph Steppe had never been with a woman.

"How did you like that numis . . . mis?" Ciano began when they were in the car.

"Nu-mis-ma-tist," Dugan said slowly, as if Ciano were an idiot child. "Four syllables."

"Whatever," Ciano said, annoyed. "What did you say to the little bastard?"

"I told him what he wanted to hear," Dugan said.

His smile irked Ciano all the way back to Staten Island.

They arrived after 3:00 and checked in with the station house. Nothing new had happened, so Ciano told Detective Marty Abel to check out private mints to see if any of them sold leptons. He also told Abel to call the city's many prop houses and theatrical supply companies to look for a three-pronged whip.

"It sounds like Ben Hur is back in town," Dugan said when they were back in the car. "Or maybe the whip's an S&M item."

"Who the fuck knows?" Ciano said.

"You want to stop at Hanratty's for lunch?" Dugan asked. He wasn't used to being this sober so late in the day.

"No. I want to talk to that little girl who saw the 'troll' at the church party," Ciano said, consulting his notebook and giving Dugan the directions.

Kathy Santini, a fourth-grader at Tysen Elementary School, was an obedient child who did precisely what her mother told her to do. Without question. Alone from 3:30 until her mother arrived at 5:00, she was under strict orders not to let strangers into the house.

"How do I know you're policemen?" Kathy Santini shouted through the thick oak door.

"Put the chain on and I'll show you my badge," Ciano shouted back.

"Mother says never allow strangers in!"

"Please, honey. This is important. Open up," Ciano said. He was tired of arguing with the damn kid. He and Dugan had been standing outside the white frame house on Elmont Street for ten minutes, trying to convince the little girl to let them in.

"Let me try," Dugan said. "We're friends of Father Layhe, Kathy. He said you'd seen something at the Halloween party last Saturday."

"What if I did?"

"We'd appreciate talkin' to you about it, darlin'," Dugan said, slipping into his brogue.

"Well, I'll open the door a little way and you show me your identification," Kathy said. She couldn't believe anyone with an Irish voice like that could be bad.

The door creaked open slowly and a small blond head peered out through the storm door. She took one look at Ciano and slammed the front door shut again. He looked like a gangster, she thought, just like on T.V.

"This is ridiculous," Ciano said. "We'll come back when her parents are home."

"Let me try it one more time," Dugan said. "But you stand back. You'll scare her."

It took another ten minutes of pleading and coaxing, but finally Dugan charmed their way into the Santini house.

The living room was covered with a yellow-orange shag rug, the floral print furniture with heavy plastic. A twenty-five inch television was centrally located for easy viewing.

"What exactly did you see?" Ciano said, sitting down beside Dugan on the couch. The plastic groaned under his weight.

"When?"

"At the party."

"Nothing."

"Come on kid. Layhe said you saw a 'troll'," Ciano said, his voice deep and rough.

The little girl, curled up in a chair, wrapped her arms around herself and shook her head. She was wearing a pink turtleneck and blue overalls; her feet didn't come close to reaching the floor.

Ciano stood up suddenly and Kathy Santini cowered deeper in the chair.

"Uh, Lew," Dugan said. "Let me." He leaned back, crossed his legs and spread his arms out on the back couch, relaxed.

"It will only take us a minute, darlin'," he said with an accent thicker than a Dublin fog. "We know you saw somethin' and we believe you. We're lookin' for this troll guy ourselves, we are."

Kathy unwound a little just hearing Dugan's voice. She looked at his open Irish face, wanting to like this man. He seemed sympathetic—unlike the dark man with the scowl.

"It's very possible you can be a big help to us in catching this man . . . so he won't frighten anyone ever again," Dugan coaxed.

"Well," Kathy hesitated. "I did see something, but everybody says I'm crazy . . . they don't like me."

"Now how could that be?" Dugan said, astonished. "A pretty girl like you and all. Why I'll bet all the boys think you're sweet as me old mother's homemade apple cider."

Ciano winced. Kathy giggled and slowly began to open up to Dugan, telling him more than he needed or wanted to know about herself, the party and life in the fourth grade. Finally, she got to what she had seen.

"His face was all pinched up and horrible," she said. "Kind of mashed in, like. He had these big floppy ears and kind of pointy teeth and all."

"How much of him could you see?" Dugan asked.

"Well, just his head and neck. At first."

"At first?"

"After I screamed, he disappeared and I went to the window and looked out. He was dressed, uh, all in green, I guess. Like Peter Pan or something," Kathy said. "It was pretty dark, but I think . . . I'm sure he was in green. And he ran funny."

"How?" Dugan asked.

"Like he had hurt his leg or something."

"A limp?"

"Yeah. A real bad one."

"Okay," Dugan said. "When he was in the window, did you notice what color his hair was?"

"Sure. It was orange. Like a pumpkin," she said.

"How about his eyes?"

70

"I couldn't really see them," Kathy said. She frowned, then asked Dugan, "Do you *really* believe me?"

"Well, you never know," Dugan said. "I've heard tell of some pretty strange things in my time. Take the little people, for example. . . ."

"Thank you, Kathy," Ciano interrupted. The last thing he wanted to hear about was leprechauns. "Do you think you could describe this man to an artist for us?"

"Like on TV?"

"Yeah, like on TV. We'll send a man out to your house tonight when your parents are home," Ciano said.

"I can do better than that," Kathy said. "I've got a picture that looks just like him. In a book."

Ciano and Dugan looked at each other. "We'd love to see it," Dugan said, and Kathy jumped up from the chair and ran down the hall. They could hear her taking the stairs two at a time.

"You're a wonder with children, Lew," Dugan said.

"Fuck you," Ciano growled, reluctantly admiring the way Dugan could handle anyone. Including me, he thought.

Kathy came back clutching a large, thin red book. At her heels was a beagle puppy. The pup took one look at Dugan, raced over to him and jumped in his lap.

Christ, Ciano thought. Kids and dogs.

"Hello, there, boy," Dugan said, petting the dog on the head. "What's your name?"

"His name's Captain Pew," Kathy said.

"Ah, named after Blind Pew, the old pirate in *Treasure Island*, right?" Dugan said, letting the puppy lick his face.

Kathy frowned. "No. We call him that because if you don't wash him all the time . . . *phew.*"

Ciano laughed. "Got ya on that one, Dugan. Read my lips. One syllable. *Phewww.*"

Kathy, Dugan, and Pew all looked at Ciano, offended. Captain Pew growled at him.

"Here's the man," Kathy said, ignoring Ciano and rifling through the book of fairy tales. "On page twenty-three. 'The Troll Who Lived Under the Bridge.' "

Ciano and Dugan looked at the artist's conception of a troll. He had a big round head, squinty evil eyes, and a twisted, crooked body. He was dressed in a green jerkin with a hood and his sharp, pointy teeth were wickedly uneven.

"May we borrow this from you?" Dugan asked. "We'll send it back soon as we get a copy."

"Oh, sure. That's a baby book," Kathy said. "I never read such things anymore." She waved her hand with an easy sophistication.

Dugan looked at the well-thumbed pages and wondered.

Joseph Steppe was worried. He had been rubbing himself on the cat for more than an hour but nothing had happened. His penis felt limp and unresponsive. He was being denied his pleasure.

The softer he became, the more his anger grew, until it became rock-hard resolve. It was the kitten's fault; it had deliberately frustrated him. He gripped it tighter and it squeaked with pain. He felt a slight pulse in his penis and squeezed the cat again. This time it yowled and Joseph Steppe once again felt himself become aroused.

He smiled. His sharp, pointy teeth were wickedly uneven.

Chapter
Eight

Driving to Richmondtown, Vince Ciano felt more like a small-town sheriff than a New York City detective. The two-lane road he traveled dipped and twisted like a living thing as it wound through a dense tract of woods. Tall trees, heavy with leaves, arched above him, shutting out the sun and forming a tunnel of autumn foliage. There was little traffic. He felt virtually alone, especially after dropping Dugan at the station house.

A left-hand turn brought him out of the woods. Ahead, a white farm house, perched on a low-lying hill, reflected the slanting rays of the afternoon sun. Behind the house, in a still-green meadow, twin silos reared up ominously on either side of a red barn. Cattle were grazing on the parched brown remnants of a corn field. It was about as far as you could get from the Bronx, he thought. I could be in fucking Kansas.

Ciano rolled down the window to smell the warm fall air, enjoying the serenity for a moment. Then he shook the thoughts of autumn from his mind and concentrated on finding the signs to Richmondtown.

He turned right on to Arthur Kill Road, then left on Clarke Avenue where he could see the restoration up ahead. It was deserted.

Ignoring the signs that said CLOSED UNTIL FURTHER NOTICE, he drove slowly toward the main parking lot, intending to nose around by himself for a while. But before he could park the car, three enormous geese and several smaller ones slowly crossed the road in single file, then stopped and looked at him. They didn't seem happy to see him and they didn't want to move from the middle of the road. They honked at him. Ciano honked back.

Joseph Steppe's concentration was shattered by the blast of the horn. The sound unnerved him and he found himself squeezing the kitten's limp form. He looked at the lifeless ball of black-

73

and-white fur, suddenly disgusted, and dropped it on the smooth rock while he pulled on his pants.

He looked below and saw a man emerging from an old station wagon. He watched as the man walked over to Stephens General Store, which had been furnished and stocked with authentic reproductions of the merchandise that had been available during the mid-nineteenth century. Steppe loved working there, surrounded by bolts of calico, clay pipes, kerosene lamps, fresh produce and oven-baked bread. But he hated the woman who walked out on to the porch and began gesturing to the man. She was Abigail West, the restoration's general director and Steppe's nemesis.

Although he was too far away to see her clearly, Steppe knew what she looked like. He could picture her thin mouth pursed in cold distaste; see her long, stringy brown hair coiled at the nape of her neck; sense her taut, too-smooth face and dead eyes. She had the face of a skeleton, he decided, a face like the dead priest in the church.

Only last week she had screeched at him in front of a crowd of sniggering school children, making a fool of him for neglecting to empty some trash containers. Abigail screamed and the children laughed. At him. At him! He hated her! How he wanted to rip the tight sweater from her high, firm breasts; how he wanted to tear away the clinging skirt that guarded her thighs; how he wished he could think of the perfect phrase to stop the stinging flow of words from her mouth. Stuck-up pig, he thought, too good for me, too educated, too proper, too . . .

The man was a different story. He was big, and Steppe imagined he could hear the wood planks of the porch creak under the man's weight. Now he was leaning against a hitching post, his back still to Steppe. Abigail West was offering her hand.

Why don't you shake his cock like you want to, you slut? Steppe thought. He followed the man's movements, watching as he casually reached into his pocket and pulled out his wallet.

A glint of gold, a feeling of wrongness. A badge! Steppe's breath caught in his throat; he felt as if he were drowning on dry land.

The police! Fear raced down his twisted spine.

The man turned and Steppe was paralyzed. The cop, powerful and tough-looking, was staring directly at him, accusing him. He dropped down on the rock, not wanting to be silhouetted against the sky, but the cop kept scanning the treeline until he focused in on the old house.

Steppe covered his eyes in horror, as if not looking at the man would make him disappear. "Police . . . police," he said aloud, until it was almost a chant. He knew why the cop had come. He knew who had called him. Steppe's low moan was lost amid the rustling leaves.

It wasn't the lingering Indian summer that brought a warming current of human electricity charging into Abigail West's body. Weather didn't affect her at all. Men did. Especially big men. She was awed by Ciano's bulk and put a hand to her tightly bound hair, smoothing it as she went to meet him.

"We're closed," she said, smiling slightly. "Perhaps you could come back some other day." Her tone left no doubt she'd be happy to see Ciano any time.

Ciano introduced himself and flashed his tin.

"Pleased to make your acquaintance, sir," she said, offering her hand and eyeing him.

They shook, Abigail West holding onto his hand longer than necessary. He had to pull his hand away from hers.

Ciano smiled hesitantly, but he found nothing attractive about her. The way she held his eyes made him uncomfortable. Her tongue darted out between long, white teeth in an almost reptilian way. She was built almost straight up and down, with small, pointy breasts straining at the beige sweater she wore.

"Is there anything I can show you?" she asked. Her voice was high-pitched, nasal.

"No, thanks. I'd just like to look around," Ciano said, noting that she kept plucking her hair, which was coiled like sausage links.

"Oh, come now. Surely I can be of some assistance," she said. "I'll give you a short tour, then you can wander about on your own . . . if you want to."

Ciano sighed. It would be impossible to get rid of her until she was ready to go. He nodded.

"Let's start inside the store," she said. "I'll give you a map, so you won't get lost," she added, giggling.

"Thanks," Ciano said. A forty-year-old schoolgirl. Jesus.

"I suppose you're here about Miss Eddins," she said, taking up a position behind an oak counter that ran the length of the store. On the counter were a variety of dry goods from different eras; on the floor near him were three muskets from the Revolutionary War.

Yes," Ciano said. "And about Monsignor Bryan's murder."

"I didn't know him very well," Abigail West said.

"He wasn't on the Historical Society board?" Ciano asked.

"A non-participating member," she said. "A concession to Miss Eddins, who adored him."

"Adored?"

Abigail West laughed. It grated on Ciano's nerves. "Not *that* way, of course. They were both in their eighties, I believe."

Ciano smiled thinly and took out a Camel, but before he could light it, Abigail West held up her hand like a traffic cop and said, "Please. Not in here. You may smoke outside."

Ciano shrugged. He lit up outside, wondering if she'd follow him. She did.

"Here's a brochure," she said, taking his arm and leading him down the steps of the general store.

"As you know, Richmondtown was begun more than forty years ago and when it is complete—soon we hope—we will have more than thirty structures on this ninety-six-acre site," she said, as if she were giving a tour.

"We have, as you may know, more than forty-thousand artifacts currently on display, everything from . . ."

Ciano didn't know and didn't care. What he did mind, however, was the way she was massaging his arm. It made him feel like he was being masturbated. The bitch was hot, he thought. Too bad she had all the sex appeal of a DOA.

"As you look up and down the street," West continued, "you can see the evolution of seventeenth-, eighteenth-, and nineteenth-century buildings, all of them carefully furnished with authentic details.

"Normally, our staff would be here, dressed in period costume, to explain the exhibits to our visitors, but we'll be closed until after Christmas this year. General housecleaning," she said, flashing a smile that was more gum than teeth.

"Over there is the Voorlezer's House, built before 1696 by the Dutch congregation as both a church and a schoolhouse. It's the oldest known elementary-school building in the country.

"And that's the Boehm House, where we stress the traditional building methods of the time. . . . The Bennett House, where we have gathered a charming collection of American dolls and toys . . . and of course, the Courthouse. It was built in 1737 and was actually the third seat of government on the island."

Ciano looked at the Courthouse and the gallows next to it.

"Some pranksters put up the noose," Abigail West said, her

lips pursed. "As soon as I find that lazy Steppe, I'll have him take it down."

"I don't know," Ciano said. "I think it adds a certain, uh, authenticity to your complex. A few public hangings in this day and age might do some good." He waited for her reaction.

"Life was difficult in those days," West said noncommittally, but Ciano could tell she disapproved of his statement, so he decided to continue. Maybe she'd let go of his arm.

"But simpler," he said. "You killed somebody and the neighbors hanged you. No mess, no fuss, no expense. I have quite a few candidates for public hanging. Or at least a good horsewhipping."

Abigail West made a strangling noise in her throat, but refused to unhand him. Fascist or not, this man was . . . well, a man, she thought.

West's arm circled Ciano's like a boa constrictor preparing to feed. Her hand moved to his forearm, but its massaging motion continued as she looked at him through half-lidded eyes intended to be seductive. Ciano found her squint grotesque.

As they walked down the cobbled street, West pointed out the print shop, the carpenter's shop, and the basket weaver's house. Ciano endured her tour guide spiel, but history wasn't his subject. In fact, the past was something he had spent a lifetime trying to outrun.

"Everything we've done here reflects our love of the past," West cooed. "No shortcuts—just care, love, and time."

"Over there," she said, pointing, "is the Lake-Tysen House. The Tysen's were a very early and prestigious island family. They settled the land in the early 1600s and the Restoration had their house transported here from its original location on a tract in what is now the town of New Dorp."

Ciano was finding it difficult to stay tuned to the conversation. What he wanted was a quiet stroll around the perimeter of the crime scene. What he got was a lot of yammering. It was annoying and he found it hard to concentrate, hearing only key words—the Guyon Store . . . the Stephen family . . . all relocated . . . all rebuilt . . . all a slice of history.

So intent was he on ignoring Abigail West, that it took him a few seconds to realize she had stopped talking.

"I said, would you like to come back to the store with me for some coffee?" Her face was tight with anticipation.

"Uh, I'm sorry, Miss West, but I've got to get back to work,"

77

Ciano said, forcibly removing her arm from his. "Some other time, maybe."

Her smile was ghastly; he felt sorry for the old broad. "But thanks for the tour. It was, uh, most instructive."

He turned and walked quickly toward his car, not daring to look back.

The whole time he could feel her staring at him, her eyes burning into a spot between his shoulder blades.

He felt like a piece of meat.

Joseph Steppe felt nothing but relief. Seeing the policeman drive away had lifted the troubles from his crooked shoulders. He felt safe, until he realized the policeman and Abigail West had been talking about *him*. That clawed at his nerves. He knew what had to be done.

By the time Steppe limped onto the porch of Stephens General Store, his mood was savage. Coming down the hillside he had lost his balance and rolled wildly and painfully a good part of the way. It emphasized his disability, his inferiority. His clothes were stained with dirt and mud and blood from a cut on his forehead trickled into his eyes.

Hurt and furious, Steppe barged into the general store.

"You, y-y-you liar!" he screamed. "You lied about me!"

Abigail West stood behind the long wooden counter, still indignant at being turned down by Ciano. She was taken by surprise by the wild-eyed Steppe.

"Steppe? What on earth are you babbling about?" she demanded. "And look at yourself, you're a mess. Why . . ."

Steppe ignored her and advanced on the counter, his rolling gait menacing. "Bitch," he breathed. "You told the police lies."

He looked around for something to hit her with and found one of the Revolutionary War muskets. He wished it were loaded.

"What are you doing?" West said, her voice rising in agitation. "Put that down!"

But Steppe continued to stalk her, disappearing for a moment behind the end of the counter and reappearing again on her side.

Abigail West felt momentarily vulnerable, then she thought about Steppe's incredible gall and became angry all over again.

"Get out of here this instant," she said loudly, trying to maintain control. "Put that down or you're fired. Do you hear me?"

Steppe came on inexorably, the musket in his hand, looking like a deranged minuteman.

West began backing up, her hand bumping along the counter,

knocking over boxes of Quaker Oats and Dr. Westgall's Tonic for Female Complaints, until she felt it. It had the satisfying thickness of stout wood.

Never taking her eyes off Steppe, she grabbed it—an oar, dry and splintery. The wood bit into her hand, but she ignored the pain.

"This is your last chance, damn you," she said, pulling the oar over her shoulder and across her body. She twisted it a half turn, the jagged wood shredding her palms, but she managed to point the blade at Steppe.

"Stop right there, or I'll bash your brains in," she shouted at him, feeling more secure now that she had something solid in front of her. He would pay for his insolence, she thought grimly.

The makeshift weapon stopped Steppe dead in his tracks and gave him a moment to think. Now it appeared she wasn't afraid of him. In fact, she was probably laughing at him. The pole in her hand was longer than the gun in his. And that made him wish to hurt her. Hurt her bad.

Encouraged by his hesitation, Abigail West took a tentative step forward. "Get out," she hissed.

Gathering his courage, Steppe pushed the oar away with the musket, moved forward a pace, hawked up a wad of phlegm, and spit. The mucus hit West above her left breast and slid down her beige sweater, leaving a slimy, snail-like trail.

Disgusted, Abigail West stepped back and looked down at what Steppe had done to her, then swung the oar with all her might. It whistled past his head, smashing into the counter with a splintering crash; a mirror cracked, boxes and bottles were scattered around the store.

The sound of broken glass angered her even more than the realization that she had been assaulted by the twisted little janitor. Her rage was murderous. She regained control of the oar and advanced on him for a second attack.

"Get out!" she screamed, secretly hoping he'd stand his ground. She wanted to sink the oar in his ugly, gargoyle face.

Steppe came out of his crouch, and using his strong calloused hands, grabbed the oar out of the air as it came toward his head. With a smooth motion, he ripped it from her grasp, and while she looked on in horror, he broke it in two. The ancient wood cracked like a gunshot.

He leered up at her with his bloodshot eyes, then he crept toward her and pulled her down to his level, his claw-like fingers ruining the delicate fabric of her sweater, pressing into the soft flesh of her shoulders.

She could smell him now, his unwashed, sweaty body, his foul breath.

"It may not be today," he rasped in her face, his spittle flying. "It may not be tomorrow." She could see his sharp, pointy yellow teeth. "But you'll pay, bitch. You'll pay."

Before she could react, he had released her. When he was at the door, she finally found her voice. "You're fired! I'm calling the police," she cried, but there was no conviction behind the threat.

Joseph Steppe didn't stop running until he was near Holy Cross Church. Avoiding the police car parked by the entrance, he crept around to the rear of the rectory where he hunkered down, his back against the foundation, to catch his breath.

Inside the church, he knew, was a dark secret place where he could plan his next move. He pried open the small basement window and wriggled through it headfirst.

In the damp darkness of the cellar, Steppe felt comfortable and safe, something he had never experienced in the outside world.

Confidently, he moved through the gloom like a nocturnal creature, easily finding the old coal bin. It hadn't been used for decades, not since the church had been converted to oil heat, but there was still a foot of coal lining the bottom of the rotting wooden box. Steppe liked to think that if the coal stayed there for a million years, it would turn into diamonds.

Carefully, he brushed the lumps of coal away until he found the cloth-wrapped package that was worth more than diamonds to him. Cradling the bundle, he moved closer to a window for a better look at his treasure. It was three-feet long and glinted in the weak sunlight: a machete he had fashioned from a car's leaf spring. He had patiently sharpened it until its edge would slice through almost anything—a man's head, for example, or a woman's.

Hefting the weapon, Steppe put his hand to his forehead where he had cut it and picked at the embryonic scab. The blood flowed.

He hummed softly to himself, remembering the priest's blood, sticky on the church floor. The flayed body reminded him of a side of beef—the way it hung upside down and naked. He could picture the priest's eye—blue and white—lying on the bloodred

80

marble floor. It had looked at him, trying to tell him something
. . . something he could no longer remember.

Later, in his mind he saw a towering figure in a priest's cassock, but the priest had the head of Abigail West.

Her mouth was gaping open in pain and terror.

Chapter
Nine

Descending the wooden stairs into the basement workshop, former police captain Ed Hanratty felt instantly at home. It was a good warm feeling, standing there in the dark—like dropping into a favorite easy chair.

He threw a switch, flooding the basement with light. A computer hummed, waiting for instructions, an electric motor powering a small compressor whirred restlessly, and on the wall, the twelve pendulum balls of an inert clock clacked their way toward eternity.

Above the clock was a framed square of needlepoint reading: IDLE HANDS DO THE DEVIL'S WORK. It had been given to Hanratty as a retirement present by Monsignor Francis Bryan, the same Monsignor Bryan whose avulsed remains had been discovered the day before.

The workshop, a curious blend of rigid order and years of accumulation, ran the length and width of the house. It was a large, open space, except for a cement block enclosure surrounding the oil burner and the walled-off pistol range. A chest-level metal worktable dominated the room. On it stood a ballistics box, a fingerprint kit, and a clock radio. A shelf underneath held a large wooden box containing a jumble of gun parts—barrels, handles, cylinders, firing pins, and even a silencer for a .45 caliber automatic. Hanratty had taken that from a two-bit hood with delusions of grandeur.

Next to the box of gun parts were prototypes of police holsters lying on their sides; some, partially constructed, looked like metal snakes shedding their skins.

The pistol range had been squeezed into the corner farthest from the stairs. Halfway down the makeshift construction, a man-sized paper target dangled from a pulley wire, a menacing sneer on its cartoonish face, seemingly oblivious to the neat grouping of bullet holes in its heart.

Hanratty pulled on an old cardigan sweater that had once been deep blue but was now a greasy gray, then slipped into a pair of crepe-soled shoes with the backs cut out. The sweater and shoes were his new uniform, the uniform of the retired cop.

Although he could sympathize with cops who claimed that everything except the job was bullshit, Hanratty had forced himself to develop outside interests. The restaurant upstairs had been his first idea, but slinging hash didn't appeal to him. It made good money, but after the first few months it bored him, so he turned over the operation to Jean Fowler, an old friend, who did most of the work. Hanratty made only an occasional foray into the restaurant now, preferring his new hobby—inventing.

Inventing was complicated, consuming, and frustrating, the perfect outlet for a meticulous, brilliant man. In the five years since he had retired, Hanratty had turned all his energy and ability to discovering and correcting deficiencies in police equipment. He held two patents on holster design, one on a more secure handcuff, and was currently working on a new type of bulletproof vest.

Absently, Hanratty rolled a .38 caliber shell between his thumb and forefinger. The bullet wasn't unusual—except for the easily overlooked coating of Teflon, which had turned it from the last word in kitchen convenience into a convenient way to kill police officers.

Coated with Teflon, an ordinary bullet could cut through a standard-issue Kevlar vest like a hot knife through butter. It had literally shot holes in the city-wide campaign to outfit cops with bulletproof vests, making the mayor angry and the P.B.A. very angry. So Hanratty had set about to develop a vest that would be impervious to the space-age plastic.

He removed a pair of pincer pliers from the pegboard tool rack behind him, admiring his collection of implements on the wall. He had made many of them himself, odd bits of metal with edges and flanges veering off in unexpected directions; long, thin, delicate tools; heavy, squat, powerful tools; round, oblong, and triangular tools. They were important to Hanratty; they would not have displeased Torquemada.

Before he had a chance to belly up to his long worktable, he heard the doorbell ring upstairs.

Ciano, he thought, come to humor an old man and put the make on his daughter. He wondered if he should say something fatherly to Erica, but it had been so long since she had visited him, he didn't want to do anything to alienate her. She was like a blast of arctic air in his temperate life and he wanted her to stay as long as possible. She looked so much like her mother, it made his heart ache. He heard Ciano's heavy step on the stairs, followed by Erica's.

"Evening, Cap," Ciano said, abbreviating Hanratty's retired rank. His voice seemed to violate Hanratty's sanctum, but Erica's presence lit up the room. It was an acceptable trade-off.

"I'd like to apologize for yesterday. I can use all the help I can get on this case," Ciano said, offering his hand.

Hanratty took it, but he could read Ciano's motives like a neon sign. A depressed, horny, middle-aged man trying to impress his daughter.

"Mind if I stay, Ed?" Erica asked. It irritated him that his daughter called him by his first name, but then he hadn't been much of a father to her. He hadn't even attended her wedding.

He rubbed a finger over his thin white moustache and peered at both of them through his wire-framed glasses, knowing they both thought him a doddering old fool.

"This is for you," Ciano said, producing a soiled nine-by-twelve brown envelope from under his arm. "It contains forensic photos, copies of some of the 5s and a xerox of my own diary on the case."

Hanratty took the envelope and placed it gently on the work-table. He didn't want Erica to see the pictures. He remembered the nightmares she used to have as a child.

"Thanks," Hanratty said. "But what I'd really like to know is what *you* think about all this."

"I don't think anything," Ciano said. "I just nose around until the case gets solved or they tell me to work on something else." He hoped he sounded cynical enough for the old man . . . and his daughter. Erica's presence was overwhelming.

"But surely you have some opinions, some ideas?" Hanratty said.

"Don't press him," Erica interrupted. "Maybe he doesn't have an idea in his head."

"Erica," Hanratty's voice was low.

"Just kidding, Ed." Erica smiled.

Ciano stared dumbly. Some kind of game was going on and again they had forgotten to tell him the rules.

"Look, Lieutenant, why don't we sit down and we'll think the situation over. Would you like a beer?" Hanratty asked, pointing to a broken-down sofa and two mismatched arm chairs.

Hanratty spoke into the intercom and Jean Fowler answered.

"Would you please send us down some beers. . . . Bud all right with you?"

Ciano nodded.

"Erica," Hanratty said, joining Ciano and his daughter, "this will probably bore you to tears. Why don't you go upstairs?"

"Without my supper, Ed?"

"You know what I mean."

"Sure. You're trying to get rid of me because you think I'm a fragile child who would run screaming from the room at the mere mention of murder and rape."

"Well, I've got news for you, Ed. I'm grown-up." Erica's words were hard, but she smiled when she said them.

Hanratty quickly backed down and remained silent while one of the waitresses from the restaurant brought down glasses and six beers in a plastic ice bucket.

"So?" Ciano said. "You really want my impressions?"

"Absolutely."

Ciano drank his beer quickly and opened a second, while giving Hanratty a rundown on the case. It wasn't until he was almost through that he realized how expertly Hanratty had interrogated him. His estimation of the retired captain grew, along with his sense of caution.

"Well, that's about all we've got so far," Ciano said. "Some psycho offed the poor old padre."

Hanratty pressed the tips of his fingers together and looked over them at Ciano. On someone else, the pose would have been affected, on Hanratty it looked natural.

"You say a 'psycho'. What do you mean?" Hanratty asked.

"No sane person goes around crucifying priests," Ciano said, somewhat taken aback by the stupidity of Hanratty's question. "Who else could it be, if it's not some nut?"

"I've discovered that there are two types of murderers, though individual motives can vary like snowflakes," Hanratty said.

"I can think of more than that," Ciano said. Snowflakes. Jesus.

"Name them," Hanratty said.

"Well, you've got your family killers. You know, the old lady's on his case, so he ices her. Then you've got people who knock off other people for their money. Or like the guy who killed John Lennon, for fame. You've got your professionals and your psychos. All kinds," Ciano said, opening a third beer. He wasn't used to talking so much. It was thirsty work.

"What you've described to me are motives, not classifications. I've spoken with Dr. Arlen and we agree that . . ."

"Arlen! The department's quack? You don't honestly mean that you believe one word that assho—ass says?" Ciano said, remembering the insolent shrink.

"You don't?" Hanratty said.

"He as good as called me insane," Ciano said, referring to his mandatory sessions with the psychologist after the Eva Prime situation. "So, no, I don't agree with him."

Erica laughed. "Sounds like a learned man to me, eh, Ed?"

Hanratty waved her remark aside. "What matters in these cases is not motive, though I grant you that is important, but we must first establish whether the murder was psychotic or psychopathic."

"A nut's a nut, no matter how you crack him," Ciano said, hoping Erica would laugh again, but she was silent, even annoyed that he had interrupted her father. Once again, he was conscious of her beauty and sheer physical presence. Her nearness to him on the couch made him uncomfortable in an exciting sort of way.

"That's where you're wrong, Lieutenant," Hanratty continued, unperturbed. "Simply put, these are two broad categories of killers. The first is the most familiar, the psychopath. He kills for money, fame, passion or pleasure. He may be a professional hitman or a cuckolded husband; he may plan a murder or commit it on a whim. But he is driven by simple human motives, which, if we can establish them, will lead to his apprehension."

"That takes care of all the murderers I ever heard of," Ciano said. "What's left?"

"The psychotic killer," Hanratty said. "Perhaps, five percent of the total."

"What makes them different?" Ciano asked, increasingly dubious about Hanratty's analysis.

"Inside a psychotic killer's mind is a burning rage that has festered for years, decades perhaps. He has a disease, a psychosis, that tells him he must kill, that God or some authority figure is controlling him, making him commit murder. This man is sick, like Joseph Kallinger, the shoemaker, who killed those women in New Jersey. He was convinced God had commanded him to do it. Without his psychosis, he would never have harmed anyone. He was not competent."

"That sounds like a crock of sh— a crock to me," Ciano said, looking at Erica. "If the guy's competent enough to crucify

86

somebody or, in the case of John Hinkley, Jr., competent enough to stalk and shoot a president, then he's competent enough to stand trial and competent enough to be executed.''

"But you must appreciate the difference," Hanratty said. "In this case, for example, I doubt you'll find Monsignor Bryan had any enemies who wanted to kill him. I don't think robbery was a motive, either. Or passion. And if it were a cover-up for something else, it would seem rather too elaborate.

"So, I think we're dealing with a psychotic killer.''

"Okay," Ciano said. "Suppose you're right. I don't see that it makes much difference what variety of nut we're dealing with. But suppose you're right, what does that mean to our investigation?" He meant ''our'' in the departmental sense. Hanratty didn't take it that way.

"It means that our man probably has no police record, though he will no doubt have a long history of mental illness of one kind or another, most likely misdiagnosed.

"It means he will probably strike again—and soon. Or he could simply disappear, his 'mission' completed," Hanratty said.

"That's not much to go on," Ciano said, frowning. The creases around his mouth and on his forehead deepened. He lit another cigarette.

"Our man is not a run-of-the-mill, spur-of-the-moment, kill-for-thrills kind of person," Hanratty said. "He's deliberate, careful, and pays attention to details. I'm sure that when we get hold of him and look inside his brain, we'll find a reason for this murder—a reason that might not make sense to you or me, but will make perfect sense to *him*. We'll be able to see it only after he tells us what his motive was.''

"Or *her* motive," Erica said.

"Sure, sure," Ciano said, annoyed.

"But what you've told me boils down to 'Forget it, Ciano, you haven't a chance in hell of finding this guy'.''

"Person," Erica corrected. "I think you've both got over-stimulated imaginations and are trying to out-point each other: Ed with his preposterous psycho-babble and Vince with his dumb-cop pig-headedness. As for me, I think I'll leave you two to your squalid little arguments.''

When she stood up, both men watched her smooth her tight skirt—Ciano with pure lust in his eye, Hanratty with more complicated emotions.

"I think I'll go upstairs for a good cry. You were right, Ed,'' she said. "You both bore me to tears. Childish, womanish tears."

"I've got to go, too," Ciano said, thinking for the first time about his ex-wife, Diane. He had to call her tonight.

"Consider what I've said," Hanratty urged. "It's worth investigating."

"Then you could be a big help if you get together with your buddy the shrink and maybe give me a report on it," Ciano said, following Erica to the stairs. He wanted to get the hell out of there. "If it's not too much trouble," he added.

He didn't listen for a reply. He was too busy watching Erica's ass swinging sensuously as she walked up the stairs. She's one helluva broad, he thought, following her across the living room. She opened a side door for him.

The night air was cold and Erica hugged herself against the chill. Ciano noticed that her nipples rose dark and hard under the thin white blouse. Suddenly he wanted to stay for a while, if only to look more closely at this woman, but he zipped up his brown leather jacket and started to say good night.

"Are you off duty now?" Erica asked, her question surprising him, the light touch on his arm stopping him.

"Yeah, I'm signed out for the night."

"Well, I thought if you weren't too busy, maybe you'd like to go for a drink."

"With you?"

Erica laughed.

"Sure, I'd like that," Ciano said quickly, feeling he was making a fool of himself. Again.

"Good. Just give me a minute and I'll meet you out front."

When they had gone, Hanratty opened the envelope Ciano had brought him. He was expecting the worst, but even after almost forty years as a cop, he was unprepared for what he saw. The sheer rage the murderer had unleashed on Monsignor Bryan was sickening. Hanratty closed his eyes for a moment, trying to erase the horror. It didn't work. One by one the glossy 8 by 10s etched themselves into his brain, driving from his mind all the memories he had ever had of the priest. When he was through, he couldn't remember what Francis Bryan had looked like before he was killed so brutally. All he saw was the violated body and skull stripped of its flesh.

Hanratty turned each picture facedown on the metal worktable, glad to be looking at the white paper instead of the murder scene, and thought about what it was like to be crucified. He tried to imagine the fear at first, then the overwhelming pain, then perhaps the acceptance of death. Did Monsignor Bryan in his last moments of life confuse himself with Christ? Did he think he was on Calvary? Did he forgive his executioner?

Was it possible that pain lasts after death? Hanratty wondered, piling the pictures, still facedown, into a neat stack. Did anguish travel beyond the bounds of earth? He sat in one of the frayed armchairs, removed his glasses, and rubbed his eyes. Does pain always live in those you leave behind?

Later, as he sat motionless in his chair, Hanratty lost his scholarly air and the abstract expression of grief on his face, and began to get angry. Who, he wondered, would commit such a foul—evil—murder? He imagined Bryan's gradual acceptance of his plight, imagined the humiliating feeling of total helplessness before a strong, implacable enemy. How used and violated Bryan must have felt, like a doll to be tormented, then thrown away. That anyone could abuse another human being in such a way infuriated him. That someone would do it to Francis Bryan made him—he couldn't express the feeling of hatred that he felt, the need for revenge.

Ed Hanratty left his chair at last, pacing up and down on the cold cement floor. After almost an hour, he made a vow. An unholy vow? he wondered. He would find the man responsible for Monsignor Bryan's death and he would kill him. There would be no trial, no juries, no lawyers, and no psychiatrists. Just one man—Ed Hanratty: judge, jury, and executioner.

It was not an impulsive reaction to his friend's death, for Ed Hanratty was not an impulsive man. It was a calculated promise to himself to use all his remaining time and abilities to bring some justice to a world gone mad. He had no choice. It was his duty, it was logical, and it was a realistic goal. He wouldn't even consider the consequences, an uncharacteristic imprecision, because Hanratty was a precise man. He was inquisitive by nature, and liked to think that he could face the reality of any situation, understand it, and adjust his behavior to match it. While others were out chasing chimeras in the dark, Hanratty believed he basked in the pure light of reason.

Not only a realist, Hanratty had a gift for intuitive investigation, which had made him a valued member of the force. Once, in the 1960s, the department was bogged down on a murder investigation involving the strangling deaths of five young women. The murderer had been careful—very careful—and had left no fingerprints or evidence of any kind. No one could figure out a motive or discover any connecting factors between the dead girls—until Hanratty was put in charge of the case. He had spent a week reviewing the evidence, a job that normally would have taken a few hours, so scant were the clues. His bosses, furious at his inaction, were about to fire him off the case, when Hanratty looked over his wire-rimmed glasses and said, "Two. There are two perpetrators."

His superiors scoffed, but within a week, Hanratty had managed to bring in one man and was close to a second. "You see," Hanratty had told them at the time, "we approached the case from the wrong angle. Thinking we were after one man distorted our ability to reason clearly about the facts we had in front of us. If we had approached the case looking for two perpetrators, we might have solved it sooner. Each bit of information means nothing in itself, but is simply a part of a greater picture. If we think we are doing a jigsaw puzzle of the sky, for example, we arrange the pieces in a certain way to support our expectations of that sky. But if all the blue-and-white pieces are of the sea, we'll have a difficult time getting it to look like the sky. Do you understand?"

They hadn't, but they were sufficiently impressed to move Lieutenant Hanratty out of the Bronx and made him a troubleshooter for the Detective Division, a job he held until he retired. There were those in the division who said he would have been made Chief of Detectives if he had only kissed a little ass. But he hadn't. He had been completely apolitical, aloof from the bureaucratic rapids swirling around him. He concentrated on his job, on the facts, and on convincing himself he was doing something useful.

It was this abstracted air, this scholarly absentmindedness that had made him the brunt of fun at headquarters. They called him "The Professor," and would imitate his careful diction and his nervous habit of pulling at his glasses. Yet they didn't laugh at his results, which were truly amazing. In twenty years at headquarters, he had involved himself in more than five-hundred cases, solving more than seventy percent of them to his satisfaction. He didn't always get convictions, he didn't always catch the murderer, but in more than three-hundred-fifty cases, Hanratty had *known* why and by whom someone had been murdered. After he had solved the puzzle, Hanratty cared little for the consequences, for he was already off on another case. One of his detractors had characterized him by saying, "He doesn't work for the department, he works for himself. If you stopped paying him, he'd still come in every day and get on everyone's nerves.''

Hanratty was dimly aware of his colleagues' contempt, but he dismissed it as a nuisance and continued to forge ahead with his work, patiently examining every problem, trying to find a solution. Of course, he didn't succeed every time and on those occasions he fretted and fumed, unable to sleep or eat. Those were the bad times, finding himself on the verge of an answer—an answer that simply would not present itself. He felt like a woman ten months pregnant, unable to rid herself of the weight within her. But always there was a new case that demanded his attention, a new set of facts to deal with promptly, and Hanratty, who had lived most of his life alone, leaped at anything that would take his mind off his failures, both professional and personal.

It was in this spirit that he made his vow to kill the man who had butchered Monsignor Bryan. And it was with this same pragmatic attitude that he had once decided to kill himself.

It was raining heavily that morning twenty-five years before, when Ed Hanratty had decided to end his life. The streets had been flooded and the drains backed up with the last of the autumn leaves. The trees were bare and depressing, spring was almost two months away, and it had been cold, he remembered, a bone-chilling cold that had frozen his soul.

He had been in the loneliest and most deserted place he could think of—a parking lot near Great Kills Beach. The name aroused Hanratty's sense of the macabre—the isolation seemed fitting to him. What he had just witnessed had appalled him.

As he sat in his car in the middle of the gigantic lot, he had watched the endless sheets of icy rain batter the blacktop. In the distance he could see the beach and the surrounding marshland; they were wreathed in an obscuring fog, lending a dream-like quality to the scene.

As he stared at the relentless rain, he placed his hand on the revolver lying next to him on the seat. It felt cold and greasy, but functional. He had spent half the night cleaning and oiling the .38 and he knew it would perform without problem. A misfire would be embarrassing. Even a bad cop shouldn't miss when he decided to eat his piece, he thought.

Lulled by the idling engine and the rhythmic beat of the rain, he picked up the gun and hefted it. He had had it since he was a rookie, and except for qualification rounds, it had never been fired. The hammer made an audible click when he cocked it.

Hanratty took a deep breath and forced the cold, clammy air out of his lungs. He rolled down the window so that at least some of the blood and brain tissue would land outside the car and be washed away. That appealed to his fastidious nature, and he wondered if he should shoot himself outside the car. He tried to move but he seemed rooted to the seat; his mouth was dry, his palms were sweaty, and he could feel his heart beating faster than the pelting rain.

In this almost hypnotic state, he let his mind wander, a last voyage through a world he no longer cared to inhabit. He seemed to be leaving his body, traveling up through the confines of the car and looking down on his own miserable form trapped inside the car. He could see the rain beating on the roof of the car, yet he could also see right through the metal, see himself raising the pistol to his mouth and swallowing the .38's short barrel. Simultaneously, he tasted the metal, thinly coated with oil. His stomach rolled, his body fought to rid itself of the foreign object, fought to live.

From his vantage point high above his body, Hanratty could see the pain and confusion on his own face. He knew what he was thinking: that if he missed, he'd be a brain-dead vegetable. He slammed the barrel hard against the roof of his mouth.

With an air of dreamy abstraction, he saw himself reach over and turn off the engine. The wipers died, the windshield blurred quickly, rivulets of rain making the car a more private place to die.

He saw his finger tighten on the trigger and heard the report, muffled far below him. He could see the bullet ripping through his mouth, exploding in his head. A fine mist of blood, bone, and brain exploded out the window, mixing with the rain, running in puddles down the front seat, and coating the inside of the windshield. In slow motion, he saw himself slump forward on the steering wheel, the back of his head an ugly, pulsing wound.

The gun still in his mouth, Hanratty broke the vision, surprised to find himself still alive. He was disgusted to see that he was shaking all over from the power and ferocity of his . . . his dream, he supposed. He felt his courage waning as the uncontrollable shaking increased and the gun clattered against his teeth. If he didn't pull the trigger soon, he never would.

Breathing through his nose, he put both thumbs on the trigger, closed his eyes and willed himself to shoot.

Suddenly, he felt a presence near him and wondered if he was hallucinating again, this time seeing his incorporeal body from the point of view of the car. He opened his eyes and in the half-light of that stormy morning saw a blur of black moving rapidly toward the car. Death? he thought. Is death coming for me?

Fascinated, he hesitated, giving the dark figure an opportunity to get near him. Hanratty didn't recognize the intruder until after the man had wedged the edge of his hand between the hammer and the live cartridge in the gun and began coaxing the weapon from Hanratty's choking mouth.

That man was Monsignor Francis Bryan.

He would be avenged.

Chapter
Ten

Ciano waited for Erica by the Hornet, realizing for the first time how shabby it had become, but not caring because he had a shit-eating grin on his face. He plugged a Camel into the corner of his mouth to keep from smiling like an idiot. It did him good to know he still had it.

He ran his fingers through his long dark hair, wondering if he should comb it in the side mirror, but there were too many cops going in and out of the restaurant. They might see him acting stupid, as stupid as he had acted that afternoon with Abigail West. The thought of her claw-like fingers made him shudder. The silly old broad had even called him that evening, something about having a clue to the murder of Monsignor Bryan, something about a crazy employee at Richmondtown. It was a transparent attempt to get him alone again, and he was glad Dugan had caught the call. Funny, he thought, Abigail wanted to do to him what he wanted to do to Erica. He hoped his luck was better than hers.

A few minutes later the screen door banged open again. It was Erica. She moved with a coordination and economy of motion that Ciano had only seen in women athletes. He pushed himself off the car and sucked in his stomach, a reflexive action; his body was responding to hers.

Erica smiled and waved. She had changed her clothes and now wore a black pleated skirt and a jacket with a white sweater underneath. Her breasts pushed through the open jacket and Ciano could tell at once she hadn't bothered to put on a bra.

Feeling like a kid, he held the door open for her, hoping someone from the precinct would see him. He was disappointed when nobody came in or went out of Hanratty's. The passenger door creaked loudly when he closed it, as if it were laughing at him.

Despite the weak interior light, the wagon's front seat looked grimy. Ciano hoped it wouldn't soil Erica's clothes, but if she noticed the seat's condition, she didn't say anything.

Just as he was about to pull out, he spotted Detective Marty Abel slumped and shuffling toward the restaurant. Ciano called to him and the short, balding detective came over to the car.

"Hiya, Lew," Abel said, bending down to speak past Erica through the open passenger-side window. "Gotta hot date?" he said, eying Erica appreciatively.

They spoke briefly about Abel's attempts to locate the manufacturer of the leptons, but nothing important had broken on the case.

"See ya tomorrow, Abel," Ciano said, driving away from the curb.

"Make a U-turn," Erica said. There was an unmistakable chill in her voice.

Ciano cut across two lanes and a solid double line. By tomorrow he would be the talk of the precinct. He felt like a million bucks.

They drove in silence for a time until Erica said, "You know, if I wanted the whole world to know I'm going out with you, I'd have told Sergeant Dugan. I don't want this to get back to my father. He's old-fashioned and thinks his married daughter should stick with her husband."

"I'm sorry," Ciano lied. "I didn't realize." His hands were clammy on the steering wheel and he was beginning to feel clammy inside.

"You knew *exactly* what you were doing," Erica said. There was a quick flash of anger behind her eyes.

Ciano concentrated on the road. He felt like a reprimanded child. "You want to go back?"

Silence. She was thinking about it.

"No," she said at last.

That didn't sound particularly positive, Ciano thought, but he kept on driving. He could feel the anger and resentment boiling off her like steam.

"Oh, forget it," she said, finally. "Why should I expect you to be any different?"

"I am, I am," Ciano said.

"What?"

"Different."

Erica laughed, the tension suddenly broken. He glanced over at her and was glad to see her calm and relaxed.

"Well, not *too* different, I guess," he said, apologizing in his own way.

Erica directed him to a place called Limetree's. Inside, Ciano found the bar more Manhattan in atmosphere than he would have expected on Staten Island. Ferns, plants, and white wine seemed to be taking over the world. But he had to admit somebody had a pretty good idea—saving tired commuters a ninety-minute trip to the city for an overpriced drink and a goat cheese salad.

They sat in a dim corner at a ridiculously small table which brought them closer together than a matchmaker could. He could feel the warmth of her body against his and liked the sensation. She ordered a Campari and soda, which Ciano tried and told her it tasted like a Listerine cocktail. He ordered Jack Daniel's, neat, with a beer back. She wrinkled her nose at that, but at least she didn't give him a temperance lecture.

"Your old man's quite a guy," Ciano said, hoping to draw her out.

"I suppose. But he's always been more interested in his job than in me."

"That why you didn't want him to know about, uh, us?" Ciano said, not at all sure there was an "us."

"No. I just don't want to do anything to upset him," she said. "And I don't like to be put on display like some kind of prize cow."

"I'm sorry about that," Ciano said. "It won't happen again." He knocked back the J.D. "It's just that you're the most beautiful woman I've ever seen."

"Sure. And I swept you off your feet, right? I've heard that one before. I've heard 'em all before," she said. "I even married a guy who used to tell me that—before we were married. Afterward, he treated me like a piece of furniture, a valuable antique."

"You divorced?"

"Not yet."

"Soon?"

"Soon as possible."

"What's he do? Your husband."

"He's an importer."

"Rich?"

"Sure."

"You gonna pick up this tab?"

"Big spender. What's with you, anyway? I mean, are you married?" Erica asked.

"Divorced. Three years ago. I've got a son. He's six. You got kids?"

"No."

"Want any?"

"Not tonight."

"Damn."

"Bastard," Erica laughed, moving closer to Ciano. For the next hour they exchanged stories, Ciano leaving out most of the bad stuff and inventing a few episodes to impress her. He found that she was strangely drawn to exciting police stories, the kind that cops told to their Aunt Marthas on Thanksgiving to keep the old broads titillated. He would have expected Erica to have OD'd on cop tales long ago, but Ed Hanratty was apparently a closed-mouth guy who hadn't been on the street in thirty years.

He was so engrossed in telling her about Monsignor Bryan's mutilations that he hadn't noticed the time.

"It's almost ten," Erica said. "We'd better go."

"Curfew?" Ciano asked. He had a good buzz on and didn't want to go anywhere.

"In a way," she said absently. He wondered then where he had lost her. It had been a mistake to bring up the priest's death. Too gory. Shit, he thought, I should have stuck to surefire retreads.

In the car Ciano asked, "Where to now?"

"You mean, your place or mine?"

"If you like," Ciano said, trying to sound casual.

"My place is out, for obvious reasons," Erica said.

"I live all the way in the Bronx," Ciano lied, thinking about Chris and Dan's bedroom.

"How about a neutral zone?" Erica asked.

"What?"

"A motel, dummy," Erica said, laughing.

"Great." Jesus, he thought, I'm making it difficult and she's still willing.

They drove for more than an hour, trying to find a motel, but neither one of them knew where they were going. Ciano remembered a place from his youth, but when they got there, all they found was a condo. The island kept changing. Ciano could feel his passion sputtering as the night and the drinks wore away his lust.

Finally, they found a fleabag motel Ciano didn't even want to try. They were just about to give up, when Erica pointed to the parking lot across the street from the motel.

"Pull over there," she said.

"Why?"

"I think I know where we can find a room."

Ciano complied, but he was still confused when he found himself in a dark corner of the parking lot.

"Turn out the lights," Erica said, switching off the ignition key, holding it a moment longer than necessary, as if considering her next move. Ciano turned to face her.

"I want you," she whispered. "Now. Here." Her voice was husky, deep, seductive.

Ciano felt his guts churn and twisted farther around until the steering wheel pressed painfully into his side. He hadn't been laid in a car since he was a teenager and about forty pounds lighter. It was as exciting as hell.

He looked into her eyes. He had seen that look many times before, but only after he had busted his ass getting them hot. Erica was different. He hadn't done anything much; she was in charge here. His instincts told him she would be different from any woman he had ever known.

"Interested?" she asked, sliding down on the seat. The question was a tease and didn't require an answer. She kicked off her shoes before draping one leg over the seat, the other one on the floor. Her black skirt slid back onto her white thighs.

Hesitantly, Ciano stroked her leg from ankle to calf while stealing a glance between her thighs. But what he wanted to see was in shadow. Erica's leg was taut to his touch, the skin cool, smooth, and bare. He couldn't believe what was happening.

Erica raised her right foot to Ciano's groin and prodded her toes against him in a small circle. The bunched fabric of his pants absorbed most of the friction, but it was the thought alone that brought his erection up.

Ciano slid his hand over Erica's knee and up the inside of her thigh. Erica shifted quickly, like a cat. She moved her foot from over the seat to Ciano's chest and pushed, forcing him back with a jolt. Their eyes met and Ciano saw something stirring in Erica, something odd. But it disappeared before he could pin it down.

"Let me," she whispered. It was a plea.

Ciano didn't know what Erica was doing. He tried to think of a counter-move, but before he found one Erica was on her knees bending over him and tugging his belt open. She pulled his zipper down with a deftness that, by itself, aroused Ciano again. Erica peeled his pants open and leaned toward him.

"Slide down," she said, and he obeyed. Her cool fingers

pulled his penis out of his shorts and she used her nails with the skill of a surgeon. Ciano felt as if he were being touched, ever so lightly, by four tiny rakes.

Erica's mouth came down on him in a wet, warm embrace. Then she slowly withdrew, following her mouth with her nails. Now eight tiny rakes were at work and Ciano moaned with pleasure.

As Ciano watched Erica's head, he stroked her hair and neck, wanting to grasp her head and guide it. He didn't though, afraid it might offend this unpredictable woman. Still, he wanted to slow her down to make the pleasure last.

Almost as if she could read his mind, Erica stopped.

"You can fuck me now," she said. Her words sent a chill up Ciano's spine.

Shifting from her kneeling position, she slowly lowered herself onto her back. She hiked up her skirt to her waist, showing him she wasn't wearing panties.

Erica ran her middle finger over the lips of her vagina.

"Fuck me," she said.

Ciano reached for the seat lever and it grated back as far as possible. But it was difficult for him to squirm between her legs. The damn steering wheel kept getting in his way.

Finally, he got into position above her and she took his penis in her hand, squeezed it, and guided it into her. She moved him slowly, sensuously up and down her vagina, giving him just a hint of the fierce warmth inside her.

Their faces met and she kissed him hungrily, her tongue inside his mouth.

She was all business, Ciano thought. No tenderness, no words, none of the things he and Diane had enjoyed. Only sex. Hot, hungry sex. Despite his raging passion, Ciano felt unsure of himself.

Erica moved his penis in small circles against her clitoris. He could feel the small nub expand until it was almost an inch long. Curious, Ciano reached between them to feel it. But Erica pushed his hand away. "Don't do that." She wasn't whispering anymore.

Ciano jumped, his nerves jangling. She's turning me on and off like a light switch, he thought. Playing with me. He wanted to tell her to stop fucking around, but he also wanted to push himself deep into her.

She wrapped her legs around him and squeezed down hard. He felt the power of her thighs as he lunged into her.

"Fuck me hard," Erica screamed, biting his neck. "Harder, harder!"

Ciano could feel the muscles inside her contracting.

"Hurt me," she gasped, raking her nails down his back until he thought she might tear his shirt. "Hurt me, you bastard!"

Erica's head was thrown back, she was breathing hard; her nostrils flared. Her every shudder enhanced Ciano's own passion, yet in the back of his mind he also felt a vague uneasiness.

"Don't come yet, not yet," Erica breathed. "I want more, I need more."

Ciano tried, but he couldn't do it. He knew he was only moments away. "Now," he said.

"No, no," she cried, dropping one hand to the floor and reaching for her purse. "Don't come. Not yet."

"Gotta," he growled, grinding against her. He wondered if she were searching for her diaphragm. It was too late to matter.

"Damn it, stop!" Erica cried and Ciano was shocked out of his trance by a piercing pain in his groin.

"Stop it!" he heard her scream through his pain. "Take it out of me!" She had, he saw now, balled both her fists and was pushing her small, sharp knuckles into his groin.

He pulled out of her, his ass almost getting stuck between the steering wheel and the seat, but before he could say anything, she said, "Get away from me. Don't touch me!"

She swung her legs around and sat up, straightening her skirt. Except for a few strands of auburn hair streaking her face, she was completely composed.

Ciano, however, was still kneeling, frozen like stone, his pants around his knees.

"You look ridiculous," she said, gazing at his shriveling penis as he hurried to pull up his pants. "You *are* ridiculous."

Her words cut him like a knife. He felt a growing rage within him. He wanted to strike her, but suddenly she opened the car door, allowing the cold air to hit him. He watched her walk away into the night.

In the weak light of the car's interior, Ciano spent his rage on the dashboard.

The radio blared. She had left the ignition on. He wondered if the battery was strong enough to turn over the engine; he wondered if he was.

Ciano was drunk and punk-sore at the world. Three hours had passed since the incident with Erica, hours he had spent looking for someone to jump the Hornet, looking for Erica, and looking for trouble. He had accomplished two out of three of these goals, getting the old station wagon on the road and being eighty-sixed from Limetree's. But so far no Erica.

Driving aimlessly, he found himself near his ex-wife's new house and decided it would be a good idea to visit her. Although he would never admit it, he was there to get his ego stroked, preferably in Diane's bed.

Despite being profoundly drunk, he remembered with amazing clarity Erica's warm wetness. His penis jumped at the thought, but quickly relaxed again. He parked in front of Diane's house, a raised ranch, part of a tract put up in the early 1960s. The lawn was brown and the flagstone steps leading up to the front door were in need of repair. He was glad to see a light on in the living room. Diane must be waiting for him to call.

With the exaggerated care of a drunk, Ciano pulled out a crumpled pack of Camels and put a bent cigarette in his mouth. It took him a while to light it; his coordination was off.

He drew the cigarette smoke deep into his lungs and stood on the small porch by the front door, trying to get his thoughts in order.

"Crazy fuckin' bitch," he mumbled to himself, thinking that Erica had played him like a fish, reeling him in just for a good fucking laugh. While he was out looking for her, confused, amazed, and hurt, she was bursting a gut laughing at him.

He pitched the butt into the shrubbery, cursing himself for ever getting involved with Erica. I should have been here with my wife and kid, he thought, not wasting my time with some nut-job bitch.

Before ringing the bell, he ran his hands through his disheveled hair and decided he'd ask Diane if he could spend the night on her couch. He figured once she saw the condition he was in, she could hardly say no. And from the couch to the bedroom wasn't such a long walk.

He pressed the bell twice: short, quick rings so as not to wake his son. He wanted to finish with Diane what he had started with Erica. He was prepared with an alibi and a long list of lies and didn't see the late model Corvette parked next to Diane's Toyota in the carport.

The light in the hall went on.

"Who is it?" Diane asked.

"It's me. Vince."

"Vince. What the hell are you doing here? It must be three

a.m. You were supposed to call.'' She sounded startled, but awake.

Ciano squinted at his watch. ''It's only 2:15,'' he said. ''I got tied up at the precinct.''

''Go home, Vince. It's much too late for stale excuses,'' she said.

''But I can't help it if I got tied—''

''You need some new material, Vince,'' she interrupted. ''I've heard it all before. Right now I'm tired and you sound drunk, so go home. I'll tell Vincent you were here.''

''But I'm too drunk to drive,'' Ciano said, his voice had an ugly whine. ''So come on, be a good wife and let me sack out on the couch.''

''Ex-wife,'' she snapped. ''And you can't sleep here. Leave before you wake up the whole neighborhood.''

Ciano fumbled for another cigarette. This was harder than he thought it would be. He changed his tone and his tactics.

''I'm not going anywhere until you open the door,'' he shouted. ''And I don't care if I wake up the whole damned neighborhood.'' He knew she hated scenes. ''You hear me?''

He heard the lock snap and the door creak open. This is better, he thought, I'll have her in bed in less than an hour. But the door suddenly stopped opening, held by the safety chain. Through the narrow space he could see she was wearing the long, flannel nightgown he had given her several years ago. She looked sensational. Her ripe body and oversized breasts filled the nightgown—and Ciano's mind—with promises of sex. Her dark hair flowed over her bare shoulders.

She wasn't as pretty as Erica, he thought, but he wouldn't kick her out of bed . . . assuming he could get her there.

''Here's Johnny,'' he said, imitating Jack Nicholson imitating Ed McMahon, as he pressed his face into the open space between the door.

Diane wasn't buying it. In fact, the look of hatred on her face made him pull back as if he had been slapped.

''I want you away from this house and out of my life, Vince, or so help me, I'll call the police and have you locked up.'' Her voice was low and dangerous.

''But I am the police,'' Ciano sputtered, not joking.

''Don't joke with me, Vince. I'm in no mood for your crap. Just leave.''

She started to close the door when he heard a man's voice. ''Shut the door on him and let's get back to bed.''

It took a few seconds for the voice to register, then he felt his life begin to crumble away. He had been on a roll since that damn Eva Prime shit, a no-luck roll: transferred, stuck on a lousy murder case, laughed at by Erica, and now rejected by his wife. Rejected and replaced by some goddamned cocksucker boyfriend. The fury, the frustration, and the bourbon boiled up inside him.

Diane didn't slam the door on him, although it might have been better if she had. Instead, she closed it firmly but quietly, snapping the lock afterward. That sounded to Ciano like she was shutting him out of her life forever, while on the other side of the door, some stranger had taken his place in her world and now shared all the things with her that he had lost.

Driven by drunken self-pity and anger, he launched himself at the door, bursting both lock and chain. The force of his entry propelled him through the foyer and into the living room. He barreled past Diane, knocking her like a rag doll into the man standing behind her. When he staggered to a stop, the three of them stared at each other in silent surprise.

Ciano steadied himself on a folding director's chair with the words, "Vincent Ciano, Jr., Superstar" stenciled on the cloth back.

Diane was so incensed she couldn't speak, but her eyes told the story. The man with her, younger than she, much younger than Ciano, held her from behind. Ciano noted that he was wearing only jockey shorts.

"You're fucking my wife," he roared, advancing on the man, his fists balled menacingly.

"I'm not your wife," Diane hissed, trying to keep the two men apart.

"Let him come," the man said, eager to get at Ciano.

"I don't need this, Teddy," Diane said, imploring both of them to stop.

At the same time, Vince, Jr., appeared in the living room, hugging a tattered Snoopy doll and rubbing the sleep from his eyes.

"Hi, Daddy," he said.

"My God." That from Diane.

Ciano knelt down on one knee by his son and held out his arms. The boy, pretending to be shy, hid his face behind the Snoopy doll, then ran to his father.

"You were supposed to call, Daddy," the boy said, squirming into Ciano's arms. "Mommy's mad."

Ciano stood up stiffly, using the director's chair as a crutch.

"As a hatter," Ciano said.

"Mommy doesn't have a hat," Vince, Jr., said, his large brown eyes serious.

Ciano hugged him again and felt the boy respond immediately. Though he welcomed the affection, he wasn't prepared for the guilt. He had forgotten how to be a father . . . if he had ever known.

Diane emerged from the bedroom, tying the sash of a blue terry-cloth robe. Teddy was behind her wearing khaki pants.

"Back to bed, Vincent," Diane said, using her mother-in-charge tone. The same tone she had just used on Ciano. "You have school tomorrow and you don't want to fall asleep in Sister Theresa's class."

The boy listened to his mother, but still clung to his father. "Please, Mommy, let Daddy stay. He didn't wake me up. I wasn't really sleeping. I heard a monster in your room. That's why I woke up."

Ciano knew the "monster" was probably Diane and Teddy thrashing around in bed. Diane's look confirmed it.

"Come on," Ciano said. "We'll piggyback to your room and I'll tuck you in."

The boy started to protest, but Ciano held up his hand. "Nope. No arguments. I'll come back tomorrow after school and we can play. I promise," Ciano said, realizing his promises were worth dog shit. He knew it, Diane knew it, even Vince, Jr., knew it, but it was all he could offer the boy at the moment. He was totally drained and he put the child down, suddenly exhausted. All he wanted to do was make a quick exit, drive around the corner and sleep it off in his car.

As Ciano stood there looking at the little boy with the red-and-white striped pajamas at least two sizes too big for him, Teddy decided to assert himself.

"You heard your mother," he said, "it's bedtime." Teddy scooped up the child and started to carry him to the bedroom.

But he didn't move quickly enough. Ciano had already lost his wife to this man. He wasn't about to lose his son. He caught Teddy by the shoulder, spun him around and pulled Vince, Jr., away, nudging his son toward Diane.

"Go to your mother," he said to his son, not taking his eyes off Teddy.

"Motherfucker," he growled at Teddy, unaware of the pun.

104

For a moment, nobody moved. Diane tried to stop them, but they were like two dogs fighting over a bitch in heat.

Size and brute strength had always been Ciano's forte as a fighter and he saw no reason why it wouldn't work now, drunk or not. He figured he outweighed Teddy by a good fifty pounds, though the younger man's sinewy muscles indicated he was in good shape. *Probably much faster than me*, he thought, though a good, big man can beat a good lightweight, anytime. That's why it was a complete surprise when he found himself lying on the floor. He had never seen the kick to the head Teddy had landed.

More dazed than hurt, Ciano got back up, but the confidence in Teddy's gray eyes was unnerving. This guy was sure he'd kick Ciano's butt with some kind of karate or something.

Ciano brought his hands up quickly and faked a short jab. Teddy ignored the punch and answered with a kick to Ciano's stomach that sent waves of nausea through his body and a teaspoon of half-digested Jack Daniels into his mouth.

Behind the kick, Teddy threw two quick punches that snapped Ciano's head back like a speed bag. Then, another kick to the chest, and Ciano found himself lying on the floor again looking up at Teddy's cold eyes. He decided Teddy could handle himself around the gym. But there was something almost feminine about his blown-dry, razor-cut hair and delicate cheekbones.

Ciano shook his head to clear it, then got up slowly, knowing Teddy wanted the pleasure of knocking him down again. Teddy looked at him with a detached gaze, as if the fight warranted only half his attention.

Ciano heard Diane say something. It sounded urgent, but the words were garbled. *Later*, Ciano thought, *not now*. He staggered against the director's chair, the blood from his nose and split lip dripping onto the canvas seat. Ciano watched it distractedly, waiting for his head to clear.

"Try to use that chair on me, asshole, and I'll shove it down your throat," Teddy snarled.

The words caught Ciano by surprise. He had no intention of doing anything with the chair, except leaning on it. But it gave him an idea.

Teddy shifted from fists to open hands, light on his feet. Fast and sure. The man was contemptuous of him, urging him on.

Ciano forced his shoulders to slump in defeat. He held up his hands, palms outward.

"Ya got me. I don't want anymore," he slurred. Teddy relaxed, too. Victorious.

With both hands, he picked up the director's chair and said conversationally, "Here, Teddy. Catch."

He flipped the chair casually through the air. Teddy caught it.

He also caught the hammering left-jab, right-cross combination that Ciano planted on his jaw. The bolt of pain that shot up Ciano's arm gave the punch a ten-point rating. Teddy went down like a sack of laundry, the director's chair still clutched in one hand.

"So long, Superstar," Ciano said, reading the back of the chair.

Rubbing his hand and trying not to look too smug, he winked at Diane and patted his son on the head.

Outside, he almost screamed with pain.

Chapter
Eleven

Wednesday, November 3

Ciano didn't like the face staring out at him from the stained mirror. The eyes were puffy and bloodshot, a pale yellow and purple discoloration rimmed the bottom of the right socket, and dried blood caked both nostrils. He touched his split, swollen lip and winced.

Disgusted with himself, he opened both faucets, drawing a sputtering stream of brown water which splashed uncertainly on the gummy gray porcelain.

It was almost 8:00 A.M. and Ciano was in the shithouse of the 122nd Precinct, an aptly named cubicle on the second floor. It looked like a shithouse and it smelled like something had died in there recently.

After an impossible night trying to sleep it off in the back of his car, Ciano felt like puking.

He pulled an old disposable razor from his jacket—he kept spares in his glove compartment—and waited for the brown, tepid water to turn yellowish. It looks like piss, he thought, scooping up a handful and carefully dousing his cut and bruised face. He hoped to make a few emergency repairs, enough to keep his men from asking embarrassing questions.

Ciano pumped the dregs of liquid soap from the wall dispenser and worked up a pitiful lather. The industrial-strength hand cleaner felt like molten lead on his battered face. Tugging the dull razor across his stubborn beard made things worse, and he inflicted two new cuts on himself. He staunched the flow of blood with the now ice-cold water and applied bits of paper towel to the deepest ones.

He cleaned the remaining caked blood from his nose and lip and patted his face dry. Once again he looked in the mirror, judging the improvement slight, but considering what he had to work with, it was adequate.

His clothes were another matter. They looked and smelled like he had slept in them. Ciano knew he should have gone to the apartment to change, but after the night he had had, Chris and Dan's love nest wasn't a place he cared to visit.

The john door swung open behind Ciano and Detective Marty Abel walked out hiking up his pants. He joined Ciano at the row of sinks and began combing his thinning black hair.

"Whoa!" he said, glancing at Ciano. "Look at that shiner. Hanratty's daughter get a little rough in the clinches last night?"

Ciano turned his back on Abel, opened his pants and re-arranged his shirt. There was something about the detective he didn't like. He certainly didn't feel like discussing his sex life with Abel.

"Well, *excuuuse* me!" Abel said, trying to be funny, but when Ciano kept his back to him, Abel slunk out the door without washing his hands.

At his desk, his head throbbing, his guts growling, Ciano waited for the dizziness to pass. Before it did, Sergeant Dugan poked his head in and asked him if he wanted coffee.

"Regular," Ciano said, his eyes closed.

"Two black coffees coming up," Dugan said, ignoring his request. Obviously he looked to Dugan as bad as he felt. Ciano had just put his head down on folded arms, hoping a few minutes of sleep would restore him, when the phone rang by his ear. He grabbed it before the noise reamed out his brain.

It was Morrison, the desk sergeant. "There's a reporter from the *Post* down here to see you. Says he's a friend of yours."

Jermezian, Ciano thought. "Tell him I'm dead," he said. It was almost true. Then reconsidering, he said, "Tell him to have a seat. Joe Dugan will talk to him in a few minutes."

Closing his eyes again, he put his head on his arms.

The ring this time finished destroying his brain cells; it was like someone had scraped a metal file across a blackboard. Ciano wasn't sure whether he wanted to scream or vomit.

"Yeah," he rasped into the offending phone.

"Mr. Jermezian says you shouldn't forget old friends. He wants to speak to you personally," the desk sergeant said.

Not wanting to be blasted out of his comatose state, Ciano agreed to talk with the reporter, but not for a few minutes. This time when he lowered his head, the phone was in the bottom drawer of his desk where its muted ringing couldn't reach him. He was almost comfortable when Dugan slammed a paper bag down on the desk and began to unpack it. He took out two containers of coffee, an open Coke can filled with beer, and a large paper cup containing something that smelled like turpentine. Ciano looked at the syrupy brown liquid bubbling out of the straw hole in the large cup and reached for one of the coffees.

"Drink this first," Dugan said, shoving the foul smelling cup toward him. It fizzed and groaned like Ciano's stomach. He eyed it suspiciously before pushing it away.

"What is that shit?" he asked, reaching for the coffee again.

"Just drink it," Dugan said.

"Fuck you."

"You prefer death by hangover?"

"No, but I'm not going to drink anything that looks like shit and smells like the inside of a paint can."

"Then sit there and continue fermenting inside," Dugan said, sipping his morning beer.

Just talking with Dugan had used up Ciano's strength. All he wanted was a bit of silence.

"What's in it?" Ciano asked, slowly pulling the container toward him. "It's cold."

"Drink it quick," Dugan advised. "When the chill wears off, it becomes toxic."

Ciano held his breath and sucked down a throatful of cold liquid which immediately turned hot when it reached his throat. It was like swallowing semi-liquid steel wool.

When he finished, Ciano made a strangling sound and opened his watering eyes. Dugan was grinning at him.

"What happens now?" Ciano asked.

"Couldn't tell you," Dugan shrugged. "I've never seen anyone drink it before."

"Jesus," Ciano said and opened up a black coffee to flush the pine-tar taste out of his mouth.

"Do I dare ask you what was in it?" Ciano asked, rolling the coffee around his mouth like a wine connoisseur.

"No."

If he hadn't felt so bad, Ciano would have laughed. Dugan was a funny guy, he thought, liking the sergeant as much as he disliked Abel. Maybe it was because Dugan washed his hands after going to the toilet.

"If you're through poisoning me," Ciano said, "let's get whoever's on duty in here so we can see what we've got to do."

"A staff meeting," Dugan said, as if Ciano had just invented sliced bread. "What a good idea."

Twenty minutes later Ciano sat surrounded by most of his squad, including the smirking Marty Abel. They all took a quick look at Ciano's black eye, but no one said anything. Abel must have filled them in, Ciano thought glumly. His plan for impressing his men had backfired. They probably thought he was some kind of scumbag.

The one consolation Ciano found staring at his detectives was that they looked as tired and frustrated as he did. Hours of following up slim leads, talking to crazies who had "inside" information, and generally wearing out their shoe leather had taken its toll. They all knew that this homicide was a shot-in-the-dark situation. It would go nowhere until they got a lucky break, a freak coincidence that would go nowhere until they got a thread attached to some looney tune. They were all on a treadmill waiting for a step-in-horseshit break and the whole world knew how Ciano's luck had been running lately. He wondered if they thought of him as a jinx, a Jonah who could fuck up a wet dream.

Ciano picked up the phone and called downstairs. A few minutes later, Freddy Jermezian, the reporter for the *Post*, sauntered into the room. Even by cop standards, Jermezian was a sartorial disaster. He wore a blue pin-striped jacket—once part of a complete suit—electric blue polyester pants that flashed green or purple depending on the light, and a hand-painted tie that was so wide it almost covered his thin chest. Jermezian's thick black hair was greased into a pompador Elvis Presley would have envied; his swarthy, pockmarked face was squinty and rat-like. He rubbed his huge hooked nose, as if confirming it was still anchored to his face.

"Hiya, sweetheart," he said to Ciano in a fey voice. "Whadda ya got for me?"

A right cross, Ciano thought, followed by a couple of shots to your gut. Not that it would take that much to put Jermezian down. He was barely five-six in his elevator shoes.

"Gentlemen," Ciano said. "You all know Freddy Jermezian. He's here to get the inside story on the murder of Monsignor Bryan. Unfortunately, I can't help him because I haven't got the slightest idea of what the fuck is going on. So why don't you guys talk to him and I'll read all about in tomorrow's *Post*."

Then, turning to Jermezian, he said, "Okay, Freddy. They're all yours. From now on I'll bust *your* balls for information.'

Before anyone could say anything, Ciano was gone.

Ciano sat in the idling Plymouth, chain-smoking and biting his thumbnail. He wished he had taken the wagon. Somehow he felt conspicuous in the unmarked police car.

Every few minutes he glanced up at Holy Cross Church, wondering when Hanratty would show up. He had to be careful with the old bastard, he thought, careful to talk about business until just the right psychological moment. Then he'd work Erica into the conversation.

He lit another Camel with the butt of the last one and thought about Monsignor Bryan's murder. So far he had nothing but jackshit to go on. Nothing checked out, nothing was happening, the case was drowning in its own inertia. All he had was a crazy retired captain snooping around, an equally crazy daughter he was hot for, and crazy Abigail West who was hot for him. It was . . . well, crazy.

The priest's death, or rather the successful conclusion of the case, was the key to the mess he had unwillingly stumbled into. If he could only catch a break, the rest of his worries would evaporate.

Mentally, he checked off his problems, dividing them into two groups: work and personal. Under work, he listed finding Bryan's murderer, getting back to an "A" precinct, getting even with Captain Talbot, and hanging on long enough to cash in on his pension. Four problems, all related, he thought. Under personal, he ticked off getting a new apartment, getting Diane to love him again, spending more time with his son, and getting back into Erica's pants. God, he hoped he'd have another shot at her. He hoped Ed Hanratty would be of some help. He hoped he wouldn't blow it a second time. Blow it, he mused. Yeah, blow it, baby.

He was thinking about Erica's mouth moving up and down on his prick, when Erica and her father got out of a slate-gray BMW right up the street from him. What the fuck was she doing here? Ciano thought. He crouched down behind the wheel, feeling like a voyeur, or maybe like a teenager suffering through his first crush. She turned him on. Just walking down the sidewalk. He moved her up on his mental list, above the apartment, just below his son.

He hunkered down lower in the seat, thinking, I hope she doesn't see me. He could imagine her fixing him with her cold green eyes and laughing at him.

He peered over the dashboard after they had passed, adjusting the rearview mirror so he could see them. From this cramped position, looking at the world in reverse, he saw Father Layhe come to the rectory door and exchange greetings. Ciano felt a twinge of jealousy as Layhe shook Erica's hand longer than necessary before pulling her gently into his world.

Fucking priests, Ciano thought, sitting up straight and banging his knee on the steering wheel.

Fucking horny priests.

Father Thomas Layhe had been expecting Hanratty, but the daughter was a pleasant surprise. It seemed to Layhe that the church attracted fat, middle-aged housewives and old crones like the late Mrs. Eddins; he often wondered where the good-looking women had gone. Perhaps they were all Protestants, he thought, holding onto Erica's hand and guiding her into the rectory.

"I must say your call was rather mysterious," Layhe said to Hanratty, as he ushered them into his brown-carpeted office.

"It's very good of you to indulge an old man," Hanratty said, avoiding the implied question. "Francis Bryan was a fine man and a close friend."

Layhe shook his head and frowned sympathetically. Actually, he was tired of hearing Monsignor Bryan eulogized. Enough was enough. Bryan was a cantankerous, senile old fool, he thought uncharitably, who had let the parish fall into ruin. Layhe knew he would have to work like a dog just to pick up the pieces. He had to soothe the old guard, like Hanratty, while attracting a whole new generation of parishioners with enough money to keep the doors of the church open. He hoped Erica would be his first new convert; it would certainly be a pleasure to see her face every Sunday.

"As I understand it then, you just want to look around?" Layhe said. "The police seem to have done a pretty thorough job. Are you looking for clues?" Hanratty's call had been peculiar, Layhe thought, peculiar, vague, and laced with what he felt was a psychic undertone. Psychic phenomena didn't bother Layhe as much as Hanratty's efforts to cover them up. What did this old cop really want? he wondered.

"Not clues, exactly," Hanratty said. "Just a feeling for the crime scene; I have police permission to help with the investigation."

"Then you certainly have my permission, Captain," Layhe said. "Let me show you the way."

"I can find it," Hanratty said. "Monsignor Bryan and I used to walk the halls here at night. I know my way in the dark."

"They're both insomniacs," Erica said. "Now Ed works all night in his shop."

"At least I'm *working*," Hanratty said, a veiled dig at Erica for staying out all night.

Erica smiled benignly. "We all do what we must," she said. "And I must run. I've got an appointment in town. Sure you can get home all right, Ed?"

"Don't worry about me," Hanratty said, hoping it sounded like, "You never worry about me."

"Please stay," Father Layhe said. "It's not often I get such a lovely guest. A cup of coffee before you go?"

Hanratty felt like the father of an eighteen-year-old. He didn't like the idea of this hot-shot young priest drooling over his daughter, but after going God knows where with Ciano last night. . . .

"Why, thank you, Father," Erica said. "For the compliment and the coffee."

"It's settled then," Layhe said, rubbing his hands together. "Are you sure you can find the door to the church, Captain?"

"I'm quite familiar with the layout of the church," Hanratty said. "This used to be Monsignor Bryan's office, you know."

I know, I know, Layhe thought, and until I die, this will always be his church. His ghost will haunt me forever. But even such dour thoughts couldn't spoil his plans for a few pleasant moments alone with Erica.

She was wearing a tweed suit which would have looked dowdy on other women, but on Erica it highlighted her smooth complexion and red-gold hair. Layhe was admiring her legs and hardly heard Hanratty's soft good-bye.

Until he came face to face with Monsignor Bryan's coffin, it hadn't occurred to Hanratty that he would need time to prepare himself.

As he stood at the door behind the altar, he could see the draped coffin sitting solidly in the aisle. The half-light from the rosette window played over the coffin in a disquieting way. The dark shadows of the church were oppressive. The whole place smelled of incense and death.

Hanratty turned abruptly and walked back into the rectory, closing the door behind him. He leaned against the wall and shut his eyes, trying to forget the glossy photographs of his friend's final agony. He felt his heart beating irregularly. His face was hot and sweaty, his hands cold as ice.

"Are you all right?" a deep, disembodied voice asked.

Hanratty opened his eyes and was startled to find Father Graff peering at him.

"David," he breathed. "What are you doing here?"

113

"I was about to ask you the same thing," Graff said. "Don't have a heart attack in here, one Miss Eddins is enough."

Hanratty breathed easier. There was something comforting about Graff, something familiar and worn. The priest's face was leathery and pushed out of shape, his cheeks shot through with veins and creases, his nose bulbous and red. He smelled like tobacco and Scotch whiskey and, like Hanratty, Graff had the guarded look of a man who had seen too much misery. Unlike Hanratty, the priest had taken it all personally. Every disappointment, every crushing defeat, was imprinted on his face.

"Just paying my respects," Hanratty said, trying to gain control of himself. He and Bryan and Graff had spent many hours together discussing police work, politics, and religion, and together they had demolished many a case of scotch.

"Care to come upstairs for a short one?" Graff asked. "You look like you could use it."

Hanratty declined, but noticed that Graff had already had a few. He didn't act drunk, but then he usually didn't. Yet his eyes were a bit too bright, his voice too animated, and his demeanor a bit too cheerful. Deep inside, Hanratty knew, Graff was full of pain.

"I'm writing the eulogy," Graff said. "Trying to think of something nice to say about Francis." He ran a hand through his gray crewcut. He was smiling, but his deeply creased face was ashen, his blue eyes dull and lusterless. "It's not easy."

"It's never easy to say what you feel," Hanratty said.

"That sounds like something I should have said," Graff smiled. "Would you like to take over for me?" His voice rumbled through the rectory hall.

"That's your job, and I'm glad of it. You knew him best," Hanratty said. He had never told anyone about that rainy day at Great Kills Beach or of his relationship with the old priest.

"He was a feisty old bastard," Graff said. "And it's difficult to make him sound like a saint."

"So? Make him sound human," Hanratty said. "He was, you know."

"There's those who might disagree," Graff said, nodding in the direction of Layhe's office.

"But there are those of us who know better."

"Sure you won't have a snort with me?" Graff said. "For old time's sake."

Hanratty shook his head. For God's sake leave me be, he

thought. "I'll see you later," he said. "Right now I think I'll go back into the church."

"All right," Graff sighed. "But remember, never turn down a drink. You never know when it might be your last."

He was joking, but the words chilled Hanratty.

The access door to the church was behind the main altar and as soon as he opened it, Hanratty knew he would have to force himself to continue. He was repelled by the sight and smell of the shadowy church and the eerie feeling that someone was watching him.

He snapped on the lights behind the altar, but the small bulbs did little to dispel the gloom—he felt like he was trapped in a partially sealed vault.

The construction work had been cleaned up reasonably well. The scaffolding around the main altar had been dismantled and was stacked up neatly in the aisle to his left. The huge cross on which Monsignor Bryan had spent his last hours had been taken away and was in the evidence room at the police academy, where it would no doubt remain for years.

Hanratty ran a finger over the communion rail, remembering Bryan's complaints about the all-pervading dust. He took out his handkerchief and carefully wiped the rail clean, as if that made things better.

He pulled his gaze away from the excavation and tried to concentrate, not on death, but on revenge. He had come to this desecrated church to find a murderer.

He circled the altar until he came to the place where Bryan had been crucified. There were still deep stains on the marble floor, and recalling the harsh clarity of the forensic photos, he began breathing rapidly, afraid of his thoughts. He bore down mentally, trying to make sense of so senseless a crime, but his attention wavered. He wondered if Layhe, sitting comfortably in his office talking with Erica, was secretly scornful of his odd ways.

Ciano would laugh, if he knew. The sight of a washed-up cop sneaking around a crime scene, communing with . . . what? The ether? The vibes? A man like Ciano couldn't think beyond the tangibles. If he couldn't hold it in his hand like a gun, Ciano wouldn't believe it. Worse, he would laugh at what he didn't understand.

Forcing his mind to go blank, Hanratty made himself receptive to the air around him. There was nothing occult in his method, simply a way of relaxing and letting everything flow over him. It was a talent many people had, but rarely talked about. He liked to think that a person who committed a violent crime left behind a residue of hate and perverted passion. And he also liked to think that the victim, in his agony, left the same kind of trace. Isolating these infra-residues from the background, that was the trick. Maybe it was a trick, he thought, but whatever it was and however he did it, it worked for Hanratty. Sometimes.

Standing with his shoes just touching Monsignor Bryan's dried blood, Hanratty tried to imagine the murder from the murderer's point of view. He tried to visualize the rage, the pure hatred the killer felt, and how released and purified he must have been after inflicting such terrible pain on his innocent victim.

Outside a distant police siren wailed, rising and falling, rising and falling . . . like the murderer's arm pounding nails into warm flesh. Hanratty could feel himself begin to sweat in the cold, dank church. And he felt something else. Initially, it was just a tiny chill centered in his spine, then he received an image of the murderer, amorphous and distant, but somehow familiar. He saw a dark figure and for an instant, a pair of mad, burning eyes. Then nothing.

Gripping the communion rail to keep from falling, Hanratty took several short, deep breaths. He knew he had seen something indescribably evil, something he had seen before, something he couldn't quite place. He was sure of only one thing: he wanted to leave the church and never come back. The aura of malignancy was too overpowering.

Unsteadily, he left the church by the altar door and by the time he was back in Layhe's office, he felt almost human again. Erica was gone.

"She just left," Layhe said. "She told me to tell you she'll be in town."

Hanratty nodded.

"Are you all right, Captain?" Layhe asked. "You look like you've seen a ghost."

"I hope not," Hanratty said, but already his mind was working on the case. "I think I'll get a breath of fresh air."

"Can I give you a lift?" Layhe asked. "I'm hearing confessions today at St. Vincent's Hospital and I'll be glad to drop you off."

"No, thanks," Hanratty said, turning to leave. "I think I'll take a stroll over to Richmondtown."

"Still looking for clues?"

"Not really," Hanratty said. "But thanks for humoring me."

"Wait a minute," Layhe said, grabbing his coat. "I'll go with you."

The two men walked to the rectory steps, and as Layhe reached the bottom he looked back up at Hanratty.

"You know, vengeance isn't supposed to be in a priest's vocabulary, but I hope you find whoever you're looking for," Layhe said. "I'd like to see someone punished for this."

"Retribution? An eye for an eye?"

"Exactly."

Hanratty, still stunned at the residue of hate and violence that had nearly suffocated him in the church, watched Layhe drive away. He stood motionless for a moment, then walked slowly down the stairs, thinking.

Deep in the basement of Holy Cross Church, not fifty feet from where Hanratty had stood, Joseph Steppe was holding a large black rat he had trapped. Careful of the animal's sharp, needle-like teeth, he swung the rat by its long pink tail and rapped its head against the boiler. The rat's head made a hollow pinging sound which mixed with the animal's frantic squeals. After several attempts, Steppe managed to render the rat unconscious, a feat that made him laugh uncontrollably. His shoulders twitched and his body convulsed as if he were being electrocuted.

Steppe felt for the rat's rapid heartbeat through the animal's slick fur and finally located it. Alive, he thought, alive but dead, and he doesn't even know it.

He put the rat down on its belly and went to the coal pile behind him. There, burning red hot, were the pieces of coal he had carefully selected for their uniformity. With an old shovel he picked them up and spread them out in front of the unconscious rat.

His tongue lolling from his mouth, licking spittle across his dry lips, Steppe took the sword he had fashioned from a leaf spring and licked it. He could taste his own blood. His spit washed away the symbols he had so painstakingly drawn on the weapon. But it was all right, he thought, he would replace them soon.

Keeping an eye on the rat, ready to crush its head with his foot if it moved, Steppe thrust the sword into the coals, enjoying the hissing of blood and spit on the blade. When it was almost

117

too hot to hold, he waved the sword in the air three times, then neatly severed the rat's head from its body. The creature's blood shot across the room like water from a hose.

Steppe plunged the sword into the rat's hot blood and delicately coated a two-inch portion of the blade. Then using only the bloody tip, he rearranged the coals on the floor until they were exactly the way he wanted them.

It is almost time, he thought, hunkering down, his flesh and bones twisting at grotesque angles. It is almost time.

When the coals had burned themselves out, the neat pile of white ash formed a word that burned itself into Joseph Steppe's mind.

The word was KILL.

Chapter Twelve

The word was eschatology—the study of the last or final things: the doctrines of death and resurrection, of judgment and punishment, of heaven and hell. These concepts meant very little to Father David Graff, as he sat in the bare room trying to compose an appropriate homily for his friend, Monsignor Bryan.

Did it matter if Francis Bryan had reached the ultimate joy of eternal life and salvation? he wondered, balling up a sheet of lined yellow paper and throwing it at an overflowing wastebasket. Or was it more important that his life had affected—helped—others? Graff was no longer sure he believed in heaven. He had already seen hell.

As a veteran priest, he had unflinchingly served his Lord in some of the Church's most trying assignments. He had run soup kitchens for the homeless, counseled battered wives and abused children, and had taken scores of addicts through the horrors of detoxification. Graff had also served as a prison chaplain, attempting to give murderers, rapists, and robbers some reason for living.

In the course of his religious career, Graff had been stabbed twice and, once during a riot at Attica, had been held hostage and tortured for two days and nights before being rescued by the National Guard.

Through it all, his faith had survived, but not without casualty. To dull the pain, physical as well as psychological, David Graff became an alcoholic.

Drinking became a hedge against burnout, a cover-up, a gauze filter to make the daily pain of living more endurable. If Martin Luther were correct, and a state of grace was simply snow over a dung heap, then Scotch whiskey was Graff's snow and his life was the dung heap.

Obsessed by unwanted thoughts and emotions, half-dizzy from the alcohol he had consumed, Graff tortured himself with his own doubts and yearned for the lost comradeship he had enjoyed with Bryan. Now that the monsignor was gone, would anyone ever take him seriously again? Or would he, like so many other old priests, become useless long before he was ready to die?

The futility of these thoughts, the metaphysical lure of eschatological problems, finally drove Graff away from his poor efforts. The maggots are working faster than I am, he thought, the old man's bones will be picked clean before I finish.

Lighting a cigarette, then angrily stubbing it out in the overflowing ashtray, Graff got up from the desk and went down the long, dim hall toward the bathroom.

He was almost there when he felt a chilling sensation, as if someone were watching him. Turning quickly, he could see no one. Only the rows of dark oak doors and the bloodred carpeting. No sound. No movement. Yet . . . something.

Afterward, washing his hands of the whole matter, he examined his face in the bathroom mirror. The creases and lines that some called rugged were simply the result of worry. They couldn't tell him where he was going, but they certainly told him where he'd been.

Graff splashed cold water on his face and scratched his gray crewcut hair, carefully avoiding the growing bald spot.

I'll give it one more hour, he thought, one more hour to finish the homily. Then, like most writers, he found a way to avoid it. He went to see Monsignor Bryan.

The church was as quiet and deserted as an empty film studio. It was dark and cold: The limits of the interior space were lost in the darkness.

Graff genuflected before the altar of the Sacred Heart, and was comforted by the red sanctuary lamp. That meant the Sacred Hosts were stored in the tabernacle, symbolic of Christ's presence.

The rosette window over the main altar provided the main source of illumination inside the church; the play of the colored lights on Monsignor Bryan's coffin was almost theatrical.

Graff slid into a front pew and knelt. Before him the altar loomed in gloomy shadows, while next to him, in the center aisle, the coffin gleamed in the strange light.

The coffin was plain, polished wood. Across its center lay a white resurrection cloth, a symbol of the priest's baptism and a testimony to the immortality of man's soul.

Graff thought about how the church would soon be filled with parishioners and clergy. More than fifty priests would come, including the Cardinal. Few of the priests would have known the dead monsignor, most would be put out by the imposition the funeral made on their time, but they were bound by honor to go—like cops for a fallen brother officer.

The coffin caught Graff's attention and he was reluctantly drawn to it. Standing by it he caught himself touching the cross motif woven into the resurrection cloth. Suffering and pain, the symbols of Christianity, he thought, tracing a cross with his finger. The body inside, Graff knew, had suffered greatly, though the police had been vague about precisely how Monsignor Bryan had been mutilated.

Perhaps they thought they'd shock him, Graff thought ruefully. He had seen bodies blown apart by Chinese rockets in Korea, had held the victims of knives, guns, bricks, and fists in his arms. He had extracted a bottle from the vagina of a nine-year-old prostitute. He didn't believe anything could shock him anymore.

Licking his dry lips, he wished he had a drink to steady him for the next few hours, but he had already finished the liter of Dewars he had brought with him that morning.

Imagine, he wondered again, they thought they'd shock me. *Me.* He got up from the pew, looked around the empty church, then feeling like a thief, or worse—a desecrator—he opened the lid of Monsignor Bryan's coffin.

A hiss of escaping air stopped him; he immediately recognized the odor—dead human flesh. The smell brought back a hundred tortured memories. He forced himself to look at Bryan's earthly remains.

The monsignor's body had been completely wrapped in a white shroud. His hands, folded across his stomach, were wrapped in the same white cloth he had held decades before at his ordination; Bryan's ruined fingers clutched his rosary beads.

He put his own hands over the dead priest's and tried to think about all the good times they had enjoyed, but his mind was blank. When he removed his hands, they were damp, a combination of his sweat and the seeping bodily fluids from the corpse. Monsignor Bryan hadn't been embalmed—there hadn't been enough flesh left on his bones.

Wiping the moisture off his palms, Graff closed the coffin lid and returned to the pew. He wanted to pray. He wept instead.

When he had sobbed himself dry, Graff intended to return to the empty room and finish the homily.

He never made it. He heard something. From the back of the

121

church. A clicking sound. No, he thought, a tapping sound. The difference made his heart race. Clicks were made by machines, settling wood, contracting metal. Taps were made by human beings. Suddenly, he felt he was being watched again.

Then the noise stopped, plunging the church into an even more oppressive silence. Graff twisted around to look behind him, but the darkness appeared solid. There was nothing to be alarmed about, he thought, trying to convince himself.

He moved from the pew to the center aisle, his hand touching the smooth, cold coffin as he passed.

A quicksilver chill brushed his nerves. The sound again. A scratch? A tap? He couldn't tell. It all happened so quickly, yet the message seemed clear. Come, it beckoned.

I'm being called, he thought, and I have to go. The illogic of the idea appealed to him, but he found his legs were like jelly. He had to stop and bolster his courage to continue walking down the dark center aisle toward the back of the church.

One step at a time, he told himself, gripping the hard back of each line of pews, pulling himself from row to row. He wondered what he was afraid of in this deserted church. He had faced savage gangs of homicidal kids, fought hand-to-hand with North Korean sappers, braved the midnight streets of Harlem where even the cops refused to go.

When he reached the two arched doors in the vestibule, he felt better. The doors didn't meet perfectly along the hinges and center seam: thin shafts of light entered the church, painting soft, liquid shadows. It was enough to see there was no danger.

He tried one door. It was securely locked. Then he pressed one eye against the center of the doors. Outside, he could see the hood of a blue-and-white police car, and that made him feel safe—and foolish.

He searched the rear pews, two on either side of the aisle. Nothing. He walked briskly to a confessional, his heels clicking purposefully on the marble floor for courage. The penitents' booths were draped and he swung the left side open. It was empty, as was the right side. He opened the door to the priest's compartment between the two penitents' booths. No one was there.

Relieved and confident once more, Father Graff stepped back into the center aisle. He looked toward the altar. Suddenly his blood froze.

The coffin was open.

Squinting in the gloom, he could see the resurrection cloth

puddled on the floor. Worse. Much worse, Monsignor Bryan's body was propped up against the lid of the coffin. His shrouded figure was caught in a halo of light from the rosette window.

Graff wanted to run, but he couldn't. His legs wouldn't obey him. He stood still, mesmerized by his friend's corpse. Monsignor Bryan looked as if he had suddenly woken up. Except . . . except there was something wrong, Graff thought, something he had missed in his terror.

What is it? he chided himself, his curiosity overcoming his fear.

He took a hesitant step toward the altar, then another. Out of the corner of his eye, he saw the Seventh Station of the Cross. The alto-relievo sculpture of Christ falling the second time under the weight of the cross. It burned into his mind as he staggered on, the stations becoming mileposts on his journey to the dead.

The sound again.

A tap. Behind him.

His heart pounding, his legs weak, Graff kept heading for the coffin.

The Tenth Station: Christ stripped of his garments. Graff felt exposed and naked. His mind and body were an unwilling sacrifice. He walked on.

Tap. Tap.

Now the noise was on his left. Still behind him.

Tap. Tap.

Closer still, coming to meet him.

The Eleventh Station: Christ nailed to the cross. Graff felt Jesus' pain, mingling with his own. His breath was coming in gasps. He couldn't stop. He had to go on.

The Twelfth Station: Christ dies on the Cross. His vision blurring, his heart pounding in his ears, Graff heard the rasping scrape of metal on stone.

Like a man jumping into the cold surf, Graff turned around suddenly, determined to face his unseen tormentor.

Nothing. Only the darkness, silent and impenetrable.

"Christ Jesus," he prayed aloud. His words were hollow in the empty, desecrated church.

He kept moving toward the coffin, as if drawn by an invisible string.

The Thirteenth Station: the Pieta. The dead Christ in Mary's arms. Comfort, security—how he longed for them. Graff wanted to run, but he couldn't resist the pull of the open coffin.

Tap. Tap.

The noise spurred him on.

The Fourteenth Station: Christ buried in the Holy Sepulcher. The end of the journey for Father Graff.

He reached the coffin and looked closely at the corpse. He felt his bowels loosen, his bladder give way, the bile rise in his throat.

He was staring at an eyeless skull covered with dead-white shreds of flesh and tangled wisps of hair. Someone had unwrapped the shroud.

Before he could scream, he heard the tap again. Only inches away. The hair on the back of his neck stood up—he could feel and smell a presence behind him.

In the eternity it took him to turn around, he regretted his study of eschatology had been so slight. Soon he would *know* the truth.

He stared blankly at the figure near him. His eyes peered blindly into the face . . . the face of . . .

But he didn't have time to comprehend anything—he didn't have any time at all—as the shining metal blade whistled toward him.

"Bless me, Father, for . . ." he groaned, as the cold steel sliced across his neck, opening a gaping wound that resembled the grinning red mouth of a toothless shark.

Father David Graff didn't feel the dripping blade as it hacked through the remaining cartilage of his neck, severing his head from his shoulders. All he felt was pain.

Then darkness.

Then death.

PART II
The Judas Voice

". . . woe to that man by whom the Son of man is betrayed!
good were it for that man if he had never been born."

—MARK 14:21

Chapter
Thirteen

Ciano's shoes slid in the coagulating pool of blood: If he hadn't grabbed a pew he would have fallen.

"It's like a skating rink in here," he said to James Young, the Assistant Medical Examiner, who was crouched beside Father Graff's headless corpse.

"Why don't you play some organ music?" Young said, not looking up from his grisly task. "Skaters away."

"Why don't you stop pulling my organ and tell me what's happened here," Ciano said, wanting a cigarette badly.

"It's incredible," Young said. "The viciousness of this murder is beyond comprehension."

"Yeah, yeah." Ciano looked at the headless corpse. It was carefully arrayed on the floor of the church, its legs and arms gracefully arranged to simulate a dancer's movements. A dance of death, Ciano thought.

"Where's the head?" he asked Young.

"Give your stomach a break and wait for the eight by ten glossies," Young said, probing the hole between Father Graff's shoulders with a number ten scalpel.

Ciano's silence was ominous.

"In the coffin," Young said finally.

Ciano picked his way carefully through a sea of slippery blood, steeling himself for what he was about to see. He thought he was ready for anything. He was wrong.

Monsignor Bryan's body was propped up in the coffin as if he were about to step out and greet the world. His empty eye sockets, deep and black, seemed to stare at the detective menacingly. The strips of hanging, decayed flesh that had been torn from his skull trembled gently like tinsel on a Christmas tree. Ciano bit the inside of his cheek to keep his stomach from heaving. But he hadn't seen the worst yet.

In the coffin, Father Graff's head had been positioned between the monsignor's legs, the mouth open in a grotesque parody of oral sex.

"Jesus," Ciano whispered. But that still wasn't the worst. The killer had cut out Father Graff's eyes, ears, nose, and tongue and rearranged them. An eye peered out of Father Graff's open mouth, his tongue poked out of one eye socket, an ear from the other. . . .

Ciano backed away from the coffin, his own ears filled with a roaring sound. Helicopters, he thought wildly. What are the choppers doing here in this church?

"You okay?" Young called to him.

"I've seen this before," Ciano said softly, the roar of the helicopters drowning out his words, the stink of blood, shit, and death in his nostrils.

"Where?" Joe Dugan asked, coming up behind him.

"In Nam. A prison camp we liberated. They took heads and changed things around, then stuck the heads on spikes to remind the prisoners not to escape," Ciano said, the memories throbbing and vivid.

"Let's get out of here," Dugan said. "You need a drink."

"*You* need a drink," Ciano said. "*I* need a suspect."

They drove slowly back to the precinct house, the silence almost palpable. Ciano could smell bourbon on Dugan's breath. Finally, Dugan asked, "You in Nam?"

"No, I was a rioter at Kent State," Ciano said. "Of course I was."

"You see any similarities between the prison camp and the murder of the priest?" Dugan asked.

"Except for the insanity, no."

"Tough over there?" Dugan asked.

"It's tough everywhere," Ciano said. "In a war there are no rules. You kill or you die—no matter what the generals say about rules of war, no matter how squeamish the politicians get, you got to do what you think is right. Or you commit suicide."

"What did you do? In the prison camp?"

Ciano was silent, remembering. "I did what I had to do. What was right," he said. "I went crazy. As crazy as the fucking gooks. There was only one survivor, and on the chopper back to base camp he caught fire at five thousand feet and we had to toss him into the river to put out the flames."

"Jaysus."

"His name was Ky, and once in a while in my dreams, I get

128

to throw him out of the chopper again. And you know what? For days afterward, I sleep like a baby."

Dugan cleared his throat. "If anyone can catch this perp, it's you Lew."

"Yeah?"

"Yeah, because you're as nuts as he is," Dugan said, wheeling into the parking lot behind the station house.

While Ciano busied himself cutting the paperwork for the new homicide, Dugan, unnerved and half-drunk, decided to respond to Abigail West's hourly calls for help.

"She'll eat you alive," Ciano said. "Dick hungry."

"Ah," Dugan responded, a stupid grin on his face.

"I'd rather fuck your grandmother than that broad," Ciano said, shrugging.

"Granny'd be pleased, I'm sure," Dugan said, waving good-bye. He had to leave the swirling activity of the squad room for a while, just until his head cleared, or until he got past the fluttering, semi-drunk feeling and into a stable stupor.

Driving with exaggerated care, he made his way back to Richmondtown, purposefully avoiding the jam of police cars surrounding Holy Cross Church. Unconsciously, Dugan crossed himself to ward off the evil and the memories, and before he got out of the car, he took a swig from his hip flask to steady himself.

In the distance, near the millpond, he thought he saw something move, but when he rubbed his eyes, whatever it was had gone.

Now I'm seeing ghosts, he thought, heaving himself up wearily from the driver's seat, and walking through the deserted restoration, whistling an ancient Gaelic dirge.

Approaching Stephens General Store cautiously, he noted immediately that the lock on the door had been tampered with, and when he tried the knob, it fell to the wooden porch with a dull thud. Dugan drew his service revolver and pushed the door open an inch or two with the barrel. Suddenly sober, he peered into the darkness. No movement.

Dugan fumbled with the flask in his hip pocket and took a swig while braced against the doorframe. He cursed himself for cowardice, then kicked the door open the rest of the way.

"Police!" he shouted as he crouched by the side of the door, his .38 held in both hands.

No one shot or shouted. He couldn't see a damned thing.

129

His stomach churning, his hands shaking, Dugan stormed into the store, knowing he should have called for backup. He spotted a glint to his left, hit the floor and squeezed off a round. He expected to feel the bite of a bullet at any moment. Instead, he heard a voice behind him saying, "Is anything wrong in there?"

Dugan spun around on the floor and aimed his gun straight at the voice. Father Layhe was silhouetted in the doorway.

"It's all right, Father," Dugan said, getting to his feet. "It's me, Sergeant Dugan."

Layhe fumbled for the switch and suddenly the high-ceilinged interior was bathed in soft light, illuminating the antique implements and products of a bygone era.

"What's going on?" Father Layhe asked. "Were you shooting at somebody?"

Dugan sighed, holstering his .38. "No, I just slipped and the gun went off," he said, wondering how he was going to fill out the Firearm Discharge Report.

"Oh."

Dugan looked around curiously at the store. Three of his four children had toured Richmondtown with school and church groups, but none of them had been impressed. Dugan was fascinated.

"Quite a place, this," he said to Layhe.

"Yes, Miss West is a stickler for authentic detail," Layhe said. "Which reminds me, I was looking for her. Have you seen her?"

"Never had the pleasure," Dugan said. "Though we've talked on the phone."

"Well, I've got to get back to the church," Layhe said. "Poor Father Graff."

"Poor, indeed," Dugan said. "You don't seem particularly upset."

"I hardly knew the man," Layhe said, shrugging.

Dugan nodded, thinking Layhe must be the coldest son of a bitch he had ever met. Two priests killed—slaughtered—in his church and the man was traipsing around like nothing had happened.

"Well, see ya," Layhe said, waving.

"Sure," Dugan said. "And have a nice day."

When the priest had gone, Dugan began to examine the store thoroughly, looking for other signs of a break-in. To his left, perched on a shelf was a stuffed owl with one glass eye. Above the bird was a .38 caliber bullet hole—his own.

"I'd be dead meat if owls could shoot back," he said aloud. "Shoot instead of hoot." He laughed, but he was feeling scared inside.

Behind the long wooden counter, he noted the open cash register drawer, but that meant nothing. The store had been closed for weeks. Then he saw a stain on the rolling floor beneath him.

Blood?

He bent down and fingered the stain.

Blood.

Two hours later, Dugan was back at the station house. He had notified the watch commander about Abigail West's presumed disappearance and had scoured Richmondtown looking for her. Not a trace. No one answered her home phone.

He was wondering if he should pay a call on her apartment in Todt Hill, when he heard a roar.

Dugan's head hurt, his feet stank, and he didn't love Jesus at that moment. He wanted sleep. Instead he got Ciano. A roaring Ciano.

"Where the fuck have you been?" Ciano asked, his voice on edge. "All hell is breaking loose around here and you're out scouting up some deranged bitch."

"And a good afternoon to you, too, Lieutenant Ciano," Dugan said, smiling.

"Goddamn it, Dugan! Get into my office."

"If you'll give me a moment to catch my breath, I think I might have something that will interest you," Dugan said, following the lieutenant into his office and sitting down heavily in one of Ciano's gray plastic chairs.

"Well?" Ciano was impatient.

"You know, Richmondtown Village offers solid testimony to the existence of the little people."

"What?"

"The little people—"

"I'm warning you—"

"Now, now," Dugan said. "You'll remember the troll we inquired after? Well, he's not a troll, at'all, at'all."

"I'm sick and tired of this crap, Dugan. You get out of here and check into detox center," Ciano yelled.

Dugan's smile broadened as he reached inside his jacket and tossed a crumpled manila folder on Ciano's desk.

"What's this?" Ciano said, opening and smoothing the bent folder.

131

Dugan remained silent while Ciano examined its contents. It contained a police artist's sketch, a blurry xerox of a troll, and a black-and-white photo attached to Joseph Steppe's employment application.

"You'll note that friend Steppe is only four-foot-eight—a little person," Dugan said. "I give you young Kathy Santini's Peeping Tom."

"You give me a pain in the ass."

"I also give you something else to think about," Dugan said. "Stephens General Store has been broken into and Abigail West is missing."

"That's a relief," Ciano said.

"Not necessarily," Dugan said. "I found blood behind the counter."

Ciano threw the folder across the desk. "You thinking what I'm thinking?"

"I think we've got a live suspect and a dead woman."

Abigail West was not dead. When Joseph Steppe had burst into the general store brandishing a sword, she had laughed, long and hard. The flustered expression on his evil little face was priceless. She had sneered at him, her eyes cold and cunning. "Get out of here, you pathetic little scum. I've called the police and they're coming to lock you up."

But he hadn't stopped. In fact, he had put his head down and charged at her. Like a matador dodging a scrawny bull, West sidestepped him and laughed again as he crashed into the counter.

"Scum," she had taunted. "Pathetic scum."

There was blood in his eye and blood coursing down his face, but Steppe was up and running at her again. This time leading with the spring leaf sword, and this time Abigail West couldn't avoid him. The sharpened steel opened her right arm to the bone. She stood looking at the dead white bone poking up through the blood and muscle before she felt the agonizing pain. She started to scream, but the scream was cut off by a burning in her left calf. She turned around to see Steppe slashing at her leg.

He's trying to hamstring me, she thought calmly, remembering the nature movies she loved so—remembering small, tough wolves bringing down a magnificent buck. They nipped at its legs until it was unable to run, then they took their time feeding on its still-living carcass.

Abigail West swung at Steppe with her fist, but he was too fast for her, ducking her blow easily. She felt the sword slash into her other leg, then, mercifully, she collapsed to the floor and into oblivion.

When she awoke, she was naked and spread-eagled in a dank basement room. On her arm, she could see a crude bandage, soggy with blood; her legs felt like they were asleep. She strained at the ropes that held her, but blacked out for a few minutes before returning to consciousness. She groaned.

"Hello, Miss West," Joseph Steppe said, looming over her. The first thing she noticed was that he was naked, too—naked and erect. He was a lot bigger down there than she had imagined, but it was nothing to brag about.

She tried to speak, but only managed a croak.

"What's that you say, Miss West? You want me to fuck you?" Steppe said in his unnaturally high-pitched voice. "You want it, don't you." It wasn't a question.

Abigail West tried to speak again, but all she could manage was a gasping scream. Never in her life had she been so helpless—trussed up like a chicken waiting for the oven, at the mercy of an insignificant mutant. She wasn't afraid, she was furious, outraged. She struggled against her bonds, writhing furiously.

"I can see you do," Steppe said, stroking his penis. "I like the way you move."

He suddenly sat down beside her, resting the sharp leaf spring sword between his legs. He smiled at her, his pointy little teeth yellow and gleaming; then he rubbed his hands together in ecstasy. Like a cannibal sitting down to a banquet, Abigail West thought, and I'm the main course. She tried to spit at him, but her mouth was too dry.

She felt his short, stubby fingers begin to play over her skin, probing, pinching her cold flesh.

"You love it, bitch," he breathed. "Say you love it."

She tried to spit at him again, and this time she had enough saliva, but it only rolled down the side of her mouth.

"You think I'd kiss you? No way. Fuck you, maybe, but I'd rather kiss your pussy than your ugly face," Steppe said, resuming his exploration of her body. He ran a finger from her left nipple to the space between her legs, then back up to her right nipple. "That's where I'm going to cut you," he said, giggling. "A nice triangle."

Abigail West pulled furiously at the ropes that held her.

She screamed, a strangled cry.

"Shut up, bitch!" he shouted, hitting her across the breast with the flat of the sword. "If I hear one more word from you, I'll slit your throat."

Abigail West had lost her fury. It had been replaced by mind-numbing terror. She subsided.

"That's better," Steppe said. "You did something for me, now I'm going to do something for you."

He positioned himself between her legs and lay down on top of her. She could feel his coarse, hairy little body covering her and thought of spiders. She could feel his hardness on her belly.

"You like this, don't you," he whispered in her ear.

She turned away from his foul breath, and tried to concentrate on saving herself from this madman. If he wanted to screw her, she'd let him. That way she might have a chance.

But when she felt the head of his penis begin to probe for an opening, she made the greatest—and last—mistake of her life: she laughed.

"Too small," she whispered. "Too small."

Enraged, Steppe leaped up from her as if she were on fire. Rage darkened his normally saturnine face.

"Bitch!" he screamed. "You don't want me, but we'll see how you like my friend."

Grasping the sword, he knelt down between her legs and ran the sharp point over her labia.

"See how you like this," he said, fury and glee etched on his face. "See how you like it!" He pushed with all his might.

Chapter
Fourteen

Thursday, November 4

After a night of restless sleep in Chris and Dan's mirrored bedroom, Ciano couldn't wait to get to work. They have aspirins there, he thought, and coffee and reasonable people.

He was right about the coffee and aspirins, but he had highly overrated the reasonableness of the police department. A groggy Dugan gave him the word.

"You got a visitor," Dugan said. "In the cap'n's office."

"Shit."

"In the form of Sally the Shit DeFeo. He's there, too, along with Captain Talbot."

"Wonderful."

"Shall I tell them you're sick?"

"That's no lie," Ciano said. "But come on, let's get this over with."

"Whaddya mean 'we'?" Dugan asked, heading down the long green corridor toward Captain Smith's office. Ciano followed behind, trying to work up the enthusiasm for a confrontation.

The three men—Smith, DeFeo, and Talbot—were standing amidst the captain's picture gallery murmuring to each other when Dugan and Ciano walked in.

Talbot, wearing a gray flannel suit that was too small for his body and a sneer too large for his patrician face, turned toward the door.

"It's about time you got here, Ciano. I've got a homicide investigation to run, and when I run an investigation, we work around the clock," Talbot said.

Ciano spoke to Dugan. "This piece of shit crawl out of the toilet or did you bring it in on your shoes?"

"Excrement, Lew," Dugan said. "Always say 'excrement' when addressing a superior officer." He had just thrown his lot in with Ciano, and had left his own ass hanging in the wind. They would rise or fall together.

"Who the hell are you?" Talbot demanded.

135

"A worker in the vineyards of justice," Dugan said.

"A nut case." This from Salvadore DeFeo. "You work here?"

"Last time I checked the In/Out Book," Dugan said, referring to the ledger containing the names of cops transferred in and out of the command. "Sergeant Dugan."

"You better go look again, because your papers just came through," Talbot said, his sneer becoming more grotesque. "You're out of here."

"Now just a minute—" Captain Smith began, but was cut off by Talbot.

"I'm in command of detectives here," Talbot said. "I say who goes and who stays, and this asshole's out."

"Excrement, indeed," Dugan sighed, and turned to leave.

"Hold it," Ciano said. "What's going on here, DeFeo?"

"Vince, Vince," DeFeo said, pretending to be sad. "I'm afraid we're all puppeteers in the hands of our masters."

Puppets, you asshole, Ciano thought, but he said, "Am I being fired?"

"Heavens no," DeFeo said, running a fat finger over his oily, flattened nose. "Is that what you think?"

I think you set this up, you shit, Ciano thought, but he stared mutely at the short, squat inspector.

"My heavens no," DeFeo repeated. "Captain Talbot, here, has been assigned as task force commander to investigate these murders. That means more bodies, more overtime and a captain or deputy inspector to command such a big operation. You're still boss of detectives here at the 122nd."

Big fucking deal, Ciano thought, I'm as good as canned. "Well, if I'm boss of detectives," Ciano said, "I want the money and I want Dugan."

"No way, Ciano. No more of your prima donna act. Until these homicides are cleared, you work for me, and I can promise you you'll work hard or you'll finish out your career as a clerk downtown."

"I want the money," Ciano repeated, meaning the extra five thousand a year a detective lieutenant received for being in command of a precinct detective unit. "And I want Dugan." He was unyielding.

"That sounds reasonable," Smith said.

"Okay with me," DeFeo said.

"Who the hell cares?" Talbot said, after looking into Ciano's dark, brooding eyes. "I want a briefing tomorrow morning at

0700 hours. I'll use your office to set up my command post. Dismissed.''

"Dismissed?" Ciano said, clenching his fists and starting for Talbot.

Dugan grabbed Ciano's arm and spun him around. "Come on, Lew. We've been dismissed from better places.''

"I should have clocked him," Ciano said to Dugan for the tenth time.

It was after ten p.m. and they were sitting in Hanratty's drinking as fast as they could. The place, as usual, was filled, but there was a certain strangeness in the air. Word of their humiliation had spread throughout the precinct; Dugan felt like a bug under a microscope. He kept checking his fly to see if it was closed.

"Thanks for saving my job, anyway," Dugan said, also for the tenth time. "I'm too old for an 'A' precinct, too smart for a desk job, and too young for retirement.''

"And too drunk to remember you've already said that a thousand times. I didn't do you any favors, Dugan. Your name's now on somebody's shit list," Ciano said.

"Which reminds me of a story," Dugan said.

"Spare me."

"No, I think you're going to like this one. It's about a police sergeant who drinks so much, he misplaces the files. Not all of them, mind you, but one skinny little file marked, 'Joseph Steppe.' How do you like them apples, Lew?''

Ciano laughed. "I like that story a lot. It's got—"

"—a certain inner logic to it," Dugan said. "The Joseph Steppe-Abigail West case is beyond the scope and purview of Captain Talbot. And as whip of us poor dicks, it's your job to follow up on the case even though you're spending most of your time on the homicides of half the clergy in Staten Island," Dugan said.

"What the hell's going on around here?" Ciano asked. "Just why the hell is this Joseph Steppe knocking off priests all over the place? And where is he? The address he gave on his employment application doesn't exist anymore. Where does he live, *how* does he live?''

"We'll find him, Lew," Dugan said. "It may take a while, but we'll nail him.''

"And why, if he hates priests, doesn't he shoot 'em or knife

137

'em or run 'em over with a car? Why all this . . . elaborate ritual?'' Ciano asked, more to himself than Dugan.

They lapsed into an uncomfortable silence, each thinking his own thoughts, when Erica James appeared and lit the table's citronella candle.

"A romantic evening for two deserves candlelight," she said in her hard, husky voice. She was dressed in tight-fitting stone-washed jeans and a V-neck blue sweater that was bursting with the fullness of her breasts. Her perfume brought a rush to Ciano's senses.

"You two seem very chummy tonight," she continued, smiling sleepily.

Ciano tried to remain calm, but this woman had an effect on him he didn't want to acknowledge.

"Ah, darlin' Erica. What a rare and temptin' treat you look tonight," Dugan said, warming up his brogue.

Erica smiled faintly at Dugan and said, in a passable Irish accent, "Can you be doin' me a favor, Sergeant Dugan? Can you take your malarkey to another table while Vince and I talk?''

"A sad day for Dugan—thrown out of two private conferences in one day," Dugan grumbled, picking up his beer.

"The drinks are on me," Erica said.

"As well they might be," Dugan sighed, slumping away, dragging his coat, chair, and holstered .38 to a table across the room.

Erica sat down across from Ciano. "Don't pout," she said.

"Don't break my balls," he said. Her smile mocked him.

"You've got a right to be angry," she said. "But your technique leaves something to be desired. You can't shove it into a woman like you do into a condom."

Rage surged inside Ciano, gathered and coiled, but he knew he was outclassed. Erica used words like he used his fists—with brutal efficiency. Trying to counter her verbally would only make things worse. He lit a cigarette.

"Waitress," he said, and a young woman approached the table. "J.D. on the rocks."

Erica waited a moment, then said, "And I'll have coffee, Cindy. Do you want something to eat?''

"I want to be left alone," Ciano said.

Erica shrugged, and said to the waitress, "In that case, make it separate checks."

The waitress disappeared into the kitchen.

"Do you want to try again?" she asked him.

"No."

"Bullshit."

Ciano leaned back in his chair; Erica leaned forward following his movement.

"Tell me you don't want to make love to me," she said with just a trace of contempt.

Ciano didn't speak, but his nerves jangled like a fire alarm. He felt his face flush, and then there was someone else with them, standing over the table, listening. They looked up together. It was Ed Hanratty.

Ciano cleared his throat. Hanratty's face was an expressionless mask.

"I'd like to go back to the church, if it's all right with you," Hanratty said, his water blue eyes vague behind the rimless glasses.

"Whatever you say, Captain," Ciano said, glad they were all pretending not to have heard Erica's proposition. "Dugan can run you over right now."

"He probably would—in his condition," Erica said. Then she ran a shoeless foot up Ciano's leg and pressed her toes softly into his crotch. She smiled at him suggestively.

Ciano glanced at Hanratty, then said, "Better yet, let me take you over there. I'd like to look around some more." He stood up before his hard-on was noticeable.

"I appreciate the offer," Hanratty said. "I know you're busy."

"Just restin'," Ciano said. " 'Night, Erica."

The expression on her face was worth the ache in his groin.

Joseph Steppe was paralyzed with fear. All day long, from his hideaway in the basement of the church, he had listened to loud voices and heavy footsteps. They were going to find him and punish him, he knew, and it made him shiver with fright. Twice, the police had broken into his secret room and had taken cursory looks around. But each time they failed to discover him or the corpse of Abigail West hidden under a layer of coal in the old furnace room. One cop, a big beefy man with white hair and a red face, had poked his nightstick into the coal bin and it had struck Abigail West in the throat, but she hadn't uttered a word of protest. She was long past caring.

He shifted position slightly. It was time to move, he thought. Time to get Miss West and himself to a safer spot, away from the police.

Like a wolf spider emerging from his den, Steppe pushed

139

himself out of the coal bin, and thoughtfully covering Abigail West's bare leg with handfuls of anthracite, he crept silently to the window, hoisted himself up, and peered into the night.

A long squad car stood guard, its interior as dark as the sky.

He was about to begin the laborious process of moving Abigail West's heavy body when he saw the beams of an approaching car. Mesmerized by the light, he held his precarious perch by the basement window, watching and waiting.

The man who emerged from the driver's side of the old station wagon looked familiar to Steppe. He racked his brain trying to remember. Suddenly he froze. He heard his heartbeat accelerate when he recognized the policeman who had seen him on the hill overlooking Richmondtown, the man who had spoken to Miss West. There was something God-like about the big cop, something in his bearing that made Steppe think of power, violence, and death. He scurried back to the coal bin, fighting the immediate urge to relieve his bowels, hoping that the coal dust he had spread over the cold concrete floor had been enough to camouflage the quarts of blood Abigail West had pumped from her veins.

He climbed into the bin and nestled himself next to the woman's rapidly stiffening body. He curled into a fetal position and waited. As an afterthought he gripped Abigail West's cold rubbery nipple between his teeth and sucked noiselessly.

For over an hour he waited, cringing with terror. Then he heard two men outside the door and the terror turned to mindless passivity. He snuggled up to Abigail West, and in a soft voice told her not to worry.

Suddenly the lights went on and Steppe could hear two men talking.

"This is just the furnace room," one man said. It was the big cop. "It's been searched."

"Thoroughly?" the second man asked. "Do you remember that case in the diamond district several years ago? The investigators overlooked a body in a three-foot-long box." The second man's voice was more soothing to Steppe. It was well-controlled and cultured. Like a college professor's or a doctor's voice.

"Where's to hide?" Ciano asked. "The furnace?"

"Don't you feel it?" Hanratty said, closing his eyes, suddenly faint.

"The cold? The damp? What?" Ciano was impatient with the old man.

"No, no. Something . . . not quite right. Something evil," Hanratty said.

"Come on, Captain. This isn't Dracula's castle. It's a church. And when I get a hold of that scumbag Steppe, I'll plant his stinking carcass so deep, he won't have to go to hell, he'll *be* there."

Steppe groaned. He felt a trickle of urine run down his leg.

"Are you sure you've got the right man?" Hanratty asked.

"As sure as shit, Captain. Everything fits, like a dick in a condom." Where had he heard that? he wondered.

"No holes?" Hanratty asked. He might have been smiling. "How about the motive. Why?"

"A crazy little fuck. Iced 'em. Who knows why," Ciano said. "I'm going to nail the little bastard and this case. Then I'm going to get the fuck out of Staten Island and leave it to the commuters. And you're going to help me."

"I am?" Hanratty asked.

"Yeah, because you've got a vested interest in this case," Ciano said.

"I do?" Hanratty was being deliberately obtuse. What did Ciano know? he wondered.

"You sure do. You want me to stop sniffing around your daughter," Ciano said. "And if I clear this case, it'll be the last you'll ever see of me."

"You're both adults," Hanratty said. "But you're right. I don't want to see Erica hurt again."

"Like I'm going to hurt her?" Ciano said, laughing.

"Or the other way around," Hanratty said, shivering. He snapped off the basement lights.

Steppe waited for another hour before he dared move. Then he re-emerged from the coal bin and began pacing the cement floor. After a quick look outside to make sure the cop and the college professor were gone and that the lights were still out in the patrol car, he moved a broken-down wheelbarrow next to the bin. Its rusted wheel creaked ominously in the silent basement.

With a strength borne of frenzy and fear, he managed to shove Abigail West's stiff body into the wheelbarrow and cover her with a tarp.

He knew where he was going to put her and he knew where he was going to hide. It would be a long, tiresome night, but he looked forward to the tranquility of the old house on the hill.

From there he could watch the events on Richmondtown unseen, feeling himself above all those people and especially the cop who knew his name.

He retrieved the leaf spring sword from the coal bin and threw it into the wheelbarrow. He wanted something to remember Abigail West by, a memento. A nipple? A whole breast? An eye? Her lips? Either set? he giggled to himself.

But there was plenty of time for that when she—and he— reached their final destination.

Joseph Steppe picked up his heavy burden, and with the squeaking wheel sounding like a wounded animal, he pushed Abigail West toward the basement door and freedom.

Chapter
Fifteen

The secret room in the basement of the old house comforts me like a womb. In fact, being in the womb was probably the only period of complete happiness I have ever known. Safe, secure, unthinking, unknowing days waiting to emerge into the hell that has been my life.

As soon as the doctor separated my mother and me from the umbilical, we became mortal enemies. Me, the helpless victim, she the all-powerful torturer, the master of my fate, the loathsome icon of my despair. For it was she—who drove me into the arms of Judas.

Judas. My protector, my savior, my hellish companion. He is coming. I can hear the rustle of his cloak and the soft slap of his sandals as he ascends—descends?—to meet me. He will be well pleased.

I close my eyes and breathe deeply, allowing my feverish mind to concentrate on the smooth green surface of a lake. Or perhaps a sea. The Sea of Galilee? The water gently ripples the shore, a warm breeze blows the clammy sweat from my brow. I am his, he is mine.

Suddenly, a blinding light streaks across my consciousness, a painful reminder of his power. The light changes to crimson— blood—and I am afraid.

You have profaned.

His voice echoes endlessly in the airless room.

You have desecrated the priest's body in ways that are foul and disgusting.

"I was merely trying to show your contempt, Lord," I say, knowing it is a lie.

Liar. Cheat. Profaner of the Holy Mission.

He can always read my innermost thoughts.

There were eleven against me . . . eleven and me chosen by the Nazarene to carry his word. But only me—only Judas—is called a traitor. Did not Peter betray Him three times before the cock crowed?

"It is so, Master," I say.

Yet I am cemented alongside Lucifer as the personification of evil.

"You were betrayed, Lord," I say. I know what he wants to hear.

You know they must die and why?

"Yes, Lord."

Then why did you mutilate the body of the priest? Why did you butcher him like a sheep?

"I don't know, Lord," I say. It is best to feign ignorance. He knows I'm lying.

You know what you must do and how you must do it. There is little time for my revenge.

"Yes, Lord."

The Covenant must be kept. You owe it to me. You owe me your blood.

This last chills me, for he is right—I do owe him for liberating me. But he has cast me into another prison. I must fight him, but I cannot.

He recedes from me like the tide, leaving my body soaked in perspiration, my mind howling for release. I have an urge to suck my thumb, but I have put away childish gestures, even though Judas makes me feel as helpless as an infant. The way my mother made me feel.

The pain the old priest suffered was as nothing compared to the agony thrust upon me by my mother. Now that she is dead, I can take sensual pleasure remembering her brutality. I can almost enjoy it, like running my hand across the flame of a candle. I am free of her. One day I will be free of Judas.

As much as I hated her, as an adult I have to admire the controlled brutality lurking behind her frivolous façade—like a mouse in the wall of a mansion, ready to scurry out and ruin a sumptuous feast. Her control is now my control, her brutality is in my genes.

I remember my mother as a beautiful woman, strange as it may sound. And even when my nightmares bring back the knife-edged details of her cruelties, I also see the graceful curve of her neck, and remember her emerald eyes, even as my screams of pain provide the background music. She and Judas, beautiful and damned. Me, the clay of their hatred, the vessel of their desire.

The cold earthen floor seeps into my very core, rotting me from within. There is so much to do and so little time to do it.

When I stand, the creaking of my joints sounds like the breaking of bones.

Chapter
Sixteen

Friday, November 5

"Ciano, you're late," Captain Talbot said angrily.

"Oh, no," Ciano said with mock horror. "I missed my period and now you'll have to marry me."

"Shut up and get to work," Talbot said. "I want you to recheck all those 5s."

Ciano looked around the P.D.U. squad room and was amazed. Cops were falling all over themselves, milling around, making phone calls, typing, writing, looking busy.

"You're sitting at my desk, Captain," Ciano said.

"I'm sitting at *my* desk, Ciano. Find yourself another."

Ciano moved groggily into the crowd of detectives marveling at the frenzy of activity. Somebody upstairs was pulling out all the stops, he thought, stealing bodies from all over the city to man the special task force.

"So this is where you've been hiding," a voice said. "Pretty fucking plush."

Ciano turned to see Bill Rand, a former partner from the Bronx. It had been years, but not enough years.

"A fucking country club," Ciano said.

"Talbot's been talking about you," Rand said.

"We're in love."

"So I noticed," Rand said. "You got any leads on this thing?"

"Yeah. Talbot did it for the publicity," Ciano said, walking away.

"Still got an attitude, don't you, Ciano," Rand called after him.

"And you're still a fucking maggot," Ciano said, not turning around. He walked out of the squad room and down the hall to the men's room. Like the squad room, the shit house was bursting with cops who were bursting with excrement. The 122nd had never seen so much action; it was groaning under the weight of police mobilization. The local detectives looked shell shocked.

"Don't this beat all?" Detective Marty Abel said as he sidled up to Ciano at the urinals. "It's worse than Shea Stadium during the play-offs. You gotta stand in line for the crapper."

"Yeah, but you can save time by not washing your hands when you're done," Ciano said, zipping up.

"What? Oh, yeah. Say, Lew, I gotta talk to you," Abel said, following Ciano to the sinks. He stood watching Ciano wash his hands.

"You remember that coin and those nails?" Abel began.

"Well, I might have something."

"Like what?" Ciano asked, drying his hands on his pants because all the paper towels were gone.

"Like that coin is probably one of a set made by this company in Philadelphia—" He reached inside his greasy sport coat and pulled out a dog-eared notebook. "The Washington Mint. They sell replicas of famous coins."

"Do they make them in Philly?"

"No, they're made in Hong Kong. I asked," Abel said, proudly.

"Good for you, Abel," Ciano said, trying to shake the annoying little bastard. He followed Ciano like a dog.

"But I don't have anything on those nails, those spikes yet," Abel persisted, trying to keep up with Ciano's long strides.

"Keep working on it," Ciano said. "And tell Captain Talbot."

"I already did," Abel said.

Ciano turned to face Abel. "Somehow I knew you would," he said, then shambled off down the stairs.

In the parking lot behind the precinct, now packed with cars, Dugan was taking a nap in Ciano's battered station wagon. He had signed in, then looked with horror at the roomful of strange detectives working up a storm, and had fled. His head hurt, his eyes stung, and the prospect of facing Captain Talbot was just too much for him to contemplate. Dugan often thought that if he could just get away for a week by himself, say to an isolated mountain cabin, he could dry out and sleep for 168 hours straight. It was a dream, he knew, because if his wife, Mary, let him off his lead, he'd go on a bender of historic proportions. The thing about the Irish, he often said, is that you've got to keep them busy or they'll drink themselves to death for the sheer fun of it. Or for the horror of it all.

Dugan opened his eyes when he heard Ciano. The lieutenant doesn't look in much better shape than I do, Dugan thought, straightening up in the passenger seat.

"You okay?" he asked Ciano.

"About as good as you."

"Then we're both in serious trouble," Dugan sighed, closing his eyes again. "How about a little heart-starter at Hanratty's?"

"No time," Ciano said. "We've got to find that fuck Steppe."

With a cloud of oily smoke, they lurched out of the parking lot and onto Hyland Boulevard, headed west toward Richmondtown.

"How was your date with Ed Hanratty?" Dugan asked, his eyes still closed.

"About as exciting as my date with his daughter," Ciano said. "We looked around the church, then Ed went into one of his *Twilight Zone* imitations and said there was evil haunting the place. A fucking space cadet."

Dugan opened his eyes and peered painfully at the suburban sprawl: fast-food restaurants, drugstores, discount stores, discount drugstores.

"Don't discount Hanratty's hunches," Dugan said, wondering if there was a discount saloon somewhere. "He's cleared a lot of cases relying on his instinct."

"And I've fucked a lot of women using my dick, but that doesn't mean it has to be eight feet long," Ciano said.

Dugan was silent. Then, "What the hell does that mean, Lew?"

"I don't know, but it shut you up and that's all I want from you right now. Silence. So, please, just give it a rest, will you? Use *your* instinct and tell me where Steppe is hiding out and where Abigail is hanging her bra."

"Touchy, touchy," Dugan muttered, as they weaved in and out of the morning traffic. The day was sunny and clear, the sky was painfully blue to Dugan's red eyes. The temperature was supposed to hit sixty. He was about to remark on the incredible weather, but thought better of it and concentrated instead on Joseph Steppe.

They had checked the address Steppe had given on his employment form, but it had turned out to be a construction site. If Steppe had lived there, it must have been at least a year ago. Several people in the neighborhood remembered the little man with the club foot, but no one knew where he had gone. No one cared. Steppe had no friends, no telephone, no driver's license, no income tax returns, no passport, no family. A mystery man who had popped up out of nowhere, took a menial job, then disappeared back to where he had come from. Wherever that was.

"Why does he hate priests so much?" Dugan asked finally.

"Everybody hates priests," Ciano said.

"Not enough to kill them—to mutilate them," Dugan said. "Do you think he was in a seminary?"

"Could be, but I doubt it. The Church is desperate for priests, but I don't think they'd stoop to picking up garbage like Steppe," Ciano said.

"Then how about a Catholic school?" Dugan asked.

"Or an orphanage," Ciano said, swerving to miss a bright yellow school bus.

"It's something to consider," Dugan said. "I'll check it out today. But how about this Abigail West?"

"That I can understand," Ciano said. "She's a bitch on wheels. I almost iced her myself. An arrogant, nasty woman— think of Talbot in drag. I can see her pushing him to the wall and him going nuts. Killing her. Yeah, I can see that."

"If your instinct's as impressive as your dick, maybe we can wrap this business up and get rid of the tourists in the squad room," Dugan said. "It's too noisy up there for me."

They wheeled into the Richmondtown entrance, past signs that said it was closed, and parked by Stephens General Store.

"This is the last place where anyone saw Abigail West alive?" Ciano said, mostly to himself.

"The stains on the floor were analyzed, but so far no report. We're trying to get hold of someone who knew what her blood-type was—if, indeed, the stain on the floor is blood," Dugan said. "And hers."

"Well, what do you think?" Ciano asked.

"Blood."

"Presumably not menstrual."

"Presumably," Dugan said, producing a key and unlocking the padlock on the door.

In minutes, they were done. There was just no hard evidence, though they both suspected what had happened.

"I'll meet you outside," Ciano said. "I have to make a call."

Dugan nodded and left Ciano in the store with its strange mixture of past and present, authenticity and imitation.

Now that he had put Erica in her place Ciano knew he had to get back on with Diane. Although he had made a fool of himself the other night with his display of wounded macho pride, he

149

thought he had seen something in Diane's eyes. A flicker of interest, a gleam he remembered from the old days.

He lit a cigarette to calm his nerves before he dialed.

"Hello," he heard his ex-wife say.

"Hello, Diane, it's me." He tried not to make his voice sound too happy.

"Vince? What's wrong?"

"Nothing. I just was wondering if you and Vinny would like to go to dinner tonight?"

"Tonight?" The line went quiet and Ciano could picture Diane mulling it over.

"Tell you what," she said, "why don't you come here and spend some time with your son and I'll cook. I think Vincent would like that."

"Dinner at home sounds great. Should I pack a toothbrush?" Ciano said, half seriously.

Diane gave him a good dose of silence before answering. "I see you're still an egotistical bastard. I hope you kept your appetite, too?"

"Depends on what we're talking about." he said.

"We're talking about dinner at seven-thirty. Don't be late."

Ciano was still searching for an answer when the line went dead.

"You look considerably happier," Dugan noted, when he joined the sergeant on the porch of the general store. "Talbot commit suicide?"

"Almost as good," Ciano said. "I'm going to see my wife and son tonight."

"And Erica?"

"Fuck her."

"Yeah?"

"Come on, Dugan. Let's go pay a visit to Father Layhe and the crime scene."

They flashed their tin to the uniform on guard, and after signing the log, they entered the church. It was dark and quiet inside, almost comforting, Ciano thought. It didn't seem like a slaughterhouse, but then, little was actually what it seemed.

They worked their way toward the front of the church to where Father Graff had been beheaded and looked at the floor. Someone had mopped up the blood.

"It's all in the hands of the great Medical Examiner in the sky," Dugan said reverently.

"Come on, let's apply a little pressure to Layhe," Ciano said, as they exited a side door and headed for Layhe's living quarters in the rectory.

They found the priest in his brown office, wearing a brown sweat shirt and brown sweat pants. His Nike running shoes were brown and white.

"Hello, Lieutenant, Sergeant," Layhe said jovially. "Short time, no see."

Ciano didn't say anything, but sat down in one of the brown leather chairs and pulled out his notebook.

"How may I help you?" Layhe asked, sitting down behind the desk and folding his well-manicured hands in front of him, as if in prayer.

"There's been two murders in your church and you are the only common link," Ciano began without preamble. "You knew both priests, disliked them both, and had the opportunity, means, and motive to kill them." He let that sink in.

Layhe's handsome face went ashen. "Are you charging me?"

"Did you murder them?"

"Of course not," Layhe exploded. "How dare you accuse me . . . accuse me of such a—" He was so overwhelmed he began to sputter.

"Are you a homosexual?" Ciano asked. "Is that why you killed them?"

"Son of a bitch! How fucking dare you—" Layhe's tirade was peppered with profanity, and when it was over, it left the priest drained, his face flushed with anger.

Ciano was silent for a minute. Then he said, "Is that a no?"

Layhe began to boil again, but Ciano stopped him with a wave of his hand. "Take it easy, Layhe," Ciano said. "I was just asking. You seem rather defensive."

"Defensive! You come barging in here accusing me of murder, of being an abomination unto the Lord, of God knows what, and you call it defensive? Get the hell out of my office and don't come back. I'm calling your superiors and the cardinal—"

"Oh, just one more thing," Ciano said. "Mind if we look around?"

"Get out!" Layhe screamed.

"Is that a yes?" Ciano asked innocently.

"Get out!" Layhe screamed, even louder than last time.

"It's like the *Amityville Horror*," Dugan said, when they were in the hall. "You know, 'Get out!' "

"Yeah, but this particular Staten Island Horror hasn't got any

151

spooks in it. We're dealing with a real person, a very smart and very deadly real person who can't be shooed away by Rod Steiger," Ciano said, heading toward the basement door, retracing the path he had taken the night before with Ed Hanratty.

"That Father Layhe sure uses bad words for a priest," Dugan said at the top of the stairwell. "Was it outraged innocence or outrageous acting?"

Ciano shrugged.

"I mean even Rod Steiger would have been cool," Dugan continued, following Ciano down the steps.

They crossed the long, dim corridor to the boiler room, where Ciano stopped suddenly. He seemed to falter, to lose all his strength.

"Lew, are you all right?" Dugan asked, startled. He reached out to steady Ciano, to keep him from falling.

"Mmmm," Ciano mumbled. "Mmmm. There is evil inside this door." His tones were sepulchral; his words chilled Dugan.

"I can feel a presence in that room," Ciano said, his voice getting deeper and more hoarse. "A creature from hell."

He pulled away from Dugan and threw himself up against the wall.

Then he screamed.

"My God," Dugan breathed.

"It's coming!" Ciano screamed, holding his head as if he were being tormented.

"It's here!"

The door to the boiler room opened slowly, and Dugan reached for his service revolver. He felt like a man in a dream—his reactions were too slow. The creature would get him.

Then the door banged open and Dugan let out an involuntary cry of alarm.

A figure stepped into the light.

"What's all this noise?" Ed Hanratty asked, his watery blue eyes squinting behind his rimless glasses.

Ciano slid to the floor laughing, while Dugan and Hanratty stood looking at him.

"My instincts told me he'd be here," Ciano managed to gasp out.

Hanratty blinked. "You told me to meet you here this morning."

Ciano laughed until he cried. Wiping the tears from his eyes, he struggled to his feet.

"Not nice," Dugan said.

152

"It was great," Ciano said. "You were perfect. But let's forget this spooky shit and get down to cases." He stood. "Captain Hanratty had a hunch about the boiler room and I'm so desperate I'm willing to believe anything—as long as we get some hard evidence."

"I just might have that for you," Hanratty said. "Come inside."

The two cops did as they were told. They stood by the door while Hanratty, armed with a high-powered flashlight, began to lecture.

"You'll note the coal dust on the floor," he said. "There is no reason for it to be here. This church has been heated by oil for years. I know. I was on the board when we made the conversion. This room was cleaned at that time. I'd say this coal dust was spread around down here for a purpose. To hide something."

Hanratty squatted down slowly and put his finger in the dust. "You'll note," he continued, "that the dust is damp. It has absorbed some liquid recently."

"Blood?" Ciano asked.

"Possibly," Hanratty said. "Get it analyzed. And look here, see this wheel track? A single tire, very recent. A wheelbarrow, I would imagine."

"Or a unicycle," Dugan said, but nobody laughed.

"Handy for removing a body," Ciano said. "But whose? Was Graff murdered down here and dragged upstairs?"

"No," Hanratty said. "I don't think so. I followed the tire track. It goes down the hall and out through an unused storeroom."

"Abigail West?" Ciano asked.

Hanratty shrugged.

After a day of harassment and humiliation, compliments of Captain Talbot, Ciano left the precinct at 6:30 p.m., determined to be on time for once in his life. A loner who had been alone too long, he was looking forward to being a part of a family again. His family. But as he neared Diane's house—his house— uncertainty gripped him. What if Teddy was there? He'd have a fight on his hands. And this time the stockbroker might not go down so easily. He gripped the steering wheel readying himself for a confrontation. But when he arrived, he was relieved to see that Teddy's Corvette was not parked on the street or under the carport.

He whistled as he walked up the path to the door and pressed the buzzer. He whistled louder when he saw Diane framed in the doorway. She looked sensational in a long, pale blue dress.

She waved him in and he walked toward the dining room where he found the table set with her mother's silver and crystal, as well as flowers and candles. Set for two. That was definitely a good sign, he thought. We'll put Vince, Jr., to bed and enjoy a late dinner, then . . .

Down the hall, he heard his son's voice.

"Who is it?" Vince, Jr., called. "Daddy?"

Ciano turned and caught the boy running full-tilt down the hall at him. Vince, Jr., leaped into Ciano's arms, no mean feat as he was carrying a football and helmet.

Working his way around the equipment, Ciano managed to hug and kiss the boy, then he spotted Diane's room, particularly the king-sized bed. It had been a long time, he thought, putting his son down. But tonight would be the start of a whole new life, a comforting family life. He beamed down fondly at his son and ruffled the boy's dark hair.

Vince, Jr., ran off to show Ciano some of his other treasures, while Diane made him a Jack Daniel's on the rocks.

"You remembered," he said.

"I could smell it on your breath the other night," she said coolly.

He ignored her tone and made inane chitchat about how good she smelled. But mostly he reveled in the air of calm certainty Diane provided. He was beginning to relax for the first time in months.

As Diane talked about the menu for the evening, he concentrated on the grace of her body. When his son returned with a collection of odd-looking monster dolls, in addition to the helmet and football, Ciano pretended to be fascinated.

"Are you a Jets fan or a Giants fan?" Ciano asked his son, while the boy, now wearing his helmet, ran around the room leaping for imaginary passes.

"Neither," Vince, Jr., said. "I'm an Eagles fan."

"The Eagles, huh?" Ciano said, looking to Diane for an explanation.

"You don't want to know," she said, checking her makeup in a silvery compact mirror.

Ciano shrugged it off as nonsense and said, "You look beautiful tonight, honey."

"Thank you," Diane said, as a horn sounded twice outside.

She gave her makeup another quick look and called her son. "Come on, Vincent, give Mommy a kiss."

As the boy went to his mother, it finally dawned on Ciano what was happening.

"You be a good boy and mind your father. I won't be home too late. Now go wash up and show your father where the clean towels are."

Ciano found himself standing and wondering if he looked as ridiculous as he felt. "Where you going?"

"I have a date," Diane answered. "Didn't I tell you?"

Ciano saw a cold look in his wife's eyes that told him her actions were calculated. She was getting even, and she was enjoying it.

"You said you wanted to spend more time with Vincent, didn't you? Is this a problem?" Her tone was defiant.

"No . . . no problem."

"Okay, so wash up and eat."

Ciano was silent and stunned as he watched his wife kiss their son good-bye at the door and leave. He watched from the window as she approached Teddy waiting in the Corvette.

"Thanks again for the football and the helmet, Teddy," Ciano heard his son say and watched as Teddy waved to the boy. He kept on watching until the Corvette turned out of sight.

"Great football," Ciano said, when the boy came back into the house.

"Teddy gave it to me for my birthday."

"Your birthday?"

"Sure, my birthday. It was yesterday."

Ciano made his way back to the couch and his drink, picking up the bottle on the way.

"By the way, how come you like the Eagles?" he asked.

"Teddy's from Philadelphia," the boy answered.

Chapter
Seventeen

Ed Hanratty heard voices in his sleep: strange, disturbing voices that dared him to recognize them. The old man struggled against consciousness, knowing the answers to his questions were to be found in the shadows, not in the light of day.

He rolled over and the dream jumped a few grooves, the voices became more urgent. He heard a man's cry. It was as anguished as the sound of a nail being pulled from a board. The cry became a long, liquid howl. He knew it was Father Graff's last earthly noise.

A montage of violence swept past him: swift, brutally graphic action that splattered blood everywhere. In slow motion he saw Father Graff's head spin from his body and land with a ripe thump on the marble floor of Holy Cross. But it didn't just lie there, it began speeding down the center aisle of the church. Propelled on a wave of blood, it rushed toward the cowering Hanratty. The wave broke over his head as he tried to shield himself, and he felt the hot blood suffocating him.

Then he heard a high-pitched, insane laugh, and on the edge of waking, Hanratty felt the cold sweat leaking from his body. The insane laugh became his own.

Shaken, Hanratty ripped the soaking sheets from his bed and sat with his hands dangling between his legs. With a supreme effort he stood, dizzy at first, then queasy. It was a short walk to the bathroom, but it seemed like miles.

After he had showered and brushed his teeth, he checked the clock in the hall. After four. He had had his three hours sleep, it was time to get to work.

He walked wearily to his basement workshop, got out his notebook, and began to write. He stopped about an hour later to open the café and get a cup of coffee, then retreated to his basement lair again.

Ignoring the facts in the case, he wrote down anything that

156

came to his head: his impressions, the smell at the crime scene, his dreams, his nightmares.

The sun was just coming up when he began to write about his wife. He remembered the rainy day when he had almost taken his life; he remembered Father Bryan talking soothingly to him, uttering time-worn platitudes that had somehow soothed him; and he remembered why he had decided to blow his brains out that storm-washed day in the parking lot overlooking the sea.

It was quite simple, really. Ed Hanratty had married a woman far too young and far too beautiful for his own good. Her name was Margot Swenson and he had first met her in Times Square. He was a cop on the beat; she was a dazed tourist from Ohio accompanying her sister and brother-in-law on a two-week vacation.

It had been a steamy hot day in June and Hanratty had been sweltering inside his heavy blue serge uniform with its high, constricting collar. He had been cursed at by truck drivers, almost run over by a limousine, hassled by pimps, and bothered by irate theatre owners. He was on the verge of losing it when the young blond girl tapped him on the shoulder.

"Excuse me, sir," she said. "Which way to the Lexington Avenue subway?"

Since they were within spitting distance of the subway entrance, Hanratty was ready with a nasty remark. But one look at Margot's wide innocent blue eyes stopped him cold. She was tanned and tawny and smooth. Those were Hanratty's initial impressions: smooth and somehow unused, so unlike the tough, hard customers he dealt with every day.

She made him suck in a breath of hot, polluted air. He choked and coughed.

"Are you all right, sir?" the creamy young girl asked.

"Yes, yes," Hanratty managed to say.

She smiled at him and he knew he couldn't just let her walk away. Ten seconds after meeting her, Ed Hanratty—nearing thirty, devoted to his job, thinking himself a confirmed bachelor—was in love.

"Excuse me, miss," he heard himself saying. "But are you staying at the Taft Hotel?"

"Why no, officer, downtown at the Gramercy Park Hotel," she said. "Why?"

"Just wondering," he said. "And your name wouldn't happen to be Lincoln, would it?"

She laughed, full of fun. "Like in Abe? Do I have a beard?"

"No, miss. We've been having some trouble, uh, around . . ."

She laughed again. "If you want to ask me out, just ask. My name's Margot Swenson."

Hanratty flushed. He wasn't used to dealing with women who weren't prostitutes, alkies or junkies. It shocked him that someone so young—what was she, eighteen?—was so forward.

Stammering, he suggested he might show her, and her sister and brother-in-law, the *real* New York. The sister, Lynn, had now joined them and was practically dragging Margot away, down into the hot, fetid subway station.

"Come about six," Margot Swenson called to him as she was being hustled down the stairs. "Room 812."

And so it began, an intense ten-day courtship that had left Hanratty feeling as if he had received the luckiest break in his life or had made the greatest mistake. Such passion and unpredictability was totally foreign to his character. Hanratty was methodical, meticulous, careful, and prodding, but the incredible ten days, which culminated with her pliant naked body under his, were unlike anything that had ever happened to him. He was like a man with a fever.

On the thirteenth day of Margot Swenson's trip to New York, they were married at City Hall. Margot's sister, Lynn, kissed them both good-bye and somewhat gratefully, Hanratty thought, left for Ohio with her husband in tow and her kid sister safely married off.

Hanratty paused to wipe his glasses and press his fingers into his red-rimmed eyes. It seemed so long ago, it was almost like a dream.

"Ed?"

He looked up quickly, and in the dim light of the basement he thought for a moment he was looking at Margot.

"Ed, Joe Dugan's here to see you," Erica said.

Hanratty cleared his throat and told her to send him down. Then he cleared his throat again, cursing himself for being weak. Even after all these years he was still in love with Margot. Not the flesh-and-blood woman, he supposed, but the *idea* of Margot. Fresh, innocent, sweet, and joyfully naive.

"Morning, Cap'n," Dugan said from the top of the stairs. "Not interrupting am I?"

"No, no, no," Hanratty said. "Come on down."

"I've got some interesting bits of information for you," Dugan said, descending the staircase. "Ciano said you should check it out."

"Where is he?" Hanratty said.

"With his wife and kid," Dugan said, handing Hanratty a manila file folder.

"He's married?"

"His ex-wife to be precise," Dugan said. He didn't want to get in the middle of a Hanratty, Erica, Ciano fight. "Declared null and void by the powers that be, if not the Holy Mother Church."

Hanratty nodded and opened the folder, but before he could digest the lab reports it contained, Dugan gave him a summation.

"The substance found on the floor at Stephens General Store in Richmondtown was, indeed, human blood. Type O positive. Very common. Also the type claimed by Miss Abigail West."

He paused for a moment then continued. "Samples from the furnace room of the church are a big ditto."

"Type O, positive," Hanratty said. "Which means we have something, but not enough."

"We all want more," Dugan said. "And usually we get it whether we like it or not, if you catch my meaning."

"What?" Hanratty said. He was engrossed in his own thoughts.

"I said, what's the next step? If you catch my pun."

"I don't know, Sergeant. If this is what I think it is, we've got problems."

"You don't say."

"This Steppe character is baffling. He seems to be a psychotic killer, but he has elements of the psychopath in him. I've never seen the two mixed so oddly before. It's like oil and water coming together, it's . . . unnatural."

Dugan shrugged. He didn't know what Hanratty was talking about and he didn't care. He wanted to know what the old man thought they should do next.

"If he was hiding in the furnace room of the church, do you think he'll return?" Dugan asked him.

"If he's afflicted with a psychosis, probably not. The voice he hears in his head will no doubt lead him to bigger and better opportunities. If he's a psychopath—who can tell. I'd say the odds are twenty to one," Hanratty said.

"And if he's just a screwed-up little perp who's scared out of his mind and looking for a place to hide—what then?" Dugan asked.

159

"He'd have to be crazy to go back to the church," Hanratty said seriously.

Dugan laughed. "I suppose he would. Do you think it would be crazy for a few dedicated law-enforcement types to sit on that church?"

"Sergeant Dugan, it's like chicken soup. It might not help, but it can't hurt."

Joseph Steppe was hungry. Not for food, but for something indefinable that was gnawing away at his gut. He hadn't slept more than ten consecutive minutes since . . . since he could remember. Every time he closed his eyes he saw Monsignor Bryan's sightless skull staring at him accusingly or heard Abigail West's final agonizing scream.

He reached into the pocket of his filthy green work pants and removed his prizes. Monsignor Bryan's eyeball, drained of fluid, was merely a flat, soggy bit of rotten gray and blue flesh. It was hard to imagine it had ever been an eye. Next to it, however, was his latest trophy: a nipple—Abigail West's nipple—and a bit of the areola that surrounded it.

Steppe had been sucking on it all night, but he noticed it began to taste terrible, and the carrion smell was beginning to revolt him. He carefully tucked his two prizes away and wished for . . . something.

While he was trying to understand his own desires, he lay underneath the old house overlooking Richmondtown. From his vantage point, he could see the spire of Holy Cross Church and a few of the restored houses. But he couldn't see where he had hidden Abigail West's body. To do that, he would have to stand up and he was too tired to move. He wanted something . . . and he wanted sleep, even if the ghosts invaded his dreams.

"Wake up, Daddy," Vince, Jr., shouted, jumping up on the king-sized bed. "Wake up and play catch."

Ciano opened one eye and saw his son dressed in Star Wars pajamas, wearing his football helmet, and carrying the new football.

Ciano groaned.

"Please, Daddy," Vince, Jr., insisted. "You promised."

I promise a lot of things, but I rarely deliver, Ciano thought, reaching out to grab the boy. He thought if he could pull the kid in bed with him, maybe the boy would be quiet for a while. It had worked when his son was two. It didn't work now.

160

Vince, Jr., grabbed Ciano's arm and began pulling him out of bed with surprising strength.

"Okay, okay," Ciano said, opening both eyes and regretting it immediately. The Jack Daniels he had drank while waiting for Diane to return had soured his stomach and mashed his mind.

"Where's your mom?" he managed to croak. He could smell her perfume on the sheets.

"Dunno," the boy said.

"She leave you alone a lot?" Ciano asked, propping himself up with one arm.

"Naw. She and Teddy usually stay here."

"Glad I asked," Ciano said, falling on his back, looking at the ceiling.

"Daddy?"

"Okay, okay," Ciano said, heaving himself up out of bed. "Let me get myself together, we'll make breakfast, then we'll toss the ball around."

"Yeaaah!" Vince, Jr., yelled, sending pulses of pain up Ciano's spine and pounding into his head.

"You go get dressed," Ciano said, swinging his legs out of bed. He rubbed his hand over his thick beard, but decided he'd rather look like a derelict than use Teddy's razor, which was probably in the medicine cabinet, or one of Diane's cute little pink razors that ripped the hell out of his face.

Pulling on his pants, he walked into the living room and looked around: two glasses and a pile of dead cigarette butts. Not much of a mess, he thought, not as big a mess as his life.

The dining room, with its French Provincial table and chairs, was a wreck. Neither he nor Vince, Jr., was much of a housekeeper. He looked at the congealed remains of his dinner—untouched—and his stomach lurched. It lurched from the booze, but it also lurched with the realization that he had come to the end of the line with Diane. All his hopes and dreams were merely fantasy. Reality was shit. Reality was dirty dishes and an ex-wife who stayed out all night with her boyfriend.

"Daddy! Where are my shoes?" Vince, Jr., called from his bedroom.

"How the hell should I—" he began, then, "Look under your bed."

"Got 'em," the boy called back happily.

What a great father I am, Ciano thought. Miss the kid's birthday, never see him, but I know where his shoes are. All kids' shoes are under the bed. Big deal.

"Daddy! Where's my shirt? My Eagles jersey?"

I hope your mother lost it, he thought, but he yelled back that he didn't know. And that was the truth. When it came to being a father, he just didn't know.

Ciano's own father had been a laborer, a big hairy man who had spoken little English and had ruled his house with an iron hand. When Vito Ciano had gas, his whole family farted. He was intolerant, mean-spirited and brutal, believing that a well-beaten child was an obedient child. Consequently, Ciano was well-beaten, but by the age of six, he didn't take shit from anyone. He knew he could stand the pain, it was the humiliation that brought tears to his eyes. When his father died, Ciano tried to think good thoughts about the man, but failed.

Sitting at the funeral parlor, ten-year-old Vincent Ciano, uncomfortable in a scratchy, ill-fitting blue suit, starched white shirt, and dark, constricting tie, tried to look sad. But he was delighted. No more beatings with the buckle end of his father's belt, no more long hours in solitary under the kitchen sink with the waterbugs and silverfish, no more being made to stand naked in front of his mother while his father laid into him. No, he thought, life would be good with his father dead.

But like most events in Ciano's life, the death of his father did not bring about the unrestrained joy he always expected. Far from it. For, released from twenty years of servitude, his mother became a monster, trying to outdo the old regime with the savagery of her punishments.

She terrorized him. Always in the past, she had been a cold, distant figure, a slave like himself to Vito's whims and drunken violence. They had shared the pain, but separately, neither one acknowledging the other's pain. Then suddenly they had nothing in common, not even the mutual loathing of Vito Ciano.

It must have been a heady experience for her, Ciano thought, becoming her own master. Unfortunately, her only model was Vito, so she strove mightily to imitate his brutality. She succeeded, making Ciano's life a living hell. That fucking— He blotted her out of his mind and wouldn't let her back in.

"Let's go, Daddy!" Vince, Jr., shouted, standing at the door.

"Don't you want me to fix you breakfast?"

"No. Let's go to Mickey D's."

"Where's that?"

"McDonald's," the boy explained patiently, as if to a foreigner. "That's Mickey D's."

162

"Okay, McDonald's it is. You wouldn't like my barfburgers for breakfast anyway," Ciano said.

"Barfburgers," the boy yelled. "Barfburgers!"

"You go on outside and play with your football and I'll be along in a minute," Ciano said. He had a few things to do.

When the boy had gone, Ciano picked up Diane's blue princess phone and called the station house. He had several messages and an urgent forthwith from Talbot. He ignored them all.

Then he called Hanratty and got Erica on the phone.

"Let me talk to your father," he said.

"Why? He prettier than me?" she said. She was laughing at him again.

"It's important."

"Is it about Joe Dugan? He was over at the crack of dawn talking to Ed in hushed, official tones. Got a hot clue?"

"Dugan was there? Good. That's all I needed to know," Ciano said. "Tell him I'll be over at noon. I'll call before I come."

"Funny," she said. "Last time you almost came before you called."

Ciano hung up and searched the living room for a pen and some paper. Then he wrote:

Diane,
I am getting a lawyer and taking Vincent away from you. You have no right to keep him when you run around all night like a fucking whore. Suppose I had an emergency call? How could I have taken Vincent with me? You could have at least called.

The words lost some of their harshness on the small piece of Snoopy stationery, and that made Ciano even more furious. Diane had always been an exemplary mother and a totally responsible person. *He* was the irresponsible one, and the sudden role reversal outraged him. If there was going to be a fuck up, it should be me, he thought.

When he was finished, he slammed the door behind him and went out for a short pass from his son. The boy threw the ball end-over-end and Ciano had to dive for it. His forty-year-old body hit the turf like a freight train ramming a brick wall. He rolled over twice, stunned.

"Nice catch!" Vince, Jr., shouted. "Do it again, Daddy! Do it again!"

"Not if you want me to live long enough to buy you breakfast," Ciano said, getting up shakily. "I'm too old for this."

The boy looked at him wide-eyed.

"But I'm not too old for this," he said, charging full tilt at his son and picking him up in his arms. The boy screamed with delight as he was carried to the car.

After a cold rubbery thing called a Mac-something that Vince, Jr., claimed was his favorite food, they went to Tyson Park to throw the football around. Ciano was quickly bored—and winded—but gritted his teeth. He wondered if he liked the *idea* of fatherhood more than actually being a father.

By noon they were back at Diane's house. Teddy's Corvette was parked out front.

"Son of a bitch," Ciano said under his breath.

"Teddy's here," the boy said happily.

"It's about time," Ciano said. "Where the hell was your mother last night?"

"Oh, I forgot. She called," Vince, Jr., said. "You were asleep and I couldn't wake you up."

"She called?" Too much J.D., he thought.

"Yeah. She said she would be home today," the boy said.

"And you didn't tell me!" Ciano said, thinking about the note he had left. "Damn it!"

Vince, Jr.'s lower lip began to tremble; his smooth forehead furrowed. "I'm . . . I'm sorry, Daddy," he said, on the verge of tears. "I forgot."

"It's okay, pal," Ciano said, putting his arm around the boy. "Tell your mom I'm sorry about . . . oh, forget it."

"Okay," Vince, Jr., said, cheerful again. "I hope Teddy brought me something. Bye, Daddy."

The boy jumped out of the car and ran up the broken flagstone path to the door, leaving Ciano feeling like the piece of shit he supposed he was.

Ciano cursed himself for thinking with his dick instead of his head. It was just eight p.m., and he was in Chris and Dan's simulated-marble bathroom, looking at his battered, creased face in the makeup mirror over the sink.

When he had appeared at Hanratty's that afternoon, Erica had spotted him immediately and had taken his arm as if nothing had happened. His first instinct was to brush her aside, but the physical, animal closeness of her had overridden his good sense. And after Diane read the note he had left, he rationalized, she would probably never speak to him again. So he sighed, and wrapped his arm around Erica's waist and thought about screwing her brains out. He felt like a shy teenager in her presence, so electric was his attraction to her. But he had the feeling he was just a dumb fish and her pussy was the bait.

As he finished shaving, he inspected his battered face in the daylight, nighttime, and outdoor modes of the makeup mirror. No change. He looked haggard and worn no matter what the setting, he thought, and there was no escaping himself. Unfortunately, there was nothing he could do about his appearance and nothing he could do about reality, which had a nasty habit of slipping into place like the tumblers in a lock.

The investigation of the homicides was now totally out of his hands. Talbot had his fat fingers on the flow of information and wasn't about to share it with Ciano. His investigation of the Steppe-West connection was a dangerous game. If Talbot or DeFeo got wind of what he was doing, he was through. Canned. Cancelled. They'd break him and hound him out of the department.

Ciano had two allies, a drunken sergeant, and a crazy old man. Jesus, what a crew, he thought. Dugan would play ball until Talbot crushed him underfoot, then he'd suddenly remember his four children and his pension. Hanratty? He was an unknown, a cipher, a strange old guy who thought he was some kind of psychic.

This case is going to kill you, he said to the mirror. One way or the other, in the daytime, nighttime, or outdoors, it's going to kill you. If you had less pride, less arrogance, you'd go to Talbot and set things right. But then, he thought, washing the last of the shaving cream off his face, if you had any sense you'd have kissed off Erica and begged Diane's forgiveness.

Some people, he thought, turning out the bathroom light, don't play it safe. Fuck it.

Ciano drove in silence, painfully aware of Erica's presence next to him. He was determined not to give away any more ground; he stared straight ahead while driving, turning his head only when necessary, but he had the unpleasant feeling that she was reading him like a book. His hand clenched the steering wheel in a death grip.

"You know," she said breaking the silence, "you behave like an emotional infant. Did you use to hold your breath until you turned blue?"

165

Ciano turned to her trying to act nonchalant. "What's that?"

Erica smiled. "Okay, you want to play, let's play. I like a good game as much as anybody. So act cold and I'll whine and plead for you to forgive me, and after I've done enough begging to bolster your do-wop macho ego, we'll be friends again. So, while I grovel in the dirt, take the expressway west. I'll tell you when to get off." There was a sly, defiant expression in her eyes.

Ciano smoldered, searching for words while he imagined smacking her. "You know the difference between a pussy and a cunt?" he asked.

"No," she said, laughing. "Tell me."

"A pussy is soft, wet, and warm. A cunt is who owns it and you're a cunt."

"That's it, Vincent, overwhelm me with your barbed wit."

"Fuck you."

"In time, detective, in time."

She laughed softly and leaned over to kiss his ear, working her tongue into it with a fluttering motion. He jerked away. But she would not be put off. She teased him until he forgot his anger and found himself caught up in her game. By the time they exited the expressway, Ciano felt a bulge in his pants. She had snapped his resolve like splintering bone.

"There's home," Erica said, pointing to a Howard Johnson's Motel.

Ciano parked in the lot. "I hope they have a room," he said, remembering their last bout.

"They do," Erica said, producing a key that she dangled from polished nails.

Ciano followed Erica into the motel. There was no hesitation as she strode across the lobby with her long-legged stride. Ciano kept pace with her, knowing that to fall even a half step behind would make him feel like a dog chasing a bitch.

She had not only rented the room, but prepared it as well. Ciano stood still inside the open door, taking in a flurry of flowers, champagne on ice, and a portable tape player on the night table. A black negligee was laid out on the bed. Wicked in color and fabric, it taunted him with what was about to happen.

Erica led him through a small kitchenette and Ciano saw there was food also. She went directly to the bathroom, undressing and regulating the shower. When she called to him, Ciano went. But in those few steps, an irritating thought struck him like a slap from a wet towel. She had known he'd be here tonight.

"What if I had told you to stuff it?" he asked.

"Then I would have invited someone else."

Ciano didn't like the answer, but Erica was already in the shower, naked and waiting, he had no time to think about it.

They made love like animals—her words—in the shower, on the floor, and in the bed. When it was over, Ciano felt he had had a machine under him, over him, and around him. He had tasted flesh, smelled the musk of her wetness, and felt the supple softness of her body against his, yet he had the persistent thought that some mechanical manipulation had been behind the woman's lust. Something alien and cold had driven her body while her mind remained aloof.

Ciano lay in bed and smoked while Erica moved about the kitchen area, and watching her, it struck him suddenly that the woman had muscles. Not a woman's muscles or even athletic muscles—she had muscle muscles, bunches of knotty defined muscles. Ciano pulled himself up to a sitting position. Shit, he thought, the lady pumps iron. He wondered why he hadn't noticed it before, but he supposed in the car they had been too close, and here he had been too horny, to notice details.

Muscles on a woman didn't turn Ciano off, but they made him uneasy, as if he weren't in control. Not, of course, that he had ever felt fully comfortable with Erica, but her hard, sinewy body explained how she was able to manipulate his bulk so easily. When Erica wanted him in a certain position, she would move him physically. This added to his apprehension and his feeling that her take-charge attitude was a form of emasculation.

As he lay in bed smoking, he heard her in the shower, and wondered why he was being so critical. Certainly she had the best body of any woman he had ever slept with; she was funny, although sometimes he had the feeling he didn't really understand all her references; she was a tiger in the sack, exhibiting no false modesty or timidity. She'd do anything he liked and some things he didn't. When she had produced a dildo and used it on herself with almost maniacal glee, he was amused. When she tried to use it on him, he smashed it against the wall. She had only laughed.

But what bothered him the most was her odd behavior each time she came. At the moment of orgasm, she suddenly went cold and stiff all over, as if she couldn't let herself go. Then she would grope under the bed for something and come up with her fists clenched. At first he thought she was going for poppers—amyl nitrate—to increase the intensity of her orgasm, but that wasn't it. He had once screwed a woman who couldn't get off

167

unless she put her wedding photos on the bed; she could only come while looking at a picture of her ex-husband. That was peculiar, he thought, stubbing out his cigarette. Peculiar and more annoying than this. Besides, the photo lady wasn't in Erica's league when it came to fucking.

"Vince," Erica called from the bathroom. "You want to scrub my back?"

"Sure," he said. "And your front."

Chapter
Eighteen

Saturday, November 13

"I want out and I want out now," Ciano shouted. He used what they called at the Police Academy his "command voice." It was supposed to stop felons in their tracks; it had absolutely no effect on Lillian Becker, the real-estate woman who had stuck him with Chris and Dan's love nest.

"I'm terribly sorry, Officer Ciano," she said in a high-pitched, Eleanor Roosevelt voice, "but I cannot let you out of the lease until I find someone else."

"And I'm telling you to oil that fucking lease and shove it up your ass," Ciano shouted.

She looked at him blankly for a moment, then she put a gnarled hand up to her prim lips and said, "Fuck you," in a high tremolo.

Ciano almost did a double take, and then he laughed. Lillian Becker laughed, too, a high "hoo, hoo, hoo," that cracked him up completely.

"Look, lady," he said when he had gotten control of himself. "Do me a favor. Please find somebody quick. That place is driving me nuts. Did you ever see it?"

Lillian Becker looked around to see if anyone else in the big real-estate office was listening, then she motioned Ciano to come close.

"It looks like it was decorated by Queers-Roebuck," she said.

Ciano laughed again. She was a spry old broad. "You got it, lady. It ain't good for my image, if you catch my drift." He winked, but she had gone back to her haughty, Eleanor Roosevelt demeanor.

"I'll do what I can," she trilled.

Ciano nodded and walked out into the bright sunshine. It was a magnificent day, perhaps the last warm day of the year. The weatherman on the radio had said it would reach seventy degrees, marveled at the unusual weather pattern, and urged people to get outside before the rain set in tomorrow. Ciano was game, and at Erica's insistence, he had called Diane and gotten her permission to have Vince, Jr., for the day.

He had tried to apologize about the nasty note he had left her, but Diane was icy.

"I'm glad you are taking some interest in your son," was all she said. "I'll drop him off at your place."

"Bring him to the precinct," Ciano had said. "That's where I'll be."

"What a surprise," she had said, snottily. "Can you stay away long enough to keep him for the weekend?"

Ciano didn't want to be saddled with the kid for two days. He, Dugan, and Hanratty had been spending their spare time nosing around Holy Cross Church, but so far they had no luck in spotting Joseph Steppe. Ciano wanted to clear this case, but he wouldn't admit to Diane that his work was more important than one weekend with the kid. So he had said it was no problem and had even added, "We'll take good care of him."

Diane didn't pick up on the "we" or she ignored it. He found himself wanting to flaunt Erica, to show her off to Diane as if to say, see, I can still get women, better looking women than you.

In the week since their memorable night at Howard Johnson's, Ciano had spent his time trying to avoid Talbot, find Joseph Steppe, and screw Erica every chance he got. She was always available, always willing, and now she wanted to meet his son. It seemed out of character to Ciano. Erica was somebody's woman, not somebody's mother.

He drove slowly to the station house and parked in the still-overflowing lot. If anything, there were more detectives than ever working on the murder of the two priests. Ciano's original team had been broken up and reassigned to various portions of the investigation. He was the precinct whip, but he had nobody to whip except Dugan, who was a master at avoiding assignments he didn't want.

In the station house, he found Dugan involved in a quiet discussion with Marty Abel. When Abel saw Ciano, he took off like a frightened rabbit.

"What did that scumbag want?" Ciano asked Dugan.

"A secret report on his progress with those coins, the leptons," Dugan said.

"It's taken him this long?"

"He's got a mile-long list of stores where they're sold, wholesalers, jobbers, importers, manufacturers and individuals who bought them by mail," Dugan said.

"Scumbag," Ciano said without conviction. "I got to sneak around to find out what's going on with my own goddamn case."

"Not anymore," Dugan said.

Dugan was right, of course, but Ciano couldn't back off. He was only hiding out. When the sergeant had offered Joseph Steppe as a nice, neat wrap-up of the case, it set Ciano to dreaming about upstaging Talbot and every other asshole who had ever broken his balls. But they had been working steadily—stealthily—on the West disappearance and had uncovered nothing of value. Worse, their asses were on the line if Talbot discovered their game.

"Talbot looking for me?" Ciano asked.

"Like a sailor looks for a safe port in a storm," Dugan said. "Like a dick looks for a warm pussy. Like—"

"Stop it," Ciano said. "I get the picture. Tell him that I just called in sick."

"Sure, sure, send the Irish guy into the lion's den," Dugan said. "I'll do it if you sit on the church tonight."

"Can't, I've got my kid this weekend," Ciano said.

"I got my kids every weekend," Dugan sighed. "How about we stop this silly shit and get back to normal?"

"I'll think about it," Ciano said. "You take off, anyway. Maybe Hanratty'll do it."

"I hear those Hanrattys do almost anything," Dugan said slyly.

"Fuck you," Ciano said mildly.

"Ciano!" a cold voice broke in. "Where the hell have you been?

Captain Talbot almost raced down the stairs, as if to cut Ciano off before he could escape.

"Hiya, Cap'n," Ciano said.

"Come upstairs, I want a complete report from you, where you've been, what you're doing—"

"Sorry, Cap'n," Ciano said. "I was just on my way out. Got to run."

Talbot turned bloodred. "Upstairs," he said in a low, choking voice. "That's a direct order."

Ciano shrugged. "Well, let's see, on Monday I went to the hairdresser's, on Tuesday I went to the cleaners, on Wednesday—"

"Can it, Ciano," Talbot said angrily. "What do you have to report?"

"Not a goddamn thing," Ciano said. "What have you got to report to me?"

"Upstairs."

"Look, Captain. I'm not working today, so get off my back. I gave you your report. I obeyed your order, now I'm out of here," Ciano said.

"If you're holding anything back, anything at all, I'll crucify you," Talbot said.

"Interesting choice of words," Dugan muttered.

"What?" Talbot's fierce blue eyes stared at Dugan.

"I said, I'm going now."

"Well, get the fuck out of here and take Ciano with you. I'm sick of both of you, and believe me, I won't forget this," Talbot said. He was purple.

"It's a good thing I enjoy such a rich personal life," Dugan said, as they were standing in front of the precinct house, "because I don't believe my professional life will go on much longer."

"Fuck it, Dugan," Ciano said. "You'd make a good rent-a-cop or maybe an armored car guard."

"Which reminds me of the story about two strippers, an owl, and an armored car. It seems—"

"Save it for Monday," Ciano said. "I'll probably be less cheerful than I am now." He sat down heavily on the steps leading to the station house.

"Can I drop you, Lew?" Dugan asked, looking down at him.

"Nope. I'm waiting for my wife and kid to show up."

"Big family weekend?"

"Kind of."

"Ah, one of those," Dugan said knowingly and waved good-bye.

Ciano sat on the damp stone steps and waited. The sun was hot and he took off his scarred leather jacket and lit a cigarette. Closing his eyes, he allowed the warmth to penetrate him until he suddenly felt a shadow pass over him. He opened his eyes.

"You look like a criminal, not a cop," Diane said.

"Thank you," he said. "And it's nice to see you. Where's Vincent?"

"In the car. I don't want him to be exposed to the kind of people that hang around here," she said.

"Cops or criminals?"

172

"Both. Are you sure you can keep him overnight?" she asked. It was a challenge.

"No problem," Ciano said, getting up and brushing the dust from his jeans. "You got a hot date with Teddy?"

"I've got plans, yes," she said, as they walked to the car. "And I want to be a responsible parent so I'm checking to see if my son will be all right."

Ciano winced. "Look, Diane. I'm sorry—"

"I'll call you tomorrow at your place. I wouldn't want you to think I've abandoned my child."

"You don't ever give up, do you Diane?" Ciano said.

"No *responsible* parent ever does."

Ciano didn't dare speak. He knew what he would say and how it would end. Control, he thought, control, control, control.

"Daddy!" Vince, Jr., shouted from the open window of Diane's Toyota.

Ciano waved and smiled. Control, he thought. "By the way," he said, "if I'm not home tomorrow, I'll call you."

"You're not going to do anything—anything you'll regret?" Diane's voice was icy.

"Like kidnapping? Come on, you know me better than that."

"Do I, Vince? Do I really?"

"Come on, sport," Ciano said to his son. "Let's get going."

The boy jumped out of the car, his football cocked, and tossed a hard short pass at Ciano, hitting him square in the gut.

Ciano made a noise like a deflating tire and sprawled on the ground, moaning.

Alarmed, Vince, Jr., ran over to his father and looked down at him. "Daddy?"

Ciano opened one eye and snatched the boy to him, holding the giggling kid over his head.

Diane looked perplexed. "Don't shake him too hard or he'll throw up his breakfast."

"No, I won't," Vince, Jr., cried, as Ciano put him down and got to his feet.

Diane shook her head, got into the Toyota and waved goodbye. Ciano and his son stood on the sidewalk in front of the precinct in the bright, hot sun and waved inanely.

"Let's move 'em out," Ciano said, after she had gone. "How 'bout a burger and a coke?"

"Barfburger," Vince, Jr., shouted.

"No, a ratburger at Hanratty's."

"No!"

"Well, come on. There's somebody who wants to meet you," Ciano said.

"Who?"

"A lady. Her name is Erica. You'll like her."

"Is she why you never come to see me?" the boy asked, as they crossed the street, hand in hand.

"I come to see you," Ciano said, dodging the question.

"Not hardly at all," Vince, Jr., said.

"Well, come on. We'll have a good time today. What do you say?"

"I say barfburgers."

"And I say barfboogers!" Ciano added.

That sent the boy into a paroxysm of laughter, and he tried to fulfill Diane's dire prediction: he laughed until he almost threw up.

Ciano used his jacket to clean his son's face and they went into Hanratty's. Erica was sitting at the table in the back, wearing a tight plaid shirt, rolled to the elbows and a pair of jeans that looked as if they had been sprayed on.

"Is that her?" Vince, Jr., said, pointing to Erica.

"Yep."

"She's pretty."

"You're learning early," Ciano said, walking the boy over to the table and making the introductions.

"What sports do you like, Vinny?" Erica asked, after the boy and Ciano had joined her at the table. "Is that what they call you, Vinny?"

"My friends do," the boy said, shyly.

"What about me, can I call you Vinny?" Erica asked in her husky voice.

The boy smiled, his eyes looking at the table. "Okay."

"Good. You can call me Erica."

"And you can call me a cab," Ciano said.

Both Erica and Vinny giggled.

"Are you all ready for our picnic?" Erica asked. "I packed us a lunch and I'm rarin' to go. It must have been twenty years since I've been on a picnic."

"Me, too," Ciano said.

"Me, too," Vince, Jr., said.

Richmondtown was crawling with cops, but empty of tourists, when they bluffed their way past the uniform on duty. A flash of Ciano's gold shield was all it took.

174

"Only a cop would pick a crime scene as a picnic ground," Erica said.

"I thought I might do a little moonlighting as long as I was here," Ciano said.

"No wonder your wife left you," Erica said, then instantly regretted it. A cloud passed overhead, making Ciano's dark features ominous.

Ciano was silent, but his look startled Erica with its intensity.

"There's a nice place," she said hurriedly, "over by the pond."

They carted a wicker picnic basket, a rectangular styrofoam cooler, and a beach blanket over to the edge of the small lake known as John Dunn's Mill Pond. Originally a working mill, grinding grain for bread, and powered by the stream that ran nearby, it was an attraction for school children and adults who got demonstrations of the huge mill stone in action. The flour milled was then baked into johnny cakes by the children and anointed with hand-churned butter. It was okay, the kids said, but not like Mickey D's.

They spread out the brown-and-white picnic blanket and sat down by the pond. The gentle noise of the water flowing over the spillway was the only sound they could hear. An occasional late-season dragonfly buzzed them, but the insects were too far past their time to be aggressive.

"Let's play catch, Daddy!" Vince, Jr., yelled.

"In a minute," Ciano said. "You want a soda?"

"Yeah, a Coke. Mom don't let me have them at home. They wreck your teeth," Vince, Jr., said.

"What your mother doesn't know won't hurt her," Erica said, twisting the cap off a bottle.

"Yeah," Ciano agreed, thinking the same thing. "Why don't you go see what's over that bridge?"

"Okay," the boy said, wandering off happily toward the rough wooden structure that crossed the pond over the spillway.

"This was a nice idea," Erica said, offering Ciano an iced can of Michelob Light beer.

"It sure was," he said, accepting the beer and lying down on the blanket, looking up at the clear blue sky. It was so peaceful he closed his eyes.

"Don't go to sleep on me," Erica said, poking him.

"Just thinking," he said, opening his eyes.

"About what?"

"About you. We're getting on pretty good together, aren't we?" he said lazily.

"We're getting *it* on, if that's what you mean," she said, lying down next to him and giving his crotch a nudge with her knee.

"That's not exactly what I meant," he said.

"But it's exactly what *I* meant," she said, running her hand down his arm and snuggling up close to him.

He was consumed by her closeness, he felt himself wanting more than anything to make it with her at that very instant, out in the sunlight, under the blue sky.

He wrapped his arms around her and kissed her deeply, his tongue seeking the moist heat of her mouth. He was rock hard.

"No, Vince, please," she said suddenly, pulling away from him. "Not here, not in front of your son."

"He's wandering around somewhere," Ciano said. "And it won't take long the way I feel." He moved her hand to his groin. She grasped him tentatively, then drew away.

"No, Vince. Please. It's not right. Later, tonight. When Vinny's asleep, I'll do anything you want," she said, her voice having lost its assurance, now had regained its husky, teasing tone.

Ciano turned away, disgruntled. He agreed with her intellectually, but still . . . he hated to get turned on, then have to cool off. He took a sip of his beer and felt her move up against him.

"Don't be mad, Vince," she said. "Please don't be mad at me. I don't think I could stand it."

Ciano was surprised. It was the first sign of vulnerability she had shown since he had met her. He was about to make a comment when he heard his son yelling, "Dadddeee!"

He sat up and Erica rolled off him.

Vince, Jr., was running as fast as he could toward them, his eyes wide with fright. Behind the boy he could see cops running across the sere brown grass toward the millpond race.

"What is it, slugger?" Ciano said, stopping the boy's forward motion.

"A lady," the boy gasped. "A naked lady."

"Yeah?" Ciano smiled broadly. Erica punched him.

"No. No. The policemen said you should come." Vince, Jr., breathed loudly. "Right now."

"Some kind of striptease?" Ciano said, but as he looked toward the gathering crowd of cops he suddenly felt cold.

"She was green," Vince, Jr., said. "And all kind of . . ." He didn't have the vocabulary to explain.

"Okay, you wait here and I'll have a look," Ciano said, getting up and taking the can of beer with him.

He walked slowly toward the scene of confusion, not really wanting to get there. But at last he pushed his way through the cops and saw what they saw.

It was Abigail West's mottled gray-green body. She had been crammed into a small space under the millpond waterfall. The gasses inside her body had expanded but having nowhere to go had finally blown a large hole in her belly, sending bits of rotting meat in all directions. Part of her decomposed face was visible, her teeth and jaw were set in a final rictus scream.

Ciano took a sip of his beer. The sun glinted off the silver can causing a flash of light that made Joseph Steppe, high on the hill over Richmondtown, think of church candles. And death.

Chapter Nineteen

Friday, November 19

Ciano tensed. His hand went automatically to the .38 Smith & Wesson on his hip. He held his breath. The door to the furnace room cracked open slowly, throwing a shaft of light onto the concrete floor. Ciano's hand gripped the wooden handle of the .38, wishing with all his might that the next face he saw would be Joseph Steppe's. He let his breath out slowly and pulled the revolver out of its holster, bracing it against a cold metal pipe that was connected to the furnace.

This is it, he thought, the payoff. He cocked the hammer and strained to see in the darkness.

The door opened farther, and in the doorway stood a silhouetted figure. It didn't look human to Ciano. It was short, hunched, and panting. But it was definitely Joseph Steppe.

Do I kill him now, Ciano thought, or do I let him spend his days getting fat and enjoying his civil rights in a nice, warm hospital? His hand tensed on the trigger.

"Hold it, Steppe," Ciano shouted. "Police!"

Joseph Steppe froze in his tracks; he could feel his bowels loosening. His worst nightmare had come true. He knew it was the big cop who had been chasing him.

Steppe threw up his hands. "Don't kill me. Don't kill me, please!" His voice was a shriek of agony, a high-pitch howl that was not unlike Abigail West's last scream.

Ciano, hidden in the dark behind the furnace, was calculating. He wanted more than anything to kill Steppe. A mere six pounds of pressure on the trigger would blow the sack of shit away and save everybody a lot of trouble.

"In the name of God, don't kill me," Steppe wailed.

Ciano snarled, "In the name of God, I ought to kill you."

Steppe sank to his knees, his hands clasped in prayer; Ciano tightened his grip on the trigger, knowing his decision was crucial for Steppe and for himself. It seemed so simple before, he thought, so clear.

• • •

In the six days since the discovery of Abigail West's bloated, exploded body, Ciano had literally haunted Holy Cross Church He had spent long, uncomfortable hours crouched behind the furnace. Once he had almost iced the custodian who had arrived to inspect the boiler, and had had a difficult time explaining to the terrified man why he was lurking in the shadows.

At work, he was under intense pressure from Talbot to devote fourteen hours a day to task force paperwork, but he had managed to avoid most of that boring and annoying duty and had concentrated on finding Steppe. It had been easy to divert Talbot's attention because the captain and borough detectives were convinced that West's homicide had nothing to do with the priests'; Ciano let them keep thinking that.

His problem with Diane had eclipsed his problem with Talbot. When she had discovered that Ciano's idea of a picnic was to take her son to a murder scene and let him discover a dead body, she swore he'd never see Vince, Jr., again. "And as for that floozie of yours, I don't think it is *responsible* for a parent to expose his child to a prostitute," she had said. When he had told this to Erica she had only laughed.

It was no coincidence that Ciano had finally brought Steppe to bay. It was persistent, unimaginative police work, he knew. When the weather had turned cold after the picnic, Ciano had figured a furnace room would make the ideal place to hide out during the winter.

Steppe twitched.

"Freeze, cocksucker!" Ciano said, coming out from behind the furnace.

Ciano watched with rapt fascination as the grotesque figure kneeling before him babbled out a stream of saliva-punctuated words that made no sense. But he was certain he had the priest-killer, as well as Abigail West's murderer. Looking closer, he could also see Kathy Santini's troll.

"Lie down on the floor and put your hands behind your back," Ciano ordered. It was rote . . . and if Steppe had obeyed, it would have saved his life.

But Steppe, beyond terror now, sprang up as Ciano approached him and rammed the cop low, sending him crashing to the cement floor and the .38 skidding across the room.

Stunned and almost paralyzed by the blow, Ciano watched

179

helplessly as Steppe produced the leaf spring sword. It whistled over the little man's head and descended in a killing arc.

Ciano lunged away from the sword, but it caught him on the left shoulder, ripping through his leather jacket and biting deep into the bone.

In the dim light, Ciano could see Steppe's eyes practically sparkling with triumph. He was drooling.

The sword cut through the air again and this time missed Ciano's head by inches. Sparks flew upward from the cement floor.

Ciano rolled into Steppe, trying to bowl him over, but the demented little man swiped at him, cutting into Ciano's thigh. The pain streaked through his body like lightning.

Gasping with the effort, Ciano threw himself out of the way, thinking of the hot rooftop where he had battled another maniac, wondering if this was the knife that had severed Father Graff's head from his shoulders.

Steppe was slow in following up on his advantage, giving Ciano time to look for a weapon. But all he could find was a splintery piece of wood about a yard long. He hefted it as Steppe came toward him, windmilling the leaf spring sword. The tempered steel bit into the cop's flimsy weapon, slashing through the wood as if it were made of paper. Ciano threw the stump into Steppe's eyes, but his toss was too soft. The light piece of wood glanced off Steppe's forehead as he swung the blade side-arm, hoping to catch Ciano in the kidneys. Ciano dodged and felt the blade rip into his side, deep.

Backpeddling, Ciano ripped his jacket off, wincing as it snagged on his wounded arm; the sleeve was soggy with blood.

Steppe swung again. Wildly. Ciano ducked. He could feel the hot breeze of the passing blade. His back to the wall, Ciano wrapped the blood-soaked jacket around his arm and prepared to ward off the next blow.

Steppe, sensing triumph, unleashed a two-handed, over-the-head cut aimed at Ciano's nose. The cop took a shuffling step to the left, raised his right arm with its leather protector and prepared to deflect the blow. The sword cut through leather, skin, and bone, but Ciano brought his left hand up and seized Steppe by the throat. His thick fingers sank into the crazed man's scrawny neck. He squeezed.

Steppe emitted a high-pitched wheeze of pain and dropped the sword, while Ciano, using Steppe's throat as a handhold, smashed the little man's head into the cinder block wall. Steppe's scream became a low moan when Ciano slammed him into the wall a second time, trying to subdue him. He was about to repeat this move when he slipped on his own blood and went tumbling to the cement floor, releasing his grip on Steppe's throat.

Desperately Steppe crawled toward the door. Ciano lunged for him, but his wounded arm seared him with pain, and his fingers slipped off Steppe's built-up corrective shoe.

Steppe crawled out the door while Ciano lay back against the wall, catching his breath and checking his wounds. The cut on his shoulder was deep, but it was clotting nicely; the wounds in his side and thigh were also not dangerous—if he didn't exert himself. But the wound in his forearm looked bad. He could see the dead white bone through the tear in his skin.

"Son of a bitch almost broke my fucking arm," Ciano said out loud, more in wonder than in anger.

He knew he should call for backup, but he would be a laughingstock if word got around that he had had the shit beat out of him by a gimpy gnome.

Ciano stood up shakily, looked for the light switch and flicked it on. His blood had pooled on the floor in several places. That made him mad. There was only one thing to do, he thought, as he retrieved the .38 that had scuttled away harmlessly under a broken, three-legged chair. "You're dead, Steppe," he whispered to himself. "You may be breathing, but you're dead."

He ripped off his shirt and tied it around the wound on his forearm to staunch the flowing blood, then retrieved his torn, blood-soaked leather jacket and wrapped it around his neck in a makeshift sling.

He was as good as he was going to get, he thought, lurching out the door calling to Steppe, as if to name him would defeat him. His first stop, however, was his car where he had incautiously left his off-duty piece.

Ed Hanratty was prowling Richmondtown on his own, seeking answers to questions he dared not ask aloud. He paused by the Voorlezer's House, built in the seventeenth century by the Dutch as the village school, church, and home for the schoolmaster. In the moonlight, its brown clapboards seemed to recede into the dark; its white trim was startling bright. Hanratty shook his head and walked toward the millpond to see for himself where Abigail West's body had been found.

The grass under his feet was wet and icy and he could see his breath. Another winter, maybe his last, he thought. When he reflected on his life, he realized that everything good that had ever happened to him had occurred during the warm weather. Or was that just because so few good things had happened, it was all coincidence?

He had entered the Police Academy in summer, been promoted to captain on a hot day in May, retired in July; he had met Margot in June. Erica had been born almost two years later. For the life of him, he couldn't think of one good thing that had ever happened to him in the spring, fall or winter. He shivered. He had tried to kill himself in the spring when he had discovered the truth about Margot on that awful day. That was the year he had withdrawn from the world, and like a bear, had begun sleeping out the winter of his life.

Up ahead he heard the rush of water over the spillway and shook off all thoughts except those related to the case. Why the hell did Steppe plant West under a waterfall? Was there some hidden message there? Her death was seemingly unconnected to those of the priests, yet together, all three homicides had to have some phantasmagoric significance to Steppe's demented brain. Or did they?

Hanratty stood on the wooden bridge over the spillway and looked down at the water flowing past. The white foam glowed eerily in the moonlight.

Free of the hot, stuffy basement, Steppe let the night wash over him. Soon the density of the darkness would seep into his pores, making him invisible.

In his curious loping gait, he struck out across the cold, wet grass toward his hideaway high above Richmondtown Village. He would be safe there, he knew, safe from the big cop who had tried to kill him.

He exhaled a lungful of air and inhaled the darkness, feeling the "shadow power"—his childhood term for the ability to pass among people unnoticed. Death in life for the shadow man. For that's how he thought of himself, as the human shadow. Even now, searching the darkness with his poor eyesight, he felt a surge of strength and optimism. When he was invisible, he could do anything.

Behind him he heard the door to the church basement slam shut. He knew the cop was after him, but it didn't matter now. The cop couldn't see him.

Ciano, his mangled arm in a blood-soaked sling, leaking blood from multiple wounds, staggered to his station wagon. He could see Steppe quite clearly in the moonlight, but the killer was too far away to risk a shot. Ciano reached under the seat for his throwaway piece, a .32 caliber automatic he had taken from a dead holdup artist five years before. The gun was cold by now, he figured, but just to make sure, he had taped the handle. There would be no fingerprints if they found it near Steppe's bullet-riddled body.

Ed Hanratty was still staring at the foaming water pouring over the spillway when he detected movement out of the corner of his eye. A figure was moving steadily toward him. Even in the moonlight, Hanratty knew instinctively it was Steppe. The lopsided gait confirmed it. He immediately got off the bridge and waited in the shadows ready to surprise and apprehend the man.

Steppe came puffing out of the darkness and from his place of concealment at the far end of the bridge, Hanratty suddenly felt fear. There was a glinting madness radiating from Steppe's eyes, a madness that Hanratty recognized. He cursed himself for not being armed and for being forty years older than Steppe. He wondered if he should let the little man pass. Then he remembered Monsignor Bryan's flayed body. That was enough.

Steppe's corrective shoes sounded like a horse's hooves on the plank bridge. He smiled, exhibiting his sharp, pointy teeth. He could almost see the house on the hill; safety was only ten minutes away.

That's when Ed Hanratty jumped out in front of him and shouted for Steppe to stop. It had to be a dream, Steppe thought, no one can see me. He put his head down, his arms pumping, and charged into the tall, insubstantial figure in front of him, determined to shatter the disturbing illusion.

They collided with an audible crunch and went down together in a jumble of arms and legs. Hanratty, stunned by the force of the blow, was gasping for breath and attempting to get Steppe off his chest. He failed. He heard a rib crack.

Steppe, howling with frustration, tried to disentangle himself from this all too real apparition. When he managed to get himself free, he sat astride Hanratty, his legs pinioning the old man's arms to his side. Then he pulled the sharp sword from his belt.

Hanratty saw the flash of metal in the moonlight, but without his glasses, which had been knocked from his face, it was a blur. But he could still recognize death. So it ends here, he thought. Hacked to death by a madman on a cold autumn night. He closed his eyes and prepared to die.

As Hanratty pressed his ear to the wooden planks, exposing his neck, he heard the sound of footsteps. Someone was coming. He opened his eyes in time to see the blade descending and he kicked with all his might, trying to pitch Steppe forward, over his head. It didn't work, but he caused Steppe to miss the killing blow. The sword bit deep into the wood beside Hanratty's head. As Steppe bent forward to pull the blade from the wood, he drooled on Hanratty and the old man could smell the stench of the psycho's stinking, unwashed body.

Then suddenly the weight was lifted from Hanratty's chest. He had the distinct impression that Steppe was flying. He could see stumpy legs dangling in the air, rising out of sight.

"Got ya, cocksucker," Ciano growled, ignoring the pain and lifting Steppe off Hanratty with a strength born of rage.

Steppe, suspended from Ciano's big hands, lashed out with the sword, but he aimed too low. Enraged, Ciano slung the little man through the guard rail and into the millpond.

Steppe screamed as he hit the icy water.

"Help, help!" he called out. "I can't swim."

"Good," Ciano called back. Then he helped Hanratty up. "You okay, Cap'n?"

Hanratty shook his head and said, "Glasses."

"For what I'm about to do, you don't want your glasses," Ciano said, pulling out the untraceable .32 and his police issue .38.

"Don't," Hanratty mumbled. "He's not worth it."

"Help!" Steppe screamed, splashing around in the water. It was almost six feet deep, but that was a good foot over his head, and his green fatigue jacket, green woolen work pants, and heavy corrective shoes were pulling him down.

"Leave me alone, Cap'n," Ciano said. "It will end here."

"Don't be a fool, Ciano," Hanratty said, groping on the ground for his glasses.

Steppe disappeared under the water, then reappeared closer toward the shore. He was trying to bounce his way to shallow water.

"Get back out there, cocksucker," Ciano shouted, firing a round from the .32, so that it kicked up a waterspout near Steppe's head. The killer disappeared under the water for a few seconds, then popped up screaming, "Don't kill me! Help!"

His head then plunged beneath the water for a longer time.

When he reemerged, Ciano loosed off another round in front of him. This time Steppe, his mouth full of water, could only gurgle incoherently.

"Ciano, stop it," Hanratty said. "I can get him out of there."

"Stay where you are or so help me, you'll join him," Ciano said, his voice cold and unemotional.

"I'm going to get him," Hanratty said, amazed at his own courage.

Ciano sat on the bridge looking for Steppe's head. When it bobbed up, he squeezed off another round. "Die, cocksucker," he said.

Hanratty tossed off his coat and pulled off his shoes and began wading into the pond.

"If you go out there, I'll put a round through his eye," Ciano said. "It won't do you any good to try to help him. Just keep thinking about what he did to your friend Bryan."

Steppe's head broke the water for the last time, but he had ceased calling for help. His lungs were full of water and the oxygen wasn't getting to his brain or his heart. He had only minutes to live as Ciano fired again. Steppe didn't notice as he rolled over slowly, facedown, into what Ciano knew as a dead man's float.

Entirely satisfied, Ciano tossed his throwaway piece into the millpond and closed his eyes.

"Help me, Ciano." Hanratty's voice jolted him awake. For a moment he thought it was Steppe, but then he saw that Hanratty had retrieved Steppe's body and had him supine on the shore of the pond. He was attempting artificial respiration.

"Help me," Hanratty gasped. "I think we can save him."

"Not likely," Ciano said, closing his eyes again.

It was the smell that woke him: antiseptic and disinfectant. Ciano opened his eyes to see Inspector Sal DeFeo staring at him.

Christ, what a nightmare, he thought.

"Ciano, you awake?" DeFeo asked unnecessarily.

Ciano tried to move, but his whole body hurt. He had bandages up and down his arms and there was a drain in his forearm. He was hooked up to an IV, his mouth was like cotton, and his head throbbed.

"You're an honest-to-fucking-goodness hero, boy," DeFeo said. "You got that little cocksucker."

"Yeah," Ciano managed.

"And you know what we found in his pocket?" DeFeo asked.

Then he answered his own question. "Monsignor Bryan's missing eyeball and Abigail West's tit. We got his sword, too."

"Her tit?"

"Well, her nipple anyway. You did real good and I'm here to tell you that. Like I said, we're one hell of a team, you and me. Supercops," DeFeo said, laughing.

"Yeah," Ciano said again. The little fuck is trying to horn in on my publicity, as usual. If Talbot had iced Steppe, DeFeo wouldn't give me the snot off his handkerchief, he thought.

"Where's Hanratty?"

"They sent him home. A broken rib. He told us all about how Steppe was trying to kill him and how you saved him by throwing the little scumbag in the drink. Great move!" DeFeo said, excitedly. "Too bad you couldn't save him for a trial, but at least you tried."

Ciano nodded. So Hanratty was a stand-up guy, after all. At least now he knew what to write in his report. All he needed was a few minutes alone with Hanratty to get their stories straight. Not that many people would be too upset about the death of a white, Anglo-Saxon, priest killer. No special interest groups to stir up trouble.

"So hurry up and get better so we can go on TV. The mayor wants an all-out publicity campaign. You know, New York's Finest Crack Big Murder Case. That sort of thing," DeFeo said.

"How about a transfer out of here?" Ciano asked.

"Kid, you name it, you got it. Card blank," DeFeo said, meaning carte blanche.

"Fort Apache, Brooklyn, Manhattan, you pick the precinct. You'll get a medal, too, and letters of commendation and . . ." Suddenly, DeFeo stopped and spun around.

". . . Who the hell," DeFeo began. Then, "Oh, Miss Hanratty."

Erica strode into the room as if she owned it, a mysterious smile on her perfectly made-up face.

"Good morning, Inspector," she said. "How's the hero?"

Ciano foolishly tried to straighten up and the needles in his arm shifted. He groaned.

"Poor thing," Erica said, mockingly. "Drowned a midget murderer and got all cut up."

"If you'll excuse us for a moment, Miss Hanratty," DeFeo said.

"If you'll excuse *us* for a moment, Inspector," Erica said.

"Well—"

"Please," Erica said. "Just for a moment?"

DeFeo looked confused, but he decided if Ciano was planking the broad, maybe he ought to mention that Diane was outside.

"Your wife's outside," he said to Ciano.

"All I need is a minute," Erica said, smiling.

DeFeo shrugged. "I'll go get your wife."

When he was gone, Erica reached inside her purse and produced three tightly written legal-size pages.

"Ed said I must give this to you immediately," she said, handing the papers to Ciano.

He took the sheets, his hand pausing for a moment on hers.

"How's your father?" he asked.

"Sleeping. Ed's too old to go out at night and play with the boys," she said. "He'll catch his death."

"He almost did tonight," Ciano said, scanning the copy of Hanratty's statement.

"And if it hadn't been for you, he'd have gone to that great precinct in the sky," Erica said. "I know. I read it."

Ciano frowned.

"Someday you can tell me what *really* happened," she said. "If you want."

Ciano was silent. He was thinking about his deal with Hanratty. He'd be transferred now. He looked at Erica, knowing for the first time how much he'd miss her.

"Well, I'd better get out of here before your wife arrives," Erica said. "See you soon."

She left Ciano feeling like a piece of shit.

Chapter
Twenty

Monday, November 22

Eating a sandwich, Inspector Sal DeFeo resembled a weasel gnawing on a fresh kill. He only half-listened as Captain Talbot rattled on about how he had been screwed by Ciano.

"It was a setup, Sal," Talbot said, passing a file folder toward the inspector.

DeFeo reached for it with short, stubby, mayonnaise-greased fingers. "It's empty," he said, revealing a mouthful of tuna salad.

Talbot sighed. He thought DeFeo was a dull-witted jerk with all the substance of a coat hanger, but the man had incredible clout in the department, and if DeFeo had the golden eggs, it was worth kissing the goose's ass.

"Of course it's empty. It's the file on Abigail West. Ciano and his butt-boy Dugan knew about the connection between the deaths of the priests and the woman's homicide. They were playing their own game, impeding my investigation, and I want them up on charges."

DeFeo took a huge bite of his sandwich, and a glob of tuna salad plopped into his lap.

"Shit," he said, his mouth full.

"Well?" Talbot demanded.

"Well, what?" DeFeo said.

"What are you going to do about it?"

"I'm going to eat my sandwich, then I'm going to the press conference and introduce Ciano. If you want to be on TV, you'd better practice smiling. This is a happy and audacious occasion," DeFeo said.

Auspicious, you asshole, Talbot thought. I hope you choke on that fucking sandwich. "You mean you're going to do nothing?" he asked.

"I already told you what I'm going to do," DeFeo said. "And I already told you what *you're* going to do."

"But—"

"But shit. Don't fuck with me, Talbot. I know who you know

and who I know is bigger. You're out-classed and out-gunned, so loosen up and go with the flow or I'll flush you down the fucking toilet,'' DeFeo said, pleased with his phraseology. He had no doubt Ciano and Dugan had been running some sort of elaborate disinformation game. Hell, Talbot would have done the same thing.

DeFeo hawked up a mouthful of tuna and saliva and spit into the wastebasket to make his point.

Talbot winced.

Thirty minutes before the press conference hit the air live at 5:04, Ciano was being interviewed by Internal Affairs. But armed with Hanratty's statement and his own eighteen years experience in covering his ass, it was enough to keep the shooflies at bay.

Telling his story wasn't his concern, it was a different worry that lurked in his mind, waiting to ambush his conscience once he dropped his guard. It was annoying and worrisome that he was having second thoughts about Joseph Steppe's death. It was self-defense, he thought. Sort of. Maybe he should have . . .

"I said, that will be all, Lieutenant," the Deputy Inspector from Internal Affairs said. "And congratulations."

Ciano tried to smile, but it was more of a grimace. He said good-bye and walked out into the media circus that was developing in the precinct's downstairs conference room. Five camera crews were standing around looking bored and unconcerned; five on-air personalities, looking like movie stars, were being made-up, and a gaggle of disheveled print reporters were waiting to pounce on him.

Freddy Jermezian, wearing a maroon three-piece suit, a black shirt, and no tie, spotted him first and shot across the room toward Ciano.

"Gimme an exclusive and I'll make it worth your while," he said, trying to be confidential. His breath stank of onions.

Suddenly, five sets of camera lights flashed on, blinding Ciano and forcing him to cover his eyes.

"Beat it, Freddy," Ciano said.

"You owe me. I saved your ass last summer."

"You saved nothing," Ciano said, pushing his way to the conference table where the Police Commissioner, the Chief of Detectives, DeFeo, and Talbot waited for him. They were all smiling except Talbot, who looked as if he had eaten a pound of dog crap.

Ciano couldn't let well enough alone. He walked up to Talbot and said, "Cheer up, Captain. Your mighty task force was close. Very close." He held out his hand, but Talbot showed no desire to take it. Instead, DeFeo leaned over and shook hands. "Well done, Vince. Very well done."

Ciano smiled for the cameras and the popping flashbulbs.

"Make this real quick, DeFeo," Ciano said under his breath. "I hate these fucking things almost as much as I hate this asshole." He nodded toward Talbot.

DeFeo, his wide weasel-like smile never wavering, ushered Ciano around to the place of honor at the table. The Chief and PC nodded and smiled.

"Where's Hanratty and Dugan?" Ciano asked, sitting down.

"Resting and on vacation. You are the star of this show and we don't need distractions," DeFeo said in a stage whisper.

"You should have taken him alive," Talbot said, loudly.

"Shut up, Talbot," DeFeo whispered.

"You should have taken him alive," Talbot repeated.

"You been assigned to Internal Affairs, Captain? Or are you just running off at the mouth?" DeFeo said, keeping it light.

But the reporters had heard and were closing in.

"A problem, Inspector?" Jermezian asked, licking his greasy chops. What a story, he was thinking. "Use of deadly and unappropriate force, perhaps? Endangering a suspect? A civilian? Police brutality?"

"No, no Freddy," DeFeo said smoothly. "Nothing like that."

"You got some facts we don't, Captain?" Jermezian asked Talbot.

Talbot looked at DeFeo's wild-eyed glance. "Just a personal opinion."

"It was a stupid opinion and one that warrants an apology," DeFeo cut in.

Talbot bristled at the reprimand, but the thought of apologizing to Ciano was too much. He turned abruptly and stormed out of the conference room.

DeFeo turned to the assembled reporters. "Just a family tiff that will be kept off the record, I trust. To insure departmental cooperation in the future. Am I clear on that point?"

The reporters grumbled, but nodded in agreement.

"Well, then, we've got it all settled and we're about twelve minutes to air time, so I suggest we go over the background material. Sergeant Williams from public affairs has a printed copy for each of you," DeFeo said, and a young, dark-haired woman holding a blue loose-leaf binder walked to the dais. She began reading in a polished voice.

DeFeo turned to whisper to Ciano, "I'll have his ass for this. He was out of line."

"No, let him alone. Maybe he'll choke when he stops to pull his foot out of his mouth," Ciano said.

At Hanratty's there was a party building. Cops, because they worked the thin edge dividing life and death, sanity and insanity, needed little reason to party. "Ciano's Roman Collar," as it was now being called, was a reason and a half. Cops from other precincts were pouring in, joining friends from the 122nd to help them celebrate the death of Joseph Steppe. They kept toasting each other as if they had personally tossed Steppe into the pond. They were having one hell of a time.

Upstairs, Erica had switched off the lights in the front room and stared down from the darkness at the flow of cops on the boulevard separating Hanratty's from the station house. She hated these coarse, loud-mouthed buffoons, and had never understood why men like her father and Ciano found themselves at ease with these bleary-eyed, red-faced maniacs.

She felt the noise drift upstairs, assaulting her senses, actually making the floor tremble beneath her feet.

Although she desperately wanted to go to Ciano, she knew he'd be drunk by now. Abusive, probably, and wanting to show her off to his friends to convince them she was his whore.

Almost against her will, she found herself dialing the phone. She heard the familiar ring at her Connecticut home, then Ron's voice saying there was no one home and please leave a message. She waited for the beep, then hung up. Her husband was in Istanbul, or Caracas or Timbuktu, she thought, traveling around the world looking for bargains to import to the U.S. At first she had gone with him, delighted with the gypsy life and enjoying the excitement of discovering new countries and strange cultures. But it soon paled, for she was as much alone on the road as she was in her million-dollar Greenwich home. Ron James thinks of me as a desirable import, she thought, but he would trade more for someone else if the price was right.

A cop downstairs let out a war hoop that set her nerves on edge. Excessive noise and unrestrained behavior were childish, she thought, and her own childhood had been devoid of everything except rules. Strict rules. Rules that had to be obeyed.

She sat still for a moment, then went downstairs, past the

roaring cops and into the basement looking for Ed. But the basement was dark; even the comforting green glow from the computer was absent. She turned on the lights and opened the door to the storage room. It was cluttered with open boxes of electrical equipment, technical manuals, and file after file of Ed's past cases. In the corner were two large cardboard boxes labeled "Erica" in Ed's small, precise hand.

Feeling like a fugitive, she opened the first one, discovering a collection of old clothes she had made Ed promise to keep when she had gone off to school in Switzerland. She pulled out a gray flannel skirt with a poodle embroidered on the side. That wasn't even hers, she thought, it had been her mother's. It felt strange touching Margot's old clothes and she tossed the poodle skirt aside. Then she reached into the box again and pulled out a plaid tartan skirt with a gold pin at the hem. She remembered that skirt, but like her old life, she had never come back to claim it. Until now.

She opened the second box, knowing what she'd find. Lying on top of each other, seemingly engaged in a fully clothed orgy of some kind, were her dolls. There's Taffy and Barbie, and Christmas Carol, she thought, naming them to herself.

Look at all these damn things. Ed should have told me to shove it instead of buying me all these, she thought. But she knew why he had done it. As a small child she had not been allowed to play with dolls. Then her mother had died and Ed, immersed in his own profound grief, had simply done anything to shut her up and shut her out. The dolls, for the both of them, had become a substitute for love. Instead of loving each other, Ed had given her money and Erica had received the dolls to love.

Pathetic, she thought, plucking a Barbie doll from the riot of doll arms, legs, and heads. She looked at the doll's stupid smile and felt herself on the verge of tears. All those years, she thought, all those fucking years. She smoothed the doll's auburn hair—and the head popped off in her hand.

Disgusted, she tossed the doll into the box with the others and fled the storeroom. She almost knocked Ed over.

"Erica!" he gasped.

"Sorry, Ed. I was just rummaging around in some of my old stuff."

"You scared the life out of me," he said, removing his rimless glasses and wiping them on the black wool tie he wore with a plaid shirt.

"That's my task in life, Ed."

"Well, I was just looking for you. Ciano's upstairs." The way he said it, Ciano might have been synonymous with garbage.

"Made your day, huh, Ed?" Erica said.

"I'll make no secret about it," Hanratty said. "I don't like the idea of you, uh, going out with him."

"Funny, you never cared that much about me before," Erica said.

"What makes you say that? You know I am somewhat undemonstrative."

"Undemonstrative? Like a stone is quiet?" Erica said.

"Please." It was a cry for peace.

"See you later, Ed," she said, heading for the stairs. "Ciano can take care of himself."

Hanratty shook his head, then walked into the storeroom and immediately spotted the poodle skirt. He tried to quell his unease. It was as if Margot had suddenly come back to life, and he didn't know if he liked the idea or not.

He picked up the heavy gray skirt and took it out to the long workbench. He looked at the pink embroidered poodle with the attached leash, and remembered telling Margot she was too old to wear such a dress. But Margot hadn't listened. She was like Erica: headstrong, beautiful, and reckless.

He retrieved his notes on the case and began jotting down random thoughts. He reread what he had written about his wife and thought that his characterization had been too glib, too shallow. He had called her "childlike," but that was an incomplete description. It indicated a sweet innocence that was sunny and appealing. Certainly she was that, but she had other childlike traits that weren't as desirable. Her lack of attention span meant she could not concentrate long enough on one subject to think it through. She lived only for the moment and could not see the ultimate consequences of her actions. She was moody, flighty, and easily driven to heights of rage and joy, states she could not control. For someone like Hanratty, moderate in all things, these swings of emotion were as mystifying as they were frightening.

At the beginning of their marriage Margot had been an obedient child, content with her husband, happy to listen to all his plans, to dream his dreams, and to show her love the only way she knew how—with her body. It never occurred to him that the sexual fulfillment she gave him could easily be transferred to another man. Or men. But that would come later.

The child in Margot needed to play, he thought, giving up all pretense of writing. She needed to be praised and loved and protected from any responsibility. Her passion to play—to party, to dance—was inexhaustible and to Hanratty, overwhelming. He could not keep up with her physically or mentally.

On the odd evening when they were at home alone together, she would devour romantic movies on TV and dig hungrily into chatty magazines that discussed the private lives of movie stars. She longed for the glamorous world of handsome men in tails and beautiful women in long gowns—a world that was as foreign to her as it was to Hanratty. On a cop's pay, the formal tea dances were few; on a cop's pay, the disappointments were many.

Hanratty got off the stool, and taking the gray poodle skirt with him, walked to the furnace. He stood there for a moment, then went into the storeroom and placed it carefully in the cardboard box. He turned out the lights.

Walking wearily upstairs, he heard Ciano shouting for him and almost retreated to the basement.

"Ed!" Ciano shouted. "Come on up and have a drink." His voice was slurred.

Thank God, he'll be gone in two weeks, Hanratty thought. The man's a murderer, and I should have turned him in instead of lying for him.

"Ed!" Ciano shouted when Hanratty appeared at the top of the stairs, wraith-like. "How's the death ray coming?"

The cops, gathered around Ciano in an admiring and drink-buying circle, laughed.

"I'm going to bed," Hanratty said, looking around for Erica, but not seeing her.

"And miss all the fun?" Ciano shouted. "Come on, let's have a few shooters in honor of Joseph Steppe, priest killer, deceased."

"I don't drink to death," Hanratty said coldly. "Especially this one."

The cops around Ciano were silent for a minute, then one said, "Screw it, Vince. Let the old fart toddle off to the sack. It's your day."

"Yeah," Ciano said, but he could no longer feel the effect of the Jack Daniel's. He was stone-cold sober and even his triumph had a bitter taste.

Chapter Twenty-One

Thanksgiving
Thursday, November 25

The church bells rang by themselves again, and as much as he wanted to, Father Thomas McKenna couldn't shrug it off. He was dozing in Monsignor Rosselli's private offices, reclining on the worn leather lounger, sipping Glenlivet and smoking one of the monsignor's ruinously expensive Monte Cristo cigars. He felt it was scant compensation for his devotion.

The Sacred Heart Academy had emptied out days earlier for Thanksgiving vacation, and on the holiday itself not even the custodians were around. It was an eerie feeling to be entirely alone in the six-building complex, Father McKenna thought, using the remote control to shut off the Lions-Bears game on the school's new 27-inch TV.

"Here, Rusty," McKenna called to his miniature poodle. The little dog, who had been lying on his back in front of the fireplace, jumped up at the sound of his master's voice and leaped into the priest's arms.

"Let's go for a walk, boy," McKenna said. "And see who's ringing our bell."

He didn't bother to put on a coat because he could walk all the way from the rectory to the bell tower without going outside. He peered out the window at the mottled gray clouds and shivered. The bare trees rocked back and forth in the cold wind, occasionally scraping against the clear, leaded-glass windows.

"A fine day to stay inside," he said to the dog, wishing he had made other plans for Thanksgiving. "But I wonder who's up in the bell tower. Do you think we've got bats in the belfry?"

The dog yipped once in confirmation and licked the priest's face.

"Well, then let's roust 'em out, boy," McKenna said. "I hope you remember your attack training."

The dog licked his face again.

195

Ed Hanratty, wearing a frilly pink apron, adjusted his rimless glasses and began reading Jean Fowler's directions.

Jean had prepared the Thanksgiving meal the day before, but the finishing touches were Hanratty's responsibility. It was four o'clock and his guests—if that's what you'd call them—were due at six. Just Erica and Ciano.

Hanratty lined up the ingredients on a white enameled table and inventoried them: turkey, potatoes, chestnut dressing, yams, creamed onions, green beans, cranberry sauce, biscuits, mince pie, pumpkin pie, and apple cider. All accounted for. He made a note on Jean Fowler's hastily scribbled instructions. Now that he had all the food arranged in neat rows, it would be easy to cook and serve them in their proper order. He made adjustments like a chess player, then wiped his hands on the ruffled apron and poured himself a stiff shot of Remy.

He took the drink into the dining room, and sat at the table. He put the glass of brandy in the center of a white-and-gold Spode dinner plate, and looked out the bow window at the overcast day. How long had it been since he had had any sort of holiday spirit? How many Christmases, Easters, Fourth of Julys, Thanksgivings, had he skipped? How many had he merely pretended to enjoy? And this was going to be one of the worst yet. He took another sip of the brandy.

Setting the Thanksgiving table had been Erica's idea and she had done a splendid job. She had carved a pumpkin and made it the centerpiece, surrounded by brightly colored leaves and Indian corn. It was beautiful and reminded Hanratty of his first Thanksgiving with Margot, but he was determined not to dwell on the past on this day of all days.

Hanratty drained the glass of brandy in one gulp and went searching for his black trenchcoat. He had work to do before the feast could begin.

Father Thomas McKenna, his poodle, Rusty, in his arms, walked down the long, deserted corridor toward the bell tower. The heat had been shut off in the school and McKenna was cold despite the gold cardigan sweater he wore. Rusty was a comfort, he thought, hugging the dog's tiny body to his chest for warmth and to dispel the eerie gloom that had overcome him.

When he arrived at the door to the bell tower, deep in the basement of the church, he almost talked himself out of going inside. He was ready to leave when the massive oak door creaked open and a blast of cold air enveloped him. It should have been locked.

"Kill boy," he said to the dog. But Rusty began to tremble and whine.

"So much for the attack training," he said, patting the dog's head.

"Who's there?" he called out weakly.

There was no answer, but a sudden draft slammed the door in his face.

"A sign," he said. "A sign that we should go back to the football game."

He turned on his heels and headed back in the direction of the rectory. But less than halfway down the darkened corridor the bells rang again stopping McKenna dead in his tracks. He looked at the door. "Did you hear that?"

The dog whimpered.

"Neither did I," he said, walking back the way he had come.

James Young, the Assistant Medical Examiner, had a problem. It had nothing to do with the fine Chinese meal his wife had prepared for him and their parents. It had to do with his boss, the Medical Examiner of New York City. Young had been told to mind his own business and keep his mouth shut, actions that were very much in keeping with his retiring personality, but actions he felt could cause harm to someone in the future.

It had to do with the Staten Island murders and his forensic findings and conclusions.

"No more, Mei Ling," he said in his faltering Chinese. "You will make me a bloated whale."

His guests laughed, mostly at his accent and incorrect choice of intonation. Both his parents and her parents thought he had become too Americanized. They would have objected to the very idea of celebrating Thanksgiving, but he had promised them a traditional Chinese dinner. What they didn't know was that the squab appetizers were actually turkey appetizers. It was his convoluted way of including his unwilling relatives in what he regarded as a pleasant holiday.

He picked at a small dish of bean curd and reflected that people were divided into two groups—rowers and boat-rockers. His relatives put their backs to the oars and never looked up from their toil. They resented anyone who disturbed the pattern of their inexhaustible rowing by introducing them to new ideas, new experiences, new ways.

The M.E. was like that, too, he thought, a political creature whose decisions were written in stone and whose brain had turned to concrete. He would not listen when Young had told him that whoever had cut Monsignor Bryan to ribbons, wasn't a person as short as Joseph Steppe.

"Maybe he was standing on a box," the M.E. had said. "Maybe he wasn't sanfordized, and shrunk in the pond."

Young couldn't believe it. When he had continued to pester the M.E., he had been told to keep his opinions to himself or get another job. Bryan's eyeball in Steppe's possession was proof enough, he had been told.

"Try this, uncle," he said to his father-in-law's brother. "It is the testicle of an octopus."

The older man laughed at Young's ignorance and lack of culture, but he accepted the proffered food. It was delicious. He didn't know he was eating Stove Top Dressing with oysters.

Young bowed his head in disgrace, wondering how he was going to disguise the mince meat pie.

"Well, maybe I did hear something," Father McKenna said, turning around and walking back to the door of the bell tower.

"Don't be afraid, we'll just run up the stairs and see what's wrong with the bells."

He pulled open the big oak door and peered inside. It was pitch-black.

"Anyone home?" he called. Silence.

"Not even any chickens?"

There was nothing but the whistle of the wind as it snaked its way down the circular, metal staircase.

"Come on, Rusty, it's probably only some kids screwing around," he said, mounting the stairs tentatively. Just before the holiday recess, he had had a run-in with a group of seniors who had smuggled in a case of beer. He had reported them to the Prefect of Discipline, who had taken his usual hard line. The bell-ringing was probably a teenage plot to get even, he told himself. He kept trying to picture the boys in the tower, beer cans in their hands, giggling. It was an insubstantial vision, but it got him up to the first landing.

He paused there to brush off the cobwebs and grime he had accumulated on the way up. He was angry now, thinking up punishments for the boys who had taken him away from his afternoon nap and had sent him out into the cold on Thanksgiving.

The level he was standing on was little more than an empty, brick-walled room with a standard cement staircase against one wall. Above it were six more levels, all similar, then another circular staircase leading to the bells themselves. The only light came from louvered windows, one on each of the far walls.

"It's a tomb with no view," McKenna said to Rusty. But the dog tried to bury his head in the priest's sweater.

One thing, McKenna told himself, as he began the long climb up the tower, was that whoever was up there had to pass him on the way down and that would be the end of that boy's career at Sacred Heart Academy.

As if in defiance, the bells rang out again.

James Young excused himself from the low table in the living room of his Elmhurst apartment and went into the bedroom to make a phone call. He knew he was being rude and foolish, but he didn't care any longer. He just couldn't wait. Linking crimes like sausages was a dangerous absurdity.

"Precinct. Auxiliary Patrolman Floss speaking."

"Lieutenant Ciano, please," Young said into the phone.

"Are you kidding? Everybody but a few guys are out," Floss said. "Ain't no brass around."

"How about Sergeant, uh, Dugan?"

"You kidding?"

"Not what you'd call a full house?"

"Nope. If ya got an emergency, call 911. If ya just wanna talk, call your shrink," Floss said. He was enjoying himself. He was thirty-seven and lived at home with his mother. Any day away from her was a treat.

Suddenly, there was the sound of a muffled argument, then Young heard, "This is Captain Talbot, may I help you?"

"I'm James Young, an Assistant M.E. I'd like to talk to someone about the Steppe case. I was looking for Lieutenant Ciano."

"I'm his superior, may I help you, Doctor?"

"I'd like to see you about some, uh, matters relating to the case. Off the record," Young said.

"You're playing my tune," Talbot said, his grin reminding a rebuked Floss of a movie he had seen once on TV. It was called *Jaws*.

Father McKenna could not believe the throbbing pain in his legs. He still had one more flight of steps to climb before the final circular stairway to the bells, and already his legs refused to go any farther. They had frozen themselves into two columns of aching stone. McKenna sat down on a step, spread his legs in front of him and began rubbing his thighs to dissipate the agonizing buildup of lactic acid. He had to breathe through his mouth and nose, just to catch his breath. At forty-nine, he felt like an old, old man.

The bells rang.

The shock of the noise echoed around the brick enclosure like thunder, but it was enough to push McKenna into action. Grabbing Rusty, he struggled into an upright position and found to his amazement that each step seemed to lessen the pain in his legs.

By the time he reached the trapdoor at the end of the metal staircase, he had little strength left in his arms. But he was furious—furious with himself for going to all this trouble instead of calling security and furious with the boys, whom he vowed would pay dearly for their prank.

He used the back of his head, his neck, and shoulders to force open the ponderous wooden trapdoor. It gave slowly, then a gust of wind caught it and smashed it open on the roof, raising a torrent of dust and debris, sending nesting rodents scurrying. Rusty, aquiver, wormed his way into McKenna's sweater.

He pulled himself through the opening and into the belfry. The brickwork was open on all four sides, admitting the damp, cold wind. Four bells, he counted. They hung black and silent in the dying light.

"You'd better show yourselves," he called out breathlessly. "Now!"

Silence.

It was light enough for McKenna to see the electrical circuitry that allowed the bells to be rung from the church, and for a second, he felt like a fool. The bells could have been rung by a short circuit in the wiring, he thought. But closer inspection showed that the wires had been torn out, leaving little doubt that the bells had been rung by hand.

From the corner of his eye, he caught a tiny movement.

"Come out at once," he shouted over the noise of the wind. "You've done enough harm for one day." Rusty began to whimper again, a sobbing sound, not unlike an infant in distress. In spite of the cold, McKenna was sweating.

Except for inky shadows in the corners of the square belfry he could see he was alone. His eye was drawn to an object to his right. A statue? he wondered. A graven image? His heart beat faster as his eyes and brain tried to decipher the meaning of the dark, pyramidal shape.

Hugging the poodle, he walked shakily to the object and rubbed his tired eyes. There was a pile of stones on the floor in the form of a crude cross. The centerpiece, a fist-sized block of concrete, had a piece of glass embedded in it. Embedded on the jagged glass was a rat, the blood still pumping from its mouth.

Rusty yelped with terror and McKenna started. Behind him the heavy trapdoor slammed shut. His heart jumped.

He took a moment to calm his nerves, then walked to the trapdoor. Even before he bent down to grab the iron handle, he sensed a movement in the shadows. He was not alone in the tower.

McKenna straightened up and called out, "Stop right there. I've had enough of this. Come out now."

He expected to see one or two sheepish-looking students reveal themselves. What he actually saw was a piece of shadow detach itself from the corner on his right and glide toward him menacingly. Instinctively, he backed away, muttering a Hail Mary and dug into the pockets of his sweater for his rosary beads.

McKenna tripped over the door handle and landed on his back, looking up at the monstrous black shadow coming toward him. Rusty was shaking so hard, he made McKenna shiver, too.

"Who are you?" he managed to whisper.

"Death," was the answer, and at the same time a white hand holding a large stone appeared from behind the black shape.

McKenna recoiled, but the hand, moving at blurring speed, smashed the rock into the priest's face, breaking his nose and fracturing his cheekbones.

Unable to react in any way, McKenna felt a hand grab him by the hair and yank him to a kneeling position. Then another stone smashed into the top of his skull, and the darkness deepened. After that, the stones pounded his head with increasing violence and regularity, but McKenna could no longer see or think; his eyes, nose and mouth had been pulverized; and his features were reduced to dripping gore—unrecognizable. He listened to the sound of the blows until his brain leaked from his ears in a slimy, gray trail.

Erica James arrived home wearing soaked sweat clothes and collapsed on the living room couch.

Ed Hanratty was in the bathroom down the hall, carefully

hanging up his unused umbrella, and smoothing his windblown gray hair. He straightened his tie and called out his daughter's name.

"I need a cold one," Erica called back.

"Where the hell have you been?" he asked.

"The gym. Half-day workout for diet defying turkey eaters."

While Hanratty went to the kitchen to get her an iced tea, Erica emptied the contents of her black nylon gym bag onto the couch. Strewn about on the chintz sofa was a wide leather weightlifting belt, fingerless gloves, a tank top emblazoned with the New York Giants logo, and a pair of cutoff jeans. She found what she was looking for, a box of tampax, and tossed it on the mahogany coffee table, just as Ed Hanratty brought her iced tea.

Hanratty stared at the box of tampons, but was determined not to say anything. He didn't have to, Erica did.

"Am I offending your sensibilities, Ed?" she asked glancing at the coffee table. "Do women disgust you so?"

Hanratty winced, and handed Erica her iced tea silently.

"Or is it that *I* disgust you?" she continued, unrelenting.

"Erica, the bitch kid of your bitch wife."

"Please," Hanratty said. "Not today. I'm not in the mood."

Erica gulped down the iced tea, then got up carrying all her equipment into the kitchen. She dumped her dirty clothes into the washing machine and laid out her belt, gloves, and gym shoes to air on the windowsill.

"That should make the turkey redolent," Hanratty said. "White meat with sneaker sweat."

Erica laughed. "If old Jean Fowler fixed it, it'll stand all the spicing up it can get. She's definitely a white bread cook."

"She was very nice to do all the work," Hanratty said defensively. "She didn't have to."

"She's hot for you, Ed," Erica said. "Only a woman in love goes to all this trouble."

"I suspect you're wrong there," Hanratty said, wondering if it could be true. "She's just a, uh, good employee and a friend."

"I knew it!" Erica said. "You're blushing."

Hanratty could feel his face redden. "If you start singing, 'Ed and Jean sitting in a tree,' I'm leaving," he said.

"You remember that song?" Erica said, laughing again.

"As a child you used to sing it all the time," Hanratty said.

"I was just testing the waters—for you," Erica said. "After mother—"

202

"Give me a hand with some of this food," Hanratty interrupted.

"Sure. Just let me take a fast shower." She grabbed the box of tampons and headed for the bathroom, leaving Ed standing in the middle of the kitchen looking for the pink frilly apron.

He had just tied the strings of the lacy apron when the doorbell rang. It was Ciano carrying a cardboard box.

"You look fetching, Cap'n," Ciano said, hefting the heavy carton.

Hanratty backed out of his way and let the lieutenant in. "What's that?" he asked.

"My clothes. I'm moving in," Ciano said.

Hanratty's outraged look said it all.

"Chill out, Cap'n. I'm just joking. It's wine. I didn't know what to get, so I got everything." He dumped the filthy carton on the chintz sofa and opened it.

Hanratty peered at Ciano's selections and was amazed at the man's bad taste. No, he corrected, not bad taste, lack of taste in any detail of civilized life.

"Will they do?"

"Your penchant in cooking wines and salad dressings is without equal," Hanratty said. "You are a true connoisseur of the inappropriate."

"Well, maybe you can use this stuff instead of Ben-Gay or to strip the paint off the bedroom floor," Ciano said, shrugging. "I don't drink nothing but Guinea Red mixed with Coke. There's a bottle of that somewhere in there. That is, when I can't get Jack."

"One Jack Daniel's coming up," Hanratty said, snatching the carton from Ciano. "I'll give this stuff a decent burial." He carried the heavy carton to the kitchen as if it were empty.

"Where's Erica?" Ciano called out to the old man.

"Taking a shower."

Ciano could picture her lathering her long, lean body with soap and he had to quickly put it out of his mind. Never walk around with a hard-on in front of your girl friend's father was an adage that sprang to mind.

Hanratty returned with Ciano's drink and a brandy for himself. They sat staring at each other, neither willing to say what was on his mind. Ciano had tried to thank Hanratty for his cooperation, but the old man wanted to pretend the death of Joseph Steppe had never happened. There was nothing to say, really. Ciano had allowed Steppe to drown, no, encouraged him to drown, and Hanratty had been his accomplice. They were locked in an intimacy that neither one wanted; they were at each other's mercy. It was excruciating for both of them.

Finally, Hanratty excused himself to check on the dinner and Ciano suggested he check on Erica, too. He didn't know how much more he could take of Ed Hanratty's silent accusations. Thank God for sour mash, he thought, draining his third.

In the steamy bathroom, Erica looked at her face in the mirror, liking what she saw. There wasn't a mark or a blemish to mar the clean lines of her face, no trace of the exhaustion she felt. She ran an index finger under her right eye, then her left. They were a bit puffy, she thought, but no sign of any discoloration, no god-awful dark rings under her eyes. She was relieved.

She slid open the box of tampons and pulled out a thin, tightly-rolled joint. Brushing her long tawny hair out of her eyes she lit it and inhaled deeply. The smoke from the marijuana mixed easily with the cloud of steam from the shower, enveloping her in a warm, comforting haze.

A few minutes later she could barely see herself in the mirror anymore, and that was what she was seeking—to lose herself completely.

After she had finished half the joint, she stubbed it out on her calloused palm. She felt like a schoolgirl, but even smoking a lousy joint in front of Ed would bring on World War III. He was too much of a puritan to approve, she thought, too much of a cop to pretend he didn't notice, so she was reduced to hiding in the bathroom.

From the box of tampons she took out a simple gold crucifix on a gold chain and put it around her neck. Then she dropped the roach into the box and closed it. Even Ed's prying cop mind wouldn't think of looking there for her stash, she thought.

When she made her appearance, Erica lit up the room. She was wearing a gray dress that swirled around her like an angry cloud, suggesting the lush body underneath, but revealing nothing obvious. Her hair was like burnished gold in a violent sunset. Ciano felt his heart race.

"Well, aren't we a glum group," she said observing the two men looking at their glasses of booze. "What a treat for me being at this wake. Maybe we should find a saloon somewhere and just get drunk."

Both men watched her intently, but neither one said anything.

The phone rang.

"Saved by the bell," Erica said, and went to answer it.

"For chrissakes, Cap'n. Let's cheer up a little and have a party," Ciano said, while Erica was on the hall phone.

"Sure," Hanratty said. "Some party."

Ciano was about to tell the old man where he could stick his party, when Erica came back in the room.

"It's for you, Vince. Captain Talbot. Another priest's been murdered."

Hanratty's usually pale face went ashen. He put his fingers to his mouth in horror, then raced for the bathroom to vomit.

Erica shrugged. "Ed never liked to party much, anyway."

Chapter Twenty-Two

Sergeant Joe Dugan was up to his Irish ass in children. His wife, Mary, a nurse, was working overtime at the hospital and wasn't expected until eight. They had planned to have their Thanksgiving dinner then.

Dugan was content, however, to be sitting in his brown fake-velvet recliner, watching football, and allowing his four kids to use him as a jungle gym. The four of them—three girls and a boy, all with red hair and freckles—scrambled over and around him while Dugan sipped a beer and pretended to be engrossed in the final minutes of the Bears' rout of Detroit.

Seven-year-old Sean, the youngest, had started hitting his sisters, and Dugan, after draining the beer, leaned forward and cuffed the boy across the back of his head, sending him sprawling and laughing to the floor.

"Get your old dad a beer, lad, and mind your mitts," Dugan said, handing his son the empty.

"Mind your own tits," the boy yelled, running off. The girls cuddled up with their father, delighted with his undivided attention, and glad that their little brat of a brother was occupied for the moment.

Tired of the slaughter, Dugan switched off the game and switched on the news. He was sorry he had.

". . . Staten Island again. Father Thomas McKenna, assistant rector of Sacred Heart Academy was found dead this afternoon . . ."

"Here, Dad," Sean said, holding out a can of beer.

"Shhh," Dugan said, taking it. He hefted the can. "Where's the rest of it?"

"Spilled," said Sean.

"Spilled my ass," Dugan said. "I'll blacken your eye if I catch you drinking my beer again."

Sean burped, then laughed, dodging his father's arm, pretending to be scared. Dugan turned his attention back to the TV.

". . . raising grave doubts about police claims that the murderer of Monsignor Bryan and Father Graff has been apprehended. Back to you, Steve," the reporter said on TV.

"Jaysus, Joseph, and Mary," Dugan said. "Get your coats, kids. We're going for a ride."

It had begun to rain when Ciano and Hanratty neared Sacred Heart Academy, their Thanksgiving dinner uneaten. Ciano was still furious at Talbot and cursed himself for letting the bastard call him every name in the book without retaliating. The truth was, Ciano knew the overbearing captain was right. He, Ciano, was a fuck-up.

"Slow down," Hanratty said, locking his grip on the plastic dashboard of Ciano's station wagon.

"Maybe it's a copycat," Ciano said hopefully, and increased his speed. He could hardly see the road through the cracked and clouded windshield. The worn wipers and dim headlights reinforced his belief that he was in some kind of nightmare, traveling as fast as he could into the void, but never reaching his destination.

"Could be a copycat," Hanratty said. "You've received a lot of press recently."

"That some sort of insult?"

"No. I just meant—"

"I know what you meant, but what do you mean?" Ciano asked.

"You mean, what if we've killed the wrong man," Hanratty said. "Do we turn ourselves in?"

"Something like that," Ciano said. "Are you going to recant your statement?"

"I don't know."

They parked by a blue-and-white, its lights flashing furiously. As they got out of the station wagon, the rain began to change to sleet; each droplet of ice caught the reflection from the whirling patrol car lights, giving the crime scene an eerie, luminous glow. Ciano pulled up the collar of his nylon windbreaker, thinking that the weather matched his mood.

Hanratty grabbed his arm before they pushed their way into the knot of cops gathered around the body. "Don't lose your temper, Ciano," he said. "You saw how far that got you."

Ciano shrugged him off. "I'll take care of it, Hanratty," he said.

Father Thomas McKenna's body had landed partially on a

cement walkway and partially on the muddy fringe of grass inside the Sacred Heart Academy compound. The top half of the priest's torso, from what was left of his head to his waist, was embedded a full eight inches into the rain-soaked loam.

Ciano looked up sixty feet to the top of the bell tower, then back at the body. McKenna's hips were on the curb, jutting upward in an obscene parody of a bump and grind movement. His legs, shattered on impact, were splayed at an odd angle. His pants were dark with blood and rain; a crust of sleet was beginning to form on his cold body.

"Somebody tossed him off the bell tower," Ciano said.

Hanratty nodded. "But look at his face," he said.

McKenna's face was merely a pulverized bloody mass of skin and protruding bone. His head seemed too small to be human. There just wasn't much left of the original shape. It had the condensed crushed quality of a paper cup that had been crumpled and thrown in the garbage.

"Somebody did a number on him before they tossed him," Ciano agreed.

"What amazes me is that the body is still intact," Hanratty said. "He should have been severed at the waist."

"Maybe he's got a tight belt," Ciano said, shrugging. "Maybe—"

"Hey, over here," a voice from the misty darkness called out. "I found something."

The circle of staring cops melted and flowed over toward the sound of the voice, some cops anxious to see another horror, others, moving slowly, afraid of what they might find. Ciano and Hanratty followed the crowd.

"Keep it on the concrete," Captain Talbot called out. "Stay off the grass, stay away from the corpse."

This crime scene's shot, Hanratty told himself. Talbot really screwed it up. It looked more like a carnival than a homicide investigation.

"Rubbernecks," he muttered to himself.

"Look who's talking. If this was my investigation, I'd kick your ass out, too," Ciano said, as if reading Hanratty's mind.

"What the hell is that?" a cop said.

Ciano and Hanratty looked at the pool of light formed by several heavy-duty flashlights. There was something on the ground, a lump of meat, a few pounds of gristle.

"He lose somethin' on the way down?" a cop said to no one in particular.

"Looks like he lost his lunch," another cop answered, pointing at the dark puddle of gore.

"Keep me away from McDonald's," a third said.

"All right, you men, make way for the Assistant M.E.," Talbot called out. He had found a bullhorn somewhere and was attempting to gain control of the crime scene.

James Young, fresh from his interview with Talbot and an hour from his Sino-American Thanksgiving dinner, moved in, his black medical bag dangling at his side. He bent down to look at the object lying on the concrete.

"It's a dog," he said. "A poodle, I'd guess."

"The priest musta landed on him," a cop called out.

Hanratty glanced around. "The angle's about right," he said quietly. "They threw the dog out of the bell tower, too."

"An easier toss with a lighter object," Ciano confirmed, moving away from the gawking cops and back to the priest's body. He was glad he hadn't eaten any Thanksgiving dinner.

"I fucked up," Hanratty said.

"Well, what are we going to do about it?" Ciano asked.

"It depends on whether Steppe killed West. If he did, we keep quiet. If he didn't—" Hanratty didn't have to finish.

"I was so sure," Ciano said.

"Maybe he jumped," Hanratty said, trying to be helpful.

"And maybe I'm the King of Siam," Ciano said. "His head hit the nice, soft dirt and at worst it should have broken open like a ripe melon—in two or three pieces. But look at it, it's like he got his head caught in a vise, or drill press. He was probably dead before he hit the ground."

"So where does that leave us?" Hanratty asked.

"Without a paddle," Ciano said. He walked around the body trying to clear his mind of everything except the case. He almost succeeded when he felt a tap on his shoulder and spun around.

"Looks like you offed the wrong perp, hotshot," Talbot said. He was dressed in a tan car coat and porkpie hat, and was wearing the supercilious smirk that made Ciano's blood boil. "Looks like our media star, DeFeo's pet, iced an innocent man."

Ciano stood his ground and took it, but he felt as hot as a stove and wondered why the sleet didn't hiss when it touched his face.

"Looks like you're suspended, Ciano, until we hold a thorough investigation and find you guilty of murder one," Talbot continued, relishing the moment. "Looks like—"

"Break my balls some more, Talbot," Ciano cut in. "And I make you and the priest a matching pair."

Talbot moved back a pace and recoiled with mock terror. "Oh, a threat. Write that down, Donnen," he said to an aide nearby. "I want this cocksucker up on charges."

Hanratty stepped between them, but Ciano moved the old man aside.

"Not a threat, Captain," he said to Talbot. "It's a favor, a citizen's duty to clean up the fucking garbage."

"Write that down!" Talbot roared.

"Write this down, asshole," Ciano said, grabbing his own crotch.

That's when all hell broke loose. Ciano lunged for Talbot, but Hanratty had him in an iron grip and managed to pivot him out of the way. Talbot feinted toward Ciano, but made sure Donnen grabbed him before he was close enough to mix it up with Ciano. It saved Ciano his pension and Talbot his life.

Like seconds in a duel, the cops at the crime scene divided themselves in two groups and surrounded the antagonists, putting considerable distance between the two and trying to calm them both down.

Finally, Hanratty got Ciano away from the cops and shoved him in the old station wagon.

"That was really a fine move, Ciano," he said. "You've got yourself in serious trouble now."

Unexpectedly, Ciano laughed. "Yeah. I was doin' real good before, wasn't I?"

"I'll drive you home," Hanratty said.

"Like hell you will," Ciano answered. "I may be a suspended cop likely to go to the slam, but I can still drive my own fucking car. I'm not dead or crippled yet."

"You're in no condition—" Hanratty began, but he was interrupted by the bright glare of approaching headlights.

A silver Ford Turino wagon pulled up next to Ciano's car and Dugan poked his head out the window.

"There you are, Lew," he said. "What's happening here?"

Ciano could see four small faces pressed against the glass in Dugan's car. "What are you doing, Dugan? Going for a ride in the country?" Ciano asked.

"Just thought I'd see if you needed any assistance," Dugan said. "Moral support? A drink?" He flashed his flask.

"That's a good idea," Hanratty said. "Why don't you go get a drink with Dugan and I'll drive your car back to my place."

Ciano shrugged. He could use a drink, then on the pretext of picking up his car, he'd pick up Erica, and lose himself in one of their wildly exotic lovemaking bouts.

"You can fill me in on the way," Dugan said, as Ciano got into the wagon. "And here," he continued, handing Ciano an unopened can of Bud, "you can start with this."

Ciano took the beer and tried to pop the top, but his hands were shaking so badly, he dropped it on the rubber mat at his feet. The beer began to hiss out of the partially opened can.

"Mind your tits," Sean said, looking over Ciano's shoulder.

Ed Hanratty drove Ciano's car with great care over the slick streets. Meticulous as always, he kept his speed at least ten miles an hour under the limit and braked the heavy wagon gingerly so as not to spin out. It took him almost a half hour to reach Holy Cross Church.

He had to ring the bell several times before Father Thomas Layhe answered. The priest was visibly upset.

"I've been calling the precinct all night," he said. "And watching the news. Is it true?"

Hanratty nodded solemnly.

"Well, come on in and tell me about it," Layhe said, ushering the old man inside.

In the priest's study, they made themselves comfortable; Layhe behind his desk, Hanratty in a brown leather chair. Hanratty gave him a brief rundown on Father McKenna's death, sparing no detail. As he talked, he watched for the priest's reaction.

"I didn't know him," Layhe said. "But I'm worried that the same person who killed him, killed Monsignor Bryan and Father Graff."

"We all are," Hanratty said.

"What do you think?" the priest asked.

Hanratty made a snap decision and said, "Do you remember Ichabod Crane in *The Legend of Sleepy Hollow*?"

"Vaguely," Layhe said. "The headless horseman?"

"Right. Well, you know that Ichabod Crane, the cowardly schoolmaster, really existed, here on Staten Island. Only he wasn't cowardly or a schoolmaster, he was a colonel in the army and served with Washington Irving in the War of 1812," Hanratty said.

"Interesting," Layhe said, bewildered.

"We found his tombstone a few years ago behind the Asbury Methodist Church on Richmond Road, and the Historical Soci-

211

ety was trying to persuade the late Jeanette Kidder Eddins to restore the monument and to move it, along with Colonel Crane's house, to Richmondtown.''

"Mmm," Layhe murmured, unable to see where the old man was headed. The radiators hissed and grumbled loudly in the brown-carpeted office; the sleet beat against the windows. A perfect night for a ghost story, Layhe thought. He hoped Hanratty had some purpose, however eliptical, in rattling on so.

"Anyway," Hanratty continued. "Irving loved the name 'Ichabod Crane' and appropriated it for his character, an act of creation that ruined their friendship and made Crane his mortal enemy.''

"As I said, that's an interesting story, Captain Hanratty, but how does it apply here?" Layhe said.

Hanratty took off his rimless glasses and rubbed his watery blue eyes. "You see, a legend is often based on reality, even if that basis is tenuous. Sometimes the reality is more interesting, sometimes the legend is more interesting, sometimes real people are mixed up in both, like the sensitive Colonel Crane.''

"And?" Layhe prompted.

"And sometimes a mind can gather a fact here and piece of fiction there and concoct a montage of the two, as Washington Irving did. To the uninitiated, the story is simply that, a single story,'' Hanratty said, putting his glasses back on and squinting at the priest.

"I'm sorry, Captain, but I've lost you somewhere along the line," Layhe said.

"Well, think about the deaths of Monsignor Bryan, Father Graff, and Father McKenna.''

"I haven't been thinking about anything else," Layhe admitted.

"Don't you see what's happening?" Hanratty asked.

"You mean a pattern?''

"Precisely. It's like the old mathematical puzzle with progressive numbers. You ask a person to give the next number in sequence. For example, 2, 4, 6 and the next number is 8. Then you ask 23, 28, 33 and—''

"The answer is 38. The numbers are progressive by five,'' Layhe cut in.

"That's where you're wrong, Father," Layhe said. "The answer is 42.''

"How can that be?''

"Those are stops on the Lexington Avenue subway. No matter

how brilliant you are mathematically, you'd never get the right answer because it's a trick. Perfectly obvious when you see it, but impossible to solve unless you have the key,'' Hanratty said.

"And you have the key to the murders?'' Layhe asked.

"I think so, but I want your opinion before I say anything to anyone else.''

"Try me,'' Layhe said.

"How did those priests die?'' Hanratty said.

"Well, Monsignor Bryan was crucified and flayed to death, Father Graff was beheaded, and Father McKenna was attacked and pushed off the church steeple,'' Layhe said. It made him shudder to think about it.

"Precisely,'' Hanratty said.

"Precisely what?''

"Don't you see the pattern?''

"I may be obtuse, but all I see is that they died horribly,'' Layhe said.

"They certainly did,'' Hanratty said. "But the key is that they died like the Apostles.''

Hanratty reached into his suit coat pockets and pulled out his notebook. "I've done some research, and according to what I've been able to find, Simon Peter was scourged and crucified upside down, James the Greater was beheaded with a sword, and James the Lesser was stoned to death and thrown from the pinnacle of a temple.''

"My God,'' Layhe breathed. "That's—''

"These are traditions, legends if you will, that are subject to interpretation and confusion. But they are facts in one clearly sick but creative mind,'' Hanratty said, closing his notebook.

The wind howled outside and despite the straining radiators, Layhe was cold.

"Someone is killing priests like the Apostles were killed. Can it be true?'' Layhe said.

"I'd say it's not only true, but that with three dead, there are at least seven to go,'' Hanratty said. "Since Judas hanged himself, and John narrowly escaped a violent death, that leaves seven Apostles' deaths to reenact.''

"What are we going to do?'' Layhe asked, still stunned.

"Go to Ciano, I guess. I wanted to see if you could talk me out of this idea first,'' Hanratty said. He looked at the bearded priest. "But obviously you can't.''

"That bastard Ciano,'' Layhe said. "Why don't you go to someone else.''

"Because if I'm wrong, they'll put me in a rubber room. And I agree with you about Ciano, he's a first-class bastard, but he can keep his mouth shut until we can verify this theory," Hanratty said, getting up from the chair. "Besides, he's just been suspended."

It was well past 2:00 a.m. when Ciano and Dugan came screeching to a halt outside Hanratty's.

"Thanks for the drink," Ciano said.

"Drinks."

"Yeah, them, too."

"Aren't you going to invite me in?"

"Are we on a date?"

"You shy?"

"Fuck you."

"Not on the first date," Dugan said. "You grab Sean and Carolyn, I'll take Ann Marie and Lucy, and we'll all say hello to Erica."

"You're out of your mind," Ciano said. "She'll kill us both, that is if we're still alive after Hanratty gets through with us."

"Well, I can't leave them in the car," Dugan said.

"You can take them home."

"Naw. My wife will be, shall we say, outraged," Dugan said. "And if I have to die at the hands of an outraged woman, I think I'd choose Erica." It was almost a sigh.

"You're crazy as a psycho-junkie," Ciano said, but he hefted the sleeping Sean into his arms and got out of the car. He opened the back door and grabbed a little girl, which one, he didn't know, and hoisted her sleeping form up next to her brother. Dugan had the other two girls in his arms, and together the two cops marched unsteadily toward the private entrance at the side of the building.

Ciano managed to ring the bell without dropping the children, and almost instantly Erica opened the door. "You two look like bag boys at the supermarket," she said, observing the scene. "Bring the groceries in."

She was still wearing the gray dress and every hair was in place. To a rumpled and half drunk Ciano, she looked almost too perfect, as if she had been preserved in acrylic.

Once they had arrayed the kids, head to foot on the living room couch, Erica told them that Ed was waiting for them in his basement workshop. "I'll stay with the children," Erica said, "on two conditions."

"What?" Ciano asked.

"One, that you tell me what's going on. And two, you come back upstairs when you're done."

"Me, too?" Dugan asked.

"Just to get your kids, Sergeant Dugan."

"No fun for the wicked," Dugan moaned. "No rest and no fun."

"Oh, by the way, Vince," Erica called after them. "Thanks for the truly wonderful Thanksgiving."

As they walked down the hall, Ciano could see that the dining room was still ablaze, the table set for guests who would never sit down to enjoy a meal. So much for holidays, Ciano thought.

They found Ed Hanratty perched on a stool at his workbench cleaning a .38 caliber Smith & Wesson.

"Looks like he expected us," Dugan said, putting up his hands.

"Sit down," Hanratty said, pointing the unloaded gun at two identical stools on the other side of his workbench. "We've got a lot of ground to cover and not much time." His tone was professional. "I believe I've figured out these killings."

"Who done it, Cap'n?" Dugan asked.

"It certainly wasn't Joseph Steppe," Hanratty said.

"How can you be sure?" Ciano asked, suddenly feeling sober.

"I can't. Not really. But look at the facts. Steppe doesn't fit the profile. Oh, sure, he haunted that church, actually had a lair, a nest there. But—"

"How did he get a hold of the priest's eyeball? We found it on him," Ciano asked.

"I can only surmise that he happened on the murder scene—he had opportunities, certainly—and picked himself up a souvenir," Hanratty said.

"Then he was a witness, not the perp," Dugan said softly, almost to himself. "Then, I repeat, Cap'n, who done it?"

"I don't know the who, but I think I know the why. You'll remember I explained about the difference between the psychotic and a psychopathic killer? Well, we're definitely dealing with a psychotic killer, one afflicted with a psychosis, a person who would never dream of killing anyone if it weren't for his mental disease," Hanratty said.

"What a relief," Dugan said. "We're dealing with a truly crazy person, not just your average killer."

"The perpetrator in this case will probably turn out to be a

215

David Berkowitz-type, an inoffensive postal worker who receives messages from Satan via his dog," Hanratty said. "The profile of this type of killer calls for an authoritarian personality, someone with an unhappy childhood, a domineering mother, perhaps—"

"What," Ciano said. "That could be anyone. You, me, Dugan."

"Captain Talbot," Dugan chimed in.

"True, but perhaps we can draw up a profile for the department," Hanratty said.

"Fuck the department," Ciano said. "Weren't you listening? I was suspended."

"Maybe we can be of some help, anyway. As a way of making amends," Hanratty said coldly, staring directly at Ciano. He cleared his throat. "As I was saying—"

"Hold it, Cap'n. You said you knew why these homicides were being committed," Dugan said, feeling uncomfortable suddenly. Hanratty and Ciano were about as transparent as two lovers sharing a longing glance that excluded the world. Only in this case, it wasn't love, it was disgust. He felt left out, and it made him nervous.

"Yes, I was coming to that," Hanratty said, and, consulting his notebook from time to time, repeated what he had told Father Layhe. He concluded by saying, "So somewhere out there, working as a clerk for an insurance company, or a construction worker or a fireman, is a person who thinks he has been commanded by God or the Devil or his dog to kill priests in the manner in which the Apostles were martyred. He's killed three and there are at least seven to go."

Dugan wiped the sweat off his brow. The last ten minutes had been the most frightening in his fifteen-year career. The idea that somebody could be that—disturbed wasn't a strong enough word—that viciously insane, ate at him like acid. It was monstrous, inconceivable, but Hanratty had made a damn good case.

"Let's get to work on this profile," Hanratty said, "and get it to Talbot today."

Ciano yawned. He was exhausted and could feel the effects of all the drinks he had had. Dugan wouldn't leave him, and while they were tossing them back, the children were amusing themselves with video games in the back room of the ramshackle Irish pub on Brian Avenue.

"You wouldn't consider postponing this, would you?" Ciano asked.

Hanratty shook his head. "It must be done at once. I want your input on this, your experience, and Dugan's. In a few days you'll be busy defending yourself against Internal Affairs, and so will I. We must make a breakthrough before then."

"And save our asses?" Ciano ventured.

"And save our asses," Hanratty confirmed. "I feel we can make a valuable contribution to the apprehension of this perpetrator—"

"Spoken like a bureaucrat," Dugan cut in.

"—if we can get Talbot some answers," Hanratty said.

Ciano yawned again, resigned, but Dugan seemed to suddenly get his second wind. "I'm afraid I don't quite see it that way, Cap'n," he said. "And that reminds one of a story I once heard—"

"Do we have to hear this?" Ciano asked. "It's late. Or early."

"I think you'll find it instructive," Dugan said. "And I won't stop bothering you until I get to tell it."

Ciano put his arms on the table and lowered his head. "Go away," he said, his voice muffled.

Dugan nodded, then began, "Well, it seems that young James Terrell got the heavenly callin' one day not long after making a hasty exit from Old Man Flynn's bedroom window, where Mrs. Flynn was poised in a most peculiar position, her being kind of naked-like and astraddle the bed.

"At any rate, young James' mother and Old Man Flynn decided that such a randy youngster—he was only about fourteen at the time—should have more wholesome outlets for his energies. So they upped and sent him off to St. Patrick's Seminary over in Galway.

"Now, they weren't expecting any miracles or nothin', but low and behold the boyo is suddenly struck with the callin'—a voice from God, he said—and sure enough goes on to become a priest, much to the delight of his poor old mother and much to the consternation of the widow Flynn, as the woman unhappily became sometime after young Jimmy received the nod from God."

"Get on with it, for chrissake," Ciano prompted, lighting a cigarette, knowing it was no use interrupting Dugan once he got started.

"Well, James, being a reformed hell-raiser, was one strict priest. Wouldn't stand for no fooling around a-tall. And with the seriousness of his twenty-one years behind him, he stepped into a tiny parish church near Connemara to become its new pastor.

"Now, this little town hadn't seen a priest in twenty years. Its small size and lack of funds made the bishop eager to sell the church to a supermarket chain or turn it into a disco. But he thought James might benefit from a little professional experience before they converted the altar into a deli counter. And so it was done.

"James arrived on a Saturday, pulled out his trusty priest's guide and discovered that this was the day for confession. Ah, confession, thought James, at last I'll be of some use to these poor, down-trodden wretches. And I won't let them get away with nothing, seeing as how I know all their tricks.

"So the word went out and the people flocked to the church with twenty years of sins on their consciences. This was in the days before television, of course."

"Of course," Ciano said. Dugan was driving him crazy.

"Well, this being a small town and all, the sins weren't that great—a few lies, a couple of steals, and a truckload of jealousy, envy, a smattering of miscellaneous transgressions, mostly of the venal variety.

"But much to his horror, he discovered a pattern developing in the confessions of the menfolk. It seemed that every male from twelve to ninety-two—there were a dozen of them—admitted to having intercourse with a woman named Pussy Green, the tailor's daughter. Old men and little boys, all enjoying her favors.

"Well, now, as you might imagine, this news terribly upset our reformed hellion, who had not even thought about a woman in seven years. He was very stern, indeed, in handing out suitable penance. All that night and into the dawn, the men of the town were Hail Marying and Our Fathering themselves hoarse.

"In fact the noise was so loud, Father Jimmy couldn't sleep. So he got up from his bed and began to compose a sermon on the evils of fornication, adultery, and sex. He consulted learned texts, ransacked the Holy Bible, and even called the bishop in Dublin to check his citations. He was going to throw the fear of God into those backsliders simply by using the power and majesty of his arguments. He was going to put Pussy Green out of business.

"And what a spellbinder of a sermon it was! For over an hour he cited examples of fornication, lust, and adultery for his mesmerized parish, many of whom began taking notes for future reference. Those were the days, by the way, before *Playboy*,

218

Penthouse and *Screw*, so those folks had a lot to learn—and avid they were.

"Anyway, as he's banging away at the sinners, he happens to look down in the front row of pews. And what does he see? A woman. A beautiful woman. She's about twenty-five, blond, and possessed of the biggest and most beautiful pair of knockers he's ever seen. Puts the widow Flynn's to shame, they did. He thinks immediately, that's the whore, Pussy Green.

"Well, he's ranting on about lust and such and he notices he's getting pretty lustful himself. He can feel his cassock getting drastic. So he gulps a few times and runs his finger around his collar to give himself more breathing room. Then he plows on.

"But before he can even damn the Whore of Babylon, he notices that the girl in the front pew, who's wearing a short white dress, is beginning to tug it slowly up her thigh.

"His voice breaks, it does, him not being much more than an adolescent, and he finds himself looking down at the girl's quiff, which is moist and all fluffy-like with blond curls. The girl's got one of her fingers moving toward the crack and poor old Jimmy can't stand it any longer.

"So he calls a halt to the proceedings, just to catch his breath and figure out what to do. But he can't keep his eyes off that beautiful snatch.

"Finally, he tells everybody to pray silently, and while they've got their heads down—all but the girl, that is, who is running her index finger in and out of herself—he calls to one of the altar boys.

" 'Son,' he says to the boy not much younger than himself. 'You see that girl in the front pew?'

"The boy looks down and smiles. 'Oh, yes, Father.'

" 'Well, tell me, son. Is that Pussy Green?'

"The boy takes another look, then shakes his head, 'Oh, no, Father. That's just the light coming in from the stained glass windows.' "

Ciano choked on a lungful of smoke, laughing and gagging at the same time.

"Jesus, Dugan," he rasped.

"So you see, Lew," Dugan said, his smile beatific. "Two people can look at the same thing and arrive at different conclusions. We did that with Joseph Steppe. So begging your pardon, Captain, it's the questions you ask that are important, not the answers."

PART III
Innocent Blood

"... I have sinned in that I have betrayed the innocent blood. . . .
And he cast down the pieces of silver in the temple, and departed, and went and hanged himself."

—MATTHEW 27:4-5

Chapter
Twenty-Three

I wake up suffocating in blood. My soul is polluted with the innocent lives I have taken. I long for the cleansing power of reconciliation—with my Church, with my God, with myself.

Iscariot is quiescent for the moment, though I can feel his fiery presence at the periphery of my consciousness. During this brief oasis of sanity, I must attempt to repair the damage he has done to me.

I want freedom from fear, freedom from Iscariot, freedom to love and be loved in a human sense. I long for the touch of someone who loves me. It is a childish wish, I suppose, but one that dates back as far as I can remember.

I never really knew my father, but I loved my mother, and she in turn hated me with a fierce passion that bordered on love— the love of inflicting pain and humiliation.

When I was young, my mother would take me into her bed to play a game she called "Hide and Seek." She would place a piece of hard candy somewhere on her body and encourage me to find it. I would explore her lush body, running my small hand over her breasts, feeling her nipples harden and hearing her gasp as I gently massaged those rosy buds. Then my hand would travel down her smooth stomach to the silky softness of the hair between her legs. I would search and feel around in that forest of hair, concentrating on finding the elusive piece of candy. Slowly, my tiny hand would intrude into the sticky wetness at the base of her belly and I would be rewarded with a soft moan of pleasure.

All I knew then was that my mother enjoyed this game and that while she was amused she would hug and kiss me, stripping me naked and taking my flesh into her mouth. The sensation of her hot breath on my naked skin excites me even now.

Later, when I was older, she and I would play this game less frequently, but with more intensity, usually while one of my surrogate fathers looked on, grunting with thick alcoholic desire.

Sometimes these men, hairy and so much bigger than I, would join in the game, their thick fingers exploring every part of me, their engorged maleness searching my smooth hairless body for any opening.

I am disgusted and ashamed, but I learned to play the game in self-defense. For when my mother was naked and panting at my touch, she would not be hitting me or pinching me or locking me under the kitchen sink for hours at a time. Sex, even in my unformed imagination, was not so much a substitute for love as an alternative to pain. As degrading as it was, sex was better than the daily beatings my mother dispensed during those times in her life when she decided our game was wicked. I would crawl into bed with her and begin to work my hand under her nightdress, hoping for her approval or at least her acquiescence. But she would grab my arm and twist it viciously, calling me disgusting, a devil-child—and worse.

For in her spells of repentance, she turned to religion as her solace. Not the religion of a just and loving God, but the religion of a terrible and vengeful God who could be placated only through flagellation, mutilation, and self-abnegation. She prostrated herself to the God of Abraham, the God who lusted for human sacrifice, but this God refused to give a last minute reprieve. I identify with Isaac, but he was luckier than I was, for the knife slashed through me many times, as did fingernails, burning cigarettes, scalding water, red-hot needles, and worst of all, the absence of love.

My mother hoarded her love for the God she called upon to save her, for she thought of herself as unique in his eyes. He tested her, she believed, more than others, demanding from her proof of her devotion, demanding the torture of her child as a sign of her righteousness.

She prayed a lot in those days, out loud, often screaming for the grace of God to protect her from the Hell of her own making. I was dragged to my knees to pray alongside her, aping her words, repeating phrases I didn't understand to a deity I despised. Sometimes, when I didn't pray loud enough or with enough piety to please her, my mother would strip me naked and whip me with a strap until my back and buttocks bled. It was a lesson, she said, a lesson in humility. Humiliation, perhaps.

My mother didn't teach me the Passion of Christ so much as indoctrinate me with it. I was brainwashed on the Crucifixion and inculcated with the Passion. The suffering of Christ became my suffering at the hands of my mother.

From an early age I was made to memorize and repeat in minute detail the scourgings, crucifixions, and tortures the Saints were subjected to by unbelievers. She taught me out of a book long revered for its sensational and gory illustrations of man killing man for the greater glory of God. It was a kind of ecclesiastical pornography that excited and disturbed me more than the magazines filled with naked women that my surrogate fathers would occasionally leave around the house.

I remember one picture in particular, printed on two pages in purple, garish tones. It showed an angry blue-black sky with jagged lightning bolts, obviously a sign of divine agitation, and on one side stood a gaggle of men dressed in multicolored robes looking smug and fulfilled. On the other page was a man hanging from a spiky, bare-branched tree, his eyes closed, his tongue protruding from his thin lips, his entrails hanging from his exploded stomach like snakes slithering from their nest. Beneath his skinny shanks was the entrance to Hell. Demons with pointed tails and horns lunged at the dead man with three-tined pitchforks, and the souls of condemned sinners wailed imploringly from the licking flames for Iscariot to join them in their everlasting pain.

To my childish mind, Judas didn't look happy to have betrayed Christ, but I could never understand why, if God were so forgiving, He didn't forgive Judas? After all, without Iscariot, Jesus would have lived to a ripe old age and retired to Heaven with nobody the wiser. Without Judas, there would have been no Christ to die for my sins. Without Judas . . . life would be tolerable.

Shaking off the past is difficult, for sometimes it seems much more real than the present. Especially when I am in the old house, hiding in the priest hole in the basement, waiting for him to come.

But I feel something extraordinary now, I feel his presence growing nearer, though I have not willed him to come. He is intruding on my mind while I am in my car, driving on an ordinary road intent on completing an ordinary task.

I am stopped at a traffic light, waiting for it to change, when the sudden hateful resonance of his voice penetrates my thoughts like surgical steel.

Lies, he hisses, and I think of his snake-like entrails crawling down his thighs. Lies and deceit, he says in his deep sibilant tones.

I look into the rearview mirror, expecting to see him, but I only see my own haunted eyes. I am frightened. This is the first time he has come uninvited. His power is increasing, I can feel it grow within me like a nova, expanding, filling me with raw power, unbridled heat, and incredible hate.

Car horns blare at me from behind, a grateful distraction from the urge to turn and face him. I coax my paralyzed body into action, anxious to pull over to the side of the road and face him. I feel his hateful eyes burning into the back of my neck.

Fool, *he says.* You thought you could break the Convenant.

His voice overwhelms the soft music on the car radio; I try to turn it up louder, but Iscariot's voice becomes unbearable, filling the car with a roaring laughter that makes the hair on the back of my neck stand up.

Desperately, I pull the car over, crunching through the brown leaves and beer cans that litter the side of the road. Wet evergreen branches envelope the windows, dimming the daylight. I close my eyes and the laughing gradually diminishes.

Encased in the cocoon-like arms of the tree, he speaks to me. You must strike again. Soon.

"Haven't I always done your bidding?"

You must strike before they catch you. They are close.

This is a new idea. As far as I know, no one has ever seen me, no one knows who I am or whose will I am performing. It cannot be.

Fool! *he whispers.* You must be more careful.

His voice is high-pitched, almost feminine. Like my mother's.

There is no escaping your destiny, just as there was no escaping me.

The words trail off, leaving me wracked with doubt and fear. But just for a moment I thought I detected a certain weariness in his voice. Does he grow tired of this game? This torture? Or perhaps his hate, which I believe fuels his existence, slowly dissipates, and he with it.

Suddenly, like a weight being lifted from my shoulders, I feel him depart. That makes my spirit soar until I realize he can now come to me at any time, any place. He is still lusting for innocent blood.

I start the car and drive away from my Tarsus, for I have many implements of death to acquire.

Chapter
Twenty-Four

Friday, December 3

"Is this the church where all the priests were killed?" Vince, Jr., asked Erica before plunging his face into an oversized ball of pink cotton candy. They were at the Christmas Carnival in the parking lot of St. Ann's and the boy was having the time of his life.

"Is this where?" he repeated.

"If you get any more of that stuff on your face you'll end up as human flypaper," Erica said lightly, trying to ignore the boy's startling question.

"I know," Vince, Jr., said. "My mom says I can get dirty just taking a bath."

"She gets angry when you're messy?" Erica asked.

"Sometimes," the boy said, taking another huge mouthful of cotton candy. "But not as mad as when I mess up my room. Then she *really* yells."

"Does she hit you?" Erica pressed on.

"Sometimes."

"Hard?"

"Sometimes."

Erica took him by his sticky hand and dragged him over to her car. "Let's go meet your dad," she said. She was uneasy with the child now, wondering if he had been abused by his mother. The thought terrified her.

She unlocked the door of her gray BMW and considered warning the boy not to mess up the leather seats and dash with his sticky fingers, but decided to say nothing. She didn't want to be as strict as his mother; she wanted him to like her.

"Is it?" The boy asked for the third time, unwilling to let it go.

"Is it what?"

"Is it where the priests got killed?"

"No, that was somewhere else," Erica said.

"Good," said the boy.

"Yes," Erica said. "I suppose it is."

Eight days after the murder of Father Thomas McKenna, Ciano was a beaten man. Always on the verge of despair even when things were going smoothly, he had been pushed too far this time. Taking away his job had taken away his life. Erica had tried to cheer him up, but he remained morose and had begun to let himself go in small ways: not shaving for days at a time, drinking too much, not eating, exploding with anger at the slightest provocation. He was clearly unhappy with his life and himself, and unable to pull himself out of his misery.

He had been scheduled for an IAD hearing after Christmas, but had managed to wipe the approaching proceedings out of his mind. He wouldn't see a lawyer or talk to Talbot. He dodged DeFeo's calls, and had even stopped talking to Hanratty.

His ex-wife, Diane, however, had suddenly become more important to him than ever. He found himself drawn to her physically and emotionally; he discovered that he wanted to be closer to his son. Perhaps it was a longing for the past, a kind of nostalgic relief from his present troubles. Or perhaps he had just lost confidence in himself and his judgment. Whatever it was, he felt that being with Erica, although exciting and fulfilling sexually, was an intrusion on his romantic nostalgia. And that was all it was, for Diane seemed perfectly content with Teddy, escaping for long weekends and leaving Vince, Jr., in Ciano's care. Six months ago he would have resented this loss of mobility, but he now had plenty of time on his hands and, strangely, Erica seemed to enjoy his son's company. He wondered if she were being nice to the kid to get closer to *him*. But that was ridiculous, he told himself, she could have any man she wanted, not just a beat-up ex-cop.

Maybe she wanted to get married, he thought, and she's showing me what a great mother she'd be. But that seemed a little farfetched to him. She wasn't even divorced yet, and he knew in his heart he'd marry her even if she hated Vinny. He was that horny for her, and he had a sinking feeling this was his last chance with a woman of Erica's special beauty.

He checked his watch—five p.m. He was late. Groggily, he went into the bathroom and turned on the shower. He rubbed his thick beard and supposed he should shave, but it seemed like too much trouble. The mere thought of stepping into the shower seemed like climbing Mt. Everest. How much easier it would be to crawl back in bed and drift. He was about to do just that when he remembered Erica's stern warning: *Shave. Don't be late.* For her, and his son, he would make the supreme effort.

He had his orders, and like a good soldier, he followed them, arriving at Hanratty's before six. He found Ed Hanratty seated on the chintz sofa watching the local news. The old man looked more tired and more emaciated than ever.

Hanratty glanced up from the television, saw who it was, and turned his head away from Ciano.

"Not home yet?" Ciano asked, standing in the living room, feeling foolish.

Hanratty shook his head. His eyes never left the TV.

"Mind if I sit down?"

Hanratty said, "Shhhh."

The pretty black woman on the screen was talking about a fire in Brooklyn that had killed a family of seven. Obviously those deaths held more interest for Hanratty than Ciano's company, but the cop sat down anyway, not taking off his new leather coat, a present from Erica to replace the one that had been slashed to ribbons by Joseph Steppe.

They sat in uncomfortable silence until Ciano said, "You ever give that psycho profile to Talbot?"

Hanratty nodded.

"What did he say?"

"Thanks."

"That's all?"

"That's all."

"You going to offer me a drink?" Ciano asked.

"No."

"Can I look at the report?"

"What for?" Hanratty said, his eyes glued to the screen. He seemed to have an abiding interest in an Alka-Seltzer commercial.

"So I can wipe my ass with it, Hanratty," Ciano said. He stood up to go.

"That's about what Talbot did with it," Hanratty said, getting up, too. He looked at Ciano closely for the first time. "Do you really want to see it?"

"No, I just wanted to bust your balls," Ciano said. "Of course I want to see it."

"I have a copy downstairs. I'll get it," Hanratty said. "Do you want a drink?"

"Sure." The old man was losing it, Ciano thought. He's off

229

in some other world doing his Houdini bit or practicing for Alzheimer's Disease.

"Help yourself," Hanratty said. "You know where it is. I'll be right back."

Ciano rubbed the closely shaven stubble on his chin and decided he'd hate to wind up like Hanratty—alone and losing his mind. That thought made him nervous and he walked to the well-stocked liquor cabinet and took out a bottle of Jack Daniel's and a glass. He poured the sour mash to the top, drank off about a quarter of it, and refilled it. He shuddered. It was his first drink of the day. It wouldn't be his last.

Hanratty came up the stairs, out of breath, carrying a manila folder. On the outside, in black marker, was written Ed's code name for the case, "Judas." He motioned Ciano to sit next to him on the chintz sofa and began to explain the results of his study.

It didn't mean much to Ciano, but he thought that if he could learn one positive bit of information from all of Hanratty's work, it would be more than he had now. He felt a gripping need to clear this case and clear himself in the process.

While Hanratty droned on, Ciano concentrated on his drink, mumbling the appropriate noises at the appropriate times, but thinking about the way everything had come down on him all at once. It was his own fault, he thought. He relied too much on gut instinct, his own sense of justice, and not enough on bureaucratic self-survival. He had gone as far as he would ever go in the police department and many felt he should be grateful to retire as a lieutenant. It wasn't gratitude he wanted from the department, however, it was action—action and some measure of respect.

"That must be them," Hanratty said, at last. Ciano heard a car turn into the private driveway at the side of the house.

He got up and went to the bay window and sat looking down at the driveway. Across the street the lights in the station house burned brightly in the cold night air; there was a hazy ring around the half moon.

Below, Erica shut off the engine of her BMW and called to Vince, Jr. Ciano watched them fondly from his perch in the window, marveling at Erica's beauty and his son's easy acceptance of her.

As he was watching the quiet domestic scene unfold beneath him, Hanratty came up beside him. He looked out the window and said, "You know, Erica's never had much experience with children."

"She's got the kid wrapped around her finger," Ciano said.

"That may be," Hanratty said, "but you shouldn't hand your son over to anyone, even to my daughter, without—"

"Without what?" Ciano snorted. "Doing a background check? Aren't you being a bit paranoid, Cap'n?"

Hanratty shrugged and sat down again at the coffee table, rearranging his report. "Let's get on with it before Erica gets here," he said.

This man's not too crazy about me fucking his daughter, Ciano thought, sitting next to Hanratty. Well, screw him. He was going to say something when he heard Erica and the boy climbing the steps.

"I'll just take this Xerox and study it," Ciano said, wadding up the paper as Erica came into the room. He shoved them into the back pocket of his jeans and caught Vince, Jr., as he came hurtling across the room to greet his father.

"How ya' doin', partner," Ciano said, hoisting the boy up into his arms. "Thanks for the drink, Cap'n. Would you like to join us for dinner?"

"Thank you, no," Hanratty said, politely, but with a hint of distaste in his voice. "I have other plans."

"Getting it on with Jean Fowler tonight?" Erica asked.

Hanratty's black look was fierce.

"Well, see you later then," Ciano said. "I'm glad everyone's safe and sound."

"You should be," Hanratty said, turning away.

"What's got into him tonight?" Erica asked. "What were you two whispering about?"

"Not much," Ciano said. "Poor Ed's got skin thinner than a ten-dollar rubber."

"Rubber what?" Vince, Jr., asked.

"Don't ask," Ciano said, leading the two of them out of the house.

They took his station wagon. "Where to?" he asked, having no real plans.

"I'm hungry," Vince, Jr., said from the backseat.

"You *can't* be hungry," Erica said. "You spent the whole afternoon pigging out on junk food."

"Yeah," Ciano said. "You mix that with real food and you could start a chemical reaction that will turn you green. And who wants a green kid?"

231

"The Jolly Green Giant!" Vince, Jr., screamed with laughter.

Ciano joined in, then Erica with her deep-throated laugh and Ciano thought he saw a whole new dimension in her. She had a vulnerable innocence at that moment that was devoid of the hip, glib, façade Ciano had come to dislike. If only it could always be like this, he thought.

"Where am I going to sleep tonight, Daddy?" Vince, Jr., asked suddenly. "With you and Erica?"

"Your father won't let anyone see where he sleeps," Erica said. "He's like a vampire. He sleeps in a coffin filled with his native soil."

Vince, Jr., looked wide-eyed. "No. You don't do you?" he asked.

Ciano laughed. "I'm going to drink your blood," he said in a bad Transylvanian accent.

Vinny laughed, but tentatively.

"Nope, we'll grab a bite, of food that is, then I'll take you back to your mother's," Ciano said.

"Can't we see your house? Please!" Vince, Jr., insisted.

"Yeah, Daddy, please!" Erica chimed in.

"Let's eat first, then we'll see," Ciano said.

"No! House first," Erica and Vince, Jr., howled in unison.

Ciano made a snap decision and headed toward Stonehenge. "But don't say I didn't warn you."

"My God," Erica said when Ciano turned on the lights in Chris and Dan's love nest. "And I was only kidding about the coffin."

"It's neat," Vince, Jr., said, looking around.

"It's more than that," Erica said. "It's a Hollywood conception of a French *maison de joie*. I can't tell you how much red-and-black velvet does for me. And all the leather! It's heaven."

"Hey, Dad. Look at all the leaves," Vince, Jr., said running over and stepping on the inch-thick layer of dead leaves that had fallen from the unwatered plants. "They crunch!"

Happily, the boy stomped the leaves into the filthy black carpet.

"This place could use a rake," Erica said. "Unless you want to turn the leaves under for fertilizer and grow corn here next year."

"I don't like plants," Ciano said.

"Well, you sure managed to kill these," Erica said. "You've got the original black thumb."

Ciano shrugged. "Wait until you see the bedroom."

Erica took one look at the round bed, and the mirrored ceiling and walls and began laughing.

"Why you old smoothie," she said. "You lure your women up here to your 1950s Playboy pad. Or do you prefer little boys?"

"Shhh. Not while my own little boy is walking around," Ciano said. "Besides, I warned you."

They moved back out into the living room, and Erica said, "I can't stand it, it needs to be cleaned. Or maybe tilled. But you can't live like this."

She peered around the kitchen looking for a broom, but couldn't find one. "You got a vacuum cleaner?" she asked Ciano.

He shrugged.

"A hoe?"

"Let it go. I told Diane I'd have Vinny back by six. It's almost eight," Ciano said. "Come on, kiddo. Time to go home."

"No," Vince, Jr., whined. "I want to stay with you, Daddy."

"Can't do, partner. Some other time. I've got to get you home before you turn into a pumpkin," Ciano said, his attempt at humor falling flat.

"I'm hungry," the boy said, stalling.

"See if there's a soda in the refrigerator," Ciano said, as Erica tapped him on the shoulder.

"She hits him," Erica whispered.

"Who hits who?" he asked.

"Your wife. She hits him."

"Nonsense. Diane's a good mother," Ciano said.

"He told me," Erica said.

"Kids will say anything," he said, pulling away from her. "Just forget it."

"I can't," Erica said. "It's so . . . so cruel."

Before he could reply, Vince, Jr., came racing around the corner holding the monstrously erect statue of David.

"Look what I found in the refrigerator, Dad," the boy said. "His dingaling's showing."

"And quite a dingaling it is," Erica said to Ciano, as the outraged cop reached for the statue. He was too late. The boy ducked under him and ran shrieking back to the kitchen. Just then, the bell rang, and the six-year-old, clutching the statue of David, streaked to the door to answer it. It was Diane. She was with Teddy and she was not happy.

"Mom, Mom, look what I found," the boy said. "Can I keep it?"

Diane's look of anger turned to horror and she said icily, "No you may not. It belongs to your father."

"Thanks, Diane," Ciano said. Of all the times, he thought.

"What are you two doing to my son?" she demanded, acknowledging Erica for the first time.

"Well, we're just through beating him and now we're going to rape him," Erica said coolly.

"For God's sake, Erica," Ciano said. "We just got here, Diane. The previous tenants left it in the refrigerator. I forgot about it."

Teddy laughed. "Sure," he said, a smirk on his face. "Hey, Vinny, let's beat feet," he called to Ciano's son. "Time to head out."

"You keep your mouth shut or I'll shut it for you," Ciano said, his hard eyes narrowing.

"You're two hours late," Diane said. "I called, I was worried."

"You're getting upset over nothing," Ciano said.

"I was *right* to be worried," Diane said. "God knows what goes on here with you and your sluts."

"It's James, Erica James," Erica said. "And I'm obviously not the only slut Vince knows."

"Come along, Vincent," Diane said. "Let's go before you get a disease."

After making a show of kissing his father and Erica, Vince, Jr., went along quietly.

"Well done," Ciano said. "You really handled that well."

"I'm not going to stand here and be insulted by that woman," Erica said. "What nerve, what— I don't know how you could have lived with her all those years. She's let herself go, she's not even pretty anymore—"

"Hold it, Erica," Ciano said, wondering why he was furious with her. "Let's not trash her all evening. Forget about it. Diane's one tough broad."

"She's one jealous woman," Erica said. "You may be divorced, but she's still in love with you."

"Yeah, sure," he said. He almost said something stupid like, "Do you really think so?" but he managed to refrain and led Erica into the bedroom.

"I can tell these things," Erica said. "She still loves you, she's jealous, and I don't like the way she's been treating Vinny."

"Well, I don't like the way you've been treating me recently," Ciano said, desperate to change the subject.

"You don't?" she asked, smiling.

"Nope. But you can fix that tonight."

Chapter
Twenty-Five

Saturday, December 4

Ciano woke up with a headache and a hard-on. There was nothing he could do about the headache without getting out of bed, so he rolled over and began caressing Erica's bare back, running his thick fingers up and down her backbone, counting the vertebrae. She shivered slightly and pushed her firm ass into his groin, mumbling, "Already?"

"Always ready," he said, misunderstanding her, and positioning himself to enter her. He thrust his hips forward in a fever to get inside of her. For that's what it was with Erica, he thought, a feverish yearning to screw her, a compulsion of some kind.

She was dry and tight and hot. He lunged forward carelessly, trying to ram it into her, trying to slake his thirst for her.

"Stop it, damn it," she whispered fiercely, pushing off him and trying to get as far away from him as possible.

"Come on," he pleaded, feeling ready to explode. "It won't take long."

She sat up suddenly on the edge of the bed, and for a moment she was terrified to see hundreds of blurry images of herself staring back. It was like seeing a reflection of herself in an insect's compound eye: alien and frightening.

"You can't leave me like this," Ciano whined, his cock purple and straining.

"The hell I can't," Erica said, getting to her feet and trying to remember where the bathroom was in Ciano's crazy apartment.

She padded groggily to a door and opened it to reveal the nude poster of Chris and Dan. Ciano hadn't bothered to take it down because he didn't use the closet. His few clothes were strewn around the bedroom, on top of the dresser and on the floor.

Erica moved to the next door, knowing Ciano's resentful eyes were staring at her. She opened the door to the bathroom, went in and shut out his prying eyes. She felt safe in the confined area.

When she came out of the bathroom, Ciano was asleep again; he still had a hard-on, she noted smugly, but he was breathing regularly, snoring a little.

She went over to the chair where he had thrown his tan cords and reached into the hip pocket. Ed's mysterious report, she thought, bringing forth a wad of typing paper. With her prize in hand, she retreated back to the bathroom and locked the door.

Sitting on the toilet, she unfolded the paper and began to read:

MEMO

From: Edward J. Hanratty, Capt. N.Y.P.D. (ret.)
  To: Captain Talbot
  Re: Psychological Profile of a Psychotic Killer

1) This memo has been prepared as a guide in the search for a suspect in the homicides of Msgr. Bryan, Fr. Graff and Fr. McKenna.
2) This profile is speculative and is in no way definitive.
3) *Background:* In my long experience in law enforcement, especially during my years reviewing homicide cases for the late Chief of Detectives, I have found that killers fall into two broad categories: the psychotic and the psychopathic killer.

  A. We are concerned here, we believe, with the psychotic killer, i.e., the person afflicted with a psychosis. This disease, for it can only be called a disease, is a mental disorder brought about by specific incidents in the victim's life. To wit: child abuse, sexual dysfunction, psychological and physical abuse, etc. These incidents become the origin of the psychosis and crimes committed by such an individual are inseparable from that psychosis. As one eminent authority has said, "Crimes as symptomatic of psychosis are as a particular rash is a symptom of measles."

  B. We believe that the elaborate, ritualistic murders of the Staten Island priests were committed by a psychotic killer, and that in addition to standard police procedure, some effort must be made to address the identity of the perpetrator *vis à vis* the contents of this report.

4) Elements of A Psychotic Personality

    A. The psychotic killer is generally male, though women have been known to fall into this category. Age: 28 to 40. We would estimate, that because of the extreme brutality of the crimes and their Byzantine elaborateness, that the rage inside the perpetrator has been festering for years—many years. Race: Caucasian, most probably. Religion: Catholic, almost certainly. Social Class: middle to lower middle. Occupation: Uncertain. Because of the duality of the psychotic killer's nature—at once a victim and the victimizer—his occupation may be an authoritarian one (teacher, policeman, supervisor) or one of little power (clerk, postal worker, utility worker, etc.).

    B. Education: High school graduate at least. Because of the religious nature of these crimes, perhaps we should investigate a failed seminarian. Military Training: very possible. The killer knows how to kill his victims quickly and also how to make them suffer. Perhaps a medic in the armed services. Marriage: Since many psychotic killers suffer from child abuse and cold, threatening parents, they seek to create fantasy families of their own. They inevitably fail. Life is not an episode of *Father Knows Best.*

Erica, sitting on the edge of the cold bathtub, chuckled. *Father Knows Best,* she thought, unable to think of Ed as knowing anything at all about families or children, little girls, in particular. She wondered if her aloof, austere father had ever watched Robert Young do his thing on TV. She continued reading:

Outwardly, the psychotic killer may lead a normal, if somewhat eccentric life. Only his family may suspect a mental disorder, but they are usually cowed by the psychotic, either physically or emotionally. Families, in many cases, have become a part of the psychosis and unable to see what is really happening.

    C. Sex: Although there was no overt sexual significance in the Staten Island homicides, the psychotic himself is generally sexually inadequate. Whether through childhood molestation by a parent, sibling or a stranger, or through disease, and mutilation, the—

Erica rubbed her eyes. Ed's dry, academic style was putting her to sleep. She scanned page after page of what she considered psychobabble, wondering if she was supposed to feel sorry for demented people who killed and to hate rational people who did the same thing. Dead was dead, she thought, the end was always the same, no matter what—or who—the means might be. Still, she read on, fascinated. The idea that someone was murdering priests—martyring them—was strangely compelling. She had no use for priests, considering them borderline psychos and closet homosexuals. Even her father's dear friend, the late Monsignor Bryan, had given her the creeps.

One portion of the report, however, caught her eye. It was listed under the title "Domination." Ed had written: "The psychotic has a compulsion to dominate, to be the final arbiter of all decisions that affect him, his family, and all those who work for him or even come in contact with him casually. He will deny that unpleasant topics exist and ignore any questions that might serve to undermine his authority."

Erica laughed softly. That would apply to every man she had ever met, she thought. Especially Ciano and her father. She read on: "The psychotic is torn apart by two sets of powerful and opposing orders. On the one hand is the Voice of the Devil, pleading, tempting, cajoling. This voice must be denied. Then there is The Voice of God, the voice that must be obeyed no matter how bizarre it appears to others. Noah obeyed God when others scoffed and he was saved. The psychotic knows this and believes implicitly that he is different from others because he has been chosen to be the Child of God."

She continued to scan the report, stopping to read that the psychotic often made chewing and sucking sounds in his sleep, an attempt to regain the breast that was denied him as an infant. She put the crumpled papers on the sink and opened the door to peek at Ciano. He was grinding his teeth. She shook her head and closed the door softly, admitting to herself that Ed's report—not so much his arguments, but the sheer weight of his material—had spooked her. She told herself to stop acting so childish and finished by reading the section Ed had called, "Disassociation.'' What it said was that the psychotic could experience a total blackout during attacks of his psychosis. His conscious mind would be unable to deal with the horror of his crimes and consequently he would simply forget. Was it possible that the killer of three priests could be walking around perfectly content and guilt-free because his mind didn't accept what he had done? Erica marveled at the concept. To her it seemed the perfect panacea. Imagine, she thought, having the unlimited freedom to—to do anything and not even be aware of it.

"Erica?'' Ciano's voice intruded on her sanctuary and her thoughts. She got up and went to the door. "Be out in a sec,'' she said, looking around for a towel. After what she had read she wanted a long, hot shower; the thought of sex with Ciano repulsed her at that moment.

At 9:00 A.M. Ed Hanratty checked his daughter's room and found it empty. Fuming with an unfocused anger, he tramped downstairs to the café. Jean Fowler, as always, was in the kitchen keeping everything together. He looked at her lithe figure and swept back salt-and-pepper hair, wondering if Erica was right about her. Could she be interested in him as a man? Hanratty sucked in his prominent potbelly and thought to himself that he should have shaved the white stubble from his face.

"Morning, Jean,'' he said.

"Hi, Ed,'' she replied. Her even white teeth were her own, he thought. His came out, like the stars, at night.

"Good crowd?'' he asked, as he asked every morning. And she answered as usual, "The best.'' She truly liked cops, he thought. She liked everything about them. He wondered why she had never remarried after her husband, a sergeant, had died ten years before.

Satisfied that everything was in Jean's capable hands, Hanratty wandered out into the café, saying hello to the cops he knew, shaking hands with some, patting others on the shoulder as they ate or drank breakfast, depending on whether they were coming on or off duty.

When he had made what he thought of as his glad-handing rounds, he retreated to his corner table. A waitress—he could no longer remember their names—took his order and disappeared into the kitchen. He had told the girl he wanted fried eggs, a buttered bagel, pancakes, home fries, and coffee. When she returned, she presented him with a half-grapefruit and decaffeinated coffee, compliments of Jean Fowler. Maybe Erica was right, he thought, maybe Jean does care for me. Or maybe she feeds me this crap because she hates me.

Hanratty was stabbing distastefully at the sour grapefruit when Joe Dugan pulled out a chair next to him, spun it around, and sat down, his arms resting on the back. "Howdy, Cap'n," he said. "Seen Ciano?"

"No," Hanratty said. "He's out with my daughter. Somewhere." Dugan's question had brought it all back. He could feel his blood pressure rising.

"Rather early isn't it?" Dugan said, consulting his watch. "Or rather late?"

Hanratty ignored him and sipped the weak instant coffee. "What's the point of drinking coffee without caffeine?" he asked. "It tastes like mud and water. The only reason to drink coffee is to wake up."

"Speaking of wake up," Dugan said, corralling the waitress. "Let me have a cold, frosty one, sweetheart."

"You're not working?" Hanratty asked.

"Still on vacation," Dugan said.

Hanratty regarded Dugan's pink cherubic face, his upturned Irish nose and prematurely gray hair. He looked like a stereotype, Hanratty decided.

"Say, Dugan," Hanratty said, making a sudden decision. "Have you got a couple of minutes?"

"I'm on vacation, Cap'n. I got lots of minutes," Dugan answered.

The waitress arrived with Dugan's beer. He took it with him, following Hanratty to the basement workshop.

"I won't keep you long," Hanratty said, bending down to unlock the gun box under the workbench. He pulled out a smaller box, gray and locked.

"I want you to keep this for me," Hanratty said, handing it to Dugan.

"What's in it?" Dugan asked, hefting it. It was not heavy.

"Personal papers," Hanratty said. "But please don't open the box until I'm dead."

"You planning on dying soon?"

"You never know," Hanratty said.

"Now wait a minute, Cap'n," Dugan said. "If you're sick or something, shouldn't you give your papers to your daughter?"

"I'm not sick," Hanratty said, irritated. "But as you may know, I've not been the best of fathers to Erica over the years, and I just don't want to burden her with these . . . papers."

"Well, okay," Dugan said. "I'll put the box in a safe place, as it were. Where's the key?"

"I'm not going to give it to you," Hanratty said. "When I'm gone, break it open."

"You're hoping that it will be too much trouble for me to peek," Dugan said. "That I'll let your secrets, like sleeping dogs, lie?"

"Something like that," Hanratty said, his watery blue eyes unfocused.

"Memoirs?" Dugan guessed.

"Bad memories," Hanratty said.

"Let's go skating," Erica said with an enthusiasm that was uncharacteristic.

"Vinny's with his mother this weekend, in case you forgot," Ciano said. He was tired, grumpy, and pissed off at having made a jerk of himself in front of Diane. But most of all, he was horny. That damn Erica had been up and dressed before he could lure her back to bed, he thought, feeling betrayed.

"No, just you and me. We'll drive into town, have lunch at Rockefeller Center and skate," she said. "You do skate, don't you?"

"Is a frog's asshole waterproof?" he said. "I'm a countryboy from Staten Island, remember?"

"I'll bet you'll fall on your big, fat, waterproof ass," Erica said, laughing.

They spoke casually on the way into Manhattan, both fearing silence, neither caring what they said as long as the conversation kept going. Several times Erica had tried to get Ciano to open up about his coming interdepartmental trial, but he brushed her questions aside. Disassociation? she wondered.

As they headed uptown on the FDR Drive, she tried again. "Vince, I'm not about to stick my nose where it doesn't belong, but if you'll at least listen for a minute, then you can tell me to mind my own business."

Ciano felt a twinge of uneasiness. She had been on him all morning. Obviously there was something bothering her, something she was having difficulty expressing. "Okay," he said. "I'm listening."

"It's about Vinny," she said. "He said yesterday that his mother hit him." She waited for Ciano's reaction; it was not what she wanted.

"So?" he said, his hands tightening on the wheel of the old

station wagon. "If he gets out of line, a smack on the ass may be necessary."

Erica looked out at the gray choppy water of the East River. "She hits him hard."

"What are you trying to say?" he asked, staring straight ahead.

"You don't discipline a child by hitting him. It's criminal. Not even animals should be treated like that," she said.

"I think you're getting a little carried away," Ciano said. "Besides, what the hell do you know about it?"

"I'll mind my own business," she said, wishing she had never brought it up at all.

"No, you want to make something out of it," he said angrily. Sensing her defeat, he couldn't help trying to make it a rout. "Are you saying Vinny's an abused child? Is that it?"

"I'm not implying anything," she said. "I'm only repeating what he said." She felt anger and resentment burning in her cheeks.

"Just what *did* he say?" Ciano asked, his voice cold.

"He said, and I'm paraphrasing, that his mother beat him when he messed up his room. And for other things. She hits him hard, and that's wrong. Terribly wrong," Erica said, not daring to look at Ciano.

"Look Erica, I think I know my ex-wife and I know she loves Vinny. If she hits him, it's for his own good," Ciano said. "A kid has to learn. God knows, I did."

Erica was silent, watching a squat, red tug glide by on the river.

Finally, Ciano said, "Okay, I'll talk to Diane tomorrow."

"Don't talk to her, Vince. Confront her. I can't tell you how important it is," she said. "I like Vinny and I'm concerned. You can understand that, can't you?"

"I guess," Ciano said, unconvincingly.

"Child abusers are usually victims of child abuse themselves," Erica said.

"You an expert?" he asked, thinking about his own father's big fists.

"Yes."

Ciano snorted. "You're telling me old Ed cuffed you around?"

Erica's eyes went dark. "My father never touched me. At all," she said.

"Well, my father used to beat the crap out of me and I didn't turn out so bad," he said. "I'm rich, charming, a genius—"

243

"It's nothing to joke about, Vince," she cut in. "I know. I've seen it. Seen the results."

"So have I," he said, wheeling off the Drive at 42nd Street and heading west. "On the streets. I've seen nine-year-old prostitutes, eight-year-old murderers, and forty-nine-year-old perverts who should have been stopped when they were ten. I seen it all, Erica, and Vinny's not like them and won't ever become like them. Believe me, I won't let Diane or anyone fuck him up."

The flags at the skating rink were cracking in a stiff breeze; the seventy-foot Norwegian pine stood tall and proud in its place overlooking the skaters. It had been there since early November, but had been lighted only three days before during the traditional ceremony. Like tourists, they joined the tourists, gawking.

Erica wrapped her arms around herself and the extravagant fur coat she was wearing. "Now this is the real New York," she said.

Ciano agreed, but he couldn't help scanning the swarms of people, looking for pickpockets.

They sat in a glassed-in restaurant looking out at the rink, and enjoyed a brunch that cost twenty-nine dollars each. Ciano would have complained, but Erica said it was her treat, and as long as she was paying, he thought, what the hell?

"It's nice to know a rich broad for a change," he said, demolishing his overcooked Eggs Benedict that reminded him of a kind of slow-food Egg McMuffin.

"Not so rich," Erica said. "My husband's lawyer sends me money every month and pays my credit card bills until—"

"—until you divorce him?" Ciano asked, drinking coffee.

"Or until I go back to him," Erica said.

"Yeah? You'd go back?" Ciano felt the eggs curdle in his stomach. He didn't know if it would be a relief or not.

"Could be," she said. "It depends."

"On what?"

"On many things. I want children, he doesn't. I like to stay close to home, he loves to travel. I like to fuck," she said, lowering her voice. "He likes to make love."

"So why don't you hit him with alimony that will knock his socks off and find somebody else?" Ciano asked.

"I thought I had," she said quietly.

"Me?" Ciano almost choked on his coffee.

She was silent.

244

"You mean, like marriage?" he asked.

She shrugged.

"How can I support you?" he said. "That coat of yours alone is about three months salary. And—"

"I'm not proposing to you, and I'm not putting you on the spot," she said. "I just think we ought to clear the air a bit and see where we stand." She paused, wiping her chin with a pink linen napkin. "I don't know the first thing about you."

"Like what do you want to know?" His hooded eyes were guarded.

"About your childhood, your marriage, what you believe, what you like and dislike. Everything. I want you to break down that wall you've built around you and share yourself with me," she said.

"Waiter, six Jack Daniel's," he said to no one. "That's one tall order, lady."

"Too tall?" she asked.

"Let's skate," he said. "Maybe the wind will blow my words away." He didn't know if he was flattered or pissed, a not uncommon problem when it came to Erica.

They rented skates and gingerly entered the counter-clockwise procession of little kids, tottering grandmothers, show-off teenagers and professional-looking couples Ciano figured were ringers or escapees from the Ice Capades.

Joining hands in the traditional crossover, they gradually picked up the rhythm.

Ciano knew he could lose her forever, but he took a chance and told her what he really thought. "You want to know about me," he began. "I'll tell you, but you won't like it."

"Go ahead," she urged, squeezing his hands.

"Okay, I was born in Staten Island. My old man was a Guinea bastard. He beat the crap out of me and my mother for years. Then he died and that was the happiest day of my life up to then. After that my mother beat the crap out of me until I was big enough to beat the crap out of her. She died and I've been on my own since then. I was raised a Catholic, but I hate the fucking priests who used to beat the crap out of me in between the beatings by my parents."

Erica stared wide-eyed at him. He looked away.

"When I was old enough, I joined the Navy, and because I was big and stupid and not afraid to die, they made me a SEAL. That's the Navy's equivalent to the Special Forces, but tougher and more elite. I can kill a man with my hands, with any weapon

245

ever made, a paperclip, a piece of paper—anything. You understand? That's what I do best; and I don't mind it."

Erica continued to stare at him. In horror? he wondered.

"Instead of staying on in the Navy saluting a bunch of fucking asshole civilians pretending to be officers," he said, "I looked around for a profession where brains were considered optional and killing was respected. So I became an accountant," he said, hoping she'd laugh. Erica did, but it was a nervous laugh.

A little girl about six, wearing an oversized red scarf, red mittens, and a red beret, shot between Ciano and Erica, almost toppling them. She was trying to escape her older sister similarly dressed, who was chasing her; they giggled hysterically.

"I married Diane and we had Vinny," he said, dropping Erica's hands to right himself. "She didn't like me to like my job so much and divorced me. You said it yourself, she's a jealous woman—jealous of my job, not me," Ciano said.

They skated half a circuit before he continued. "I believe that life sucks and then you die. That ninety-nine percent of the people on earth are either too stupid to talk to or actively out to hurt you. That the line between civilization and barbarism is thin and blue, and that I'm on the goddamn front-lines. Life may be shit, but there are moments—and I want all the moments I can get before I spend the rest of time rotting in a cold grave."

He finally got up the nerve to look at her. A tear coursed down Erica's cheek. "That's—that's the most cynical, corrupt philosophy I've ever heard," she said, skating away from him as if she were being pursued.

Ciano slowed down and watched her go. "Hey!" he shouted after her. "I still like to fuck." But she didn't hear him. He had blown it again.

Chapter
Twenty-Six

Ed Hanratty looked down the barrel of a Charter Arms .357 Magnum and squeezed off two rounds into a dressmaker's dummy wearing a bullet-proof vest. The sound of the big gun was thunderous in the confined basement shooting range. He walked slowly to the target knowing what he'd find, but somehow hoping he was wrong.

The teflon-coated bullets had passed clean through the vest, the dummy, and into the padding at the back of the range. Another failure, he thought, used to it by now. His new type of body armor was just not good enough. That meant his materials were faulty or his theory of wave modulation was wrong. At this point, he didn't care which. He found it impossible to shake the troubling thoughts that dominated his waking hours and prevented him from getting a good night's sleep.

He carefully unloaded the bullets from the Magnum and cleaned the inside of the barrel with cotton swabs; then he put the gun in a locked box under his long workbench.

Valiantly, he tried to shake off his depression by telling himself that he was at last taking action; that his days and months of quiet introspection were coming to an end. He knew who killed Monsignor Bryan, Father Graff, and Father McKenna. Now all he had to do was prove it.

He sat in the disintegrating armchair and thought about Erica and Margot, and about how one man could ruin so many lives when all he had ever tried to do was help. His, he decided, had been a sin of omission, a sin that could be atoned for.

He had already insured his salvation by passing information along to Dugan. Now he would try to save his soul. He called Father Layhe and made an appointment to see him immediately.

Father Layhe opened the rectory door for Hanratty. He had been dreading the moment, and although he wouldn't admit it, Hanratty's aloof, otherwordly manner made him uncomfortable.

He couldn't decide if the man was a saint or a devil pretending to be a saint. Hanratty's wan, ravaged face, his crooked, bent-over posture and watery blue eyes reminded Layhe of a picture he had once seen. It was in a book of religious paintings. It was called *Guilt*.

Layhe led Hanratty to his brown-carpeted office; they sat as far away as possible from each other. Layhe was determined to keep this unpleasant business as short and as impersonal as possible. "The housekeeper is not due until one, so I can't even offer you coffee," he said to Hanratty.

Hanratty could smell the faint aroma of brewing coffee coming from the kitchen. "I understand," he said, smiling sadly. He did.

"Shall we begin?" Layhe asked, shifting uneasily in his brown leather chair.

"Of course," Hanratty said. "I won't take up much of your time, but first I have a few questions about Monsignor Bryan."

Layhe made no effort to hide his annoyance. "Mr. Hanratty," he said. "You requested the sacrament of reconciliation and I agreed to hear it because it is my duty as a priest and because, let's face it, you're an important person in this parish. But I won't be questioned about Monsignor Bryan again. I have told you and the police all I know. I am drained of information. If any questions remain unanswered then it's safe to say that they went to the grave with Monsignor Bryan. *Requiescat in pace.*"

Like an actor, Hanratty paused for effect, trying to upstage Layhe's outburst with his silence. Finally, he said, "Was a head-stone ever erected for my friend, Monsignor Bryan? Since the funeral I had been meaning to ask. But you know how busy we have all been."

Bryan had been buried at St. Mary's Retreat on Long Island. The priest was embarrassed.

"St. Mary's provides. Nothing elaborate, but sufficient for the monsignor's simple tastes," Layhe said.

"You know nothing of his tastes," Hanratty said. Then to soften his ill-considered words, he added, "but I'm sure that whatever was provided will, indeed, be adequate."

"And now for the confession and reconciliation?" Layhe asked.

An hour later, a confused and frustrated Layhe was in his car driving across Staten Island to Sergeant Dugan's house. He had had enough of cops, enough of murder, and enough of his calling. Sometimes, he thought, he just couldn't stand it another minute. He felt like a vulture, feeding off the carrion of other people's misery, gorging himself on their sins, and drinking in their petty, shameful secrets.

Ed Hanratty's reconciliation had been an excruciatingly slow process. To Layhe it wasn't really a confession at all, but a massive expenditure of decades of unspecific guilt. He had forced himself not to scream with boredom as the old man had rattled on about his unfaithful wife, ungrateful daughter, and some kind of overwhelming guilt he felt about them both. Layhe had asked enough questions to feign an interest and to keep himself from going mad with ennui. Mercifully, it had come to a sudden conclusion when Hanratty mentioned the murder of Monsignor Bryan. There had been something in the retired captain's voice, something hard and determined, that had shaken Layhe out of his lethargy. He tried to question Hanratty further, but the old man had evidently disgorged enough sins for the moment and indicated that he was through.

Layhe had administered absolution, and when they had shaken hands, the priest had noted a change in Hanratty. The ex-cop seemed more relaxed, his face was curiously smooth and unlined, his eyes positively ethereal—the look of a religious martyr or a fever victim. Layhe didn't like it.

"I am going to spend some time with the monsignor," Hanratty had said.

Layhe didn't like that either, but he had decided he had bigger problems to worry about. The police had asked for his help, and as much as he hated the idea, he hadn't been able to think of an excuse when Dugan had called. Kicking himself mentally, he drove recklessly toward a fate he couldn't imagine.

While Father Layhe was fighting the traffic and his own unsettled emotions, Sergeant Joseph Dugan was lying on the floor of his living room, trussed up like a chicken ready for the oven.

"I may be your Gulliver," he said to his children, "but for heaven's sake, free my right hand so I can get my beer."

The three girls laughed and Sean, Dugan's seven-year-old son, used the opportunity to jump on his father's stomach. "Bombs away!" the boy yelled before he landed.

"Jesus, Mary, and Joseph," Dugan gasped. "You'll wreck my kidneys and I'll be unable to put out your fire later on."

Ciano sat on a plaid, discount-house couch and watched Dugan playing with his children, thinking that they got along so well, there must be a reason. Then it hit him. "You got the brain of a child," Ciano said.

"And the disposition of a saint," Dugan said, straining to sit up to sip his beer.

"No, seriously, Dugan. You think like them and act like them. You *are* a child," Ciano said. "And this plan of yours is childish, stupid, and dangerous."

"Perhaps," Dugan said. "Maybe that's because it was Sean's idea."

Sean, hearing his name, looked up and grinned at Ciano. "You're next," the boy said.

"Come near me with that rope and I'll shove my size eleven Italian shoe up your size four Irish ass," Ciano said. "I'm not into B & D."

Sean laughed and stuck out his middle finger at Ciano when his father wasn't looking. "Your kids are a powerful argument for birth control," Ciano said.

"To tell you the truth," Dugan said. "My wife and I use the bucket and turnip method."

"What the hell is that?" Ciano asked, intrigued, in spite of himself.

"Well, as you know, the Mother Church frowns on the use of mechanical devices and chemicals to prevent conception. My wife and I use an ancient Irish form of birth control that is one-hundred percent as natural as the rhythm method." Dugan paused, tried to get to his beer, but Sean had somehow tied his right hand to the leg of the glass-and-chrome coffee table. Dugan sighed and continued. "Now, as you know, my wife's a great tall woman and I'm but a shrimp of a man, not much bigger than Sean here. So when we're in the mood to procreate I stand on the bucket—for leverage and position."

Ciano wasn't fooled, he could hear the punch line coming. "Okay, Dugan. What about the turnips?"

"Well, we go along nicely until my eyes get as big as turnips, then she kicks the bucket out from under me," Dugan said, laughing. "No muss, no fuss—"

"And no more Seans," Ciano said, defending himself from a full-fledged charge by Dugan's kids determined to tie him to the couch.

"That's the bucket and turnip method," Dugan said. "Though some say we should have practiced it sooner."

"Keep practicing it until you get it right," Ciano said, trying to act disgusted, but he admired Dugan's closeness with his children. He and Vinny were getting to know each other, but a barrier remained, an uncharted area of unquestioning trust. It was something, Ciano imagined, he had to earn.

"Okay, Dugan," Ciano said, grabbing Sean with one hand and tossing him softly to the other end of the couch. "Enough fooling around. Tell me why you wanted me to come here. And don't give me more crap about that stupid plan of yours."

Dugan smiled as two of his daughters escaped Ciano's clutches and ran to their father. One of the girls looped a rope around Dugan's neck. "Ah, I have two visitors coming," he said, keeping a wary eye on the girls. "Visitors bringing gifts of incense, frankincense, and information." One of the girls tightened the noose.

"You shouldn't be doing that, darlin' " Dugan said. "If you throttle your dear old dad, they'll be no Santa Claus this year."

"Choke him," Ciano told the girl. "I got a hook at the North Pole."

"Gads," Dugan croaked. He closed his eyes and stuck out his tongue in mock death. Sean, seeing his father in trouble, jumped off the couch to go to his rescue. He leaped on his sisters and the three of them went tumbling and rolling on the floor.

"Saved at last," Dugan said, untangling himself and sitting up. "Children," he said. "Enough." But they paid no attention to him. Dugan struggled, rescued his beer, and sat on the couch next to Ciano. "It will work, you know," he said to Ciano.

"And you'll never work again if they catch you. You can't run your own police department," Ciano said. "Your brain is destroyed from too much booze."

"Childlike perhaps," Dugan said. "But not destroyed. I've got Father Layhe and Marty Abel coming over."

"What a fun day," Ciano said.

"We can work this out," Dugan said.

"We can all go to jail."

"Have you ever thought that to catch this perp, we have to use unconventional means?"

"Unconventional, yes. Stupid, no," Ciano said.

"We've got to stop this soon," Dugan said, suddenly serious. "And this is the only way I know. I think we are close to knowing who did this, and I think that we're confused by what we've seen so far. We all agreed it was Steppe, then that didn't pan out."

Ciano winced. He still couldn't shake the scene on the bridge from his mind. He knew the little fuck was guilty of something and the death of Father McKenna seemed to confirm it. "You mean the two perps?" he asked.

"A possibility," Dugan said, finishing his beer and sending Sean for two more, one for Ciano.

"I think we're looking right at the answer, but we're too dumb to see it," Dugan said. "Which reminds me of the story about a couple of boyos out on the town in Dublin. They had just shared a winning lottery ticket and decided to keep this news from their darling wives. Wives, as you know, tend toward the practical and abhor the ephemeral. They loathe the spiritual but insubstantial pleasures of drink and sex."

Ciano leaned back on the plaid couch and closed his eyes. He didn't have the strength to stop Dugan.

"So, not wanting to invest their windfall on a telly, or some such foolishness, they decided to blow the whole wad on a magnificent night on the town—a legendary pub crawl that would leave them minus a few million brain cells, but happier than they had been in a long, long time.

"So they rented evening clothes and hired a car, and as the sun sank down behind the gray stone buildings of Dublin, they started out.

"Well, it was a hell of a night. Along about nine o'clock, Michael and Costello, for those were their names, were tighter than a parish priest's purse. For being country boys, they were not used to the strong brew of Dublintown, and they were sore amazed at the sheer number of pubs, restaurants, hotels, and cafés where the Devil's own brew was sold. The money was holding up fine, but they were pretty well gone.

"Well now, they're in a pub called O'Casey's, and Costello looks down at the end of the bar and spies this tall, lanky bugger with a derby hat and a bright red muffler.

" 'Say, Michael,' Cos said, 'Ain't we seen that git down at the end of the bar someplace before?'

" 'You're right, by God. I remember that scarf and derby,' Cos said. 'We've seen him twice now.'

"So they went on to the next pub and sure enough, after a pint or two, they see the same fellow at the end of the bar—red scarf, derby hat, and all. 'Jaysus, save us,' Michael says. 'It's the Shaun Vaughn.'

"Now for uninitiated Eye-talins like you," Dugan said, grabbing the two beers from Sean, and handing one to Ciano, "the Shaun Vaughn is the Irish Angel of Death, and as country folk

252

would have it, if you set eyes on him thrice in one day, you're the next to go to your reward.

"Now being from the country and all, and being plastered like a wall, and feeling guilty about spending their ill-gotten gain, Michael and Costello were scared out of their shoes. 'It's the will of God,' Michael wailed. 'He's sent the Angel of Death to fetch us to his bosom!'

" 'I'd be happy enough with that,' Costello said. 'But I think by the looks of that red scarf, we're headed in the other direction.'

"Well, they drank their drinks as fast as they could, knowing their time was up and the brew they were drinking might be their last. Then, screwing up their courage they approached the Shaun Vaughn, who was sipping away on his drink like nothing in the world.

" 'Oh please, yer Majesty?' Michael says, falling down on his knees. 'I've a wife and five youngsters to care for. Please don't take me.'

"And the man in the red scarf looks down at him and says, 'I'd say it's time I took you out of here.'

"Well, with that, Costello also falls to his knees and pleads for mercy. But the man in the derby is adamant. They have to go.

"So now they're both down on the floor, their arms wrapped around the Shaun Vaughn's legs, cryin' and beggin' and in general making fools of themselves. Finally, in desperation, Michael cries out, 'Oh, my mighty Angel of Death, spare us, save us, we'll be your willin' slaves!'

"And with that, the man in the derby and red scarf pulls himself away from the clinging drunks and looks down at them in disgust.

" 'What did you call me?' he asks.

" 'Why, you're the Shaun Vaughn, aren't you?' Michael says. 'The Angel of Death.'

" 'Why you poor lunatics,' the man in the derby says. 'I ain't no angel.'

" 'That's not so,' Cos cries. 'We've seen you in every pub we've visited.'

" 'Well of course you have, you silly bastard,' the red-scarfed man says. 'I'm your fooken taxi driver, and your time's up. We gotta go!' "

Ciano groaned. "Thanks," he said. "I didn't need that."

"But you see the point," Dugan said. "We've been looking

at the wrong perp. We thought Steppe was the man because we saw him everywhere we looked. But he was no angel of death, just the taxi driver. We're letting ourselves be carried away with the exotic, when the mundane is usually the answer.''

"I was right," Ciano said.

"About what?''

"About your brain being destroyed. I'm getting the hell out of here before I catch whatever mental disorder you got,'' Ciano said, putting his half-full beer down on the coffee table and getting up.

Dugan looked at his watch. "Just five minutes more.''

Grudgingly, Ciano sat back down and took a long pull on his beer. "The meter's running.''

Fifteen minutes later the bell rang and Detective Marty Abel arrived. He stood awkwardly in the hallway, shifting his weight from one foot to the other and blowing on his hands. "Cold out there,'' he said, stupidly.

After a minute of watching Abel stew, Ciano said, "Don't mind me, Marty. I'm just the maid.''

"I didn't, uh, expect—''

"Nobody expects Lieutenant Ciano,'' Dugan cut in. "He's like death, rather than taxes. Always unexpected. Get you a beer?''

"Huh? Uh, sure,'' Abel said, not understanding much of what was going on. His only concern was to cover his ass in all directions. He knew Ciano was on Talbot's shit list, but then he had seen Ciano best Talbot by catching up to Steppe. He didn't know who was going to win the current battle, but he wanted to be sure to be on the right side.

"Talk to me,'' Dugan said, after he had returned with a beer and had shooed the children out of the room.

Abel cleared his throat. "We got a rundown on that coin, that Lepton,'' he said. "It was brought into the country by a local importer, but the records from there get all screwy.''

"Screwy?'' Dugan asked.

"The guy who runs the company is nowhere to be found, and apparently nobody else in his office knows where the coins went,'' Abel said, taking a bird-like sip of his beer. "The nails they used on that first priest were dated as antique—about two thousand years old, but nobody knows where they came from.''

"Any other physical evidence?'' Dugan prompted.

"No,'' Abel said. "That's what makes this case so hard. No

physical evidence left at the scene of McKenna's homicide. No prints, anyway. And if anybody was up in that bell tower, the wind and snow blew the evidence away. We only got coins and nails. Mrs. Eddins died of a heart attack and the West woman, by the way, died of internal hemorrhaging.''

"Anything new on that one?'' Ciano asked, trying to be casual.

"Yeah, you'll be glad to know that she was killed by Joseph Steppe, according to the M.E. He matched the knife wounds on her body with Steppe's leaf spring sword. But it was not used to whack off Father Graff's head, so that one's still up for grabs.''

Ciano felt a hundred pounds of guilt lift from his shoulders. At least Steppe hadn't been an innocent bystander.

"That ought to make you happy, Lew,'' Abel continued. "Knowing Steppe didn't die in vain.''

"Never thought he did,'' Ciano said. "It was an accident, anyway. His own fault.''

"Sure,'' Abel said, with a smirk. "Whatever you say.''

"Yeah, Abel. That's what I say. You got a problem with that?'' Ciano wanted to smash the little fuck's face into the wall.

"Whoa, Lieutenant. I don't want to start nothing with you,'' Abel said, putting his hands up, palms forward, as if he were pushing Ciano away.

"Get out of here, you little shit,'' Ciano shouted at him. "Get the fuck out of my sight!''

Abel rose and sidled toward the door. "All I was doing was helping you. Jeeze. That's always—''

Ciano flung his empty beer can at Abel; it hit him on the chest. "Hey! Lew!'' Abel yelped, grabbing for his coat in the hall.

"Go back to Talbot and tell him he can kiss my ass,'' Ciano roared. It had been a long time since he had felt confident enough to piss off the cops. Abel was a worm, and Ciano was tired of being dumped on by the Talbots, DeFeos, and even the smarmy little slimes like Abel.

"Well, now you've done it,'' Dugan said, when Abel was gone. "Ruined my reputation as a host.''

"Fuck him,'' Ciano said, smugly.

"Fuck him,'' Sean Dugan yelled, running into the room. "Neat-O. Can I throw a beer at you?''

"No,'' Dugan said. "Get up to your room.''

"Fuck him,'' Sean said.

"The back of my hand to ya,'' Dugan threatened.

"Aww," Sean said, but he wandered out of the room, completely unintimidated.

"And I'll thank you not to be teaching my children them bad words," Dugan said.

"We all got to recognize shit so we don't step in it," Ciano said, leaning back on the couch totally satisfied. He wondered how long it would take Abel to report this to Talbot.

"Seriously, you shouldn't have done that," Dugan said. "As miserable a little swine as he is, Abel was my best link with the task force operating out of the precinct. It will make my plan a lot harder."

"Your plan sucks—" Ciano started, but stopped when the door chimes rang out a short rendition of *Danny Boy*.

"Jesus," Ciano said. "Abel's lost the way to his car."

"Father Layhe, no doubt," Dugan said, getting up. "Our Judas goat. You know what that is, don't you?"

"The national bird of Ireland?" Ciano said.

"Come in, Father," Dugan said, from out in the hall. "Welcome to my house."

The priest's reaction to Ciano was similar to Abel's—shocked—but he hid his feelings better than Abel.

Ciano, however, was feeling cocky, justified. He ignored the priest and stood to go.

"I'll tell you one last time—forget it," he said to Dugan.

"I got to do what I got to do," Dugan said.

"It will kill you," Ciano said. "And you, too." He looked at the priest for the first time.

Sean Dugan ran back into the room to inspect the new visitor. "Say hello to Father Layhe," Dugan said to his son.

"Fuck him," Sean said, and ran from the room.

Ciano laughed, while Dugan and Layhe looked embarrassed. "I'm sorry about that, Father," Dugan said. "Sean's an impressionable child—"

"Who's been keeping bad company," Layhe said, returning Ciano's stare.

"What's the matter Layhe?" Ciano said. "You so out of it you never heard that a little child shall lead them? He's only expressing my feelings, and the feelings of half the world about you priests. Fucking parasites, sucking the blood out of old ladies and little kids by telling them lies about heaven and hell. You make a comfortable living for yourself by scaring the shit out of them. If there is a God, he ought to curse you and make you burn for all eternity."

Layhe said nothing; instead he looked accusingly at Dugan, burdening the Irishman with the job of defending him.

"I invited the Father here to discuss my plan," Dugan said. "Not to be insulted by the likes of you. You owe the good Father an apology."

Ciano saw Dugan's anger, but there was no way he would weasel out of it. "I don't apologize for the truth," Ciano said.

"Then, I'll ask you to leave," Dugan said.

"Please, Sergeant Dugan—" Layhe began, but Ciano cut him off.

"Your kid was right, Dugan. Fuck both of you. There's a sick, dangerous nutcase running around out there, and he won't be suckered into your crummy plan. You and your fucking Judas goat here better wise up to that or you can catch a real bad case of death." He grabbed his coat and left without saying anything else. There wasn't much to say. In one short afternoon he had alienated Erica and Dugan. Now he was alone and that's the way he wanted it.

Chapter
Twenty-Seven

Absolutely alone. *My God, what a glorious feeling! To be cut off from the snorting, squealing pack of pigs that call themselves human, to be hidden from the great mass of evil energy known as God, that is the pinnacle of human experience. Alone.*

My entire childhood was spent seeking peace. Whenever I found it, as I was hidden away from life and death in my secret priest's hole in the basement of the old house, something would always jerk me back to my mother's version of reality. I can still feel her short, stubby fingers probing my naked body, intruding into areas that were never meant for her—or for anyone. I can smell the whiskey on her breath and feel the obscene strength of those men with whom she shared her bed. All I wanted, all I ever wanted, was to be left alone.

Even when she was not playing her sick games with my immature body, she was manipulating my mind, fucking me with her insane religion, filling me with visions of a fiery hell. Leave me alone, I screamed. But that only whipped her into a fury, a fury that could be stilled only by my physical torture.

Unloved. No, that is not sufficient, for it indicates neglect. I was never neglected. No, I was actively hated—physically, sexually, and mentally abused by a woman who should have been put away. So it was little wonder that I withdrew into myself, seeking comfort from the only source available to me—him.

When he first came to me, I was eight years old. (Though if you looked into my eyes, you would have sworn I was a hundred times older.) He had no solid form then—nor does he to this day—only a generalized shape, like smoke and shadow. He was my only link with a world in which there were no punishments, no mental cruelties, no disgusting sexual perversion. He was alone, too. Misunderstood and hated, he said. Just like me.

Judas promised me freedom, but we never discussed the cost. He spoke of our common persecution, but he never spoke of taking my soul. That was understandable, for I was so young, I was easily influenced. Caught up in his words of sympathy, I saw him as my surrogate, a whipping boy for the false God. His love—and hatred—infected me with a heart-hammering need to toss off the yoke of my enslavement, and walk with him in the deep shadows of eternal peace.

Once convinced his tactics were working on me, he intensified my indoctrination, much as my mother increased her unhealthy demands on me. He kept asking me to sign the Covenant and he would free me from my torment. I didn't know what a Covenant was then, but I knew it was a bargain. He would make my life bearable, and I would be required to do something for him. I offered him my body, but he had only laughed at me, calling me wicked. It was the only thing I had, I told him, the only thing about me people seemed to want. What was done to me was sick and unnatural, but I was being attacked sexually, at least I wasn't being beaten.

He scoffed at my puny offering and told me he would demand much from me when I was grown older and stronger. I willingly allowed myself to be carried forward on the wave of his malignancy. I submitted to him. What choice did I have?

The time of action occurred two years after he had made himself known to me. My mother had been gone for two days leaving me to glory in my solitude. Her return would bring me many things, all of them painful.

I slept fitfully that night, moaning in my sleep, until I heard the sound of her car in the driveway. Instantly, I was awake. I listened carefully. If I heard two car doors opening it meant she was not alone. I crossed my fingers, my skin crawling with sickening anticipation. I would no longer be an offering to some drunken man she had picked up. But that night I heard no car doors open or close. I heard only the whisper of his robes and the slap of his sandals on the wooden floor of my room. His voice was deep and reassuring.

It is time, time for the Covenant to be initiated.

I rose from bed. The room was cold enough for me to see my breath. The furnace had broken before Thanksgiving and there had been no money to fix it. I looked out the window; there was an icy ring around the moon. Something ominous and permanent was about to happen, I knew.

Come, I will show you the way.

Mesmerized by his calm, insistent voice, I forced myself to move, alternately trembling and stopping dead in my tracks for moments at a time. Then I would feel his hot breath on my neck, and I would jump forward once again, my heart and lungs laboring.

When we reached the damp chill of the living room, he told me to stop. I obeyed.

Remove your clothes, for the Covenant must be signed.

The black cold of the air shriveled my feverish skin, but I threw off the oversized pajamas I always wore. They had belonged to my father—the father I denied existed.

Naked and shaking with fear, I turned to face him, but of course he was always just out of my sight. I did see, however, what he wanted me to see: the razor-sharp letter opener by my mother's chair.

I sat in the burning cold chair, shrinking with fear and the cold, and picked up the letter opener. It was in the shape of a miniature crusader's sword. Holding it by the point in the moonlight, the letter opener resembled a silver cross. Iscariot spoke:

Give me your blood and I will give you your freedom.

I hesitated.

Give it to me now, that you may be free.

"There is no Covenant," *I whispered.* "No paper."

The Convenant is in your heart and mind.

"Then why do I have to cut myself?" *I asked.*

To fulfill the Covenant.

I closed my eyes and let the silver-sharp blade rake across my wrist. Oh God, I can still feel the intense pain, see my blood, black in the dark room, form along the line of incision. Snakelike it pooled, rich and sluggish as molasses in the freezing night air.

Carefully I wiped the blade clean on my stomach and sat with my left arm extended, waiting for what was to come.

It is a start, a new beginning. Close your eyes.

I complied, and for a moment I was warmed by a great source of heat close to my naked, insubstantial body. I felt as if I were being enveloped by a pair of great wings—comforted, warmed, encouraged. But before I could revel in the comfort, the presence seemed to recede from me, leaving me once more only a small, shivering child sitting naked in a chair.

"Where are you?" *I asked.*

With you. In you.

"What—" *I began, but I looked down at my wrist. The blood had disappeared, the wound had miraculously healed. I caught my breath. Had I even cut myself at all? Was it all in my mind?*

Suddenly, the silver moonlight turned emerald green, then to red, as if it had somehow absorbed my blood. I felt the room expand around me until I was only an atom in the midst of infinite space. My mouth was dry, my eyes twitched and jiggled in their sockets, my head was pounding furiously in the void.

Once I had experienced my own nothingness in the cosmos, the world rushed back to me at an incredible speed, and suddenly I was bigger than the house, bigger than the earth, bigger than the universe. I was power unlimited, I was God, I was everything. *I laughed at the insignificance of what I was about to do, for it meant less to me than the falling of a leaf. I was invincible, absolute. Then he broke the spell.*

It is time.

My bare feet never felt the killing cold of the hard ground. The next thing I remember was finding myself in the garage, but not really in the garage. It was more like a dream. In the rusty red moonlight, I was watching myself from afar. He spoke:

You know what we must do.

I knew. I switched on the garage light and was not surprised to find that it was red like the moonlight. I realized later, that it was like seeing everything with infrared goggles.

My mother was alone, and as I expected, lying drunk, slumped over the steering wheel. While I watched from above in my dream-like trance, I saw my naked childish figure walk up to the car and peer in the window. My mother opened unseeing eyes, said something, and fell sideways into the door. She snored, and snorted like a pig.

Usually, when she got like this, I would help her to bed, always careful to stay away from her hands which would inevitably probe for my groin. If she were too drunk to walk, I would put a blanket over her and retreat into the house.

Without thinking, I went to get the beach blanket she kept in the garage.

Not tonight.

His voice cut through the frosty air like a fiery torch.

Open the door carefully. Don't let her fall.

I did as I was instructed, revolted as always by the smell of whiskey and perfume and—sex? Beneath the sweet odor of perfume was a rottenness and filth that was overpowering. She had a moral gangrene that could not be disguised by cosmetics or liquor. She stank to high heaven. An apt thought, I remember thinking.

I opened the door slowly and with one hand kept her unpro-

testing body upright. She coughed and a bit of saliva dribbled out of her mouth and ran over her thick, sensuous lips—lips that had sucked my—

Do not think about it. All will be peaceful soon.

His voice reassured me and gave me courage to continue to work his will. My will?

My mother mumbled incoherently and belched up a revolting stink from within her diseased soul. I shrank away, but suddenly felt Judas' hand on my neck. I almost fainted. It was the first time he had actually touched me. My head and heart pounded so loudly I could hardly hear him.

I will help you. And you will help me.

With his hand on mine, he guided my small fingers to the ignition key.

One turn and you will be free of her.

The key seemed to throw off sparks at our combined touch; his powerful hand squeezed mine reassuringly as the engine roared to life. The cold, clammy air was immediately filled with the stench of gas fumes.

With his help, I eased my mother sideways on the seat. She placed her palms together, as if praying, and tucked them under her head. She said my name. Quite clearly. And I felt a sudden rush of guilt.

It is done. The Covenant has been validated.

I took one last look at her, so beautiful and peaceful in her final sleep, and was suddenly unable to remember anything bad about her. Only the good. Could this sleeping woman be the cause of all my pain?

The bitch is gone. You owe me. Your part of the Covenant must be kept.

"When?" I whispered.

When I choose. You live on borrowed time. Your life is mine, your actions belong to me. Remember the Covenant until we meet again.

I closed the car door and shut off the garage lights, acutely aware that Judas was no longer with me, and amazed that everything seemed normal.

Outside, the moon had lost its bloody tinge and had regained its silvery glow; it quickly disappeared behind a cloud, and in the utter blackness of a winter night, I pulled the heavy garage door shut. I looked through the grimy window at the car, thinking that perhaps I would see smoke or fumes. But carbon monoxide, like Judas, is invisible, and even when I look hard, I can see nothing.

Walking back to the house I searched for Judas but he was as good as his word. He was gone.

I stood by the door to the house, naked and shivering. I was ten years old, I had just killed my mother, and I was alone.

I went inside and went to sleep.

Chapter
Twenty-Eight

Saturday, December 11

Eyes followed the priest's every movement with rapt attention. The priest removed his Roman collar and black shirt before slipping on a brown sweater embroidered with reindeer and snowflakes.

It was cold inside the rectory office, cold all over Holy Cross Church. Whether it was the residue of three brutal deaths or not, the priest couldn't decide. He slumped into the brown leather chair behind his desk and switched on a small television. The choice was limited: news, talk shows, old sit-coms, and even older movies.

The priest settled for a movie starring John Wayne, and propping his feet on the desk, he took a sip from an open beer can. In the dim light of the flickering television, his face looked ghastly—like a dead man's.

The watcher's pupils darkened, not from a trick of the light, but as if some inner demon were taking possession. One pupil, the right, became larger than the left, and then the confusion in the watcher's brain increased dramatically. The eyes continued to watch the priest watching the television, but the watcher was waiting for final instructions. They came at last:

—*He will die.*

"*He will,*" the watcher confirmed.

—*He is Jude.*

"*He is Thaddeus. He is Jude.*"

—*He is dead.*

As if he knew he was the center of attention, the priest suddenly pushed himself up from the chair and went to the window. He parted the drapes and stared into the night. Moonlit shadows loomed across the parking area like prehistoric creatures.

The window was open at top and bottom and the frigid air whistled in. Now he knew why the office was so cold; he pushed the bottom window down and continued to stare into the night as if he expected the shadows to come to life. Then he yawned, rubbed his beard, and tried to decide whether to continue the vigil. Less than four feet from the priest, the watcher lay totally hidden in the shadows, camouflaged by black clothing.

Unaware he was being watched, the priest sucked in the night air gratefully. He was tired of being the Judas goat—or more precisely, the lamb, the bait. For a week now, he had exposed himself to great danger, but instead of increasing his anxiety, it had simply made him tired. Sometimes he wished the killer would strike just to get it over with and allow him peace.

Unseen, the watcher melted silently from one shadow to another, working carefully around the rectory like a fighter looking for an opening. It wasn't difficult to find: an unlocked window. The watcher eased it open, slowly and noiselessly. No sound, no movement. The watcher hoisted a canvas bag through the window. Inside the bag were three long, thin, aluminum javelins, their tips sharpened to a razor's edge.

The watcher stood for a moment in the pitch-dark room, waiting for help. Then came the terrifying sound of sandals on the bare floor.

—*There is another close by.*

"*I know,*" the watcher said. "*I can feel him. He is dangerous.*"

—*He will die if he interferes.*

"*Don't be too confident. I am not.*"

—*Does it matter? Strike now!*

The watcher crept down the long, dark corridor, guided by the sound of the television and looked inside. The priest had his back to the door, engrossed in the John Wayne movie.

—*Do it now!*

Somehow, the watcher could hear Iscariot's voice over John Wayne's terse pronouncements.

—*You must hang him on a cross, then run him through with the javelins.*

He will not be easy to kill, the watcher thought.

—*I will help you.*

"*I will kill him first, then crucify him.*"

—*It is not important. It is only important that the priest dies as his predecessor did. It is my revenge. It is the key to your freedom.*

"*Then we will do it my way.*"

In the brown leather chair, the priest checked his watch and wrapped his arms around his chest. He wanted to sleep, but

265

knew he couldn't. He raised the volume of the television. *Hondo*, the announcer said, would return in a moment.

The hate that festered inside Iscariot flowed through the watcher like a potent drug, infusing the watcher with a grotesque mask of pain and rage.

The watcher looked for Judas, for such a sacrifice demanded an audience. The curtains billowed inward for a moment, sounding like the rustle of robes, and the watcher smiled in the dark. Pulling a javelin from the canvas bag, the watcher hefted it like a professional athlete. But instead of throwing it, the watcher charged forward, ramming the wicked pointed weapon through the back of the brown leather chair.

The priest had just taken a sip of beer, but he never had a chance to swallow it. He looked almost surprised as the point of the javelin burst out of his chest right under his eyes. He watched, curiously removed, as the blood and gore poured from the wound. He opened his mouth to speak, but a torrent of blood mixed with beer poured over his lips and down his chin. Frustrated and unable to comprehend that he only had minutes to live, the priest twisted in the chair like a fish on a spear. He caught a glimpse of a face, a contorted face, a face that was oddly familiar. Just before he blacked out, the priest suddenly remembered what was happening to him, but by then it was much too late.

Then two things happened almost at once. The watcher realized that Iscariot had made a terrible mistake, and simultaneously, on the television screen an Indian stuck a lance in John Wayne's dog. It howled; so did the watcher.

Before dawn, Ciano woke up and got out of the round bed and staggered to the bathroom. He had had a terrible dream about his mother and even semi-conscious he could hear her sweet, threatening voice. When he looked into the bathroom mirror, he almost expected to see her face. But all he saw was his own.

Since his harsh words with Erica and Dugan, he had lived like a hermit, attempting to ignore everyone and everything. It wasn't working, he thought, looking at the dark rings around his hooded eyes. He was bored out of his mind.

As he was shaving he made a decision. He would try to square things with Dugan, and if that worked, he'd call Erica.

It was still dark outside when he drove out of Stonehenge on his way to find Dugan. He knew he'd find the sergeant sitting on the church with Father Layhe as his bait. That stupid, Irish bastard, he thought, wheeling onto Victory Boulevard. Maybe I can help him catch the priest killer.

The parking lot on the side of Holy Cross Church was deserted. But then, Dugan wouldn't park close to the church, Ciano thought, getting out of the old station wagon. The air was dry and cold, the sun just beginning to lighten the sky. For the first time in a week, Ciano felt confident.

His mood quickly evaporated when he found the rectory door unlocked; he pulled his service revolver and nudged the door open cautiously. The long hallway was dark and deserted. He heard voices from the office and chided himself for being too careful.

"Dugan?" he called out. "Layhe?"

No answer.

As soon as he cracked open the door to the rectory office he smelled it. Death. The odor of blood, feces, the residue of fear and pain. He gripped his Smith & Wesson .38 like a talisman.

Ciano heaved the door open all the way and stepped onto the brown carpet. In front of him was a man in a brown sweater watching television, his head turned. Behind him the door banged closed. Ciano whirled to see a gaunt, hollow-eyed Layhe staring at him. The priest started to say something, but Ciano turned quickly to the figure in the chair. "Shit," was all he could say.

Sergeant Joe Dugan was slumped in the chair holding his stomach, his dead eyes staring at the television.

Dugan had let his beard grow and was wearing Layhe's usual muted brown clothes. The deception had worked, Ciano thought, only too well.

Gently, Ciano moved the chair; Dugan's hands fell to his sides and a torrent of black blood and bluish entrails fell into his lap with a wet noise. Dugan had been stabbed so many times, he was a human pincushion, Ciano thought, a dead pincushion.

Ciano walked to the couch and surveyed the blood-splattered room. Then he put his head in his hands and wished he could cry. It was a minute before he remembered that Layhe was standing mutely by the door, staring at Dugan's tortured features.

"It should have been you," Ciano said. "If there is a God, he should have taken you."

"I, uh—" Layhe began, but he couldn't finish.

"You didn't call anybody?" Ciano asked.

267

"Uh, I—"

"No, you didn't, did you? *Bastard!*"

Captain Talbot was in a fury. "What the fuck have you done here, Ciano?" he demanded.

Ciano sat in his car wondering if he'd ever be warm again.

"You set this up, didn't you?" Talbot said. "You couldn't work with us to clear this case. No, not you, you fucking prima donna. You get Layhe and Dugan to go along with your fucking plan and you killed one and left the other ready for the nuthouse. *You* killed Dugan, you and your goddamn insubordination!"

Ciano thought about turning on the heater in his wagon, but it took so long to work, it didn't seem worth the effort.

"Answer me, goddamn it!" Talbot roared.

"Not my idea," Ciano mumbled.

"Sure," Talbot said. "Blame it on the dead. That's your specialty, isn't it, Ciano? Blaming everyone but yourself."

Ciano wondered if he had a pair of gloves in the glove compartment. That's where gloves ought to be, he thought.

"Get out of my sight," Talbot said. "I'm going to hang you, Ciano." He turned and walked back toward the rectory.

Ciano didn't find any gloves, but he smacked the dashboard of the old wagon; music blared from the radio. He lowered the volume and began to drive up one suburban street and down another, pursued by demons he wouldn't acknowledge. He was seeking shelter, going to ground, trying to escape the wild thoughts assaulting his senses.

Concentrating on keeping the car on the road, he instinctively headed for the one place that would have him—home.

"What are you doing with all that garbage?" Ed Hanratty asked his daughter an hour after Ciano had found Dugan.

"I collect it," Erica said. "Garbage is my life." Arrayed in front of her, taking up the whole of Hanratty's long workbench, was Erica's entire collection of dolls.

"Some sort of nostalgic fugue?" Hanratty asked sourly.

"The invasion of the doll people," Erica said. "You know, I once thought of these toys as my only friends. After mother—"

"Everybody has problems," Hanratty said quickly. "And mine is you. Please throw those things away or put them in the storeroom or give them away. I'm going to work down there."

"Why don't you just admit it, Ed?" Erica said suddenly. "Mother was a whore. A bitch and a whore."

The blood drained from Hanratty's pale face. "Don't say that!"

"She was fucking every guy she could pick up, making a fool out of you," Erica said.

"Erica!"

"Well, it's the truth, damn it," she said. "You go on carrying a torch for a woman who gave you nothing but shame and humiliation."

"But I loved her," Hanratty said.

"She hated your guts, Ed. Why do you think she drove you away? Why did she offer herself to your so-called friends?" Erica was venomous.

"Stop it," Hanratty said softly.

"That's what you should have done years ago," Erica said. "Instead, you deserted us—me—and left us—"

Hanratty spun on his heels and walked away.

"Run, Ed. Run away from everything," Erica called after him. And with a vicious blow of her hand, she knocked several dolls to the floor. Then methodically she stomped in their heads.

By 9:00 a.m. Ed Hanratty had crossed the Verrazano-Narrows Bridge and was looking for the signs announcing the Belt Parkway. The early morning mist had burned away and the day promised pale blue skies and bitter cold. The weak yellow sun made Hanratty squint and pull down the visor to block it out.

Still reeling from his encounter with Erica, he knew he had to get away, had to put his daughter, his problems—hell, Staten Island—behind him. He was on his way to visit Monsignor Bryan's grave at St. Mary's on Long Island. The way he drove, it would take more than three hours, and during that time he hoped he would have a sudden insight. Or perhaps, he thought, find the courage to do what he knew had to be done.

In the rearview mirror he caught sight of Staten Island looming behind him, the trees dappled like an impressionist painting in the winter light. A station wagon crowded with kids passed him, and a little girl, about three years old, waved to him and smiled. Suddenly touched by her innocence, he waved back, but his thin, bloodless lips were locked in a grim, tight line.

In fact, he couldn't remember the last time he had smiled or why. He tried it, but his face became a leering horror. Margot had always said he didn't smile enough, and he had always countered, truthfully, that he had nothing to smile about.

Margot had always smiled, even when he was trying to teach

her about life, and finances, and duty. Lessons she was apparently incapable of learning. All she ever wanted to do was laugh and dance and party all night long. She didn't understand that life was real and earnest. Even the baby didn't change her, he thought.

In the second year of their marriage, Margot had discovered she was pregnant. Ed Hanratty had never once questioned the paternity of the child, but in later years he wondered if Erica—tall, beautiful, cold Erica—was really his child. Certainly she wasn't like him, a person of almost fanatical moderation. Nor was she the childlike innocent her mother had been—or seemed to have been. No, Erica was something different: demanding, forceful, emotionless. He knew her shortcomings were his fault—and Margot's.

Until Margot's pregnancy, Hanratty had deceived himself and the world about his marriage. His colleagues in the department, however, began to hear rumors that eventually got back to him, rumors about Margot's rather *too* friendly kisses at departmental functions and her sudden, mysterious disappearances with handsome young cops. The men who worked with Hanratty ignored the stories, refusing to listen to any gossip about a man they admired and respected. Still, it worried him.

In time Margot gave birth to a baby girl and Hanratty hoped the rumors would subside, and that his wife would devote herself to the child's care. But, of course, it did not happen.

Hanratty turned off the Belt Parkway and onto the Southern State, thinking that, from the very beginning, Erica had driven a final wedge between him and Margot. Even the baby's name had precipitated an argument. Margot wanted to name her Amber Dawn, a whimsical name made with his wife's usual immature enthusiasm. Hanratty, in a rare moment of assertiveness, insisted on Erica, which had been his grandmother's name. In a desperate attempt to get her way, Margot made up a story about conceiving the child one beautiful, amber dawn. But since he only made love to Margot at night, Hanratty had persisted and prevailed.

To his surprise, it was Margot who arranged to have the child baptized. She had met a priest who had agreed to administer the sacrament and had even gone so far as to ask Hanratty's cousin and his wife to act as godparents. A priest in Margot's life was a ray of hope for Hanratty, so he simply enjoyed the situation, never questioning how or why she happened to know a priest.

He hoped Catholicism would steady her and give her a new and moral outlook on life.

Perhaps he had expected too much of her, he thought. The priest she had selected to perform the baptism was Father Francis Bryan. Energetic, handsome, and in his prime, Bryan had brought a new sense of vitality to Holy Cross parish. And because of his craggy good looks and dark, curly hair graying at the temples, Bryan had become the darling of the female parishioners. Even austere Jeanette Kidder Eddins became enamored and opened her heart, as well as her purse to him.

Hanratty had unexpectedly found himself drawn to the priest, and encouraged by his wife's seeming rebirth became friendly with him. He felt certain that the subtle changes he detected in his wife were the result of Bryan's good offices, and his friendship with Bryan grew.

Hanratty had a sudden urge to pull over to the side of the road and sleep, but he pressed on, trying to shake the thought that kept running through his mind: he had known Francis Bryan from baptism to crucifixion.

He drove with precision until he neared St. Mary's, then he pulled over to the shoulder and closed his eyes for a moment. It was past noon and the sun had reached its inefficient apogee. Clouds were moving in from the west as Hanratty rubbed his eyes and drove slowly ahead, looking for the entrance to St. Mary's.

Two imposing stone pillars and an open wrought-iron gate marked the beginning of the two square miles of property owned by the Benedictine order. The land and the imposing Victorian mansion at the end of the long U-shaped driveway had been given to the order by two maiden sisters at the turn of the century. They were the last tender flowers of a once robust family of Irish land swindlers, stock manipulators, gunrunners, and slavers who had grown fabulously wealthy and had used their wealth to buy respectability.

From the late seventeenth century to the twentieth century, at least one member of the family, usually a second son or a plain daughter, was encouraged to enter the order, bringing with him or her a dowry of hard cash and, until the line was finally overbred, a legacy of hardheaded business sense. This symbiotic relationship, medieval in many ways, was finally snapped when the last two women in the family failed to breed and the order inherited the money and the land. Since then, the Benedictines had hung on tenaciously, opening up the great old pile as a retreat, conference center, rehabilitation center for disabled nuns and priests, and even as a summer camp for the disadvantaged children. The cemetery where Hanratty was headed was actually a Potter's Field for destitute priests. In most cases, Hanratty knew, the families of priests paid for their plots and headstones, but some, like Bryan and Graff, had no family, and the church had to provide.

Hanratty drove past the enormous old house built solidly of gray stone and wood. In the distance, beyond the house, he could see the ocean. The wind had freshened and was whipping up frothy whitecaps.

He drove for more than a mile on a winding blacktop road until he came to the cemetery. It was dominated by an imposing stone cross, at least thirty feet high. Heavy and oppressive, it seemed to threaten Hanratty with its presence. The graves in the newer section of the cemetery were laid out in precise rows—modest headstones of white stone, shaped like crosses, spread out for several acres. To the right, were the flamboyant markers of a bygone era, memorials built at great cost by the family who had donated the land. Against a rolling grass-covered dune was a pagan mausoleum built to resemble a doric temple. Near it stood a sixty-foot-high obelisk with a rampant lion perched on top, and most curious of all, a triangular slab of granite, twenty feet tall, thirty feet long, topped with a bronze model of a sailing ship. Hanratty shook his head, wondering if people were more insane in life or in death. He passed under the shadow of the cross and went looking for his friend.

Hanratty found Monsignor Bryan's grave easily. It was a bare patch of ground, slightly convex. Pushed into the raw earth was a temporary aluminum tag the size of a twelve-inch ruler. Stamped in the metal were the numbers, 3847-AX8, and the name, misspelled: "Brian". The final indignity, he thought. Would they carve "Brian" into the soft white marker?

Behind Bryan's final resting place was a similar grave with aluminum tag stamped "Graff." Hanratty crossed himself and said a prayer for the tough, alcoholic priest who had endured the horrors of the world and had been shattered by them.

Looking back to Bryan's grave, he knelt in the cold dirt and willed himself to think about the priest as he had been in life. He thought about the friendly arguments they had engaged in, the long talks on obscure religious doctrine that had appealed to Hanratty's analytical mind.

And, of course, he thought of Margot, of how the three of them had dined together, went to cocktail parties and fund raisers together, and had even spent two weeks in a rented cabin in the Berkshires together. They grew close, inseparable.

Hanratty stood up stiffly to wipe a tear from his translucent cheek. Damn it, he thought, they *had* been friends. He felt the rage building and tried to calm himself. He turned away and walked toward the ocean.

Since the nineteenth century, the shoreline had moved inexorably toward the cemetery, which had been sited too near to the water. Eventually, he supposed, the entire cemetery would be only a flooded memory.

He looked out at the rolling waves and thought about that cold, cold day in February. Erica had been a child, and Hanratty had returned home early for some reason he could no longer remember. He had found Margot in bed with the seventeen-year-old kid who delivered the groceries. He had been too shocked to get angry. He had simply retreated from the bedroom, a shattered man. He knew she had been unfaithful to him for years, but she had always taken great pains to hide it from him. As a detective, he found himself looking for evidence, clues to her infidelity and every time he failed, he felt strangely reassured. If she cared enough about him to hide her lust, then she still loved him enough to care about his feelings. That was his tortured rationalization.

But after the grocery boy, Margot no longer bothered with pretense or discretion. The child-woman turned vicious. She brought her lovers home to Hanratty's bed, and made it a point not to change the sheets afterward. He railed at her, and on one occasion struck her, but she had only continued her humiliation of him, indifferent to his jealousy.

Hanratty had poured his heart out to Father Bryan, but the priest had had no comfort for him. He had had to suffer his punishment alone. What mystified him more than anything else was why Margot continued to live with him. She could have moved out at any time. The only conclusion he could come to was that she had a permanent lover somewhere nearby, a man who was married, and although he was free to bed her, he couldn't support her. It was this man that Hanratty set out to find—and kill. He didn't give a damn if she screwed every me-terman, delivery boy, and gas station attendant on Staten Island, but Hanratty couldn't stand the thought that there was someone she loved—really loved—more than she loved him. That someone was not difficult for a detective to find. That someone was Father Francis Bryan.

Hanratty walked to the beach and stood there watching the gray, oily waves crash into the shore. He felt like screaming into the wind, but he knew that if he ever started, he could never stop.

But he was my friend, Hanratty thought. *A priest.* He had found them naked and thrashing on the bed at the old St. George Hotel in Great Kill. He had had no trouble following them, no trouble convincing the manager to give him a passkey. No trouble at all.

Damn you both! he had shouted at them, *damn you, damn you!* He had pulled his .38 and was about to kill them when he had had a better idea. He holstered his service revolver and went to his car in the parking lot. A second away from eating his gun, Bryan had saved him. He had said, "Kill me. I deserve it. You don't."

Simple words, Hanratty thought, watching the seagulls wheel and turn above the surf, inadequate words, perhaps, but the words he needed to hear. Now, all these years later, he wondered if he had done the right thing. Perhaps if he had pulled the trigger, he could have saved many lives.

The sky had changed from blue gray to gray flannel by the time Hanratty crossed the bridge back into Staten Island. He knew where he was going and he knew what he had to do. Thinking about his eventual reconciliation with Father Bryan and their mutual efforts to help Margot, had finally made up his mind. As big a bastard as Bryan may have been, he had repented, and no one deserved to die the way he had, crucified and flayed alive. Hanratty shivered.

He drove carefully through the city streets, past Richmondtown and up behind the restoration to the crumbling Victorian house. He found a side door open, but before he entered, he pulled his .38 Smith & Wesson from the small of his back. He had much to answer for, he thought, much to atone for. But he had made a holy vow. Bryan's killer would be brought to justice.

The house was deserted, but Hanratty could feel a presence—an evil presence, the one he had felt in Holy Cross Church—pervading the wrecked and ruined house.

Always logical, he decided to start with the basement, determined to cover every square inch of the crumbling ruin. He descended into the blackness, and as he did so, he felt the force

274

of evil growing stronger and more virulent, and he gripped the revolver tighter, his knuckles white.

He heard a soft sound and strained his weak eyes searching for it.

"You knew it was me all along, didn't you?" A voice cut through the darkness, sending shivers up Hanratty's spine. He swallowed, dry-mouthed. "Not at first," he said.

"What are you going to do?"

"I have to stop you," he said.

"Will you kill me?"

"No."

"Then why the gun?"

Hanratty put the .38 back in his holster. "Will you come with me?" he asked. "We will get you help."

"I have all the help I need," the voice said.

"I must do this. You understand," he said.

"Should I put my hands up? Assume the position?"

"No. Just follow me out of here," Hanratty said. Into the light, he thought.

Hanratty turned around and put a foot on the creaking wooden stair.

"Your intelligence and your—what do you call it?—your hunches have impressed me," the voice said.

Hanratty shivered again. The quality of the voice had changed: deeper, more in command. It was a voice he had never heard before. "But, in the end, you are just a stupid man."

"I won't hurt you," Hanratty said, uncertainly. He wished he still had the .38 in his hand.

"That's the difference between us," the voice said. "You wish me no harm and I am going to kill you."

Hanratty was already reaching for the Smith & Wesson when he felt a sharp pain in his temple. Son of a bitch, he thought, sapped by— But he didn't have time to finish the thought before the darkness swirled around him.

Hanratty awoke to a world of pain. Somewhere in the back of his mind he could hear hammering, but he couldn't connect the pain with the hammering. Not yet. It was too confusing.

All around him was blackness, but he had the impression he was standing up. How could that be? he wondered.

The hammering ceased, but the pain continued unabated. Then a shadow, darker than the surrounding blackness, appeared to him.

"We have learned much," a deep voice said. "We now know that the feet should overlap and that a single spike must be driven through both. This concentrates the weight in one spot, yet allows the legs to support the body. The hands must be nailed to the crossbeam between four bones in the wrist, the so-called 'Destot space.' A nail driven through this area will pass through without breaking the bones and will support the weight of a body suspended from a cross."

Hanratty heard the words, but his brain could not decipher them. He tried to move his arms, but the pain was excruciating.

"You'll note," the voice said, "that a nail driven through the Destot space will cause the thumbs to adhere tightly to the hand."

Hanratty tried to move his thumbs; he felt nothing but pain. He was, however, beginning to understand. He had been crucified.

"However, death by crucifixion is long and tedious," the voice continued. "The cause of death from crucifixion is asphyxiation. Plain old asphyxiation. Those who were crucified were supposed to writhe in agony for their crimes, then die. Unfortunately, a man in good condition can endure for long periods of time. That's when we would administer the *cruvifragium*, the breaking of the legs. This causes the body to slump on the cross, making it impossible for the lungs to function properly. The heart is strained, lack of oxygen causes unconsciousness and eventual brain death. It would all be over soon and everyone could go home, chastened and thrilled with horror."

Hanratty tried to scream, but no sound came out.

"In your case, Captain Hanratty," the voice said, "all this is simply a briefing—background information to satisfy your curiosity. And, as you know, curiosity killed the cop."

A deep, evil laugh echoed through the basement. "You shall die quickly, Captain."

"Margot . . . Erica," Hanratty gasped.

"Why not call for your God?" the voice said. Then a rustle of robes, a flash of metal, and the tip of a long silver javelin pierced Hanratty's throat, nailing his head to the back of the huge wooden cross he was pinned to. Blood welled from the wound and bubbled down his chest. He never felt the second javelin that ripped through his thin chest and destroyed his aging heart.

When he had ceased convulsing, the voice said:

"It was a mistake."

—It had to be done.

"He was not a priest."

—He will do. His death is my life.

"And mine?"

—And yours. Cut him down and let the maggots consume his rotten flesh.

Chapter
Twenty-Nine

Sunday, December 12

It was after midnight when Ciano pulled up in front of Diane's house. He parked and looked up and down the block; Teddy's Corvette was nowhere in sight. He breathed a sigh of relief, a sigh saturated with bourbon, a sigh that could have started a forest fire. Yet for all he had had to drink, Ciano felt acutely sober.

"You look like shit," Diane said, pulling her blue terry cloth robe tighter against the night air. "But you better come in."

Ciano felt better immediately. He had expected to catch hell for showing up so early in the morning, but it was as if she were expecting him.

She led him into the kitchen. "Hungry?" she asked, putting a pot of coffee on the stove.

He shook his head and slumped gratefully into a vinyl-and-chrome chair.

"I heard about Dugan on TV," she said, rummaging around in the cupboard. "He was your friend?"

Ciano nodded again. "Yes, I guess he was."

Diane put a shot glass and a bottle of Jack Daniel's in front of him on the Formica table.

"And I suppose you think it was your fault that he died?" she said.

"Yeah. He wouldn't listen. He had to go off on his own and—" Ciano began to talk, relieving himself of his guilt. As she had so many times in the past, Diane became his sounding board as he unloaded his emotions on her. He talked for five minutes, telling her about Dugan's plan, about his refusal to have any part of it, about Layhe's involvement, about Talbot's accusations. Then he stopped, suddenly remembering he had no right to burden her so. "I'm sorry," he said, pouring himself a shot of sour mash. "I didn't mean to bother you with all that."

"It's all right," she said. "It's just like the old days."

"The good old days?" he asked.

"Not particularly," she said. "A cop's wife always goes for the coffee pot and jug when the shit hits the fan. It's instinct, especially in the middle of the night."

"I wonder why?" he asked.

"Because a cop's wife spends a lot of time drinking coffee in the middle of the night waiting for a knock on the door—like the one Dugan's wife just got. I've often imagined how I'd react if I had to face a police chaplain standing at my door."

"You'd bear up," Ciano said.

"What makes you think so?" she said. "What makes you think that just because you're some kind of iron man, I am, too?"

"You'd find someone new," he said.

"Like Teddy?"

"Yeah, like him," Ciano said.

"Is that what this is all about?" she asked, sitting down, joining him.

"Isn't it?"

"No, it's not. It's about the kind of life you lead—all of you damn cops. You're a supervisor, for heaven's sake, you should be sitting behind a desk, giving orders, not crawling around on your belly in the sewers looking to get shot or clubbed or knifed."

"You're really serious about this aren't you?" he asked.

"Serious!" she said, raising her voice. "What the hell have I been talking about all these years, for God's sake? I want a husband that comes home to me every night, a husband who will live long enough to see his son grow up."

"Like Teddy?" he asked.

"Fuck Teddy," she said. "I mean you, you damned . . . damned—" She suddenly broke into tears, and Ciano got up to comfort her, but she shrugged him off. "You'll never change," she said, getting control of her tears. "You—all you cops—you like the danger and the excitement. It makes your wife and kids at home seem pretty damn tame."

"But don't you see?" he said, returning to his chair. "We need both—the excitement and the certainty of a family."

"You relegate us to second-class citizens. We're expendable," she said. "How can I compete with the department?"

"It's not a question of competing," he said. "It's a question of, what-do-you-call-it? Co-existing?"

"Is that what we are?" she asked. "R and R from the war?"

"That, and more," he said. "I can't really explain it."

"And I can't really accept it," she said, getting up and pouring them both a cup of coffee.

"Truce?" he asked.

"Truce," she said, sipping her coffee. Then, "Did Dugan have kids?"

"Thousands," he said.

"Have you seen the wife yet?"

Ciano shook his head and rummaged through his pockets for cigarettes. "I never met her," he said, not finding any. "You wouldn't have any cigarettes lying around, would you?"

"I don't know, I'll look." She got up and began searching through kitchen drawers.

"Did you know Dugan for a long time?" she asked.

"Only a couple of months. Since I was transferred here," he said. "But he was a stand-up guy."

Diane pulled a rumpled pack of Kent IIIs from a drawer and tossed them to Ciano.

"Kents? Who the hell smokes Kents?"

"They were Teddy's."

Ciano said nothing as he snapped the filter from the low-tar cigarette before putting it into his mouth. "I'm going to miss that crazy Irish son of a bitch," he said, saluting the air with a shot of bourbon, then tossing it back.

"You want to talk about it some more?" Diane asked, sitting back down at the table.

"I don't know," he said honestly. "I don't think so. Not right now." He felt the tears well up in his eyes and was embarrassed.

"Why don't you lie down for a while?" Diane said. "Vinny will be up at six and he'll kill me if you leave without saying hello to him."

Ciano nodded, and wiped the moisture from his eyes with the back of his hand.

"You look just like your son when you do that," she said. "Both of you are tough guys."

Ciano stood and headed for the couch in the living room, but Diane caught his hand and tugged him in a different direction. "The bedroom's this way," she said. He followed her numbly.

On the way to the bedroom, he looked in on his son. The boy was sleeping soundly, and on an impulse, Ciano walked into the room and kissed him on the forehead. He was feeling queasy now, afraid he'd let himself go into shock like Father Layhe.

In Diane's bedroom, he sat on the bed to take off his shoes. It seemed so natural, yet so strange at the same time. This is how an LSD flashback must be, he thought. Still fully clothed, he lay back on the bed. It seemed like weeks since he had last slept.

"Why don't you take off your clothes and get under the covers?" Diane said.

Ciano took off his socks, then stood to remove his pants. Diane was close to him and unexpectedly they came together in an embrace. Their mouths met and Ciano felt his wife's tongue search urgently for his; her body pressed against his and he squeezed her gently, just before they fell backward into bed.

The phone rang incessantly, drawing Diane and Ciano slowly from sleep. As Diane turned to answer it, Vince, Jr., dressed in Smurf pajamas, charged into the room and dove onto the bed.

"Daddy! Daddy!" the boy screamed as he tried to get under the covers with them. But Ciano made a valiant attempt to keep his son above the covers because both he and Diane were naked. While Diane fumbled with the phone, Vince, Jr., pointed to something on the floor. "That your undies?" he asked his father.

Ciano nodded, and the boy jumped from the bed. "You should put your dirty clothes in the wash," he said, disappearing from the room, Ciano's jockey shorts clutched in his hand.

Diane gave the phone to Ciano, her voice as cold as ice. "It's for you," she said.

Ciano took the phone. It was Erica.

"Vince, I'm sorry if this call is inconvenient, but I'm desperate. It's Ed. He's missing."

"My God!" Ciano said, exaggerating his concern, in the hopes that Diane would understand the importance of the call.

"He's been gone since yesterday morning," Erica said. "We had a fight and—I don't know. I've been looking all over for him and I don't know what to do next. I hate to lay this on you, but I don't know where else to turn."

"Maybe you're getting worried for no reason," Ciano said. "Ed's a—"

"Don't tell me he's a grown man, Vince," Erica snapped. "He's not a grown man, he's an old man and he's missing. He may be dead of a heart attack, he may have been hit by a car or lying in some hospital bed. Or—"

"Have you called the station house? He might have gone there. Or to Dugan's?" Ciano asked.

"I've called everywhere, Vince. No one has seen him," she said. *"Help me."*

"What do you want me to do?" he asked.

"Come here."

"Where are you?" he asked.

"In his workshop. I know it sounds dumb, but I thought being here, surrounded by his things, might give me a clue as to his whereabouts," she said.

Ciano sighed. "I'll be there in an hour," he said.

"Hurry, Vince. I miss you," she said. "I love you."

"I understand," he said.

"She's there, isn't she?" Erica said. "Is she listening to us?"

"I'll be there soon," he said. "Maybe I can get some help at the precinct."

"Never mind that crap, Vince," Erica said. "Tell her to mind her own damn business."

"I'll see you later," he said, hanging up.

Diane's eyes blazed at him, but before she could say anything, Vince, Jr., came running back into the room. "You coming to see me sing?" the boy asked. "At choir."

"I'll try," Ciano said. "What time?"

"Three o'clock," Diane said, her tone still frigid.

"Sure, if I can," Ciano said.

"Yaaa!" Vince, Jr., shouted, and ran from the room again.

"You're getting all tangled up in the strings that woman pulls," Diane said when the boy was gone.

"Jesus, Diane," Ciano said. "Weren't you listening? Her father's missing, she needs my help."

"Since when are you assigned to Missing Persons?"

"You're being unreasonable," he said, embarrassed.

"Then go help her," Diane said. She got out of bed and wrapped her naked body in the blue terry cloth robe.

Ciano followed her out of bed. Dressing, he asked, "Can I come back later? I've got to pick up my underpants." He waited for her to smile but she didn't.

"Sure," she said frostily. "But try not to wear yourself out playing two positions at once."

Erica answered the door, her damp hair loosed, her lush body barely contained in a black lace teddy and a sheer, red kimono. She took his arm and dragged him inside.

"I was going crazy," she said. "So I took a shower just to have something to do."

He followed her up the steep, narrow stairs, unable to keep his eyes off her gently swaying ass. He felt like a bastard, thinking about making it with her fresh from Diane's bed. But you didn't have to be a rocket scientist, he thought, to know she wanted him, too. Why else the Frederick's of Hollywood get-up?

"Have you heard anything?" he asked her after he was seated on the living room sofa.

"Heard what?" she asked, sitting beside him.

"About your father."

"Oh! Ed. No, nothing at all. I'm so worried, Vince. Really worried," she said, snuggling up next to him.

Ciano was aware of his growing uncertainty about Erica. She was unpredictable in the extreme, and unpredictability was something he knew all about. An hour ago she was pulling her hair out worrying about her father, now she seemed to have forgotten all about him. Of course, he thought, an hour ago I was warm and comfortable in Diane's bed dreaming of a reconciliation, and now I've got a hard-on for this broad. Unpredictability was something he cherished in himself and loathed in others.

"I'm sorry about last week, Vince," she said. "I was upset about my divorce and I took it out on you. I love you, baby."

Her words rang hollow to him, like dialogue from an afternoon soap opera. "Where do you think he might have gone?" Ciano asked, trying to get her back on the subject.

"I mean it, Vince. I love you and want you," she whispered. Her tongue darted out and caressed the cavity of his ear. He felt his whole body tingle, but he pulled away.

"If you've notified Missing Persons and wised up the precinct, there's nothing much I can do," he said. "It's better left to the pros."

Erica moved closer to Ciano and wrapped her arms around him. He could feel the damp heat of her body pressing against him. "Please help me, Vince," she said. "I know I'm being silly, but I've got a premonition that something terrible has happened to him."

Ciano held her close while the doubt within him grew. Had she gone to all this trouble just to get him back?

"What's wrong?" Erica asked sharply. Ciano could tell that she was changing from the sexed-out whore to the critical, aloof bitch. "What's wrong?" she repeated.

"Nothing," he said unconvincingly.

"Then what? You pulled away from me. Are you too tired from fucking your wife all morning?"

Ciano pushed her away and stood up. "I came here to help you," he said. "Not to listen to you shoot your mouth off. You ought to see a doctor. Your mood swings would make a Ferris wheel jealous."

For a brief second, Erica's look of hatred and rage shocked Ciano. He had seen that face before—on cornered homicide suspects. It was frightening in its intensity, but suddenly, as if Erica had thrown a switch, the look changed. Her face regained its regal composure, and all Ciano could think of was her incredible beauty.

"I'm sorry, Vince," she said. "I really am. I'm frantic with worry. Friends?" She offered her hands to him.

Ciano took them. Her hands were cold as ice; she was trembling. He drew her into his arms, wondering if he had misread the situation. Erica was a physical person and sex would keep her mind off her problems.

She clung to him in unfeigned desperation, her body wracked with sobs. He held her tight until he felt her hand pull his zipper down. "Fuck me, Vince," she whispered. "I know this sounds crazy, but I need you in me."

Ciano tried to kiss her tenderly, but she was beyond tenderness. Her mouth and tongue devoured his face; she bit into his neck painfully; she was out of control. At the same time, her hand fondled his penis, working and shaping it.

There was nothing sensual about what Erica was doing, he knew. Her manipulation was rough, and he was feeling as much pain as pleasure. He wanted her to stop, but he didn't dare fuel her passion.

Erica stopped long enough to push Ciano down on the couch. "I want your cock in me," she whispered. "Deep inside me— until it hurts!"

Ciano allowed himself to be dragged down on the couch, but he made a feeble attempt to stop her. "I can't," he said. "I have to meet Vinny at St. Mark's. He's in the choir."

"What time?" she asked breathlessly.

"Three o'clock," he said automatically, then he cursed himself for not lying about the hour.

"We've got plenty of time," she said, unbuckling his belt and pulling off his pants. His cock was like steel. She went down on him hungrily.

The living room was surrounded by windows, and Ciano was

worried about being seen from outside. He imagined an audience of uniformed cops clapping and shouting while Erica was sucking him off.

"Let's go to your room" he said, running his fingers through her damp, red-gold hair. She let his cock slip out of her mouth. "No! Here! Fuck me here!" Her voice was deep and commanding.

She got up from her knees and lay back on the couch, her legs spread wide. "Now!" she demanded.

Ciano kicked off his shoes and pants and got between her legs. She spread herself wide to accommodate him. He entered her quickly, unable to resist. She let out a strangled cry and clasped him to her, as if she wanted to absorb him completely. The heat inside her was intense, almost painful, but just as he was getting his rhythm, she pushed him off her. She turned on the couch, knelt, raised her buttocks to him. "Fuck me!" she said breathlessly. "Fuck me from behind—like a dog."

Ciano didn't hesitate. He was as hot as she was, but he was also determined to get it over with as quickly as possible.

As Erica bucked against Ciano's cock, she groped for something hidden between the pillows of the couch. It was a box of tampons, Ciano could see. She opened the box and took out a small gold cross. Ciano stared uncomprehendingly.

Without losing a beat, she wrapped the cross in her fist and reached between her legs and began massaging his balls with the cold metal cross.

That did it for Ciano. He pulled out of her, feeling his erection wilt almost immediately.

Still on her knees, Erica shifted, and with a triumphant smile, replaced his cock with the cross, masturbating with it.

"I don't need you," she almost growled. "I don't need anyone!"

Ciano dressed quickly and left, Erica's moans still echoing obscenely in his ears.

Ciano drove back to Chris and Don's apartment in Stonehenge trying to figure out what had happened. He was worried about Erica. What was she up to? He wondered if Ed Hanratty was really missing or if it was just an elaborate excuse to get him there.

"Crazy fucking whore!" he shouted into the rearview mirror, and having released his rage and—what, fear?—he tried to formulate his plans: take a shower to wash the smell of Erica off

285

his body, call Diane, call the precinct to see if Erica had reported Hanratty's disappearance, call Erica to tell her to fuck off, get over to St. Mark's to see Vinny. That was enough to keep him occupied, he thought, pulling into his assigned parking place.

Wearily, he got out of the old station wagon and concentrated on different versions of the next time he would meet Erica. Each time he imagined putting her down brutally, leaving her in tears. He was smiling when he pushed through the glass door of his building and ran head-on into old Mrs. Stabille, who gasped and crossed herself. Ciano rubbed the rough stubble on his cheek and realized he didn't look very respectable. He peered down at the frightened old lady, and putting his thumbs in his ears and waving his fingers like antlers, said, "Booga-booga!" Mrs. Stabille screamed, dropped her metal shopping cart with a clatter and ran for the safety of her apartment.

"Merry Christmas," Ciano said, shrugging, and walked up the stairs to his apartment. Inside, he tossed his coat in the dusty, unused sink and picked up the phone. There was no answer at Diane's. Pushing aside sudden thoughts of Teddy, he hung up and decided to take a shower. Just as he was lathered up, the phone rang. He rinsed off as best he could, wrapped a towel around himself and went to the bedroom to answer.

"Ciano, this is Freddy Jermezian."

"So. Big fucking deal," Ciano said, wondering why the obnoxious reporter was calling.

"It may be. If I was you I'd hustle my butt over to Dugan's house," Jermezian said.

"Fortunately, you're not me," Ciano said.

"They're trashing you."

"Who? Dugan's kids?"

"Talbot and DeFeo. They got you tried, convicted, and executed. You got any sense, you'll haul ass over here and defend yourself," Jermezian said.

"So you can defend me in the paper?" Ciano asked.

"Could be," Jermezian said. "You're a shithead, Ciano, but so are Talbot and DeFeo. I don't give a rat's ass about any of you, but it makes good copy. Also, it might be fun to watch a fistfight at a wake."

"You got some sense of humor, Freddy," Ciano said.

"Yeah. It's the Armenian national trait."

"Hey, Freddy," Ciano said. "Fuck you and fuck Armenia."

"Good. I'll see you in about twenty minutes," Jermezian said, hanging up.

It might be fun at that, Ciano decided, rubbing the towel into his groin.

Father Thomas Layhe sat in his small bedroom at the back of the rectory. The lights were out, and he was softly chanting "Hail Mary" as a penance for his cowardice. He had heard the intruder, or at least he thought he had. He had come treading quietly down the long corridor, ready to help Dugan subdue the man whom he supposed was the murderer of Monsignor Bryan and Father Graff. But when he had rounded the corner, suddenly everything went blank. He was unable to move or see—he felt as if the hand of God had suddenly struck him down.

A rational, highly motivated priest who believed in the doctrine of helping his fellow men here on earth, Layhe was suspicious of miracles, visions, and prophesy. He was an accredited psychologist and was familiar with the quirks and foibles of the human mind. In private he scoffed at the incredible bilge that coated his religion like pond scum: fiery chariots in the sky, miraculous cures and resurrections, gossamer-like souls floating in ether, virgin births and improbable acts attributed to even more improbable saints. All these things, he thought, could be explained psychologically or as a by-product of the monstrous Christian public relations effort, a juggernaut that had been rolling along ceaselessly for almost two thousand years. He believed in a Prime Mover, an Alpha and Omega, a First Cause, not in some old bearded guy wearing a sheet.

But what he had seen near the rectory office had shaken his faith in everything he held dear. Even twelve hours later he was unable to think about it clearly. He had seen a vision from hell, a black robed figure who should have been a myth, manifestly alive and undeniably dangerous. The figure was howling, a sound Layhe would carry in his mind until he died. He had tried to move, but he was rooted to the spot; he had tried to speak, but he was mute. It was a hallucination, a mental trick played on him by his overwrought imagination, he had told himself. Then he had slumped to the floor, unconscious, while the robed and cowled figure continued its wailing. He was sure he had not been seen.

When he had awakened, it was morning. Stiff and aching, his head a burning cauldron of confusion and pain, he had staggered down the hallway to finish the journey he had begun earlier.

In his office he saw himself seated at his desk, his bearded face contorted in agony. He stared for a long moment, mesmerized; then he knew by the utter stillness of the body, that he was surely dead. He blinked. But if he was dead, then how . . .

Then for the second time in his life Father James Layhe had fainted; this time he was only out for a few minutes. When he woke, he knew he was alive and that the dead man in his chair was Sergeant Dugan. He also knew he had been resurrected. God had given him a sign. God had torn the scales from his eyes and had shown him the light.

He had gotten up from the floor and gone to the window to greet the first day of his spiritual awakening, but before he was able to contemplate his rebirth, he had stepped on something. Bending down he picked up a multi-pronged whip. Its wooden handle was more than sixteen inches long; attached to the well-worn handle were six rawhide thongs, each ending with a T-shaped piece of sharpened bone. This instrument of torture, he knew from his studies, had been designed to rip out chunks of flesh from the victim. It was a *flagrum*, the whip the Romans had used on Christ, perhaps the very whip that had been used on Monsignor Bryan.

Layhe took a deep breath. Where had it come from? Had the robed figure dropped it? Or had God left it for him? He had held it away from his body, wondering what it meant when he heard a car engine and looked out the window. Ciano.

Layhe had tucked the Roman whip into the back of his pants and covered it with his shirt. It was cold and alien on his skin, but he knew what it wanted. What God wanted. God wanted him to scourge himself of his pride and weakness of faith. When Ciano had entered the room, Layhe had been too overcome with his miraculous transformation to speak. Even when the doctors had tried to talk to him, he pretended to be sleepy so he could be alone with his thoughts.

In the darkness, he pulled the blood-stained *flagrum* from beneath the mattress and contemplated the fiery pain—and fiery salvation of his soul.

Chapter
Thirty

Freddy Jermezian opened the door of Dugan's house wearing what Ciano supposed was his funeral suit: it was forest green, dark and ugly as opposed to his normal taste for the loud and ugly.

"Your St. Patrick's day get-up?" Ciano asked.

"Let me talk to you in private," Jermezian said, grabbing Ciano by the arm. Ciano stared at the little man and Jermezian quickly released his grip. "Come in the dining room."

Ciano followed him and nodded to a few patrolmen who were standing around, their plates piled high with homemade salads, casseroles, and sandwiches. They were drinking beer and talking in muted tones.

"Try some of this dip," Jermezian said, helping himself. "It's real good."

"I'm going to dip you in shit if you don't tell me what's going on," Ciano said impatiently.

"I heard something pretty interesting," Jermezian said, blowing cracker crumbs on Ciano. "They're gonna send you before an interdepartmental trial board for Dugan's death. Reckless something-or-other."

"I didn't do that one," Ciano said. "I yelled my fool head off trying to stop him from playing cops and killers on his own time."

"Yeah? You got witnesses?"

"Only Marty Abel," Ciano said. "And Layhe."

"Abel, the brown-nose and Layhe, the looney," Jermezian said. "Big fucking help."

"Layhe hates my guts, but he's not looney," Ciano said.

"He is now. We're talkin' fruitcake city," Jermezian said, stuffing his mouth with more crackers. "I mean this guy's one sick puppy."

"Well, that's it, Freddy," Ciano said. "My only two witnesses."

"They'll probably leave you alone if you pull the pin," Jermezian said.

"I wouldn't give them the satisfaction," Ciano said.

"It'll make good copy," Jermezian said, shrugging.

"May as well say hello to the widow," Ciano said, brushing more cracker crumbs off the sleeve of his leather jacket. "Long as I'm here."

Ciano could see the power relationships in the living room at once. The widow, Mary Dugan, was the star attraction. Surrounding her in concentric circles were the brass in order of importance. The inner circle was composed of Captain Talbot, Inspector DeFeo, Captain Smith, and the police chaplain. The next ring consisted of relatives in somber clothes and the third ring belonged to the detective sergeants who had their own little Mafia. In the final and most populous ring were the uniforms and lower-ranking detectives, who were paying brief, obligatory homage to a fallen superior. They couldn't wait to leave and the brass couldn't wait for the photographers.

Ciano cut through protocol and introduced himself to the widow, seriously angering DeFeo and Talbot. The precinct commander, Captain Smith, tried to look neutral—the chaplain, pained, but pious.

"So you're Ciano," Mary Dugan said. "Joe talked about you often."

"I'm sorry for your loss," Ciano said. "All our loss." He could see the woman's strength. She had been crying, but was still in control. Perhaps she would collapse later, he thought, but she's determined to see this through.

"Thank you," she said. "You know these gentlemen, don't you?"

Talbot and DeFeo visibly winced and mumbled. Smith grinned.

"Of course," Ciano said. "They're the salt of the earth and they'll help you out all they can. At least as long as Freddy Jermezian keeps Joe alive in the papers."

"Ciano!" Talbot snapped. "Remember this is a wake."

"And remember this is my house," Mary Dugan said in the same tone.

"Be in my office tomorrow morning at 8 a.m. sharp," Talbot said. "That's an order."

Ciano ignored him. "If you need anything, any time, call me," he said to the widow and walked away, glad to have done his duty.

He was in the hallway, on his way out, when seven-year-old Sean Dugan, dressed in a dark blue suit, white starched shirt, and navy blue tie, came running down the stairs. He looked like a miniature Joe Dugan. He stood toe-to-toe with Ciano and said matter-of-factly, "You were my father's friend."

"I like to think so," Ciano answered, looking down at the boy.

"Then you'll kill him?"

"Who?"

"The man who killed my father."

Ciano looked behind him. Sean's three sisters had suddenly appeared, and were sitting primly at the top of the stairs, wearing identical black velvet dresses, Mary Janes, and white tights. This was obviously a group decision, Ciano thought, and Sean was the spokesman for the tiny, but bloodthirsty group.

"That's against the law," Ciano said, lamely.

"We don't care about the law," Sean said. "Daddy said you were a Mafia and that the Mafias kill people who kill their friends. So you gotta kill him."

He could imagine a half-crocked Dugan expounding on his, Ciano's, Italian heritage.

"You've been watching too much TV," Ciano said.

"You have to do it," Sean said, his face pinched and red.

Don't cry, please don't cry, Ciano thought. But the boy didn't cry, he motioned with his fingers and one of his sisters came down the stairs holding a gray metal box in both hands, as if it were an offering. Sean took it from his sister and she retreated up the stairs.

"My dad said that there was treasure in here and that he was going to leave it to you in his will," Sean said, thrusting the box toward Ciano.

"I can't—" Ciano started, but the crestfallen look on the boy's face melted him. "—promise, but I'll do my best."

Sean nodded with satisfaction and extended his small hand. "Good luck," the boy said, and walked up the stairs, herding his sisters before him.

"Ciano!" It was Captain Talbot, and Ciano's cue to depart. He opened the door and shut it securely behind him. In the car, he examined the box. It was locked and there was no key. Ciano sighed, and tossed it on the passenger seat. He had to listen to his son sing. For the first time in his life he hoped Vinny would never be a tough guy—like Sean Dugan.

• • •

Fifteen boys between the ages of six and twelve stood at attention at the back of St. Mark's Church. Dressed alike in red cassocks, white surplices, white collars, and red bows, they looked like a Norman Rockwell painting. Unfortunately for the choirmaster, they marched like the individualists they were.

"Don't slouch, Murphy," the choirmaster said. "Keep your head up, Donnato. Let's try to get this right. Lead off with your left foot. Go!"

The boys lurched forward like a snake with a broken back. "No. No. Your other left, Ciano. Come on back. We'll try it again. We've only got an hour before our performance today and only twelve days to go until Christmas."

"And a partridge in a pear tree," piped a boy in the back row, setting the entire choir off giggling and laughing.

"Hush. All of you. We're in church, so behave. This is serious business. We don't want to embarrass your parents, Monsignor Fullerton—or God."

"Mr. Caldwell, Mr. Caldwell!" a towheaded boy shouted out, raising his hand.

"Yes, Johnston?" Caldwell asked.

"I gotta go to the bathroom."

The boys all laughed and one made a farting noise. They laughed harder.

"All right, all right. Go ahead," Caldwell said, sighing.

"Me, too! Me, too!" rang out several more high-pitched voices.

"All right, all of you go, then be back in the choir stalls in five minutes and we'll practice *Adeste Fideles*."

As the boys dispersed, running for the bathroom located in the adjoining rectory, Ralph Caldwell, the overweight, balding choirmaster, trudged down the center aisle of the church, wondering how he had ever gotten involved with these children. He had always wanted a serious career in music, but somewhere along the line he had been sidetracked. He supposed he just wasn't a good enough musician and that his present position was God's punishment for being second rate. It seemed a heavy punishment, indeed.

When the boys had finally wandered back from the bathroom, he arranged them in the choir stalls and told them to turn to page seven in their music. Incredibly, it took a few minutes for everyone to find the right page. Then they began to sing. It was a bit ragged and not quite in sync, but their young voices had a purity that seemed perfectly suited to the acoustics in the vaulted church. No wonder during the middle ages they used to cut the boys' balls off to preserve their immature voices, Caldwell thought. Then during the chorus of *Angels We Have Heard on High*, Vinny Ciano sneezed. That broke the boys up and made Caldwell wonder if castration wasn't the answer to controlling these uncontrollable children. He waved his arms, demanding silence.

In a front pew not far away, Erica James watched the choirmaster attempt to reestablish control of his mutinous chorus. She caught Vince, Jr.'s eye, twitched her nose, pantomiming a huge sneeze. That cracked the boy up and he giggled hysterically.

"Vincent Ciano," Caldwell said. "What in heaven's name is so funny?"

Vinny, whose bow tie had twisted one hundred and eighty degrees and was tickling his nose, looked to Erica for help. Erica slid from the pew and approached them, her high heels clicking loudly on the marble floor. "Hi," she said, holding out her hand to the choirmaster. "I'm Erica James. I've come to pick up Vincent Ciano."

Caldwell stared at her—a tall, cool woman with extravagant red-gold hair lying luxuriously on the collar of her expensive fur. She parted the coat slightly and allowed him a glimpse of her magnificent breasts wrapped tightly in white cashmere. Her presence, her scent of flowers, made him clear his throat before he spoke. Finally he said, "Uh, excuse me. I can't let the boy go with just anyone."

"I'm not *just* anyone," Erica said, mockingly.

She's dead right about that, the choirmaster thought. "But I don't know you," he said.

"You know me, don't you, Vinny?" she said. "Or do I have to show you my American Express card?"

The boy giggled. Caldwell smiled.

"Tell you what," Erica said. "Why don't you call Diane, Mrs. Ciano, to confirm it."

"I'll be right back," Caldwell said, not wanting to leave her intoxicating presence.

When he had gone, Erica said to the boy, "Where are your things?"

"Over there," Vinny said, pointing to a mound of books, coats, and galoshes dumped at random by the boys.

"Get them and we'll go. Your Dad's in a hurry," she said.

"Okay," the boy said, undoing his tie.

"Leave that," Erica said. "You can change at the house."

When Caldwell returned, Erica and Vince, Jr., were gone. Well, I tried to call, he thought, shouting at the remaining boys who were practicing professional wrestling choke holds on each other. It's not my fault no one was home. Besides, he couldn't believe that a beautiful woman could possibly be anything but legitimate.

"Okay, quiet down," he said over the din. "We'll try not to butcher *God Our Help in Ages Past*."

"You'd better hope your God will help you if something's happened to my son," Ciano shouted at the choirmaster, before running from the church and getting into his car. It was two-thirty and he hoped that Diane had some good explanation why she allowed a stranger to take Vinny. He never considered the possibility that the stranger was Erica.

He pulled up next to Diane's house, just as she was getting into her car. One look at her face and he knew she was as frantic as he was.

"Oh, my God," she said, when he told her about his trip to the church. "Then it's true. Mr. Caldwell just called me and I was on my way there."

"He's definitely not there," Ciano said. "Let's go inside."

They went into the house together, and suddenly Diane had a thought. "The woman who took him was tall and good-looking, with red hair and a fur coat."

"Could be anybody," Ciano said, trying to think of how many enemies he had made in fifteen years on the force.

"It sounds like that slut of yours," Diane continued. "That Erica person."

"What?" Ciano was thinking of Antonio Maldonado, the one-eyed flake who was suing him.

"You mean you didn't send her to pick up Vinny?" Diane said, on the verge of tears. "Please tell me you did. I don't care, I just want my son back."

Ciano took her in his arms and hugged her. "I swear I didn't send her to pick him up. But I'll call her right now."

He steered Diane to a chair and picked up the phone. A man's voice answered on the second ring.

"Captain Hanratty?" he said. "It's Ciano. Everything all right?"

"There is no Captain Hanratty here," the voice said, and he began to recognize something about the tone that unnerved him.

"Let me speak to Erica," he said. "Is she there?"

"Yes, she is." The answer was hostile, indicating that Erica was there, but that Ciano couldn't talk to her. The thought crossed his mind that the voice might belong to Erica's husband, come to claim his wife.

"Look," he said. "This is Sergeant Vince Ciano and I'm looking for my son. Is he there?"

"He is here," the voice said flatly.

"Well, let me talk to him," Ciano said, smiling reassuringly at a relieved Diane.

There was silence on the phone, then a child's scream that erected the hairs on the back of Ciano's neck.

"Who the fuck is this?" Ciano demanded. He could see the agonizing fear return to Diane's eyes.

"Someone who will slay the priest," the voice said.

"What is it, Vince?" Diane said.

He put his finger to his lips. "I don't know who you are, but put Erica on," he said.

"The bitch is mine."

In the background he suddenly heard Erica's voice, arguing. "Vince, help us please. He's crazy!"

"Erica, what's going on?" Ciano said; he was desperate. "Who's there? Is Vinny all right?"

"He's crazy!" Erica repeated, hysterical now. "He'll kill us all."

"You will all die," said the deep voice, cutting Erica off in mid-sentence. "You will rot in hell."

Ciano felt shivers run down his spine. Although the voice kept changing distinctively, only one person had been speaking. It had been Erica all the time.

The cold sweat collected on his clammy forehead and dripped into his eyes; he could smell his own fear. Choosing his words and tone carefully, he said, "Erica, listen closely. I'm coming to help you. Just take care of Vinny."

"The bitch is mine," said the voice. "And so is the boy. They will die soon. Then it is your turn."

"Erica!" Ciano shouted loudly, his panic threatening to burst in his brain.

"Help us, Vince," Erica begged. "Come quickly before he—"

The phone went dead in his hands.

Ciano had just enough strength to hang up the phone before collapsing into a chair.

"Where's my baby?" Diane asked, absorbing Ciano's fear and spitting it back as hate. "Where the hell is he?"

Ciano couldn't look at her. "Erica has him."

"Get him back, Vince. And I mean right now!"

"I can't," he said.

"Don't give me that," Diane said, her voice rising as she spoke. "She's your whore, and you gave our son to her. Now get him back, goddamn it!"

Ciano slumped in the chair, his mind in turmoil, his gut producing acid by the gallon. What the hell could he tell her, what the hell could he do?

"It's not as simple as that," he said.

"Is he hurt?" Diane asked, taking a new direction. "Is he . . . dead?"

"No, he's fine and I'll get him back," Ciano said. "It's just that we have a problem."

"What kind of problem?"

"With Erica," Ciano said. "If I'm right, then we've got to help Vinny right now."

"Vince, what are you saying? Why are you acting so crazy? What do we do?" Diane's words were stinging.

"Erica may be dangerous," he said. "Unbalanced." That was the understatement of the year, he thought.

"Will she hurt him?" Diane asked, her voice full of disbelief.

"I don't think so, but we've got to get to them right away. Come on, let's go to the house."

Erica James held Vince, Jr.'s face between her strong hands and studied his childish features, trying to see the adult that would emerge some day.

"Do you want to be a priest when you grow up?" she asked him in her husky voice.

The boy sensed danger in the question. Not knowing what to answer, he tried to guess what she wanted to hear. Parents liked priests, everybody except the kids in school liked priests, he thought, so he answered yes.

Erica stiffened, her lips drew back and for a moment the boy thought she might howl like a wolf on TV, but she released her grip on his face and began pacing up and down in front of the boy, talking to someone he couldn't see.

Vince, Jr., loved playing in Ed Hanratty's workshop with its tools and boxes of fascinating mechanical parts. But the game

Erica was playing today was not fun. It was scary—scary because she seemed so different.

Always before, Erica was a beautiful lady who took him places and bought him things—a nice lady like his Aunt Carol. But when she had met him at choir practice she had seemed changed somehow. Rougher and meaner.

His mouth was dry, but he was too afraid to ask for water. He swallowed, feeling the thin strand of wire twisted around his throat. Every time he moved, the wire bit deeper into his neck. It hurt, but when he cried, Erica tightened the wire by turning the handles at either end of the garrote. From the corner of his eye he could see the handles were made from yellow Mongol pencils, the kind he used in school.

Despite his terror, Vince Jr., remained alert enough to understand that Erica was really two people. One he loved, like his aunt, and the other one was the one who hurt him. That bad person wasn't Erica at all, he decided, but someone else. Someone real bad.

He saw the bad person start for him and suddenly, to his amazement, the face transformed back into Erica's.

"I can't help you," she said, putting her face close to his and whispering as if she didn't want the other person to hear. "He thinks you are John the Fisherman."

Vince, Jr., was confused. He had never been fishing in his life.

"We are leaving here and you must promise to behave. It's very important that you behave," she said.

Good behavior was something Vince, Jr., understood. You were rewarded for it. Maybe if he was very good, Erica would let him go, he thought. But first he had to have something to drink.

"Water," he gasped.

Erica stood up, and in an instant, her fine, classical features twisted into a snarl. She was gone again, Vince, Jr., knew, and the other person was back.

"You *will* obey," she said in a strange, deep voice that shook the boy to his soul. Then she twisted the pencil handles on the wire until he screeched with pain.

"Do you understand?" she screamed over his whimpering cries.

" 'Stan'," was all he could manage.

• • •

"Are you going to tell me about this or do I have to guess?" Diane asked as Ciano careened through the dark crowded streets.

"Later," he said, having no idea what he could ever say. Only one thing was important, he had to get his son back.

"What's this?" Diane asked, picking up the gray metal box that had been poking her in the side.

Ciano glanced over momentarily. "A box of treasure left by Dugan. His kid gave it to me."

Diane said nothing, but gripped the box with whitened knuckles.

Using the yellow pencil handles, Erica lifted the boy from the straight-back chair in which he had been sitting and pushed him in front of her, oblivious to his gagging sobs.

"If you say one word or try to get away, I'll do this," she said, twisting the wire into his throat. He was too terrified to notice the pain.

Erica guided him up the stairs, and along the way, the boy saw his jacket and reached for it. Erica reacted with a violent twist of the garrote; the wire cut into his neck and blood the color of his scarlet robe gushed down his white collar and surplice.

"Put it on, but next time ask," Erica commanded, wrapping the boy's scarf around his neck to cover the wire.

Outside, she led him to her car, passing several uniformed cops who waved and greeted her.

"Altar boy?" one of them asked her, seeing Vinny's robes flowing beneath his parka.

"Choirboy," Erica answered with a smile, while the boy stared straight ahead, afraid even to look at the policemen. Under his scarf, her hand grasped the handles of the garrote. In the misty winter gloom it looked as if she had placed an affectionate hand on the boy's back.

Inside the car, Erica loosened the garrote slightly, allowing Vince, Jr., to breathe easier, but held one side while she fumbled with her keys.

"Where are we going?" he asked, as the car shot out of the driveway.

"To the temple. To Jerusalem," she said. The boy recognized the voice. Erica was gone again.

In a desperate attempt to get her back, the boy called her by name, "What are you going to do to me, Erica?"

"I'm going to give you a bath, young John. A bath to cleanse your wicked soul."

Ciano screeched to a halt outside the family entrance of Hanratty's house. He flung the door open and ran across the dead yellow grass to the door. It wasn't locked.

He raced up the stairs shouting, made an inspection of the living quarters, then ran downstairs again in time to meet Diane in the foyer. She was holding the gray metal box and was frightened into silence. He grasped his ex-wife by the shoulders and moved her out of the way, and calling Erica's name, he plunged down the dark stairwell to Hanratty's basement workshop.

Standing at the top of the stairs Diane could hear him thrashing around down there yelling for Erica. She had never seen him this wild before and the terror that had paralyzed her since the phone call suddenly burst. She ran down the creaky wooden stairs to the basement.

She found Ciano on his knees looking at a straight-back chair. Even from across the room she could see droplets of red blood on the chair and on the gray concrete floor. She moaned softly to herself.

Ciano wiped his index finger on his leather jacket and looked up at her hopelessly. The pain in his hard eyes, the strain on his craggy face, somehow stiffened her spine.

"Think, damn it!" she shouted. "Where would she take him? You fucked her often enough, you ought to know where she is."

Ciano stood up and walked to the long workbench, then back again to Diane.

"Is there a pattern to her insanity?" Diane heard herself asking. Her voice belonged to a rational person and she was far from rational at this moment. "Think, damn it! Where would she take my baby!"

"I don't know," he said. "I just don't know."

"Then why would she take Vincent?"

"She's insane," Ciano repeated. He couldn't think, his mind had iced up.

"Damn you, this is all your fault," Diane said, lunging toward him. Her anger and fear were funneling, laser-like. All she wanted was a target for her fury. Her hand flew up and hit Ciano across the face, drawing blood from the corner of his mouth. He tried to clear his head, but she wasn't through. She hit him a second time and a third, until he suddenly became aware of what was happening.

He reached up and grabbed her hand and pulled her to him, smothering her in his embrace. She pounded wildly on his chest for a moment, then began sobbing. He held her until she stopped.

"Oh, it's you," Jean Fowler said, standing near the stairway. "Erica's out." She looked disapprovingly at Ciano.

"Where did she go?" Ciano asked.

"She wouldn't tell *me*," Jean said, with a sniff. "I'm sure I don't know."

"When did she leave?" Ciano asked, as Diane broke away and with her back to him, fished in her purse for a tissue to wipe her eyes.

"Not too long ago," Jean said. "I saw her car in front a few minutes ago, but it's gone now."

"Did you see my son with her?"

"Nope. I didn't see *her*, just her car," Jean said. "Don't be too long. When Ed gets back he'll notice if anything has been disturbed." She went back up the stairs calling out, "And for goodness sake, turn out the lights when you go. Electricity's expensive."

"We've got to think," Diane said, when the older woman had gone.

Ciano paced back and forth, his square jaw jutting out in defiance, as if to dare the answer not to come. Suddenly, it struck him. "There's only one place she would take him," he said. "The church. That's where the first two murders took place, then Dugan. It has to be the church."

He picked up the phone on Hanratty's desk and dialed 911. It rang three times, then a recorded announcement told him to please hold on until there was an operator available.

Almost screaming with frustration, he dialed the precinct, identified himself and asked to speak to the watch commander. Instead, he got Marty Abel.

"Hiya, Lew. How they hangin'?" the detective said.

"Shut up and listen," Ciano said. "The priest killer's got my son and she's headed for Holy Cross Church near Richmond-town. Get the nearest car over—"

"She?" Abel said. "Who dunnit? Dolly Parton? Iced 'em with her tits?" He laughed.

"Damn it, Abel. This is an emergency. I'm giving you a direct order. Get a car over to the church and—"

"Direct order, huh?" Abel said, the laugh was gone. "You ain't shit no more, Ciano. Remember? You're suspended and you can't say jackshit to nobody. Especially me. Now sober up and leave me alone.'' The line went dead.

Ciano's first instinct was to rip the phone from the wall and hurl it across the room, but he was gradually regaining his coldly rational, street-cop mentality.

"Get back on 911 and tell them to send a car to Holy Cross, that's got to be where she's going,'' Ciano said to his wife, dialing the number, holding it to his ear, then handing Diane the receiver. "Bastards,'' he said under his breath, furious at the overloaded circuits and undermanned emergency source.

"I'm going with you,'' Diane said.

"No, I need backup. Stay on the phone until you get it,'' Ciano said. There was authority in his voice now, a calmness and sureness that he didn't feel.

"What if she comes back here?'' Diane asked.

"Run like hell,'' he said. "And take this.'' He handed her his back-up .38 Smith & Wesson. He would be afraid to use it if Erica had his son as a hostage.

Reluctantly, Diane took the gun. She held it as if it were something slimy and obscene.

When he had gone, she carefully emptied the bullets from the chamber of Ciano's gun, and lined them up neatly at the end of Hanratty's workbench. They were dragon's teeth, she thought, that could bring only death and destruction.

"We are here,'' Erica said, in a deep, hollow voice.

"Where?'' Vince, Jr., asked, looking around.

"Your Golgotha. Soon you will see the God you love so much.''

"God?''

"He who grows fat on the sufferings of the faithful,'' she said, her voice sepulchral and totally convincing.

Chapter
Thirty-One

Finally, Diane reached a 911 operator.

"What be the probl'm?" the operator asked.

Diane explained.

"What that number?" the operator asked, when she told her Ciano's badge number.

"Why not call the presink?"

"Why don't you dispatch the damn patrol car?"

"Hey, lady. You be quiet. Don' you talk lak that to *me.*"

"Just do it," Diane said, barely able to keep from screaming at the mental defective the police relied on to deal with the public. She slammed the phone down, hoping she had managed to convince the concrete brain on the other end of the line that she was serious.

She sat at Hanratty's workbench for a minute, then unable to stand the suspense, she jumped up and began wandering around the basement room. She looked at the needlepoint sampler on the wall and the unusual clock, she played with the keyboard of Ed's computer, she thought about her son.

She remembered odd little incidents: the time Vincent had gotten his head caught in a wrought-iron fence and couldn't get it out. How helpless he looked with the hood of his snowsuit— the blue one with the white pompom—sticking through the railing. He was funny and sad at the same time. She remembered his first tooth and how she and Vince had suffered with him, or rather, how she had taken on the responsibility while Vince worked nights. She thought about the divorce and how she thought her heart would break. She thought—

The gray metal box suddenly caught her attention. What was it Vince had said? Treasure willed to him by Sergeant Dugan? She wondered what it could possibly be—a watch, a trinket of some kind? She shook the box but nothing rattled inside.

She poked at the lock with her fingernail, then looked around

Hanratty's well-equipped workshop for a tool to open the box. Selecting a Phillips head screwdriver she dug into the lock clumsily, scratching the gunmetal-gray paint. Next she tried a ball-peen hammer, but a few ineffectual blows failed to open the lock.

Diane glanced at her watch. Where the hell was Vince? she wondered. He should be at the church by now. Why doesn't he call? The waiting was driving her beyond all endurance.

In a rage of frustration, she brought the hammer down on the lock with all her strength. It suddenly popped open.

Embarrassed by her outburst, Diane looked around the workshop as if someone might have seen her lose control of her emotions. But of course the basement was empty and silent.

Removing the lock, she reached into the box and pulled out a black leatherette diary. It was about the size of a paperback book, but only a half-inch thick. Intrigued, Diane opened it at random and read: *My suspicions grow by the hour, and I am unable to confirm or deny them. Could it be that she is guilty? All my senses rebel at the thought.*

The words chilled her, and Diane flipped to the beginning of the diary. It was dated November and signed by Ed Hanratty. She read:

She has reentered my life and I am uneasy about it. I do not know how to treat her—as a prodigal daughter, a loving daughter, or God help me, a suspect.

He was writing about Erica, Diane thought.

It was more than twenty years ago when my poor, tortured Margot was found dead in her car. I always wondered if she had committed suicide, or, if her death had been the simple accident everyone said it was. In the long run, I suppose, it doesn't really matter. What mattered then—and now—was I loved her and she grew to hate me.

Diane felt as if she were prying into Hanratty's innermost thoughts. It made her uncomfortable, but she had to continue reading.

When I questioned Erica about her mother's death, I was stunned. She broke into tears and began telling me a confused story about being abused by Margot, about an imaginary friend named Judas. And frankly I dismissed her wild comments as fantasy—a fantasy festering in the mind of a child grieving for her mother. Perhaps I dismissed her story too soon.

Diane put the diary down, trying to grasp the implications. She flipped a few pages ahead.

Her spells of melancholy and periods of intense, almost compulsive, concentration forced me to take her to a psychiatrist. He was a cold and unsympathetic man who told me I was the crazy one, though not in so many words. A child reacts differently than an adult when confronted by the death of a parent, he told me. Her fantasies are normal, he said, a hedge against loneliness and sadness. And if I couldn't give the child time to accept her loss, I was a foolish father.

Yet despite seeing him for almost a year, Erica grew more and more introverted, less and less connected to reality. She would seem normal one minute, then she would phase out, go off to some other world. Her habit of talking to herself—whispering actually—in conspiratorial tones unnerved me at first, but I grew to accept it. Perhaps I accepted too much.

Diane moved ahead in the diary and found a snapshot, yellowed with age. It showed a Victorian house on a sunlit summer day. A little girl, surely Erica, was standing on the porch. She was wearing a white frilly dress and had ribbons in her hair, but she didn't look happy. In fact, she looked positively furious.

Diane turned the photo over. Inscribed in an unfamiliar hand, it said, ''Erica. Her tenth birthday here at 26 Dempsey.'' Diane put the photo back into the diary and continued.

. . . but when she tried to mutilate herself, I knew I could no longer ignore the situation. I made an exhaustive search for the right kind of institution and settled on the Clinique D'Ambrose in Zurich. It was fabulously expensive, but I felt I owed it to Erica, owed it to her mother to provide her with the best possible care.

And also to get rid of her, Diane thought. Cops have no sense of family. She was indignant even in her fury at Erica.

She went to the end of the diary and read the final entry:

My suspicions are probably ungrounded, but was it a coincidence that the murder of Monsignor Bryan coincided with Erica's arrival here? And where is her husband? His office says he's away, but is he really? Is it some bizarre quirk that Erica's problem—her dementia—fits so neatly with my theory about the murder of priests recapitulating the death of the Apostles?

There are more questions than facts, more ''feelings'' than hard evidence. And I pray to God I'm wrong.

I am leaving a written record of my fears and speculations so that if anything happens to me, I may be of some posthumous help to the investigation.

Diane put the diary facedown on the workbench, her worst

fears confirmed. Erica *was* some kind of nut, she thought, a dangerous nut who would harm her son.

The phone made her jump. But she picked it up before it had completed the first ring. "Vince?"

"Yeah." His voice was leaden.

"He's dead," she guessed, her heart leaping.

"No. He's not here. Nor is Erica," he said.

"My God. What do we do now?"

"Pray," Ciano said, meaning it for the first time in his life.

Erica pulled the gray BMW under cover of the old elm tree by the garage. She turned out the lights and sat for a moment with her eyes closed. Vince, Jr., was absolutely still. In the moonlight, her features seemed to be made of white marble: cold and unyielding.

"I cannot do this," Erica said.

Vince recognized the voice. "Erica," he said.

"Shut up." The voice was rough and deep.

She was gone again, the boy thought.

"I will not do it," Erica said.

You cannot disobey me. The Covenant must be fulfilled.

"I will fight you."

—You are me.

Erica's face contorted in pain and rage, her lips pulled back over her long sharp teeth; drool coursed over her lips and ran down her chin in long ropy strands. She trembled all over, convulsing, her head snapped back, banging the headrest repeatedly. Her hands flew up to her head as if she were trying to keep it from exploding. She let out a shrill cry and fell forward on the steering wheel. For a moment Vince, Jr., thought she had gone to sleep.

He edged toward the door, never taking his eyes off her. Slowly, his hand reached for the door handle. He could feel the cold metal when suddenly her head jerked up from the steering wheel and she fixed him with a baleful stare.

"Come, John. It is time," she said in a voice that Vince, Jr., now recognized as the *other* Erica.

He made his move, but she grabbed him by the garrote and viciously cut off his wind. She dragged him to her side of the car and threw him to the ground. Clawing at the wire around his neck, Vincent tried to scream, but no sound came out.

"Stay there or you will know the meaning of real pain," Erica said, glaring at him. To the boy, lying on the ground, she seemed

305

ten feet tall; commanding. His throat hurt too much for him to move.

Erica went to the back of the car, opened the trunk and removed a large galvanized tub.

"A good fit," she said, eyeing the boy.

"Think, damn it," Diane said. "Where would she go?"

Ciano felt like he had a buzz on—his thoughts were racing, but he couldn't focus them.

"A nut like her would go to ground," Diane said, grasping at the first thought that came to mind. "Would she go home to her husband?" She paused. "Wait a minute, I know something about her husband," she said, flipping through Hanratty's diary. "It says here—"

"Where?" Ciano asked.

"Hanratty's diary."

"How did you—"

"Never mind. It says here he owned an import-export firm. They lived in Connecticut. They—"

"I know that," Ciano said. But suddenly he thought about the leptons and the antique nails. Who else could easily acquire them except an importer, he thought. Or an importer's wife.

Ciano was desperately trying to remember what Ed Hanratty had written in his report to Talbot. "No," he said. "I don't think she'd go back to her husband. She would return to her childhood home, perhaps."

"I'm in her childhood home, aren't I?" Diane said in an agitated voice. Then she remembered the photograph and dug for it frantically.

"Here it is," she said. "She used to live at 26 Dempsey."

"Dempsey Avenue?" he asked.

"How the hell do I know?" She was close to tears again.

"That has to be it," he said. "Dempsey Avenue is behind Richmondtown."

"It's a Victorian house," Diane said, trying to be helpful.

"I'm on my way," he said.

"I'm going, too," she said.

"No."

Diane hung up the phone, and noting the Dempsey Avenue address, walked up the stairs to the restaurant. She asked the waitress where Jean Fowler was and went into the kitchen.

"I've got to borrow your car," she said.

"Sure and why not take the keys to my house?" Jean Fowler said, laughing.

"I'm serious. It's a matter of life and death," Diane said.

"In that case, call a cab," Jean said, unable to believe the nerve of this stranger.

"No time to wait," Diane said, advancing on the older woman. She spotted a heavy-duty kitchen knife on the counter and picked it up. "Give me the keys," she said, pointing the knife at Jean Fowler.

Jean Fowler was not intimidated. "Look, hon, there's a whole roomful of cops out there," she said. "One yell from me and you're in the slam."

Diane lowered the knife defeated. "I'm sorry. It's just that I'm desperate. Please, it's my little boy."

Jean Fowler looked at her critically. "Why don't you tell me about it?"

Diane started to say something, but broke into tears before she could blurt out the story.

Jean Fowler, her frustrated maternal instinct touched by Diane's tears, put her arms around Diane. "It can't be all that bad."

"But it is," Diane insisted, drawing away. "Please. I may be too late."

"Well, I guess you can borrow my car," Jean said at last. "Just bring it back by quitting time." She reached into the pocket of her slacks and produced a key ring with a worn rabbit's foot fob. "It's the white Camaro out front."

Diane wiped her eyes and said thanks, then left, almost on the run, for the front of the restaurant. In one hand was the rabbit's foot key ring, in the other was the sharp stainless steel knife.

"Get your fucking hands off me," Ciano said, twisting out of Talbot's grasp. "I've got to save my son!"

"You've had it this time, Ciano," Talbot said. "You're going away. Cuff him."

The burly policeman watching in amazement didn't move. They were in a church, for God's sake, he thought.

"Cuff him, damn it! And take him back to the precinct," Talbot shouted, his voice echoing in the emptiness of Holy Cross Church.

"What charge, asshole? Consorting with a brain dead scumbag like you!" Ciano yelled back. "One move and I'll sue your ass for false arrest."

307

"You son of a bitch," Talbot screamed, months of hatred boiling to the surface. He swung wildly at Ciano, clipping him on the ear. Ciano brought his fists up protectively and jabbed with a left that caught Talbot square on the jaw, then a powerhouse right that sent the captain reeling into a row of pews.

Stunned, he watched Ciano advance on him and yelled to the uniforms, "Arrest him for striking a superior officer!"

The big uniformed cop shrugged and grabbed Ciano's arm. He received a one-two combination to his gut and went down like a deflating balloon.

Ciano turned his back and began to run for the door when Talbot ordered him to halt. Looking around he saw that Talbot had drawn his service revolver. "Don't move, or so help me I'll shoot."

Erica had undressed the boy. He was huddled, skinny and shivering, in a basement corner of the old house. The garrote was still around his neck, dried blood streaked down his thin chest and his choir robes and school clothes were heaped near the stairs.

Erica was in the center of the room, bent over the rectangular tub she had brought from the car. It was propped up on four stacks of four bricks each. Under the tub was a layer of lava rocks. Ringing the rocks were three acetylene torches.

She emptied the last gallon of oil into the tub, oil she had purchased from several different stores. She had mixed peanut, sunflower, and sesame; the oil gave the dank basement a heavy, not unpleasant smell.

When she had finished pouring the oil, she carefully turned on the acetylene torches and flicked a spark under each one with a flint. She adjusted the oxygen-gas mix, then stood back to observe her work. The lava stones were soon hissing and sparking—the oil would quickly start to sizzle.

"Time for your bath," she said to Vincent. "Time to wash away your sins."

Diane drove past the house on Dempsey Avenue several times before spotting it hidden among the trees. Finally, she turned into the rutted driveway. Heedless of the potholes, she pulled Jean Fowler's white Camaro next to Erica's BMW and jumped out. She didn't have time for stealth, she thought. If that bitch was in there with her son, she wanted Erica to know she was coming.

Diane tried the side door that Erica had used, but it was locked. Without hesitating, she swung her pocketbook into the glass, shattering it. She reached inside and unlatched the door. It opened with a groan.

"Vincent," she called out loudly. "Vincent!" There was no answer; her voice was muffled and dulled in the rotting house.

Diane called out one last time, then entered the silent house. A rat scurried out of her way, paused, then stood on its haunches and glared at her with evil red eyes. She stomped her foot at it, but the rat held its ground, baring needle-like yellow teeth.

Frustrated, Diane took a swipe at the rat with the kitchen knife in her hand, but it only hissed at her and stalked off majestically, not deigning to fight her.

As soon as it disappeared into the wall, Diane began her search. Trying to be systematic, she started with the dining room, then moved to the kitchen and pantry. Nothing but trash, debris, and animal droppings that gave the house a sick, diseased smell.

Fungus grew in patches on the bare walls of the living room. An overturned chintz chair dominated the vacant room because it was the only recognizable piece of furniture. In the den, off the living room, an industrious spider had webbed half the room, and Diane thought she saw the tail of a black snake slide noiselessly into the wreck of an ottoman.

The rooms on the main floor were alive with animals seeking warmth, but there was no sign of Erica or Vincent.

Diane was losing her initial fury. It had been replaced by a quiet dread of this eerie old house, and at last she began to wonder what she would do when she ran into Erica. She wished now she hadn't emptied Ciano's revolver. She didn't know if she had the guts to use it, but a loaded gun would have given her confidence—more confidence than the kitchen knife she clutched in her hand.

Changing her tactics, Diane walked up the central staircase quietly. She hoped now to surprise Erica, to catch her in the act—the act of what, she couldn't imagine. But after a thorough search of the second floor, she found nothing but rot and decay. It was cold upstairs because portions of the roof had fallen in, opening what had once been Erica's bedroom to the sky. Diane thought she saw a face in the window, but it was just a pigeon settling on the sill.

Disgusted by her own fear, Diane clenched the knife and moved back down the creaking stairs. There was only one place she hadn't checked. The basement.

Ciano looked into Talbot's eye, wondering if the captain would kill. Slowly, he raised his hands and stood quietly, waiting to see what would happen.

Talbot got up from the pew and helped the big cop to his feet. "Cuff him."

The cop, dusting off his uniform, said, "A pleasure." He spun Ciano around and made him assume the position with his legs spread and his hands resting on a pew. The uniform frisked Ciano viciously, slamming his hand into Ciano's crotch. Then he handcuffed him as tightly as he could, bearing down on the cuffs until he cut off the circulation in Ciano's hands.

"You'll get no more shit out of him, Captain," the uniform said. "He's clean."

"Get him out of my sight, Russo," Talbot said.

Russo grabbed Ciano by the elbow and hustled him out of the church.

"Tough guy, eh?" Russo said, pushing Ciano into the side of Talbot's unmarked car. He grabbed Ciano by his jacket and smashed him into the car again. "A fucking tough guy, are you?" He was incensed at Ciano for dropping him with two punches; he felt any punishment he could inflict on Ciano would earn him Talbot's undying gratitude. He smashed Ciano's head into the roof of the blue Plymouth, looked around to see if anyone was watching, then did it again.

Ciano dropped to the sidewalk, the darkness coming down on him like the lid of a coffin.

As soon as she opened the door to the basement Diane smelled it, the nauseating stench of a decomposing body, mixed with a heavy, oily smell. She gagged, bringing her arm up to her nose to cut the sickening smell.

"Vincent," she called into the blackness of the cellar.

"Mommy," came the faint reply. Then a high-pitched, child's scream that ended with a gagging sob.

Something inside Diane snapped. Heedless of the danger, she ran down the old wooden steps to save her son.

Holding the knife in front of her like a talisman, Diane reached the bottom of the stairs and stepped into something soft and disgusting. She stepped over whatever it was on the floor and looked for her son. She called out to him, but received no reply in the absolute darkness of the reeking cellar.

Suddenly a light flicked on behind her and Diane whirled

around. She looked up at a gigantic cross bolted over the staircase. On the cross was a robed figure, arms outstretched, feet together on a wooden platform, hooded head on its chest.

Diane stared incoherently at the obscene figure crucified on the wall, unable to comprehend what she was seeing. She wanted to scream. She wanted to run, but before she could move, the head of the figure on the cross rose slowly, and as the hood pulled back she recognized Erica's wide-eyed face. Diane tried to run, but she stepped on Ed Hanratty's rapidly decomposing corpse. Her shoe went through his abdominal wall, releasing a loud blast of body gasses. She looked down at the maggots crawling in and out of Hanratty's open mouth and doubled over in horror.

At that moment Erica leaped off the cross with a scream that was so high it snapped in and out of Diane's consciousness. She hit Diane with a glancing blow, sending her sprawling to the floor, her face close enough to Hanratty's that she could see small animals under his skin, eating their way out.

But as she let out a strangling cry, Erica swung a two-by-four at her head. A bolt of light exploded behind Diane's eyes and she fell unconscious into Hanratty's dead embrace.

His hands cuffed behind his back, his head reeling from having been smashed repeatedly into the roof of the car, Ciano reverted to his street fighting days. As Russo, the big cop, bent down to haul him to his feet, Ciano bit him on the nose, as hard as he could. The cop screamed and simultaneously, Ciano brought a foot up between the cop's legs. Russo's gasping cry was satisfying. He hit the ground next to Ciano and rolled around on the sidewalk holding his groin. Ciano scooted crab-like next to him and brought the cuffs down on Russo's head until the cop stopped screaming. It took a few minutes of acrobatic maneuvering to find the key on Russo's body and unshackle himself.

Fortunately Talbot remained in the church and Ciano was able to make an escape in Talbot's personal car. He drove like a man possessed.

Clumps of maggots had fallen from Hanratty's body and were swarming over Diane as she lay semi-conscious on the dirt floor. She moaned and stirred. Through her tears she was witnessing a nightmare scene from the depths of hell. A robed figure was dragging her son, naked and protesting, toward a boiling cauldron. Diane tried to speak his name, but the crawling maggots

311

covered her lips and she was too hurt and stunned to brush them away. She blacked out.

"Nooo!" Vince, Jr., cried, as Erica brought him closer and closer to the seething, sputtering oil.

"The time has come for your act of martyrdom, John. Do not cry out. Give your pitiful life gladly," Erica said as she forced the boy closer to the tub.

Diane came to again. The dream of her son being engulfed by two flaming hands faded, but the horror of the real situation sent her into action. She pushed herself up, her hands slipping on Hanratty's coagulated blood.

Erica had the boy in her arms now, holding his unprotesting body in an embrace that was both tender and blasphemous at the same time: an insane madonna and child.

Gently, she lowered the boy toward the oil, pausing to say, "For Him that I loved." Vince, Jr.'s foot touched the searing oil and he cried out frantically, just as Diane managed to stagger closer. She had the shining kitchen knife in her hand. "Get away from him you crazy bitch!" she screamed.

Then with no clear conception of what she was doing, other than defending her child, Diane charged at Erica. She hit the surprised Erica at the waist level and drove her sideways, away from the tub. Vince, Jr., went with her, spilling out of her arms and onto the cold hard floor.

Erica regained the advantage quickly, twisting grotesquely and lashing out with clawed hands at her attacker. Her nails scraped Diane's cheek, leaving four long red streaks.

She and Diane got to their feet, and Erica laughed contemptuously at her smaller, weaker opponent and struck out with two quick punches. They weren't soft feminine punches, but a hard, sure combination that had been sharpened by hours of practice. Diane's head snapped back and her nose ran red with blood; she was hurt, but more than that, she was shocked. It had never occurred to her to expect a punch from a woman.

Erica pressed her advantage, her gaze stark and pitiless, her teeth drawn back in a savage grin of triumph. Diane held her ground trying not to show her waning enthusiasm for the fight, but Erica smelled her fear and the grin widened.

Diane retreated toward her son who was lying in a corner behind her, moaning softly. Her one thought was to place her own body between the boy and Erica. She prayed for the strength to save him from this incredibly strong, incredibly evil woman.

Erica lunged forward, raking Diane's face with her long nails again, laying bare the flesh from forehead to chin. The blood that poured from Diane's wounds seemed to excite Erica, and she threw back her head to laugh. Diane, seeing Erica's unprotected neck, threw a wide haymaker that caught her by surprise. Erica staggered back a step and Diane seized the opportunity and reached forward to grab a handful of Erica's long, lustrous hair. She pulled hard, twisting it and turning her body in a short, powerful circle that sent Erica flying.

Although her attack was successful, Diane had sacrificed her position. Nothing lay between the boy and Erica.

"Die!" Erica howled, rushing toward the boiling tub of oil.

Behind her, Diane swooped to pick up her pocketbook which had been lying near Hanratty's swollen body. She reached inside it and brought out Ciano's .38.

It was a last desperate gamble, but she had come too far and endured too much to quit trying.

"Don't make me kill you," she screamed at Erica. The gun in her hand wavered, but was pointed in Erica's direction.

Erica laughed demonically. "I cannot die. My work is not done yet." She grasped the sides of the tub and was about to push it over when she heard Ciano shouting upstairs.

"Vince!" Diane called. "Down here!"

Erica faltered for a moment, as if she had regained some portion of her sanity. She could hear Ciano's heavy tread on the wooden stairs.

Ciano leaped over Hanratty's body and skidded to a stop, trying to size up the situation. Diane was next to him, the .38 shaking like a tree branch in the wind. Erica was poised over a bubbling cauldron of oil and his son, naked and helpless, lay unmoving in the corner.

"Die!" Erica screamed again, pushing over the boiling tub of oil. It hissed and sizzled as it hit the cold floor.

"Shoot!" Ciano shouted to Diane rushing toward his unconscious son.

He splashed through the boiling oil and scooped up his son before the boy's body was scalded; then he turned in time to see Erica pick up the fallen kitchen knife and flee up the stairs.

"Shoot, damn it!" he yelled to his wife, but Diane just stood there. Then the gun dropped from her hand.

Ciano examined his son carefully. The boy had deep cuts and abrasions around his neck and a red and blistered foot, but he was breathing easily and his heartbeat was slow and regular.

Ciano moved close to Diane and put his free arm around her,

examining her slashed face, bloody nose and bruised arms. "You did real good," he whispered to her. "You saved him."

Diane didn't respond, but stared at him blankly, as if her brain had overloaded and was still trying to sort out what had happened.

Ciano realized she was going into shock, and bent down to retrieve his .38. Then gently, he guided her up the stairs and outside to Talbot's car. He rolled down one window and started the car to give the heater a chance to warm them up. He took off his leather jacket and wrapped it around his son. He cradled the boy in his arms for a moment, then used Talbot's radio to summon an ambulance.

Sitting in the dark with his battered, abused family by his side, gave Ciano a groaning sense of guilt. He was the cause of their misery. His stupidity had killed Dugan and Hanratty and had almost killed his wife and child. He alone was responsible, and he alone would settle the score.

As the ambulance flashed into view, Ciano decided he could not risk any more lives. He would make Erica pay for her crimes, but he had to do it alone.

He handed Vinny to Diane and she seemed to come out of her shock long enough to hug the boy to her in a fiercely protective gesture. She held him so tightly the Emergency Service ambulance attendant had to pry her fingers off the child in order to examine him.

Letting her son go was the hardest thing Diane had ever had to do. In fact it occupied her so completely that she forgot she had something to tell Ciano. Something very important. But as the ambulance sped away into the night she couldn't remember what she wanted to say. Something about bullets, she thought vaguely.

Chapter
Thirty-Two

Ciano scanned the woods, then looked over the hillside to Richmondtown. The restoration was partially lit with flickering gaslight, giving it a magical quality that seemed wholly inappropriate. It was a graveyard, he thought, a killing ground. Erica's killing ground.

He walked slowly and purposefully in the heavy night air, following the path that Erica and Joseph Steppe had used so often. In less than ten minutes he was on the outskirts of the restoration, his gun in hand, eyes alert to any movement.

It was quiet and peaceful as a tomb, not a breeze stirred. The dark evergreen trees soaked up the traffic noises and blotted out the starlight. He cocked the hammer of the .38 and pressed it against his leg. He wondered if he could kill her if he had to; he wondered if she'd try to kill him. In the winter desolation of the woods, his sense of unreality was intimidating. Every shadow was a potential menace, every tree branch an enemy.

Approaching the wooden gates of the restoration, Ciano stopped and pressed his back against a sign that listed Richmondtown's rules and regulations. He was sure he wouldn't be doing any loud radio playing, but he couldn't be sure he wouldn't smoke, spit, curse or kill.

Concentration, he thought, was the key to survival. Concentration and caution were the hunter's best weapons. He visualized their final confrontation: Erica attacking, screaming, running at him with the kitchen knife raised over her head. He shoots once, twice, three times. The bullets penetrate her body, as three red splotches of blood appear. She jerks like a puppet on a string and falls to the ground. Case closed.

He wiped his eyes realizing he had allowed his concentration to wander, and if that happened, the outcome of the confrontation would be different. It was one scenario he avoided thinking about.

Up ahead, he saw a car parked in front of the eighteenth-century tavern. Its interior lights were on. Ciano stopped dead in his tracks and melted into the shadows.

From his vantage point, he could see that it was a patrol car owned by the private firm responsible for the security of Richmondtown. The closed door had an emblem on it: a bulldog wearing a policeman's cap and carrying a shotgun; behind the dog was a gold, five-pointed star. The firm called itself *The Buster Brigade*. In other circumstances, Ciano would have found that funny, but there was nothing funny about it on this night. Through the windshield, he could see a figure sitting in the driver's seat, smoking a cigarette.

Cautiously, Ciano circled and approached the car from behind, trying not to be spotted from the side- or rearview mirrors. He moved in a crouch, his gun held out in the ready position.

When he was close enough he could see that the driver was in uniform. The security guard was bald and had apparently fallen asleep with a cigarette between his lips. Ciano straightened up and walked normally to the side of the car.

The rent-a-cop's cigarette had a long, arching ash and the red glow from the burning end had almost reached his lips. Ciano was about to nudge the guard awake when he froze. The man's throat had been slashed to ribbons, parts of his larynx and yellowish glistening tendons poked through the wound. Erica had given him a second smile, a bloody red one. Worse still, the guard's fly was open, revealing a gory mass of tissue seeping fresh blood and body fluids where the man's genitals had been. Ciano thought about Erica's incredible anger; he didn't want to think about how many times Erica had fondled him.

He checked the rent-a-cop for vital signs and found none. But even on a cold night, the body was warm to the touch; the man's bald head was still damp with sweat. He removed the cigarette from the dead man's mouth—a final parody of the sex act—and crushed it underfoot. Erica had been here not more than ten minutes before, he thought, suddenly straightening up and scanning the immediate area. He could almost feel her piercing eyes staring at him from the darkness.

Ciano slunk back into the shadows, tasting hate and terror in his mouth. For the first time he questioned his own lunatic behavior. He could have called the precinct; they would have sent an ESU team. But that would mean turning himself over to Talbot. Unfortunately, the rent-a-cop's radio had been dangling from stripped and ruined wires. There had been no key in the ignition, no usable equipment in the car. The private security man's big flashlight had been smashed and his nightstick—the only weapon his company allowed him—was missing.

Erica, he thought, had been thorough. She wanted him to follow, but on her terms. It was too late to retreat, too early to attack, he was at his most vulnerable.

He continued his cautious pursuit, his way lit by gaslight. Above him, clouds covered the scimitar-shaped moon; Ciano didn't know if he preferred the half light or the complete darkness for what he had to do. Erica had made it personal when he had slept with her and she had made it a vendetta when she had hurt his son. There was only one possible outcome. One of them would die, and it wouldn't be him.

The restoration's two main roads intersected at what was called Richmondtown Square. Ciano felt the hair on the back of his neck rise. She was near, he thought. Still too far away to show herself, but very near. In the eerie silence, he began his second surveillance of the terrain, not looking at the shadows directly, but using his peripheral vision to catch any sudden movements.

His gaze swept the square, taking in a geometrical collection of shapes—buildings, benches, a hitching post. He noted two colonial stocks in plain sight of the benches, placed there he presumed so that tourists could take pictures of their friends serving mock colonial punishment. Slowly he scrutinized the area. Then he saw a slight movement in the shadows near the stocks. His stomach iced over with fear and excitement.

He moved closer, took a two-handed stance, and watched over the gun barrel. He saw the movement again, and this time he could see that one of the stocks was occupied. He ran in a crouch using shadows as cover until he was close enough to make out the figure in the stocks. Immediately he recognized a uniform hat. Another rent-a-cop who had gotten too close to Erica, he thought, presuming the man must be dead. But a low moan from the stocks galvanized him into action. He ran full tilt to save the man.

A few feet from the stocks, he understood his own stupidity. The top half of the stock swung open with a jarring bang. The figure rose up and the hat flew off to reveal a mane of long red-gold hair. Erica screamed, a cry of attack, exposing the full force of her rage. She wielded a large sickle, its blade a rusty curve of death.

"The Covenant must be kept," she howled in an unnatural voice.

Ciano was transfixed. Too late to shoot, he raised his arms to cover his head. The rusted sickle wrapped around his arm and dug into the flesh. The pain was sharp, but brief. Erica withdrew the weapon to strike again.

Ciano felt the warm blood spreading down his arm and back as he dove to the right to avoid her second strike. He hit the dirt hard on his shoulder and elbow; the .38 jumped from his weakened grip.

Frantically he scrambled for the gun, and seeing his intent, Erica stopped in mid-stride and flung the sickle at him. Forgetting the gun, Ciano covered his head with his bleeding arm as the flying sickle struck him. The blood welled up from his scalp and trickled into his eyes.

A few feet away Erica retrieved the kitchen knife which she had plunged into the side of the wooden stock. Ciano expected another attack, this time with the knife, but Erica laughed contemptuously at him. "You cannot stop what God has decreed." She turned and stalked off into the night with a gliding pace, as if she were wearing thronged sandals.

Ciano sat for a moment trying to understand what had happened. The woman he had just fought was Erica, he was sure of that. But it was an Erica so twisted with hate he had hardly recognized her. Her grotesque face could have belonged to a corpse, not a living person. The snarl on her lips was a rictus grimace; her laugh was not that of a human being, it was a wail from the grave.

Ciano found the .38 and started off after her, trying to deny what he had seen with his own eyes. His stomach knotted with fear, as off in the distance, in the dark, he heard her demented, inhuman laugh.

Bleeding and battered, he followed her, never quite able to reach her. It was like a nightmare—Ciano's legs seemed to be working, but he could gain no ground on her.

Erica had taken Courthouse Road, a major cross street that ended at the stately colonial Courthouse. The wooden structures that lined the street were primarily craft shops, each with a large sign out front to indicate the sort of goods sold there; the general store and reception center was on his right. Directly ahead was the courthouse with its ominous gallows.

Ciano walked to the center of the road, holding the .38 in his left hand and using his right to mop up the blood that was oozing from the wound in his scalp. He felt like shit.

Three wooden wagons, relics of the nineteenth century, were gathered together halfway down the street. They were packed high with pumpkins, gourds, several varieties of squash and dried stalks of Indian corn—out of place on a dark winter night. To Ciano, it screamed ambush.

He shifted his position from the middle of the road and approached the wagons from the right, walking as carefully as he could on the wooden planking that served as a sidewalk.

A closer inspection of the wagons revealed two decorative dummies dressed as colonists. One faced Ciano in a seated position, the other lay haphazardly, its arms covering its head. Ciano stopped dead in his tracks, thinking that Erica was running out of tricks. Instead of approaching her directly, he backed up to the wall to plan his strategy.

Keeping his back to the building behind him, he inched his way along, holding the .38 close to the side of his head.

Ciano glanced quickly into the window at his back and dismissed it. Inside were four mannequins—two male, two female—in period dress, sitting around a table drinking tea. As he crept past the window, he tried to keep his concentration on the figure atop the wagon. Once he thought he saw it move, but it was probably a cloud rolling across the moon. He rested a moment and wiped the coagulating blood from his eye, and in that second of carelessness, one of the mannequins in the window blinked.

Suddenly the silence gave way to the sound of shattering glass; a pair of long-nailed hands smashed through the window and slipped a wire garrote over Ciano's head. Strong hands pulled it tight.

Ciano cursed his slowness, both mental and physical, as the wire sliced into his neck. A violent dizziness engulfed him; his legs grew numb. I've got to stay standing, he thought, trying to focus on something, anything, to keep from falling and killing himself with his own weight. The pain, delayed by surprise, shot through him like jolts of electricity.

Erica screamed. Ciano screamed back, his crushed larynx vibrating pain, and with a supreme effort he reached behind his head to grasp any part of his attacker. He knew that if he failed, he would die, gagging and choking on his own blood.

His fingers waved helplessly in the air, then landed on Erica's hands. He tried to crush the bones in her hands, but he was too weak; his hands slipped off hers which were slick with his blood.

Contorting and gagging, he reached again, looking for any handhold. This time he brushed against her silky hair—the same red-gold hair he had caressed so lovingly during their lovemaking. He pulled as hard as he could, managing only to rip away several long hairs. Erica's grip never weakened. He could hear her panting in his ear, smell her foul breath.

Finally his left hand landed on Erica's ear. He grabbed it with his fist and pulled as hard as he could. He heard her gasp in pain and tightened his grip. Then bending forward at the waist, he pulled her over his left shoulder. He felt her body shift as her gasp became a scream; he threw himself forward, impervious to pain and heard the splintering crash as he pulled her through the window and smashed her on the street.

They both lay still for a second like exhausted lovers. Then Erica regained her feet, and vanished down the street toward the Courthouse.

Ciano ripped the bloody wire from his neck and used the side of the building as a crutch to help himself up. So far Erica had been more than a match for him, he thought. She had been shrewd, calculating, and effective; he had been stupid but lucky. Very lucky to be alive. He knew now that he had little chance of taking her alive, and for all his high-blown thoughts about vengeance he knew he had never been completely serious. Something inside him still hoped she didn't have to die; hoped that she would suddenly, magically become her old self again. He knew it was a fantasy—a weakness—but he couldn't help himself.

He walked stolidly down the street in the direction she had taken. The door to Stephens General Store was closed, but the door to the Courthouse at the end of the street was yawning open.

He tested his voice, but all he could manage was a hoarse whisper. The air around him seemed to have grown dense with fog, but he had long since given up trusting his senses. The fog might be a hallucination caused by his damaged eye or concussed brain or reduced oxygen flow from Erica's use of the garrote.

The three-story Courthouse stared at him forbodingly. The gallows in front of the building suddenly seemed like an omen. He was going to be Erica's judge, jury, and executioner, he thought, a job he had never bargained for.

Ciano entered the eerie, musty smelling Courthouse and adjusted his eyes to the darkness. He touched the gun in the small of his back, but decided he had plenty of time. At best Erica was armed with the kitchen knife, and he felt confident he could overcome her.

He held his breath, listening, and heard a creak on the stairs above him. He wondered if the noise was unintentional or if she were luring him upward. In the end it didn't matter, he thought. He had to climb those stairs.

Ciano reached the second floor quickly, and now that his eyes were used to the dark, he could see a long line of wooden doors—offices—lining the corridor.

To his left he thought he heard the soft sound of a door closing. She was definitely setting him up, he thought, but again he had no choice but to play her game.

He slammed the door open so she couldn't hide behind it. It was a wasted effort. Erica was standing in the middle of the bare room, her hand up over her head, the kitchen knife gleaming wetly in the scant light. He saw the glint of steel flashing toward his face and in an instant she was upon him.

He blunted her charge by dodging to the side and grabbed a small chair to use as a shield. Erica, an inexpert knife fighter, wielded the blade amateurishly, holding it in her palm and attacking him with overhead blows. He prodded her with the chair, daring her to attack, feeling sure he could disarm her. But she surprised him again by ripping the chair out of his grasp, as if she were taking a toy from a baby. She followed up her move with a horizontal overhand slash that narrowly missed Ciano's face. It grazed his chest, drawing blood.

He was stunned again by her snarling hatred, but it was her eyes, those dead green fires of insanity that appeared lifeless, yet were somehow alive. He had never seen such sheer demonic intensity.

"Are you afraid of me?" she asked in her husky voice, an octave lower than he remembered.

"Put the knife down, Erica," he said, his own voice a rusty whisper.

"Do you want me?" she asked. "Do you want to fuck me?"

Despite his revulsion, Ciano felt himself stir. "Give me the knife and we'll talk about it," he said in a low voice.

"Talk about it?" Erica screamed. "The woman was good enough for you before."

Ciano noticed that she now referred to herself in the third person. He didn't know if that was good or bad for his chances. Watching the hatred flow from her eyes, he was silent.

"Do I make you hard?" She had found his weak spot. He hesitated, she moved to one side, near a window. "I do, don't I," she said, her skin glistening in the moonlight. He saw the sinewy tendons of her forearms flex powerfully, and didn't doubt for a moment that she had the strength to run the knife straight through him. Wounded, she would be an even more deadly opponent. He had to get a clean shot at her or she'd surely kill him.

"You always turn me on," he whispered. "But the knife worries me."

"Fool," she said, pressing her palm to the blade. "It is not for you." The blood pooled quickly in her palm and ran through her fingers, sounding like raindrops on the wooden floor.

Ciano was sick watching this display, but he never lost his total concentration.

"I'll put the knife down if you'll fuck me," she said in a half-insane, half-coquettish voice that made Ciano's skin crawl.

"Whatever you want," he said.

Erica held the handle of the knife out, between thumb and forefinger, as if she were carrying a dead mouse by the tail. Opening her fingers, she let the knife drop to the floor. It plunged into the floor with a thud.

"Come to me," she commanded. Ciano took a hesitant step forward as Erica opened her arms to him. He embraced her with all his strength. Her once flawless skin was dripping with blood and sweat. He gagged, smelling the rancid odor of corruption about her.

He reached behind his back and smoothly shoved the four-inch barrel of the .38 Smith & Wesson into her stomach. This was it, he thought, closing his eyes. He squeezed the trigger three times in rapid succession, each time hearing the hammer strike an empty chamber.

Erica jerked back from him, screaming, "Liar!" She reached for the knife on the floor. Surprised, Ciano had a difficult time keeping his feet on the blood-slick floor. To his horror he saw Erica swing the knife at him, and as he threw himself backward to avoid the attack, he fell on his ass.

Then she was on him, the knife poised to slash through his throat. He caught her arm and twisted, rolling her off to the side. But she was on her feet faster than he was, and attacking again. He kicked her feet out from under her and she went crashing to the floor.

This time they were both standing at the same time, and Ciano, still wondering why his gun had misfired, uncorked a vicious right hook that caught her square in the jaw, breaking it. He charged, swinging a wild left and right that didn't do much damage, but forced her back to the window. A hard, desperate left caught her in the eye, and as Ciano went in low, he pushed her through the bone-dry window frame. She tottered a moment trying to regain her balance, then began to fall.

He lunged for her, reaching through broken shards of glass that cut into his arms and chest. He didn't know why he was trying to save her, when a minute before he had tried to kill her. Maybe it had something to do with Joseph Steppe or with his past relationship with her or maybe he just wasn't thinking clearly anymore. But with one hand on the sill and his other hand on Erica's arm he literally held her life in the balance. He tried to pull her up, but his hand slipped on her bloody arm. He strained, feeling his back muscles tear. For a moment he looked down and saw her green eyes staring up at him. "Help me, Vince," she said clearly, pleadingly. "Please, help me." Her eyes darted back and forth wildly, accusingly, her face had softened to child-like helplessness.

Erica's tenuous grasp on both reality and Ciano's hand began to slip, but not until she looked into a moonlit pane of glass near her head. Time seemed to stand still. For in that piece of glass she saw, not her own reflection, but that of Judas Iscariot. Eye-to-eye she had finally met her protector, her tormentor . . . herself. She stared at the bearded, cankered face in the glass and recognized it as the face of death. "What have I done?" she whispered.

Ciano sensed that something was happening to Erica; he felt her body tense in a spasm of revulsion that unnerved him. Bracing his body to adjust for her weight, he strained to haul her up. Just then she ripped a piece of glass from the splintered casement and stabbed it into the back of his hand.

Ciano groaned and loosened his grip, while Erica kicked against the side of the building to wrench herself free and, missing the concrete walkway, landed in the muddy grass.

Stunned, he watched her slowly get up and walk purposefully to the gallows in front of the courthouse. She looked up at Ciano outlined in the broken window and was sad. Mortally sad. He probably expected her to run, she thought, but she was long past running. She would walk to her death.

In that one instant of terrible clarity, when she had seen the face of Judas, Erica understood it was not the priests Iscariot had wanted. It had never been the priests. Or revenge. Not that, certainly. No, it had been her—her mind and soul—that he had sought to possess and control. Seeing his horrible reflection in the broken glass, grinning sardonically back at her, had made it clear to her.

Erica's head brushed the hangman's noose, and she recoiled slightly. But counting the thirteen horizontal knots, she realized that she had met her destiny at last. She slipped the noose over her head and tugged it tightly around her neck.

Ciano screamed from the window above, but she hardly heard him. Iscariot must die—she must die. She had known it all along.

She kicked her leg out at the lever activating the trapdoor; after a second's hesitation, the door dropped open and Erica's body fell into space. She had crossed over into Judas' world, and they were one.

From the second-story window, Ciano watched Erica's frenzied dance of death subside, watched as her flailing arms tried to grasp something, watched as her neck snapped and her body hung motionless in the misty air.

He left the Courthouse without looking at her. He didn't want to see her purplish, ruined face or protruding tongue, he just wanted to get back to Diane and his son.

As he walked away from one life into another, he thought he heard the soft slap of sandals and the rustle of coarse robes behind him. He stopped for a moment to listen, but it was only the sound of Erica's body twisting in a sudden wind.

Epilogue

The gunshots echoed early amid the marble and granite monuments of St. Vincent's cemetery. Ciano shoved his hands into the pockets of a lightweight raincoat and waited impatiently for Joseph Dugan's body to slide into the frozen earth.

It was finally over, he thought, watching the knot of mourners from a little distance away. Mary Dugan, the widow, and her four children stood erect and brittle, trying not to break, as a uniformed lieutenant ordered the four riflemen to fire another round. Ciano jumped involuntarily at the ragged report. He had had enough of guns, he thought.

A bugler played taps, slowly and painfully driving the message of death into the minds of the survivors, the sound chilling Ciano's blood. He wanted to be in Diane's arms, safe and warm in their house, his son playing at his feet. That was impossible, of course, because they were both still in the hospital recuperating slowly from the mental and physical torture inflicted upon them by Erica. But Ciano had no doubt that within a week he would completely change his life, settle down with his family, and become an exemplary husband and father. He knew it in his heart and his mind. He discounted a lifetime of false starts.

A third volley of shots rang out and the uniformed lieutenant put his firing party at parade rest. He stripped the American flag from Dugan's coffin, and with the help of another officer, he began to fold it into a triangular shape. It seemed to take forever, and the time allowed Ciano to think about Erica. He hadn't been able to stop wondering about her and her incredible sickness. He felt a mixture of shame and outrage at having been used by her, but couldn't help wondering what his life might have been like if only—

He tried to push Erica's face, contorted with insane rage, from his mind, and he wondered who would attend her funeral. Her husband was still missing—perhaps dead—and family members apparently were burying Ed Hanratty and his daughter in a cemetery in Queens. Where, he didn't know. He told himself he didn't care.

At last the lieutenant handed the folded flag to Mary Dugan and the mourners began to drift away from the grave site. Cemetery workers, lurking anonymously nearby would lower the coffin into the ground, covering up the last earthly remains of a good cop.

Stiff with cold, Ciano walked slowly behind the main group of mourners heading for the warmth and security of their cars. He hoped no one would notice him, but he was wrong.

Blocking his way was Captain Andrew Talbot, his face still bruised from Ciano's fists. He was flanked by two uniformed officers, one Ciano recognized by his bandaged face as Russo, the cop he had escaped from at Holy Cross Church. Ciano felt his gut tighten.

"You're under arrest," Talbot said.

"Fuck you," Ciano said.

Talbot smiled, revealing a chipped tooth. "You really think you're going to beat this thing, don't you? You think you're a fucking media star again. But it's not going to happen. In two days another psycho will crawl out from under a rock and you'll be old news."

"You got a warrant?" Ciano asked, knowing Talbot was right.

"Yeah, and he's right here next to me," Talbot said, indicating Russo. "Unfortunately, you're going to resist arrest and get very, very messed up."

Ciano sighed. If he went down, he'd take Talbot with him. But just as he tensed to attack the captain, he felt a tug at his raincoat. He whirled around, practically knocking Sean Dugan from his feet. He reached out a steadying hand and looked down at the boy's white, drawn face.

"I asked my mom," the boy said. "She said it was okay." He handed Ciano the folded flag from Dugan's coffin.

Ciano took it because he didn't know what else to do.

"Thank you," Sean said. "My daddy said you were the best." The boy was on the verge of letting go. Ciano wanted to pick him up and hug him, but he couldn't. Neither one of them would show any weakness, and certainly not in front of Talbot and his hitters.

"You can come over and see it anytime," Ciano said. "I'd like you to meet my son."

Sean turned away and ran toward the group of limousines waiting to take him and his family back to a cold, empty house.

"Very touching," Talbot sneered. "Fucking kill him, Russo."

Ciano feinted toward Russo, who was on his left, but came full force at Talbot, wanting to smash as many of the captain's teeth as he could before Russo took him apart. He heard the sharp splintering and felt the pain in his left hand as he snapped off the punch. Russo's giant hand grabbed his raincoat, but it ripped and Ciano fell forward on top of a bleeding, moaning Talbot.

"Boys, boys. This is a funeral, not a wrestling bout," Deputy Chief Sal DeFeo said, coming up on the group.

Talbot untangled himself from Ciano and stood up. The two hitters backed away leaving Ciano on the ground, totally exhausted.

"Hey, I've got good news for everybody," DeFeo said, smiling without humor. "Get up, Ciano. It's cold on the ground."

"I've filed charges and you can't stop me from arresting this man," Talbot said.

DeFeo considered. "No," he said. "I can't stop you, but you can stop you."

"Never," Talbot said, wiping his bloody mouth.

"Hear me out," DeFeo said. "I have a deal for you."

"No deals," Talbot said.

"Oh, you'll like this one," DeFeo said, taking a Baby Ruth candy bar from the pocket of his black overcoat. He gnawed off the paper and let it flap away in the wind, and nibbled a bite. "How'd you like to be the new Deputy Commissioner for Neighborhood Relations?"

Talbot stared at him. "Deputy Commissioner?"

"You got it, Andy. An appointed post. All you need is my recommendation," DeFeo said, chewing loudly.

Ciano got painfully to his feet and stood holding his ribs in the frigid air. It was like a dream.

"All you gotta do is forget Ciano and you got it," DeFeo said, his voice smooth as diarrhea. "You want to retire as a captain or do you want to get in with the brass—be the brass? Is this fucking guinea worth it?" He pointed a chocolate-coated finger at Ciano.

Talbot poked a finger into his mouth and pulled out a splinter of tooth. "On the level?" he asked.

"Sure as shit," DeFeo said, laughing. "Come on, you know you'd sell your grandmother for the job, and now you can keep the sweet old lady at home just by dropping your vendetta against Ciano."

"Deputy Commissioner?" Talbot repeated.

"Yep. Hot shit, DC," DeFeo said. "Press conferences, interviews, TV."

"Come on, Russo, let's get out of here," Talbot said, turning to go.

"Wait a minute," Ciano said. Talbot turned back. "If you're going to be on TV, you'd better get those teeth fixed."

"That's enough, Ciano," DeFeo said, grabbing his arm. "We're out of here."

Maybe it was over after all, Ciano thought, picking up the fallen flag and allowing DeFeo to lead him away.

"He won't bother you anymore," DeFeo said.

"Why'd you do it?" Ciano asked.

"Peace in the department," DeFeo answered. "You step out of line and I'll kill you, Ciano. Got it?"

"Fuck you," Ciano said.

DeFeo laughed, but it sounded like a death rattle in the windy cemetery.

Later that night, Father Thomas Layhe suddenly opened his eyes. He had been lying in a trance-like sleep for two days, much to the annoyance of his psychiatrist, Dr. Beldon, who could find no physical and little psychological reason for Layhe's comatose state. But Dr. Beldon hadn't been in Holy Cross rectory when the priest had confronted his deepest fears in the form of a black-robed figure.

Layhe sat up stiffly, the self-inflicted welts on his back aching dully. He got out of the narrow iron bed and went to the window. Through the bars he could see only the darkness. An asylum, he thought rationally enough, an insane asylum. I have to get out of here. I must escape.

He beat on the padded metal door for five minutes, but no one answered his calls. He was trapped. Alone. He sat down on the bed and began to cry. That's when he heard it—the soft slap of sandals and the rustle of coarse robes. A monk? he wondered. Or—his mind froze in horror. He thought he heard a voice.

"Who are you?" Layhe whispered.

—I have come to set you free.

"How?"

—The Covenant must be kept.

Layhe's hysterical laughter finally awoke the night attendant, but he didn't move from the desk. Just another psycho, he thought, going back to sleep.